3 1266 20753 1047

DISCARDED OR WITHDRAWN
GREAT NECK LIBRARY

28 DAY BOOK

```
FIC         Belletto, Rene.
BELLETTO
            Machine.
```

D1800730

DATE			
May 24			

GREAT NECK LIBRARY
GREAT NECK, NY 11024
(516) 466 8055

NOV 29 1993

M
BAKER & TAYLOR BOOKS

MACHINE

ALSO BY RENÉ BELLETTO

Eclipse

MACHINE

René Belletto

Translated from the French

by Lanie Goodman

Grove Press
New York

Copyright © 1990 by René Belletto
English translation copyright © 1993 by Grove Press, Inc.

All rights reserved. No part of this book may be reproduced, stored in a retrieval system, or transmitted in any form, by any means, including mechanical, electronic, photocopying, recording, or otherwise, without prior written permission of the publisher.

Grove Press
841 Broadway
New York, NY 10003

Library of Congress Cataloging-in-Publication Data

Belletto, René
[Machine. English]
Machine / René Belletto.
Translation of: La machine.
ISBN 0-8021-1437-7
I. Title.
PQ2662.E4537M3313   1993
843'.914—dc20   93-658

Manufactured in the United States of America
Published simultaneously in Canada

Designed by Laura Hough

FIRST EDITION

10 9 8 7 6 5 4 3 2 1

MACHINE

*L*eonard *would wait* until his mother went to bed to kill her.

He would kill her in bed.

Soon . . .

"Anyhow, I won't do it like that," he said to himself. Switching from channel to channel, he had come across a scene in a TV movie where the classic slasher was stabbing the classic prostitute right in the heart.

He, Leonard, would stab her many times.

The victim would bleed a lot, she'd whimper and writhe in pain before she died.

In a flash, he pictured himself striking right in the heart. Yes, to top it all off, he'd strike right in the heart!

"Does that really interest you?"

The boy jumped up, startled.

"No, I like *Zorro* better."

"So put *Zorro* back on," his mother said gently.

Click. He put *Zorro* back on. Marie Lacroix was surprised that he'd turned off the program a few minutes before the end. Ordinarily, an earthquake couldn't get Leonard to bat an eye when his favorite program was on. She thought back to the blueberries and whipped cream dessert that hadn't produced the usual joyous yelps.

Perhaps he was ill?

Abruptly, Leonard tossed the remote control down next to him. His mother took his hand. He gave her a smile, a kind of smile, and withdrew his hand. Usually, he was the one who snuggled up against her as they watched TV, eager to cuddle . . .

"You aren't sick, are you?" Marie Lacroix asked. "Do you hurt anywhere? Do you feel like you have a fever?"

She felt his forehead. He offered no resistance, suppressing a shiver of excitement. He'd kill her. Soon, he'd kill her. Soon, he'd be able to express all the hatred that had been building up, that was still building up at this very moment. It was as if his mother were doing everything possible to bring this hatred to its culmination.

"No. No, I promise, Mooo-mmy. I feel fine."

Marie worried too much. She knew it. She'd always made an effort not to overprotect Leonard. But right now, after all, she could allow herself to do so. The present circumstances had changed all of their behavior.

What state would Marc be in when he got home?

He was already exhausted when he stopped working six days ago—exhausted and, in her opinion, somewhat depressed since the terribly trying business with Michel Zyto. Not to mention the illness he'd suddenly discovered, which was probably bothering him more than he would admit. She regretted that she hadn't insisted on taking a vacation. On the evening of July 31, she should have told Marc that they were going to leave the next day or the day after—for anywhere; by plane, if he was too tired.

It was the same thing every year. Whenever vacation time rolled around, Marc was always worn-out but he couldn't relax. He missed his work, and had a hard time tearing himself away from it.

Yet, there was one positive aspect, an important one: during the past six days, they had started having sex again. Marie couldn't help thinking that recent events had something to do with it. There was a link, but she couldn't say what it might be.

Still, Marc had fallen back in love with her.

She'd regained hope. After this business with Zyto, everything would be back to normal. She would have to be brave and put up a good front for Leonard.

"Let's hope Daddy calls us soon," she said.

For the first time since she'd returned from the Cazanvielhs', Leonard became animated, the way boys of his age normally are. She noted it with satisfaction. He turned toward her, his eyes sparkling.

"He said not to worry!"

"That's right, darling."

She gave him a hug. It was true. If Marc had told Leonard not to worry, then there was nothing to worry about.

Considering where he is now and the shape he's in, he's not likely to call, Leonard said to himself, which softened the resentment he felt at having his face squeezed against his mother's breast like that.

Finally, she let him go.

"My poor little lamb, I'm keeping you from watching *Zorro*."

Final scene of the episode: Everyone realizes that the masked lover of justice who marks bloody Zs on the faces of the bad guys, and the perfumed, cowardly, wealthy *caballero*, are one and the same person. Every kid in the world loves the revelation of this dual personality, particularly Leonard, but not this night. He yawned twice in a row, forgetting to cover his mouth.

"I still think you're very tired," said Marie Lacroix. "We didn't sleep well in that hotel. You can never get a decent night's sleep in a hotel."

She instantly regretted having mentioned the hotel. What a terrible fright they'd had! But the child didn't seem to notice.

"C'mon, time for beddy-bye!" she said.

She stood up. The leather sofa returned to its normal shape with an almost bestial hiss, which often made Leonard laugh. Sometimes he'd stand up just to hear that sound.

Marie walked across the living room, brushing her hand against a house plant as she approached the bay window.

A view of the garden and a sky full of stars.

Tomorrow would be a nice day.

"Would you mind turning off the TV? Those commercials are boring, don't you think?"

"Yeah."

Leonard retrieved the remote control, which had slid between the cushions (as most objects that were placed on the sofa did), and fiddled with the buttons. The set went off with a nice, neat click. "I zapped it!" thought Leonard.

The vast silence of the countryside was closing in on the house. The child didn't move, didn't say a word. Marie Lacroix turned around. He was looking at her strangely. She had rarely seen his face so drawn.

"Off to bed!"

They went upstairs. She left all the lights on downstairs for Marc's return.

Leonard was ahead of her on the wooden stairs. He forced himself to perform a few antics and clown around for appearance's sake, flopping his head from side to side and making little barking noises like a puppy, much to Marie's delight.

Once upstairs, he entered his room, then his bathroom.

"Be right back," said his mother.

She went on toward her own bedroom at the end of the hall. She passed the guest room and Marc's study. Originally, this room had been meant for a second child. She thought about it again tonight. As newlyweds, Marc and Marie Lacroix had both agreed it would be better to have two children than one. Then, a year after Leonard's birth, Marie had realized that her maternal desire had been satisfied once and for all, and she didn't want to become pregnant again. As for Marc, an only child himself, he had quickly adapted to the idea, content with the domestic trio to which he had become accustomed. All of the good reasons to expand the family circle had become less pressing compared to what secretly compelled the couple to leave things as they were.

They had avoided talking about the subject in depth. Time and force of habit had done the rest. Leonard had turned ten. At this point, a change was out of the question.

They had an only child, a son.

Marie drew the heavy brown curtains of the two windows in the master bedroom. One faced the countryside and the other, the garden.

She took off all her clothes and went into the bathroom.

She took a leisurely shower. Perhaps Marc would feel like making love, even if he got home late. His desire for her had returned in a way that moved her, with all the fears and the impetuousness of an adolescent, as though he had never slept with her before. Of course, Marie had refrained from comment, she was far too modest and discreet.

These moments of peculiar passion were helping her through the present difficult period.

She stepped out of the bathtub and dried herself in front of the mirror with a blue towel that complimented her dark complexion.

She hesitated between two pairs of panties, then wondered why she had even hesitated; she preferred the white pair with the blue stripes, even if they were starting to look worn. The fabric stretched over her haunches. Her hips were narrow for her height, but her buttocks were nicely rounded. That had been the first intimate thing Marc had ever said to her—he'd once murmured that he found her round bottom very sexy.

She combed her long hair.

She had hardly changed. Her body was just as perfect, just as firm and supple at thirty-five as it had been at twenty-five, when she was still a newlywed.

She slipped on Marc's burgundy bathrobe.

Leonard was waiting in bed, wearing his white pajamas with the red musical instruments. He hated this ridiculous outfit and he'd grudgingly put it on. He hated the books, the toys, the room, and everything in it.

He kicked off the sheet and blanket.

He heard the sound of a door. It was about time, his mother had finally finished washing up. Now she would say: "Ready or not," to which he was supposed to reply: "Here I come!" and she would come kiss him goodnight. How idiotic!

"Ready or not . . ." cried Marie Lacroix.

Leonard sat up, propping himself on his elbows.

"Here I come!"

With wicked irony, he pictured himself stabbing her two times: "Here I come, here I come!"

The bedroom door opened. He registered a slight unpleasant shock, recognizing his father's bathrobe.

"Are you sleepy, my darling?"

"Yes!" said Leonard.

"Do you think you'll fall asleep right away?"

"Oh yes!"

She went over to the bed.

"Show me your teeth."

He made a horrible grimace, grinning from ear to ear so that even his molars were visible.

"My my, don't you look handsome!"

She smiled. Ordinarily, just for fun, he'd do exactly the opposite, showing as little as possible. He'd pucker his lips and open his mouth only slightly, allowing his mother to inspect the four incisors, at the very most.

"Bravo, they're nice and white."

Of course they were white, he'd brushed them with every ounce of energy he had left, as if trying to wear them down, cruelly taking out all his nervous anger on the toothbrush.

"Goodnight, darling."

She kissed him on both cheeks. He smelled her perfume, or rather the scent of her skin mixed with soap, since she never used perfume. She was clutching her bathrobe together at the neck with her left hand.

"Aren't you going to give me a kiss? You can stop making that awful face, you know!"

★ ★ ★

She stretched out on her bed and loosened the belt of the bathrobe. She felt hot. She was exhausted.

The telephone on the night table was within arm's reach, but she moved it a few inches closer so that it rested on the edge of the table. She put back the framed photograph that she had accidentally displaced. She paused for a moment to look at it. Taken eleven years ago, it was a picture of her with Marc, when they were first married. Marc still had his mustache, an homage to Jay Mortimer, the American scientist who sported one. He had shaved it off shortly thereafter: Marie wasn't too keen on facial hair. It was the year he had finished medical school. The year she had decided not to take her qualifying exams in Classics, which she definitely would have passed. But then she would have been obliged to teach for several years under contract, in compliance with the French National Education System.

There were times when she wondered what her life would have been like if she had been a teacher. A professor of French, Latin, and Greek in a high school, in Versailles . . . But she had no regrets. She had been able to devote herself entirely to Leonard.

She reached for *The Odyssey*. She was glad she could still read the book in Greek with little difficulty. She had almost finished. There were only a few pages left. She removed the thin leather bookmark.

She was having a hard time concentrating on her reading. She kept squirming and mopping her brow. She was restless. She crossed one leg, then the other. She thought about Leonard. He'd feel better tomorrow, once he'd had a good night's sleep.

The bathrobe was now completely undone, exposing her beautiful body.

After twenty minutes of total immobility, Leonard turned on the light and got out of bed.

He pulled open the bottom drawer of the dresser. He took out a sheet in which he'd hidden a pair of gloves, the two revolvers, and the long carving knife. His eyes were gleaming.

He put on the gloves, first the left one, then the right, and picked up the knife with his right hand.

He left his room. The house was completely silent. Barefoot on the carpet, he advanced without a sound. He continued down the dark hallway. He moved quickly. He stopped in front of his mother's bedroom.

Then he thought he heard a feeble cry. He wasn't sure. Had one of the two in the basement managed to untie his gag? Certainly not. It was probably an animal in the countryside. The basement door was securely locked. And anyhow, he'd be taking care of those two, soon enough. In the meantime, let them yell all they wanted.

He hid the knife behind his back.

Marie Lacroix thought she heard something, too, a dog howling from far away. She straightened up and listened. It had stopped. She heard a knock at her door, a soft rap. At the same time, she saw the knob turning. She sat up a little straighter.

"Leonard?" she said anxiously.

*A*fter making his rounds on the morning of July 31, Doctor Marc Lacroix signed out of the Sainte-Anne Hospital, where he served as acting head of the psychiatric clinic three times a week.

The prospect of taking a month's leave depressed him. Although he was devoted to pure research, he also liked being "on the scene" at the hospital. A brain specialist, physician, biologist, and clinician all in one, he was constantly trying to make connections between fields that were too often treated as separate, even opposed to one another. He was interested in every aspect of the brain, from cellular activity to psychological behavior, and couldn't say which one fascinated him the most.

In any case, the direct, personal contact with the patients was indispensable to him. Through them, he felt as if he were approaching the mystery of thought in its vaguest, most obscure, but also most exciting form. He was constantly astonished by the diversity, which was why, despite his strictly scientific work, he rejected labels and classifications. He was curious about each individual patient, as though the answer to this mystery might eventually be revealed during a session with one of them.

His Nissan Terrano was parked in the courtyard, in the shade of a walnut tree—he'd only found out it was a walnut tree three weeks ago. The vehicle, a four-wheel drive that had just been voted "The 4WD of the Year" in the States, still smelled new. Stripped of the famous "Patrol" trademark, its chassis and body resembled a King Cab. It was equipped with a curious triangular back window, adding a little bit of originality—compared to the Range Rover or other similar four-wheel drives—which had immediately appealed to Marc. His colleagues had not been able to resist kidding him the day he'd turned up at the hospital in his little red tank with enormous tires. They asked him if he'd applied for a job in Nouakchott in the Mauritanian Sahara, or if he was perhaps thinking about converting it into a clinic on wheels with eight beds, an operating room, and a recovery room—clever remarks like that. Friendly comments, most of the time, but every now and then, his colleagues acted a little strait-laced, a bit irritated by Doctor Lacroix's unusual, even eccentric, personality.

Marc was thirty-nine years old, tall and thin, and looked younger than his age despite a fair amount of gray hair. He had slender, delicate hands, and a handsome, angular face that bore a striking resemblance to certain El Greco paintings of Christ. A Schubert symphony played from the four speakers of the Terrano. He wasn't crazy about Schubert, but in the car, any kind of music was OK.

He stepped out of Sainte-Anne Hospital, nodding back at Harvey, the redheaded guy at the check-in desk who always acknowledged him.

It took him barely twenty minutes to get from Sainte-Anne to Lariboisière. Paris was half deserted. It wasn't very hot, even rather cool, and it felt good to speed along the streets with the windows open. And the Terrano, despite appearances, wasn't any bulkier than a lot of other conventional cars that looked a lot smaller. He could weave in and out of the lanes and park anywhere—well, almost, thought Marc Lacroix, amused by his own dishonesty. He was well aware that he'd purchased this car on a whim, he'd bought himself a toy. It wasn't absolutely imperative to ride from Paris to Versailles in a vehicle capable of scaling the Eiffel Tower or sailing up a mountain stream against the current at ninety miles an hour, as he'd tell his son to make him laugh.

He took Sebastopol Boulevard, which he always found sinister-looking. He concentrated on driving his Nissan. He tried to make as many green lights as possible.

Every now and then, his throat would tighten with a little wave of anxiety. He was en route to the Lariboisière Hospital not as a doctor but as a patient. This year he had experienced dizzy spells on two occasions, along with a buzzing in his ear as if it were swelling, becoming enormous. He'd thought it was an ordinary ailment, due to an imbalance of fluids in the inner ear. He'd waited, all the while knowing that these symptoms, if they recurred and became more painful, might indicate something more serious.

At the end of June, after a third attack, he'd consulted his friend Cedric Houdé, head of Ear, Nose and Throat at Lariboisière, who had suggested a preliminary scan, only as a precaution, whenever Marc wanted. July had come and gone with no other warning signals.

On Magenta Boulevard, he was passed by a vehicle like his own, with the word "Cherokee" written on it. He almost felt like racing, just to make sure he could pass it. He decided against it. Anyway, Rue Ambroise-Paré was very close by. He swung sharply turning right, then braked to let an unheeding dog trot across the street at its leisure.

He backed into a parking place in front of the entrance of Lariboisière Hospital.

"*Hi there*, big boss!" said Marc, entering the doctor's office.

"You're the big boss, pal!"

Cedric Houdé wasn't joking. Not only had he felt an instant rapport with his younger colleague, he admired Marc for his professional audacity and intuitive research. Marc had convinced a skeptical laboratory to perform a complex molecular adjustment to an existing antidepressant, for example, thus developing a new antidepressant, Minotaryl, that was more precise, more specific, and could calm the tormented ruminations of certain neurotic obsessives.

The two men shook hands. At sixty-seven, Professor Cedric Houdé was almost as thin as Marc. As for his face, Marie Lacroix had a perfect, amusing expression for it: "the ugly mug of a good guy." He looked like anything *but* a doctor; his features, as Marie would say, belonged to a man who had always been tempted to rob banks but could never take the leap, swayed by honesty and goodness at the last minute.

Marc appreciated his wife's humor. They had laughed a lot together in their life.

"It looks like the country this time of year," Marc said.

He gazed at the vast inner courtyard that faced Cedric Houdé's office—the grass, trees, and hedges. Cedric glanced out the window.

"I suppose so," he said. "Sit down." He sat down, too. "It's pleasant, I agree. But you know my dream, a small Ear, Nose and Throat clinic in the south of France, far from the big cities. I'm going there for two weeks in mid-August to do a little prospecting. What about you? You still don't know if you're going away?"

"No," Marc said. "No plans. I'll relax at home. We'll see. Maybe a week in Greece or Italy. Marie is always up for that."

"How is she?"

"Fine."

"And Leonard?"

"Great. He just gets better and better."

"I'm sure he does," said Cedric with a slightly forced smile.

They were both uncomfortable to be meeting under these unusual circumstances. They realized that it would be easier to chat once the business of the scan was over. Marc looked at his watch, a handsome nautical watch he'd inherited from his father.

"Shall we?" he said with an equally forced smile. "It's time."

Cedric Houdé stood up at once.

"Let's go."

An elevator took them four levels underground. They walked down the orange corridors, some of which turned at right angles, while others curved on interminably. Their footsteps and the few words exchanged echoed strangely, reverberating before and behind them. After a good five minutes on this labyrinthine course, they arrived in front of the scanner unit.

A patient was being wheeled out on a cart, unconscious, his head swathed in bandages. Two black orderlies were pushing the cart. The door swung closed. Marc and Cedric waited. A light came on, and they entered the radiology room.

The dome of the scanner occupied a predominant position in the room.

They drew nearer.

It was like being in the bowels of the earth, where the fates of men were decreed.

Everything was set up for the X-rays.

"Whenever you're ready," said Cedric.

Marc Lacroix buried his head in the scanner.

3

M̲ichel Zyto, *thirty-seven years old.*

A psychopath? Yes and no. Yes. A bizarre case.

Meticulously groomed mustache. A combination of self-love and hate, you can see it immediately. Magnificent dark chestnut brown hair, thick and wavy. That's the first thing that strikes you, the hair and the mustache.

Irregular features. Something slightly simian in the overall appearance—average height, strong jaw, long arms, a hint of awkwardness and hesitation in his gestures and walk.

All in all, he nearly resembles Martin Vérapoutsimila. But Zyto has an advantage over Vérapoutsimila, who's more the silent type—it's a sudden and winning smile that transforms him, lights up his face. He doesn't smile often, but when he does it lasts a long time. Rather strange.

Good attitude during the trial. The veneer of a self-made man.

Well-spoken, with occasional outbursts of vulgari[ty]...
sorts of books.

Classic anamnesis. The usual characteristics s[o typi-]
cal in the formation of a psychopathic personality: t[he father]
and feeble-minded, disappeared early on (the moth[er used to]
beat him); the alcoholic mother, an incestuous rel[ationship with]
Michel without consummation (are we sure?); in short, a total negation of the father, that is to say, of all laws of nature. Part of Michel makes him susceptible to crossing the line into the forbidden without the slightest scruple, inciting him to hurt, wound, and kill (?). And he is incapable of making any emotional connections (are we sure?), any attachments. Typical, typical. The suicide attempt during his first confinement, also typical. More than typical, in fact: he's actually extremely suicidal.

But. But but but but . . . Several atypical elements, even contrary to the normal psychopathology (ha, ha!) of these nut cases. For example:

—He doesn't lie. Or just a little. In my opinion, he's telling the truth from start to finish. In any case, he does not constantly lie, in my opinion. Impossible.

—Guilt feelings are not foreign to him, far from it.

—No real professional instability. Intelligent, a substantial education in technology. Very intelligent, even. Begins working after his mother dies (on a motorscooter, hit by a bus late one night on a major boulevard in Pantin, horrible story). Apparently, this death doesn't affect him. Taken in by a remote bachelor uncle hardly more present than his father, but who gives him the semblance of a home. Practices twelve professions in fifteen years, all different, due to trouble in the job market, not Zyto's fault; he's never the one who quits, give or take two exceptions, and for that matter, he had good reasons. In a certain way, he's the opposite of an unstable person, oddly enough. He stays with his uncle in Pantin until age twenty-eight and then moves into a small, very respectable apartment, at 30 Rue Maronites, in the twentieth arrondissement. He lives alone there for many years. No friends, no girlfriends. A mo-

...ous life, without any diversions or incidents. Though we ...ould mention the classes in the evening: he starts attending night school, and being a creature of habit, he perseveres and acquires a certain knowledge of biology and computer science.

—Another surprising element, this one remains to be verified: I watched Zyto closely during the trial, and I'm convinced that a good therapeutic relationship is possible with him.

—The disaster began at age thirty-five, that is to say, late. Until then, no acts of violence, nothing, which is exceptional for psychopaths, who begin their revolt early in life, it's practically a rule. Still, petty acts of delinquency during his youth and adolescence, like breaking pinball machines. (He boasts, in passing, about having been an ace at pinball. He is a braggart.)

So there you have it. Then accused of having stabbed four women, several times each. The fourth one died. He admits to the first three, insisting on the fact that he didn't kill them nor did he wish to kill them, it wasn't what he was after, he only wanted to hurt them. He denies the fourth, even though they found him at the scene of the crime. Besides, if he were, in fact, guilty, they wouldn't have found him at the scene of the crime, obviously he wouldn't have stayed in that sordid hotel where they arrested him in the morning. And plus, he went on, that final stab right in the heart . . . No, however aberrant his behavior might have been in those calamitous moments when he attacked the women, he wouldn't have gone for the heart. He knows that it wasn't in him. That's what Zyto claims and I believe him. Besides, no real proof against him, only presumptions, no fingerprints, no witnesses . . . At the time of the arrest, he's in possession of a Colt .38, which has never been used.

Question: why at age thirty-five, why so late? Perhaps (pure guesswork for the moment) because 1) the maternal cocoon was almost totally airtight, 2) the identification of all women with his mother was virtually complete, 3) the hatred for his mother (who didn't let him live his own life) and the fear of his mother (fear of being destroyed, fear of incest) were almost complete, 4) thus, up until the age of thirty-five, he avoided all contact with women, fear and hate overpowering desire and curiosity. Hmmm. Needs a closer look, 5) at thirty-five, he runs into a woman (a prostitute, an enterprising drunk). His "bad" side, which has remained dormant, suddenly flares up. In a fit of panic he beats her, knocks her out, goes to get a knife, and he stabs (superficial wounds) but does not kill her. With no intention to kill. Are we sure? And why? Needs a closer look, much closer.

Conclusion: I'd like to take a closer look. Michel Zyto interests me. I'll do everything to get the great Hugues d'Oléons to admit him into his distinguished Center, then I'll ask this great man for free access into that distinguished Center, and attempt psychotherapy with Zyto, etc.

Doctor Hugues d'Oléons, head of the Stéphen-Mornay Psychiatric Center, put the notes he'd just read back into the thick "Michel Zyto" file.

Just as he was turning around to slip the file back into place (the last one, to the right of fourteen others) there was a knock on his door. "Come in!" he shouted, without getting up. He stood up as seldom as possible, because of his weight. He was enormous. He'd organized his existence around his obesity: this meant remaining in his swivel chair as much as possible, and knowing his patients by studying their files.

He pivoted his chair in the direction of the door. Marc Lacroix entered his office. The room, spacious and modern, looked out onto a meticulously kept French garden, as did the patients' rooms.

Marc seemed almost melancholy despite a brief smile. But when had Hugues d'Oléons ever seen Marc Lacroix look perfectly content? Probably never, he thought, extending his hand.

"Marc, what a coincidence! I just finished rereading the notes you took on Michel Zyto after the trial. It's the first document in his file here..."

"It's just a rough sketch," Marc said. "You know, like one of those caricatures a courtroom artist would dash off. Another coincidence"—he smiled, looking slightly less unhappy—"I've come to talk to you about your model psychopath. I'd like to try another outing with him. The first one was such a success!"

It was easy to escape from the Stéphen-Mornay Center. And for some time now, Michel Zyto had permission to leave the Center as often as he liked, even every day if he so desired. But he had not gone out, except for one time, with Marc. He lived like a recluse in the comfort of his room. He didn't mix with the other patients in the clinic. It was rare to find him in the dayroom. He seemed to wait for Dr. Lacroix's visits.

Marc had taken a seat near the window, in an authentic, magnificent Louis XV chair that was out of place in this room full of metal, lacquered wood, and straight lines but added a nice touch. The chair belonged to Hugues, he'd inherited it from his brother. Marc glanced outside. The garden looked luminous rather than merely sunny, as if the rays were streaming in from every direction.

"Take him out as often as you like," said Hugues. "You know how much faith I have in you. You've never been wrong about our in-house matador, right from the start."

Marc's heart missed a beat. Yes, he knew just how much the great d'Oléons trusted him. And in a certain sense, he was about to betray this trust, wasn't he? Hugues had used his influence to help Marc as soon as the trial was over. After a thousand administrative procedures, and two months of veritable acrobatics, Michel Zyto, following his suicide attempt, had been admitted into the new but already renowned Center on Avenue Stéphen-Mornay. His anxious and aggressive state of mind, which was aggravated by the trial and two months in a hardcore mental institution (useless medicines, bad rapport with the personnel, locked doors, bars on the windows), had improved in less than three weeks.

As he suspected, Marc had been able to establish a therapeutic bond. He now knew a good deal about Michel Zyto. Not everything.

Still a few gray areas that Marc hoped to illuminate—so did Zyto, for that matter, whose vast willingness to cooperate was obvious, and at times, touching. He, too, wanted to understand, to know what went on inside himself at certain times.

Dr. d'Oléons was a serious, levelheaded, reasonable man who measured his words. Jokes and sarcasm didn't come easily to him, as they did to Marc, but he'd occasionally make an effort to get into the spirit, the "in-house matador" comment, for instance.

"Picador would be more like it," said Marc. "Some superficial goring, but no mortal wounds."

Hugues ran his fingers through his hair—already scarce, though he was barely older than Marc, and graying, or at least turning pale yellow—then scratched the back of his head. Why was it, wondered Marc, that ever since the Stone Age man has always brought his hand to his scalp when confused, and scratched it with obvious pleasure? Would science ever explain that?

"Anything new on that subject?" asked Hugues, perplexed.

Meaning: whether or not Michel was truly guilty of the murder of Marie Poterjnikof, a question that had preoccupied both of them ever since the trial.

"Yes and no," said Marc. "That's also what I'm here to talk to you about. You know how attached to me he's become. Too much so, in my opinion. I'm going to have to try to distance myself from him somehow, or the therapy will come to a standstill. If there were anything else to be learned, I would have heard about it. I really think he told me everything. On the other hand, I have my own theory that I'd like to share with you. Just a psychiatrist's hypothesis, of course, it wouldn't bear any weight with a jury, but that doesn't matter. What matters to us is to make him well."

"Go on," said Hugues, who was in fact very excited, but was forcing himself to remain calm and dignified.

"Actually, I have two theories. The first is that Michel Zyto didn't really commit incest. It never came to that. Which is to say that he's never had sexual relations with any woman. The second is that he didn't kill anyone. You already know about these two theories. What's new about them is that I believe they're linked. Let me explain. I think that Zyto's mental process is very simple, like the few, simple elements instilled early in life that form a personality. He hates his mother, thus all women, his sexual aggression being proportionate to that which he endured as the victim. In other words, if it had been consummated back then, he would be a murderer today. In his mind, the sexual act represents a loss of being, a kind of theft that the woman commits in which he is robbed of a part of himself, a part of his existence. He takes revenge by using physical violence, stealing from the woman the exact quantitative equivalent, so to speak, of what had been taken from him. One could almost establish a percentage. That's how it looks to me at this point. Our sessions over the past eighteen months have led me to this kind of diagnosis; and, from what I can tell, he is able to temporarily suppress the symptoms. Right now, he's *normal*. Aside from his hypochondria, of course, but that . . . is he still taking his antibiotics?"

Marc couldn't help smiling. Zyto, with his uncommon physical resilience, capable of eluding the police for weeks under extreme surveillance conditions, also capable of trying to take his life by flinging himself head first against a brick wall, was as shy and frightened as a lamb the moment his health was in question. He was terrified by the idea of illness; he'd fret over a simple itch. Recently, he'd been complaining of a sore throat and an earache on the left side. They had finally given him some antibiotics, just to shut him up. They couldn't find a thing wrong with him.

"Still nothing planned for the month of August?" asked Marc.

He knew the answer. Hugues hardly ever took a vacation. The Center was his entire life. He was a bachelor. He only left Avenue Stéphen-Mornay to sleep in his apartment on Rue Saint-Dominique, if one were to exaggerate slightly. Assuming that he didn't carry on any clandestine activities or have a secret life, something Marc could not possibly imagine.

"No. What about you?"

"No."

It was a categorical no. A kind of flat refusal, more straightforward than he'd been with Cedric Houdé. The results from the scan, not terribly heartening, had somewhat demoralized him.

In any case, leaving was out of the question.

The two men remained silent, each absorbed in his own thoughts. Then Marc got back to Zyto:

"As far as treating the fundamental problem, if we can manage to peel away this destructive maternal image he has for women, and probably for the world in general..."

"Which you've now come to represent for him, but in a beneficial way, is that it?"

"You're sly as a fox, Hugues. Sly as a fox. Yes, that's it. That's why, despite everything, I'm afraid to stop using eye contact during our sessions, and begin something more like psychoanalysis."

At the outset of his career, Marc had worked for a year as a psychoanalyst in a clinic in Fontainebleau, where during his internship, he himself had been analyzed by the famous Martin Vérapoutsimila.

"If he's doing as well as we'd hoped, it's not a problem," said Hugues.

"Yes. Otherwise, it's tricky. I think it would be best to wait. And, for him to get out every now and then. Cloistering himself away like this is a bit like recreating the same conditions that caused his problems in the first place."

"I'm still thinking about your hypothesis. It's wonderful," said Hugues.

"How can we verify it? We'd have to see how it all functions from the inside." Marc was silent for a moment, with a faraway look in his eyes.

"Plus, we'd have the absolute proof of his innocence," Hugues added. "If only we could step into his shoes for a minute. Be a witness to his thoughts, but remain sound and lucid."

"Ah yes. If we could take a little stroll inside his head. The psychiatrist's dream. And alas, impossible."

"Yes, impossible."

Marc gazed at the garden again. Impossible? Perhaps it wasn't. And in the next few days, he intended to do precisely that, take a little stroll inside Michel Zyto's head.

For the twentieth time since he'd awakened, Michel Zyto went to examine his throat in the bathroom mirror.

He closed the door and shut off the light to make it dark, turned on the flashlight, and stuck out his tongue. How revolting! This time it was obviously serious. His throat was covered with little white bumps; there were even some on the roof of his mouth, his uvula, everywhere. His anxiety turned into panic. It seemed like the old symptoms were still there, the pain in his ear and neck, every time he swallowed. And now, on top of that, this dry, burning sensation all through his throat. Were they two different things, or the same malady spreading, taking on new variations? So the antibiotics had served no purpose, the infection had been stronger! Or was it something else, something worse than an infection?

Panic. He put down the flashlight and went back into his room.

His anxiety had subsided. He was familiar with this phenomenon: extreme fear would drain him of all his energy and make him appear somewhat calm. Not just any kind of fear. Only one particular kind, the fear of disease, of something foreign inside that would harm, perhaps destroy him. Nothing else frightened him like that. He was fearless about everything else.

He sat down on the edge of the bed, his shoulders hunched over, hands tucked between his knees. He couldn't decide if he were still as happy as before, when he'd first arrived at Stéphen-Mornay, or if he'd had enough, enough to make him scream. Maybe both.

He glanced at his watch. Marc was late. Zyto waited for him with baited breath. He was all nerves. Lacroix would know how to diagnose it, now that there was something to see! Dr. Lacroix could no longer tell him that his fixation on a little pain was magnifying it, nursing it along. And this time he'd treat it. If only Zyto were a doctor too! He wouldn't have to go through these agonizing moments. He'd know right away how to interpret the symptoms. And he'd move in medical circles, he'd manage to become friendly with specialists of every part of the body.

The sound of footsteps in the corridor interrupted his daydream. But he didn't recognize Marc Lacroix's walk. No, it wasn't him. The sound faded away.

He swallowed, something he'd refrained from doing for a few moments. Ouch!

After looking at his throat in the bathroom one more time, he wiped his perspiring forehead with a washcloth, combed his hair and his mustache, straightened the collar of his pale blue shirt and tucked it more securely into his pants, a brand new pair of blue jeans that he was wearing for the first time. He liked looking impeccable for Lacroix's visits. He'd always been very meticulous about his appearance.

Fifteen minutes late! He couldn't hold out any longer and went to open the door of his room. He took one step into the corridor, praying with all his might that he'd catch a glimpse of the doctor, but at the same time embarrassed by the possibility of revealing his impatience. Unfortunately (or was it fortunately?) Marc appeared at the end of the corridor, on his way up from the ground floor, looking elegant in his summer suit. He waved to Michel Zyto, and advanced with large, graceful strides.

Marc immediately realized that his favorite psychopath wasn't feeling well. But he didn't let on, gave him a smile, shaking his hand as usual, and apologized for being late. Michel Zyto let him in, the way a doctor would usher someone into his office. He sometimes liked to think that Marc Lacroix was a patient who had come to consult him, a private little fantasy that gave him great pleasure.

The room was wallpapered in dusty rose, with somber wood furniture and dark green curtains made of Provençal fabric, and looked more like an expensive hotel room than a clinic. A hotel room that had been lived in for quite some time, where the guest would have arranged it to suit his taste, modifying certain details, cramming it with books, installing a small stereo. Michel Zyto had, in fact, begun to listen to music, Vivaldi in particular. One day he made a naive yet subtle comment to Marc, saying that this music reminded him of the garden at Stéphen-Mornay, only without the suffocating sensation that a well-ordered garden might give, whereas Vivaldi—Marc had helped him formulate these confused ideas—surprised him with soaring passages of solo instruments that broke through the strict symmetry.

They sat in their usual places, two small chairs facing each other between the window and a table, which was more or less used as a desk.

"So?" Marc asked.

Zyto couldn't wait to launch into his hypochondriacal tirade.

"My throat hurts," he said. "It looks really terrible. I saw it with a flashlight."

"Did you speak to Dr. Fabricant about it?"

"No."

Marc stood up with a determined air.

"Come on, let's go take a look."

In the darkness of the bathroom, Zyto obeyed Marc like a docile child. He sat down, tilted his head back, though not quite far enough; Marc gave it a slight push, putting his hand on Zyto's hair.

How thick it was! He thought about his own hair, which depressed him.

"Stick out your tongue, say 'ahhh' . . . That's it. OK, you can close your mouth. Wait, no, don't open it again, do just the opposite, bite down . . ."

Michel Zyto kept his teeth clenched. Marc rolled back his lips across the entire width of his mouth, both in front and on the sides.

"Sorry, I'm treating you like a horse. That'll be fine. I've got the whole picture now, and there's nothing wrong with you. Let me explain."

He's got more luck than I have with my ear, Marc said to himself.

Back in his chair by the window, Zyto's face had changed. Marc's words had brought him back to life, he was like a changed man.

"What you've got this morning is a yeast infection, candida albicans. A common fungus."

"A fungus?"

"Yes. A yeast infection caused by the antibiotics, believe it or not. Quite common, it happens all the time. It looks drastic, but it goes away just as fast as it appears."

"But the other pain?" asked Zyto, now divided between anxiety and hope.

"I was getting to that," Marc said in a reassuring tone. "Now I understand after looking at your teeth. I knew it wasn't serious, in any event, but I have an explanation for it. That's even better, isn't it?"

He smiled at him. Zyto wanted to smile back, but he couldn't manage it. Later, after the explanation.

"Yes."

"The jaw muscles are the muscles in the body that put out the greatest effort. They exert incredible pressure, about eight hundred pounds per square inch. And nervous people like you tend to clench their teeth, and tense their jaws."

"You think so?"

"I'm sure of it. Even if you don't realize it. Like during the night, while you're asleep. Plus, you grind your teeth, I can tell from the way they're worn down. In short, this pain is a muscular pain, purely mechanical, but one that can result in inflammation. The swallowing movements hurt your ear and throat, like the pain of a ganglion. I know what it's like, it happens to me sometimes."

Zyto felt a surge of hope. If it happened to Marc Lacroix, then . . .

"It's a bit like the tendinitis athletes get. You watch all those tennis matches on TV, you must have heard of it. It's the same thing."

"It'll go away?"

"Of course. Especially if you pay less attention to it. Excuse me for repeating myself."

"So I don't have anything to worry about?"

"Not a thing. There's nothing wrong with you."

"But that fungus?"

Here we go again, Marc thought.

"We all have mushrooms in our intestines. Armies of them, hordes. Ordinarily, they destroy themselves and the balance is restored. You know that antibiotics are bad for the intestines. They upset this balance. This army takes advantage of the situation to seize power. It invades the entire digestive tract, rises into the esophagus, sometimes all the way to the throat. A yeast infection of the digestive tract, that's precisely what you've got."

While he was speaking, he turned toward the telephone on the desk and dialed a number.

"Hello? Good morning, it's Lacroix. Do you have any Maktarin? OK. Would you bring it to Room Six? Thanks."

He hung up.

"You can take three pills right away and three more tonight. From tomorrow on, two between each meal, six in all. For three weeks. And of course, stop taking the antibiotics since there's nothing the matter with you."

"Three weeks?"

"Yes, to avoid a relapse. The enemy is fearful, but tenacious. But I can guarantee you'll feel better in a few hours. The symptoms will disappear."

"Are you positive? Everything you're telling me is true?"

"A hundred percent. Don't give your throat another thought, there's nothing wrong with you."

Michel Zyto could not hold back a long sigh of relief. He could have kissed Marc. His pale eyes shone with gratitude.

"Thanks. Thank you so much."

"Besides your throat?" Marc asked pleasantly.

Zyto concentrated for a moment, then changed his tone and posture.

"I had a hard time finding a weapon. It's difficult. You've got to stay on the right track, steer clear of the bogus tips, and believe me, there are plenty of those. You're dealing with bums who ask you for money, and then they send you god knows where. You end up in some deserted neighborhood, with no one at the address they gave you . . ."

As strange and incongruous as it seemed, Michel Zyto had abruptly launched into the continuation of his story. During the last few sessions, he'd begun to tell Marc exactly how he'd spent the weeks on the run after his third attack, that is to say, from the time he'd actually been identified. Reassured about his health, he'd taken up the story right where he'd left off the last time, and all this with such spontaniety and trust that Marc was touched.

He said nothing and listened. Zyto was relieved to be able to confess it all to someone. The most difficult part had been recounting the three attacks. Now he felt relieved talking about it, filling in the details.

"The hardest thing was finding the right connection. After five days of wandering around Paris, I found him. They told me about a guy who hangs out in a bar near Place Blanche, Le Terminus. They call him Little Rat, because of the way he looks, I guess. He has a funny mustache and little beady eyes. He doesn't do anything else, that's his job. He acts as a go-between for people who are looking for weapons; a revolver, certain kinds of knives, machine guns, grenades, everything. He doesn't ask for money. He probably gets a commission from the arms seller, that's what I figure. But you have to go through him. He calls the guy, and that's that. The dealer took a real liking to me, for some reason. He found me a hideout on Rue

Piat, Belleville, in a small one-story house with a garden. A tiny little place. Everything is small. The bedroom's on the first floor. A great little room. It's nice and quiet. The owner lives on the ground floor. His name is Jacquot, a parrot's name. It's probably because he never says a thing. He doesn't like it if you talk to him either. He's around sixty. You're safe at his place."

There was a knock at the door. An unattractive blond woman walked in, smiled at the two men, put two boxes of pills on the table, and left.

"Should I take some right away?" asked Michel Zyto.

"Yes, go ahead."

He swallowed three pills with a little water and sat back down across from Marc.

"In any case, if something happens, you can be sure it's not his fault. He has that reputation. I was able to get some rest in that little room, breathe easy for a while."

He was silent. What a pleasure it was, not having to worry about his throat anymore!

He looked straight into Marc's eyes. Suddenly, he flashed him a smile; his smooth, charming movie star smile.

Marc looked down, then looked up just long enough to return the smile, and looked down again.

Marc pulled off the Champs-Elysées and veered to the right onto Avenue Marigny. He made the turn cautiously, as though surrounded by a cloud of motorscooters.

A mean-looking guy on a motorcycle, dressed entirely in black, shot an approving glance at the Nissan Terrano, then at Marc. Marc had noticed that the traditional animosity between bikers and motorists became less hostile, even changed into complicity if the vehicle were slightly out of the ordinary, like a Jeep. As if sitting behind the wheel of a 4 x 4 were enough to turn the driver into a great athlete, Marc thought with some bitterness. He reproached himself for not taking care of his body. Lately, he had the feeling that his biceps, pecs, and waist were getting flabby. He was starting to get a belly.

But was a firm or flabby body just a matter of whether or not you were athletic? No. Michel Zyto didn't play any sports and he was as hard as a rock. Then again, so was Marc, aside from two or three little soft spots . . . that he could get rid of simply by working out.

The search for a parking space put an end to these contemplations. He went down Avenue Marigny for a few blocks, swung left onto Rue de Ponthieu, then left again on Rue Jean-Mermoz . . . Nothing. Ah, a stroke of luck, a long Citroën was pulling out, leaving a free space right in front of the Red Dragon restaurant, which Marc interpreted as a good omen. He was slightly superstitious and realized that was rather silly.

He backed into the space without any difficulty. Three Terranos would have fit in there, he thought, still amused by his own self-deception.

The four-wheel drive's imposing size, red color, and small triangular side windows tended to attract people's attention—especially children's—to such an extent that Marc, fairly shy in daily life, usually stepped out of his car like a actor making his debut.

Marie Lacroix, who was waiting for her husband's return, leapt up the moment she saw him out in the street. Marc and she had kept up the ritual of lunching alone in a restaurant without Leonard every now and then, as they had before the child was born.

He walked into the restaurant. She smiled at him, and tossed back her long black hair. She was wearing a pale sleeveless dress. She looked fresh and pretty, like a young girl, despite her height and voluptuous figure.

How could anyone not be in love with such a splendid woman? Marc thought, kissing her. But the fact remained that he wasn't in love with her anymore, and it tormented him twenty-four hours a day.

She sat down again. Marc took off his jacket and took the seat across from her.

"Aren't you cold? It's a little chilly outside," he said.

"I have my red jacket, but I left it in the Austin. No, I'll be OK."

"Our usual table?"

"No, I feel like sitting near the window. We've been reserving the same table for the past two years, do you realize that?"

"You're right. I get caught up in my routines. I'm a creature of habit."

"More like an enslaved beast," said Marie.

"A poor little lamb . . ."

He had always enjoyed joking with Marie. He liked talking to her, she was intelligent and stimulating. Already two years since they'd started coming to the Red Dragon as regular customers. And more than three months since they'd made love. Ever since he met Marianne? Right to the day, more or less. But Marianne was only a telltale symptom. Even before, way before that, he'd lost all desire for his wife. More than three months . . . Knowing Marie, there was no way in the world she would ever bring up the subject. And neither would he. The right time to talk about it had never presented itself.

"Everything OK with Leonard this morning?"

"Fine. I left him with the Cazanvielhs. I'm going to stop by there this afternoon," she added after a moment of silence.

Marc's features looked pinched. Marie sometimes wondered how he kept up with it all. He was involved in thirty-some-odd activities, his patients, all of his research—in neurobiology at the hospital, in computers at the Dumesnil Center, in physiology and cerebrovascular physiopathology at the Institute on Avenue de Verdun, plus occasional work that he didn't always discuss in detail, plus his regular visits to Michel Zyto twice a week, plus the travelling back and forth, plus a minimum of family life . . . it was too much, he didn't have a second left to breathe. Yet she understood how suddenly dropping everything could make him upset and depressed. Put him in the state he was in right now.

Even though his face was drawn, she found him more handsome than ever.

"Will Marie-Thérèse be there this afternoon?" he asked.

"No. She's got some shopping to do in Paris."

"So you'll be all alone with Marshall?"

"And with Leonard. You're still jealous?"

"Yup."

"You know how silly that is, don't you?"

"Yup."

Marc took her hand. He was trying to hide how desperate he felt. Things were getting too complicated. He was even more jealous of Marshall Cazanvielh now that he was cheating on Marie with Marianne. He needed Marie more than ever, unconditionally.

She let go and covered his hand with hers. She felt a bit sorry for him. Of course, she'd contemplated the possibility of another woman, a rival, even one in particular—her girlfriend Marianne, who'd stopped calling her. But aside from not wanting to believe it, she felt the real problem lay elsewhere. Marc was slipping away from her, and probably from himself as well. He was in bad shape.

They were going through a crisis. All couples did. It would pass, she was almost certain of it, and clung to her belief.

She reached into her purse for a little bottle of pills and swallowed two of them. She sometimes had leg pains from bad circulation. Marc had prescribed a mild, but refillable, dosage.

She kept smiling at him engagingly.

"Are you thinking about tonight? Don't worry, we won't stay long. And starting tomorrow, you've got to relax and have some fun. Even if we don't go away. We're so lucky to have a beautiful house in the country and you never even take advantage of it."

Marc appreciated the "even if we don't go away." Marie was wonderful. He knew being deprived of a vacation would disappoint her. Though he seldom took advantage of their house in Versailles, she, on the other hand, was there all the time. They didn't even mention the last week in August, which they usually spent at La Colle-sur-Loup with Marie's parents. Marie wasn't on very good terms with them, and considered the visit a chore.

"So, did you have a nice morning?" she asked.

"Not bad. What about you? What did you do?"

"The usual. Oh, I've also been rereading *The Odyssey* in Greek. Is anything bothering you? What's up? Was it something this morning?"

Wonderful, and cunning too. No, sharp was more like it, there wasn't an ounce of cunning in her. Or was he completely wrong about her? Maybe she knew about everything, his affair with Marianne, his laboratory at Louveciennes, maybe she was cheating on him every afternoon with Marshall, leaving him to flounder in his incipient madness, she had figured it all out, she was a ruinous witch, bent on his destruction. . . . He felt as if he were indeed going mad. It lasted a fraction of a second.

Initially, he'd decided not to mention his visit to Lariboisière. He changed his mind.

"Just a little something. I saw Cedric this morning."

"And . . . ?" asked Marie, immediately alarmed. "Did you go for that X-ray? And you didn't even tell me!"

"Yes. It's a bit more serious than we thought. But nothing major, don't worry." (She had turned pale.) "Cedric found a little growth, benign, of course, on the acoustic nerve. Now I know why I was having those dizzy spells. It's called a neurinome of the acoustic nerve. It's a common problem."

"What can be done about it?"

"Nothing. I can live with it for a hundred and fifty years. I'm only repeating what Cedric told me."

"It can't get any bigger?"

He hesitated.

"No, it could."

"And then what?"

"If it grows any bigger, it'll mean an operation. There's a slight risk of deafness. It's a bit tricky, the surgery."

A great risk, actually, and there were some other ones as well, even more serious, very serious. He hoped an operation would never be necessary.

"Don't worry. I've probably had it for ages. There's no reason why it should get any bigger. It has to be watched, that's all. Nothing to get upset about, I promise. OK?"

"I'll try . . ."

He pretended to study the menu.

"The usual?" he asked.

She smiled.

"Yes, the usual."

They weren't particularly fond of Chinese restaurants, except for the Red Dragon, where the food happened to be delicious.

Connie Huong, the owner, caught sight of Marc. Everytime he saw her, Marc thought of the expression, "to be all smiles." This petite and gracious Chinese woman was all smiles, a smile that came from every part of her.

"You're lucky to be able to read Homer like that," Marc said to his wife.

He'd also studied Greek in high school. He couldn't remember a thing. He wished he could. Before Marie had time to answer, Connie Huong was already moving toward them, extending a smiling hand.

Cookie, a West Highland white terrier who was really very cute (but then, they all are), looked in surprise at the sugar cube his mistress held out to him and gulped it down. He was almost never allowed to have sugar. But he knew today was a special day. First of all, his mistress was expecting someone, that was obvious. She'd taken out her nice china cups and baked a cake. She was feverish with excitement, and couldn't stay off her feet in spite of her weak legs. Yet, every so often she would burst into tears. Cookie would whine, then, and put his front paws on her knees, but this demonstrative act did nothing to calm her. Quite the contrary. She just hugged him to her breast and cried even harder.

Yes, it was a strange day for Cookie. And it wasn't over yet.

Germaine Halbronn, a very old woman who was always out of breath, lifted the chocolate rice cake (her grandmother's recipe) out of the refrigerator and, taking little steps, made her way to the dining room to set it on the table.

She'd been living in this modest, clean, but gloomy apartment at No. 12 Rue de Budapest for nearly forty years, on the ground floor, left side. And now she'd have to leave it. But one thing at a time. The hardest part was Cookie. After that, she'd see. She could be strong, if need be.

Still, to have to part with Cookie!

She held back her tears. It was 3:25. She sat down and stroked the dog with her fingertips. He didn't dare react too strongly, for fear of making her cry. But he couldn't help stretching his head upward, his eyes open very wide.

He was barely a year old.

On the telephone, the doctor-who-wanted-a-very-nice-dog had said half past three and at 3:33 the doorbell rang. Germaine Halbronn stood up and went to open the door. It took her a while to get there. She was dragging her feet and had difficulty breathing.

Marc grasped the situation at first glance, the essentials: a very elderly woman, a two-room apartment with no light, pictures of her husband everywhere (a little man with a mustache, shorter than his wife), forced to give up her dog although he was so much a part of her life.

Marc was kind-hearted. He was moved. He immediately resolved to do everything in his power to get Cookie back to this nice lady. He'd even give her an allowance if it were a question of money, or a problem with a home for the aged.

Ten minutes later, Marc Lacroix, Germaine Halbronn, and Cookie were great friends. Marc drank his coffee with the dog on his lap. But he also had to force down a piece of rice cake of unidentifiable taste. With his eyes closed, he would have had a hard time determining exactly what was in his mouth—a handful of buckshot in a thick sauce of fresh sweetish plaster, as he would later describe it to Leonard. After the succulent steamed dishes at the Red Dragon, it took great effort to get it down.

He'd detected Madame Halbronn's severe asthma right away. Alas, she would indeed have to give up Cookie. Nothing could change that, not all the money in the world.

In any case, Cookie would be perfect for the experiment. . . .

"Do you like it?"

"Very good," said Marc. "Very good."

"I'm glad. Not everybody likes it, you know. My grandmother taught me how to make it. I was sixteen. If you knew how many times I made it for my husband, poor man! And for my son! Won't you have another little piece?"

"No thank you," he said lightly. "As I mentioned earlier, I just finished having lunch. You're right though, it's hard to resist, but . . . wouldn't the dog like some?"

"No, he's never cared for it very much. Although he just loves to eat. Don't you, Cookie?"

The dog looked at her and cocked his head to the side in an amusing way: was the invitation enticing enough to leave Marc's cozy, hospitable lap?

"Ah yes, I've got to part with this treasure. My asthma has gotten even worse. The specialist told me: you cannot live under the same roof with a dog. Plus, I can't really manage on my own anymore. It's the legs, the circulation. My son and daughter-in-law want me to come stay with them. They live in Montmartre. Still, they've got a small apartment. My son is a tipster. Oh well. It's going to be very hard on both of us, isn't it Cookie?"

This time, the dog took a flying leap onto her chest and licked her face. She disengaged herself, caught between amusement and sorrow. She was terribly wrinkled, but she wasn't repugnant the way some old people were, Marc thought. It was her hands. She still had beautiful hands, hardly marred by age.

Marc was thinking. The dog was still young enough to adapt to a new master. But who? Leonard didn't want another dog, not since Baby, his German shepherd, had died. Later on, he'd said. Maybe. And some sort of retriever. Not a ball of fur, he didn't like balls of fur. So who? The tall slinky Marie-Thérèse Cazanvielh, as a present for her birthday tonight? In addition to the fabulous antique hat that

Marie had found her? Why not? It was exactly what she wanted, a dog that was already some months old, not a puppy. Otherwise she'd feel sorry for it.

Cookie at the Cazanvielhs' house. Yes, why not?

"I'm often in Paris with my car, I could bring him to see you every once in a while."

Was that a good idea? Germaine Halbronn, her face strained with emotion, was on the verge of tears at the idea of occasional reunions with her dog. She caught hold of herself. She was strong. She knew how to look on the good side of things, the positive side.

Her eyes sparkled with gratitude.

"Oh, thank you, thank you! Will you really do that?"

"I promise," said Marc.

She was silent for a moment, distraught, chewing her gums, looking off into the distance to the interior courtyard, which resembled a prison yard.

"You'll see, you'll be happy with Cookie. Westies are the sweetest dogs you'll ever find. And Cookie's the sweetest of them all. And the most handsome, look at him. People were always asking me to enter him in contests."

And when I come back with him for a visit, he may even be the most famous dog in the world," Marc thought.

"It must have cost you a lot, a purebred Westie like Cookie. At least three thousand francs?"

"Much more than that. Almost five thousand. But it's what I wanted. I don't regret it."

Marc took out his checkbook.

Madame Halbronn was shocked, almost indignant.

"Oh no! Most definitely not! I put "giving away Westie" in the ad, didn't I? You can't sell them once they're a year old. People want them when they're puppies."

"Well, as for me," said Marc, beginning to write out the check, "I wanted one that was a year old, so there you are. I wouldn't have called you otherwise."

"No, no. It would make me feel uncomfortable."

She was absolutely sincere. Marc stopped writing and looked at her.

"Well I feel uncomfortable too. Just as much as you do. So let's both try to make this simple. I wanted a dog exactly like him and I'm paying you for it, it's only right. If my wife were here, she'd tell you the same thing."

Germaine Halbronn could hardly believe that people as nice as Marc truly existed. She leaned over her chair, reaching out with her right arm. He knew what she wanted. He complied. He was probably the same age as her son. A tipster. He'd never heard of that profession before.

He leaned over at almost the same time she did, holding out his right arm. The old woman bestowed a kiss on his cheek.

They were both looking out the window.

Marianne Matys was tall and blond. She had long legs, a shade on the heavy side, slim arms, and a fairly slender torso, if it weren't for her full rounded breasts. Her knees were slightly out of alignment with her legs, giving her a somewhat languid air and walk.

Marc adored these "imperfections" of Marianne's. There were others—for example, the tiny asymmetrical irregularities in her smile, in her eyes—that made her so attractive. That's where her type of beauty and appeal lay.

She lived in a small three-room apartment, No. 14 Rue du Faubourg-Saint-Honoré, on the sixth floor. Her windows opened out onto a large courtyard that was shared with the other buildings. In the middle of the courtyard was an enormous tree.

She snuggled up against Marc, put her arm around his waist and kissed him on the forehead. Marc slipped his hand under her skirt.

He caressed her, the fabric of her panties, then her skin. He immediately wanted to make love to her.

He had never known anyone (granted, he hadn't known that many women) with whom physical rapport was as easy, natural, and exciting as with Marianne. And it had been that from the first time they'd met, in Marc's office on Avenue Verdun, on the small couch that had until then only been used for naps. A wonderful memory.

Marc had met Marianne through Marie. Marianne was the daughter of Eduoard Matys, a professor of French, Latin, and Greek, with whom Marie had taken classes at the Edouard Herriot High School in Lyon, in preparation for the École Normale Supérieure. Marie had been nineteen at the time, and an excellent student. Edouard Matys, who was a widower, was very fond of her and sometimes invited Marie to lunch at his home. He lived with his daughter Marianne, then just a girl of fourteen but already effortlessly sensual.

Fifteen years later, on a night when Marie had succeeded in dragging Marc to the theater to see *A Midsummer's Night Dream*, she had recognized Marianne Matys as the actress who had admirably played the part of Titania, the Faerie Queen. They had gone to her dressing room after the performance. The two women were happy to see one another. Eduoard Matys had since died. Marianne had launched her career in the theater at an early age. She was even becoming fairly well-known, the difficult debut a thing of the past; she was now in demand. That night in the dressing room, she kept looking at Marc and Marc couldn't take his eyes off her. Afterward, Marie and Marianne would occasionally see each other, sometimes go shopping together in Paris. Marie had invited her several times to Versailles.

One Sunday morning when Marianne called, Marc, who was alone in the house, had answered. They became lovers the next day.

Since then, she'd seen the Lacroixs as a couple only once. Her encounters with Marie became more sporadic, and eventually she stopped calling. One night, Marie had commented on how surprising it was. Marc limited his response to: "Well, you know actresses . . . maybe she's on tour," and it was never brought up again.

At first, Marc was afraid that he'd fallen for a femme fatale. But she was nothing of the sort. Marianne had had as little "experience" as he, though that wasn't the point, it was just that she behaved that way with him. Their physical intimacy had been immediate, she'd been wonderfully naive and innocent. The words "paradise on earth" had crossed Marc's mind; he'd had the thrilling sensation of the first time, a new life, total ecstasy, and absolute discovery. Sleeping with her had become like a drug. The rest of the world took on a lesser existence. Even his family, he realized with alarm.

Perhaps at thirty-nine, he was truly in love for the first time in his life.

The rest of the world, with one exception: his laboratory at Louveciennes. The machine he'd built over the course of several years, his grandiose plans for Michel Zyto in that laboratory... he'd never told anyone about it. It was his secret. Marianne was also his secret. Two secrets, two life rafts that kept him afloat, allowed him to survive.

Marianne Matys and Michel Zyto.

And, to some degree, his red jeep. Able to cross deserts, seas, rivers, mountains, he thought, always amused when Marianne brought up the subject of his Nissan Terrano.

"Still in love with your beautiful car?"

"More than ever."

Marianne had only seen the four-wheel drive twice. Marc could have parked it in the courtyard, but he didn't. He concealed his affair with Marianne as much as possible. He was never seen with her. Out of caution, but also out of profound necessity. He escaped through Marianne, the way he took refuge in his laboratory, and any contrary action, like going out in public with her, would have diminished the benefits of his secret life.

He would only see her in the private cocoon of her apartment, solely to make love. And for the time being, Marianne had no objections.

Marc hadn't told her anything about Cookie. Was the dog miserable in the car? Was he barking? No, he wasn't the barking type. Maybe he was whining. Whimpering. At a year old, he seemed to have inherited the strong, philosophical character of his mistress.

He'd wait before he started to panic. And with a little luck, he wouldn't panic at all. He would look after him, he liked that little dog, with his surprised, gentle eyes.

Marc slid his hand down Marianne's legs, then glided back up between her thighs. Her breathing quickened, she turned toward Marc and kissed him as he continued to caress her. At the same moment, they impulsively interrupted their embrace to hug each other passionately. Marianne was also very much in love with Marc, more than she'd ever been with anyone else. She loved his handsome face with its intense expressions, his intelligence, his talents; his confused manner, like a lost child; his skin, so wonderfully soft; the desire he felt for her, his adolescent admiration; yes, she was in love, won over, making her even more seductive and desirable in Marc's eyes.

She let go of him, and swiftly removed what little clothing she still wore. She lay down on the bed, her eyes turned toward Marc, struck as always by his Christ-like face, magnificently lit from behind at the moment.

He came over and knelt down beside her. He gently spread her legs, presenting her vulva to his kiss.

After giving her breasts one last kiss, first the right, then the left, Marc got out of bed. The left in particular. It was the farthest away from Marc, who always lay on Marianne's right while they were resting or talking. And since the left breast wasn't exactly parallel to the other, its nipple was less within Marc's kissing reach. As a result it wasn't pampered as much. Pillow talk. So sometimes he'd have to give it more attention. To compensate, as Marianne would say.

Marc took a shower in the bathroom, so tiny that one couldn't help bumping into everything. But everything about Marianne's apartment was too small, all of the rooms. There was a kind of storage space with a skylight, which the real estate woman had called the second room. "It's for the baby, no doubt," Marc had commented one day. "For the first few days of his life," he'd added, trying to make Marianne laugh. "A baby pygmy. An especially puny one. Even for a preemie like him." Marianne, who had a good sense of humor, adored Marc's jokes. He made her laugh even when he was tense and depressed.

Of course, the small apartment, which had been completely renovated just before Marianne had moved in, was attractive, but Marc never could have lived there the way she did, shut in for days at a time. He would have felt stifled. Marianne, on the other hand, was very comfortable there. She could have afforded something ten times larger; she had regular work as an actress, not to mention all the radio shows and dubbing for movies. She made good money. But she had a preference for these deluxe student-like apartments that were charming, impractical, and inevitably temporary. By the same token, she loved designer boutiques, and she had thousands of them at her doorstep in the Faubourg Saint-Honoré neighborhood.

She was still stretched out on the bed, her legs apart. She closed her eyes. She never took a shower right away. She always let Marc go first. She would think about him, telling herself she loved him. So far, she wasn't bothered by the fact that he was married and rarely free. She was happy and carefree.

She was getting sleepy. The sound of the shower was soothing. Marc took incredibly long showers.

The water stopped. Then she heard a thump (an elbow or a knee or maybe even a skull, slamming into a resonant wall) followed by an emphatic "Shit!"

"Oh! Poor darling," said Marianne. "Did you hurt yourself again?"

Marc walked into the bedroom, naked. He wasn't self-conscious about his slight physical imperfections in front of Marianne, he knew how much she loved him. But he sucked in his stomach anyway, trying to appear casual, and stood with his shoulders very straight. Marianne smiled at him. She was relaxed, as if she were luxuriating in her thick blond hair, her desire to sleep, and her physical well-being. Marc leaned over with both hands on the bed and kissed her eyes.

Their faces were practically touching. Marianne caressed his shoulder in a gesture of pure tenderness. Her gaze was pure tenderness as well. For a brief moment, Marc was as happy as she was.

Marshall Cazanvielh and Marie Lacroix sipped their glasses of Armagnac.

Marshall had concocted a clever strategy to keep Leonard from wanting to tag along with them on their customary walk from the house to the château.

The maid was in today. Leonard wouldn't be alone. And he'd have something to play with. That was certain! A lot of kids would have loved to be in his shoes!

Marshall, now retired from the army, was sixty years old. He was bald but it suited him well; strong, attractive, suntanned all year round; passionately fond of horseback riding, shooting, chess; a fan of American action films; and a collector of antiques and curious objects. One entire room of his villa there in the heart of Versailles was devoted to these sorts of acquisitions, with the exception of the statues, which he installed in his immense garden.

He loved puttering around the house, unlike his wife, Marie-Thérèse, who always had something or other to do elsewhere. Nothing in particular, really, but she had to get out of the house, had to "stir up the air," as Marshall put it. And when she was home, she continued to scurry about even when she was on the phone with her innumerable friends and acquaintances. She was eleven years younger than Marshall. Marc and Marie found her a bit frivolous, a little nutty, but generous and amusing. And she adored Leonard.

In fact both of them were very fond of Leonard, Marshall and his wife, and they spoiled him as if he were the child they'd never been able to have.

Marie finished her drink, and placed it on the wood coffee table decorated with fine and intricate inlays. She tried to catch a glimpse of Leonard through the window facing the garden, the window where the "phone nook" was. This little corner, comfortably and attractively arranged by Marie-Thérèse, consisted of a space bordered by potted plants, with a leather chair near the window and a six-legged oak coffee table. On this table sat a green, ornately curved telephone—a gadget right out of science fiction—several packs of cigarettes, three ashtrays—large, medium-sized, and tiny—and a pad of note paper on which Marie-Thérèse would write useless trivia. She was always taking things down when she was on the phone.

Marie caught sight of Leonard. Ten seconds later, he burst into the room. On the thin side, but tall and sturdy for his age, and very handsome, he resembled both of his parents, though no one could pinpoint exactly what came from which.

Marshall emptied his glass, stood up, and set the first part of his plan into action. He'd waited until it was time for their walk. The element of surprise, the lure of something radically new would work to his advantage, and Leonard would no longer be an obstacle.

"I have something to show you that was just delivered yesterday," he said to mother and son. "I'm sure you'll appreciate it. Especially Leonard."

The boy's eyes sparkled when he heard "especially Leonard." If Marshall said so, it was probably pretty good.

* * *

The room upstairs was crammed with bizarre objects, but the pinball machine stood out—an antique, one of the first of its kind in Paris, that was what the proprietor of the café behind Rue des Lyonnais had told Marshall. It was decorated with scenes from the Wild West. The vertical panel depicted a typical shoot-out: two men standing face to face on Main Street for the final showdown, Colts in hand, about to pull the triggers; one would soon be lying in the dust, dead.

"Wowee!" cried Leonard, his own personal expression for supreme happiness.

Polished and gleaming, the machine was in mint condition. Armed with a handful of coins, Leonard planted himself in front of it with the obvious intention, written on every square inch of his body, of remaining there until school reopened in September.

He was wearing navy blue shorts and a light blue short-sleeved shirt. His bangs fell prettily onto his forehead.

In response to his mother's tender, concerned question, he answered with a definite "No, I do not mind staying here by myself while you go on your walk, not even a teeny weeny bit."

He was thrilled to death.

Marie and Marshall left the house by the courtyard side. It was a magnificent turn-of-the-century villa that had cost a fortune, but Marshall and Marie-Thérèse Cazanvielh were rich. They had both been independently wealthy when they'd married.

As Marshall was opening the iron gate that led to an alley called Soldier's Impasse (there had been a time when he'd found the coincidence amusing), Martine, the maid, a redheaded woman about fifty, appeared at a second-story window.

"Does Monsieur still want the frozen *pommes dauphine* this evening?" she cried. "I'm going out to do some shopping."

Marshall, usually a gourmet who shunned canned and frozen food, still had a weakness for frozen potato puffs.

"Yes, that'll be fine. You won't forget to leave them in the oven for four minutes more than is written on the box?"

"I know, Monsieur. It cooks the grease out. Have I ever forgotten?"

"Never, Martine, never. You're wonderful."

She laughed, a bit too loudly, and shut the window, also a bit too loudly.

The alley ran into the Avenue de Paris, and the Avenue de Paris led straight to the château, approximately a mile away.

They walked briskly. There was a slight breeze, not very warm for the thirty-first of July. Marie had put on her red jacket. Marshall was wearing a thin wool black sweater with nothing underneath that made him look very athletic.

Marie Lacroix knew full well that he had gotten rid of Leonard. This meant he had something to tell her. She was waiting patiently. For the moment, they were chatting about this and that, the weather, the streets of Versailles, always deserted, no matter what the season. It was enough to make anybody want to stay home.

"Unless people who like to stay home settle in these kinds of places on purpose," Marie said a trifle mischievously. "They don't even notice it."

Marshall smiled. She was right. Not to mention he lived ten minutes away from the Lacroixs, and seeing Marie on a regular basis had taken on considerable importance in his life. So what if the streets in Versailles were desolate. . . .

He had fallen in love with Marie the moment he saw her. Yet he loved her in an almost adolescent way, surprising for a stable, dependable, down-to-earth man like himself. She represented the fantasy part of his life he still needed, and perhaps deep down he didn't want anything more than that. Even if he thought he did, and even if today was the day he'd decided to act on it.

Besides, he was extremely attached to his wife. At times he found her a bit childish, a trifle inconsistent, but he adored her and made love to her with passion in their stunning fifteenth-century canopy bed.

The Lacroixs had met Marshall in a real estate agency in Versailles several years ago, when they were looking to get out of Paris.

Marshall was a friend of the director of the agency, an ex-military man like himself, and happened to be visiting when the Lacroixs stopped in. They'd struck up a conversation and had taken to one another immediately. Marc wasn't terribly adept when it came to certain practical matters. Marshall had offered to help them. Little by little, he had taken charge. He would accompany them to visit the houses, or even go by himself, to save them the journey.

His flirtation with Marie was always infinitely discreet and dignified. He addressed her using the formal *vous*, and shook her hand both in greeting and saying goodbye. Never once had he said anything to her that was out of line, or even ambiguous. Marie appreciated his discretion, and wasn't entirely indifferent to his advances, knowing all the while that she would never cheat on Marc.

And what about Marc? Did he cheat on her? No, of course not . . . but what was he doing this afternoon, for instance? He'd told her he was swamped with work, that he had a million things to take care of. Marianne Matys? That was ridiculous. Still, she felt slightly distraught.

She glanced over at Marshall. Right then, she wouldn't have minded if he were to put his arm around her shoulder. She would have shied away, but the thought and the image were appealing.

The color black went well with his tan.

Marshall could feel Marie's eyes on him. Then she looked away. Now? He wondered. No, perhaps a bit later, on the Place d'Armes, once they'd arrived. It would be easier with a lot of people around. The crowd would minimize some of the embarrassment and establish a complicity between them.

"Any plans for a new dog?"

"No. Leonard hasn't mentioned it. But he still talks about Baby. He has dreams about him. He tells me his dreams."

Her voice quavered with emotion. And Marshall thought about how much he'd like put his arm around her at that moment.

The dog hadn't died a natural death. He'd been hit by a car. Leonard had been given the dog when he was very young, when the only word he could distinctly pronounce, aside from "Dada" and "Mama," was "baby," so they'd called the German shepherd Baby.

"It occurred to me that I have a friend who owns a kennel, not far from Paris. Another retired military man. We're a real mafia, you know," he said with a smile.

He seldom talked about his former profession. He'd been a colonel, which Marie had always found surprising. He didn't fit her image of the military type. Too intelligent, too refined, too gentle.

They'd arrived at the Place d'Armes. Lots of visitors, as usual. Busloads of loud tourists, a variety of exclamations, and snatches of conversations in foreign tongues.

Normally, they never stayed very long. One glance at the chateau and they would start right back. Today, Marshall stood face to face with Marie and didn't budge. She returned his gaze. A declaration, she thought. It's about time!

"Marie, there's something I've been wanting to tell you..."

He stopped. He couldn't continue.

"I wouldn't want to hurt you, Marshall. Really I wouldn't. I'm very fond of you. Let's not spoil it."

He hung his head sheepishly, like a child.

"I'm sorry. Please don't be angry with me for a few inappropriate words."

"I'm not angry with you, I swear."

He looked into her eyes.

"Well, I don't regret it. It was now or never. If I'd let it go by, knowing me, I would have been in a bad mood all summer."

Again, Marie was struck by how funny and nice he could be. She drew near him, placed her hand on his shoulder, and gave him a quick peck on the cheek. Then she immediately took his arm and steered him back toward his home.

This kiss was the most exquisite negative answer he'd ever received. Marshall remained thoughtful, filled with admiration. What an amazing woman she was! He realized he'd probably never sleep with Marie Lacroix, but he loved her now more than ever.

"*You see,* not a single black spot. A black spot is one criterion for disqualification. So are walleyes. Have a look at his beautiful hazel eyes. The eyes are supposed to be dark or hazel. Mana is a purebred. To give you some idea, there are only thirty some of them in France, bulldogs of this quality."

Beautiful eyes, beautiful eyes, that's easy to say, Marc thought. The Argentine bulldog scared and slightly repulsed him, the snowy white coat and that vague redness around the mouth, inside the ears, and on the testicles.

Aware that he was being discussed, the dog stood up and gave them a cold stare. Every now and then, he let out a little growl.

"Lie down, Mana, lie down!"

John Joseph had murmured the command. The dog obeyed instantaneously. He lay down by the window and no longer paid any attention to them.

In the distance, Marc could see the Eiffel Tower.

"He's not vicious?" asked Marc. "I've heard that bulldogs . . ."

Actually, he'd made thorough inquiries about Argentine bulldogs before answering the ad. John Joseph interrupted him.

"It all depends on how you raise them. It's true that originally, Doctor Antonio Nores Martinez wanted to create a dog that would hunt puma and peccary. The white color was supposed to help spot them from far away in the pampas. After a lot of trial and error, he opted for a cross between the German bulldog, the boxer, the pointer, and the Irish wolfhound. Naturally, he obtained an animal that was potentially aggressive. But training is the determining factor. Many of the French have raised their bulldogs to be killers, that's why they have a bad reputation. If you raise them as killers, that's what they become. But not if you train them in a gentle way, and if you don't beat them. Especially if you don't beat them. As a matter of fact, in 1972, Professor Diego Rosa published an article on the behavior of bulldogs. He explains and proves that the dog is calm and obedient if you avoid physical punishment."

From his armchair, John Joseph (who spoke French without the slightest accent, though he'd only been living in Paris for the last three and a half years) pulled out a thick magazine from the bookshelf behind him, flipped through it and found Diego Rosa's article.

"If you'd care to read it . . ."

"No," said Marc. "I trust you. If you swear to me that they aren't mean animals. I have a ten-year-old son, you understand."

Actually, he didn't trust John Joseph for a minute.

"I swear. Under normal conditions, they're fine animals. They growl every once in a while, but it doesn't mean anything in particular."

"OK," said Marc, taking out his checkbook.

He couldn't wait to leave. He didn't like the crowded living room or this pedantic nut who seemed like a real phony with his affected speech and an entire library on dogs.

Two thousand francs for a fully grown animal, and on top of that, an Argentine bulldog! This hypocrite must take me for some kind of fool, Marc thought, filling out the check.

He held it out to John Joseph.

"You don't mind me asking... uh, it's not really important, but why are you getting rid of him?"

A few moments of silence elapsed (John Joseph was reading the check), then a door opened, and an ugly child of about thirteen appeared, with eyes as cold as the bulldog's.

"Because he bit Mommy," said the child.

Marc was not displeased. What he wanted was precisely an obedient but unpleasant and vicious animal.

His search hadn't taken very long. Now he had the two ideal dogs.

10

Marc slung Cookie under his arm. The dog was hanging like a piece of rubber, and seemed to be enjoying it.

How extraordinary, for once Doctor d'Oléons wasn't in his office. Marc entrusted Cookie to Mademoiselle André, the elderly blue-haired woman in charge of all the bookwork for the clinic.

She was delighted. She herself was the owner of two poodles.

Marc had preferred not to leave Cookie in the car alone with Mana, the cranky bulldog, who hadn't stopped growling throughout the ride. Cookie had snuggled up close to Marc, trembling. Twice, Marc had reached over and pet Mana. The dog had immediately calmed down. This almost constant snarling was probably mere habit, like John Joseph had said, but it was better not to take any risks.

"And where did you get this precious thing?"

"It's a birthday present for a friend," said Marc. "What do you think of him?"

"He's lovely. Absolutely lovely." Mademoiselle André's voice quavered with sincere admiration. "He's one of the nicest-looking Westies I've ever seen. And believe me, I know all about them. I even had one when I was younger. They're my favorite dogs, next to poodles. Well, what do you know, there's a storm brewing."

A slight shudder went through her upper body as the blue-haired woman declared that it was going to storm.

"You think so?" asked Marc skeptically. "It's not too hot, the sun is shining..."

"I feel it. I get pains between my shoulder blades. Every time I get pains between my shoulder blades, there's a thunderstorm."

"You've been hiding this from us? Not the pains, the weather forecast they inspire. So about what time will it take place?"

"You're making fun of me, huh? In a little while. One or two hours... look, you can already see the clouds."

Marc went to the window. So did Cookie, and stood up on his back paws.

It was true. In the distance were thick clouds in the sky, and they were rapidly making their way toward Paris.

"*Spectacular,*" said Michel Zyto, holding a glass of grape juice. "Three hours later, the pain had already died down. I don't know how to thank you!"

The effectiveness of the Maktarin, which had fought off the fungus in his digestive tract, had put him in high spirits. But he was also glad to see Marc again. And grateful for his concern. Marc could have made a simple phone call, but no, he had come instead, making two visits in the same day.

Alas, as of tomorrow...

"Are you going away on vacation?"

The long vacation month of August had Zyto worried. He would miss Marc. And would Marc miss him? He felt a kind of jealousy.

As a psychotherapist, Marc was extremely flexible when it came to theory. He put a high value on immediate results, and as early as his second session with Michel Zyto, he'd determined that his new patient needed a friendly rapport with his therapist. It was against the rules, dangerous, perhaps, but he'd decided to take the risk. Zyto had to be made to feel that an emotional bond could be formed with someone who wasn't a woman, thereby a mother figure; he had to realize that other men existed besides his nonexistent father, and that meaningful contact with them could protect him from women—take the edge off his tremendous overwhelming hatred for them, in other words.

In response to Michel Zyto's question, Marc said no, very casually, as he'd casually answered so many questions that his protegé had asked about his family, his house, his friends, and his life in general. That way, it would help give him the impression that Marc was a total person, an equal, someone to talk to and with whom it was permissible to satisfy his curiosity.

Another question, this one, as yet unspoken, presently hung over the room.

"I'm going to relax at home, in Versailles. I've been working too hard. But I will have to come to the Center occasionally, so I'll drop by and see how you're doing."

"That would be great," said Michael Zyto.

It was clear that nothing would make him happier. He didn't attempt to hide his relief.

"I thought we might even go out once in a while. It went very well, last time."

"Yes. I'd really like to do it again."

"You'll see my new car, the four-wheel drive that I told you about. And the radio. Four speakers, forty-five watts each."

Marc had never gone this far with the "buddy buddy" approach.

"That would be great," repeated Michel Zyto.

He didn't know what else to say. Someone was taking care of him, protecting him, helping him; someone who wasn't his mother, or a nurse feigning friendliness, with a syringe of tranquilizers in her hand; someone who liked him without ulterior motives.

He gulped his drink enthusiastically, and put his glass back down on the table next to the book he was currently reading, *The Count of Monte-Cristo*, which lay next to the telephone.

Marc was in the phone book. But he had never given him his number. Zyto didn't blame him, of course. It was only natural. Would he give it to him someday? What a sign of trust that would be!

The initial lengthy stages of Marc's therapy with Michel Zyto had been terminated. The "in-house killer" was doing well. In his current state, he would never assault anyone. But establishing a physical and emotional relationship with a woman . . . that was another story. In any case, he wouldn't make a sieve out of her with the first knife he found handy. If subjected to the questions and the usual tests, any expert psychiatrist would have found him normal, aside from the hypochondriac symptoms, which were still acute.

For the time being, Marc's "method" was working wonders.

And now? Now, other issues had to be faced, potential problems, but he'd have to be very careful. Marc had already broached the first problem with Hugues d'Oléons: how to modify Zyto's attachment to Marc—his fixation, the particular nature of the transfer he'd made—how to prevent Marc from becoming "maternalized" by Zyto. Certainly by letting him go free, by progressively reintegrating him into everyday life—assuming this was his desire, which hardly seemed to be the case. Overprotecting him at Stéphen-Mornay made less and less sense, it even risked a partial setback in his improvement. He could, for example, return to the Center two or three times a week, to continue his psychoanalysis.

Let him out.

Which brought up the second problem: Michel Zyto was cured, but what did being cured mean in his case? Was a relapse possible? How long would it take and under what specific circumstances, circumstances that no one could predict?

God only knows. God, and perhaps Marc, soon enough. If his experiment was a success.

Third problem, pertaining to Marc in particular: wasn't Doctor Lacroix guilty of having kept the preparation of his experiment a secret? Why take this approach? There were several good reasons. The scientific milieu is often ruthless when it comes to novelty, originality, or true radical invention, and the ambitious researcher is sometimes better off keeping to himself. But there were several bad reasons as well: pride; an insane, inordinate pride in becoming one of the great names in science, to be considered an equal of Pasteur, Einstein, or an even greater name. And the risk of human experimentation, though Marc was certain that it wasn't dangerous—but did one man alone have the right to make that decision?

Another question tormented him now that the hour of the experiment was drawing near: By using this charming, friendly approach with Zyto, hadn't Marc tried to make him into a consenting subject, so that the idea of refusal would never occur to him? The same thing could even be said for the visit this afternoon, when a simple phone call would have been sufficient.

No. A tormenting question, but in all good faith Marc could answer "no." Experiment or no experiment, his attitude as a therapist would not have been any different.

His experiment must succeed. It was Marc's greatest inspiration, his obsession, the driving force of his life, the hope that allowed him to face his fears, that kept him from becoming too anxious, even about the tiny growth that had so rudely attached itself to his acoustic nerve.

In the rose-colored room, a soothing calm prevailed. The bushes in the garden were absolutely still, as if mesmerized by the sun. A storm! The old woman was nuts, all that talk about her shoulder blades!

Zyto was savoring his grape juice. Marc suddenly envisioned himself in Zyto's place, far from mundane concerns, protected on all sides—should the slightest problem arise, you simply pushed a button and someone came running, like Doctor Marc Lacroix himself.

He suddenly found this vision horrifying. Then it faded, he banished it from his thoughts.

Michel Zyto envied Marc as well, on the eve of his vacation. But he, on the other hand, did not dismiss the thoughts provoked by this envy. He imagined that Marc was going to be with his wife and son and remain with them all day, that he was going to see friends, have a good time, drive thousands of miles in the car whenever he felt like it, do anything that came into his head, experience all kinds of pleasures.

He felt himself choking back a fit of jealousy.

There was nothing new about this type of jealousy. But today it bore into him with a deadly violence—a violence that was killing him, or rather, made him want to kill. Kill Marc. Hit him, strangle him, take revenge on fate's injustice that had put Zyto in this wretched position. Or it made him want to kill himself, in defiance of this injustice.

His mind was in total destructive chaos, but for such a fleeting moment that he was barely conscious of it, he could scarcely recall it, like a terrible pain that instantly disappears. No sooner does the mouth open, ready to cry out, than the pain has already vanished, no sound is ever made.

He felt good here with Marc, who would be back to see him, despite his vacation.

They smiled at each other. This time, Marc did not look down.

During the first three years of their marriage, Marc and Marie Lacroix had lived with Marc's parents at Louveciennes. The two couples lived at the end of Rue du Général-Leclerc in a vast, luxurious two-story residence made entirely of wood; a kind of grand, imposing jewel (if indeed a jewel can be referred to as "imposing"). The house, all shiny with thick varnish, with balconies sculpted like lace, did in fact resemble a priceless object. André Lacroix, Marc's father, devoted a great deal of his time to its upkeep, and a great deal of money.

Sharing the house had not posed any problems until Leonard was born. Of course, Gertrude wasn't terribly fond of Marie nor did she display an inordinate affection for her: it was merely another example of the classic animosity between the spouse's mother and the woman who has taken her place beside her son. But it was rarely bothersome for Marie, and in such a large space they could all move about freely. The young couple often went out at night. During the day, Marc had work to do and Marie was still taking classes at the university. They frequently met in Paris in the late afternoon and went home to Louveciennes together. They dined alone on the second floor, while Marc's parents were watching television or were already in bed.

Things quickly deteriorated when Leonard was born. Gertrude had suddenly manifested aggressive, possessive tendencies—something Marc was already familiar with, though he had been previously unaware of their underlying hostility. Possessive toward Marc, who had escaped her control, no longer a child, since he himself was to become a father; aggressive toward Marie, the intruder, the thief; and, what was more serious, aggressive toward the baby. Gertrude Lacroix had made their lives miserable. Ironically, she always wanted to be with Leonard. She fussed over him constantly, as a means of exerting her domination, preventing what should occur after the birth of a child—the strongest possible bond between a couple. She wanted to maintain their life as it had been by taking away their child, so to speak.

Marie wanted to move. Marc agreed. But then a small catastrophe arose unexpectedly: André Lacroix died. Even though Gertrude suffered from several serious illnesses, it was he, in perfect physical health, who had passed away first, victim of a cerebral hemorrhage caused by a fall. Perched on top of a ladder, busy revarnishing the highest balustrades in the house on the garden side, he'd tumbled down two stories, and had probably died during the fall.

The three months following the accident were hellish. Gertrude virtually lived with them. It was out of the question to leave her alone. Marc was unhappy and harassed, an old guilt that he thought was gone forever stirred up in him again. He felt torn between his wife and his mother. At that time, he was finishing the technical part of his analysis with Martin Vérapoutsimila, and naturally told him about the situation. But the wise master of Rue des Arquebusiers had even worse troubles with his own mother-in-law, even though she was almost one hundred years old. Knowing how these types of problems resist the fiercest efforts of the human mind, he treated Marc with the stony impassibility for which he was famous in psychoanalytic circles.

Ultimately, a diabetes attack got the better of Gertrude three months later. Everything returned to normal and the Lacroixs promptly moved to Paris, on a dead-end street in the sixteenth arrondissement. Marie couldn't have spent another month at Louveciennes. She never spent time there anymore, for that matter, except on rare occasions, and Leonard was cut off from the house where he was raised. They later explained to him that his mother had some very bad memories associated with Louveciennes. They never actually told him what those memories were, and the phrase remained a mystery to him.

Marc inherited the house. Naturally, he didn't sell it. He didn't need the money. And he was attached to it for sentimental reasons. It was the house where he was born, where he'd spent his childhood. He had his heart set on preserving it like a jewel, just the way his father had left it, and so Marc had it properly kept up.

One day, perhaps Leonard would live there.

The house also included a basement of ninety square yards, already equipped for scientific purposes by André Lacroix, where Marc had set up his secret laboratory.

André Lacroix, a small, thin man (Marc was exactly five inches taller), mild-mannered and extremely self-effacing in daily life, had been a fairly well-known researcher in physics and computer science before devoting himself to the management of a pharmaceutical products factory. During the last years of his life, he suddenly felt compelled to take up his research again. He began working two or three hours a day in his basement. He'd attempted, in vain, to perfect the concept of perpetual motion, or what would have been almost perpetual, since a simple push of the finger every twenty-six hours would have ensured the mechanism's operation. Most importantly, he'd modified what was an already complex computer so that it could process unusual, even fictitious information—not in its content, but in the form in which this information was presented—linking it, for example, to other computers of a completely different type, by electronic or electromagnetic means. Here again, no conclusive results were found. He'd channeled his creative powers, however, in a direction that fascinated Marc—one that he was now in the process of exploring, with great success.

He had rearranged the basement to suit his purposes: the electricity (he would need a considerable amount of kilowatt power), the air conditioning, and the security system. He'd left some of the equipment where it was, had done away with the rest, then acquired some new machines—a Umay 12 computer, in particular, the latest model in the Umay series. A splendid instrument from another world, simple, cylindrical, and sleek, that emitted curious little wisps of gray smoke when in operation.

Marc had worked in secret. At times, he would tell Marie that he'd stopped off at Louveciennes to check on the house, and other times, he wouldn't say anything. On several occasions, Marie had been unable to reach Marc where he was supposed to be, but it had always been easy for Marc to invent explanations after the fact. As for the neighbors in Louveciennes, it seemed perfectly normal that Doctor Lacroix should occasionally stop at his parents' home. It would take a strict, perpetual surveillance to arouse any suspicion. Besides, what was there to suspect? That he had his own laboratory?

Marc enjoyed a perfect, undisturbed quietude. Within a few years he'd designed, created, and perfected a machine that would mark an epoch in the history of science.

12

*T*he *critical experiment* was drawing near. Marc's heart was beating wildly, his hands shook. He hadn't realized it until he let go of the steering wheel with his right hand to grab the gearshift.

The Lacroix residence, No. 101, was the last house on the interminable Rue du Général-Leclerc, isolated from the rest of the village. The rear of the house faced the street. Marc entered through the park, as he always did, and pulled up next to the stoop. That way, the car wasn't visible from the street.

The facade, an architectural curiosity, gave onto a park of twelve thousand square yards with a pond in the middle, surrounded by weeping willows. Marc got out of his Nissan Terrano with Cookie under his arm and Mana on a leash. His jacket pockets were stuffed with sugar cubes. He took several deep breaths to steady his heartbeat. The two dogs were docile and followed him with little resistance, as Cookie was naturally sweet-tempered, and Mana, proudly indifferent.

The clouds were no longer slipping by, and hung over Paris and the vicinity. The sky had taken on a dark gray hue. Within half an hour, the temperature had fallen several degrees. Had Mademoiselle André's shoulder blades been right after all?

One more deep breath, a gentle command to the animals, and Marc, using the enormous clanking bunch of keys that deformed the right pockets of all his jackets, entered the wooden house.

He descended the stairway to the basement.

He arrived at a wooden door which he opened with a large key, after setting Cookie down behind him with a kiss on the snout.

Behind the wooden door, about eight inches away, was another door made of heavy metal. On the side wall between the two doors, at eye level, was an electronic keyboard with numbers and letters.

"Everything is going to work out just fine, isn't that right, doggies? And afterwards, Mana will go to a kennel where they'll treat him like a king; you hear that, mutt? And our Cookie will go to that tall painted lady, Marie-Thérèse. Marie-Thérèse Cazanvielh. Right, my little Cookie pooch?"

Marc spoke with such gentleness, a kindness so obviously sincere, that even Mana was impressed. His tail swung several inches off course from its usual axis, a sign of intense, friendly enthusiasm.

A 2 B 3 4.

The heavy door slid open silently, as if it had disappeared into the wall.

Marc fiddled with a switch on his right. The lights came on in the huge basement.

They entered. He pushed a button. The door closed behind them.

Marc had inherited his father's taste for wood. He was fascinated by modern technology, and attracted to the functional, sophisticated beauty of the equipment that exemplified this technology. But it was right under his nose all year long, and he'd wanted wood to be predominant in his laboratory, just as his father had. Wood, a natural material, rich, noble, warm, human. Upon entering the basement, one was impressed by the light-colored wood panelling on the walls; the deeper-hued solid oak partition that divided the room in half; the two handsome booths, also in dark oak, flush with the partition. These identical booths, approximately six feet apart, were both open on one side, facing each other. Their silhouette was visible from the entrance, as each booth extended slightly beyond the curved legs of the chair inside.

In the corner to the right of the front door, several square feet had been arranged as an area for rest or relaxation: there were two chairs and a round table, a small closet, a small refrigerator also panelled in wood, and a small turn-of-the-century piece of furniture that was actually a medicine chest containing various tranquilizers. And a sink and some towels.

Above the sink, to the left of the mirror, hung a striking watercolor. It was the easily recognizable self-portrait of Marc as a boy, his thin Christ-like face, his intense gaze; a fine little painting done in mostly blues and grays. From ages fourteen to nineteen, Marc had devoted himself to painting and drawing. Then, practically overnight, he'd given it up. The only work he'd kept was this self-portrait. He'd thrown away the rest.

The floor was covered with thick, brown carpet.

Beyond esthetic considerations, Marc's choice of decor had been selected for another reason: This was where the experiment would take place. Soon, as soon as possible. Tomorrow, if everything went well! An experiment to be carried out on man, on his brain—on Marc himself, and on Michel Zyto—and the environment had to be friendly, comfortable, and soothing.

Behind the partition was Marc's machine, his life's work.

A door situated at the far right of the oak partition led to a kind of double laboratory, which covered about a third of the entire floor space.

A cool semi-darkness prevailed, imperative for the equipment to function.

Glowing in the dark, here the machines were assembled: the imposing Umay 12; two somewhat smaller Cray 6 computers, which controlled two extremely powerful superconducting magnets; two machines designed to record cerebral activity, at rest and after various electromagnetic stimuli; and several smaller but impressive machines of obvious complexity. It looked like odds and ends from an attic belonging to someone from a faraway planet, a collection of incomprehensible objects that appeared useless, waiting to be discarded—not the superbly organized brain Marc had conceived, a superior brain capable of commanding the performance of other brains.

The two booths were perfectly symmetrical in their form, size, and content, which was, in fact, minimal: a chair and an armband attached to the end of two large wires coming out of the partition. Above each chair, where the subject's head would be, the booth narrowed into a conical shape of whitish metal. It looked like the inside of a gigantic bullet.

And that's all there was in that part of the basement. No electrical wiring visible anywhere.

Between the booths, on the partition, were six small dials arranged in two rows of three. Each dial was surmounted by a corresponding circular warning light. Dials 1, 2, and 3 were connected to the booth on the right (that would be hooked up to Cookie's cute little brain), and dials 4, 5, and 6 with the booth on the left.

One exception to the symmetry: in the booth on the right, beyond the oak partition and to the right of the chair, were three large black levers, with lights above them.

The entire assemblage, the booths and the machine room, comprised a complex, revolutionary system of brain manipulation with the most scientific measures of its activity—a system Marc had temporarily named (although he knew he'd have trouble finding another name, now that he was used to it) a "psycho-computer."

Once the door slid shut, the dogs began to show vague signs of anxiety, according to their contrasting temperaments. Cookie began to whine, waving his paws in the air, and the Argentine bulldog was making sounds as if it were feeding time at the zoo, but without any particular hostility toward Marc.

Marc gave them both a sugar cube and prepared to begin the experiment as soon as possible. He was shaking like a leaf.

He started with Mana. With the help of the sugar, some petting, and a constant stream of encouraging words, Marc managed to get him to sit on the chair in the left booth, and slipped the armband around his neck. The dog was accustomed to collars, and at least from the obedience standpoint, John Joseph hadn't lied: the dog didn't budge, he even seemed to be rather enjoying himself, his guttural noises reduced to half the volume. He yawned and made himself more comfortable on the chair. Now it was time for Cookie, who, on the other hand, would have let anyone tape him to the ceiling by his ears without the slightest objection. While he was getting Cookie settled, Marc continued his watch over Mana, keeping up a flow of sweet talk into which he occasionally slipped an obscene insult. This amused him and helped him relax a little.

Everything was ready.

He took a seat between the two dogs and pushed the first button. The corresponding light turned red. A faint purr started up behind the partition.

The incredible adventure was about to begin.

The first step was to analyze what Cookie and Mana "were thinking about," which was stored in the gray matter in two fashions: first, in the form of a concentration of a group of molecules in certain brain cells; second, in the form of "facilitation" of the passage of nerve impulses in the frequently used neuronal circuits. Dials 1 and 4 lit up, three luminous orange lines appeared, grew longer, shorter, then longer again, indicating that the analysis, made possible by multinuclear spectroscopy through nuclear magnetic resonance, was taking place. The metal cones on the two animals' skulls conducted a field of several tesla—units of magnetic flux density—while behind the partition, under the complete command of the all-powerful Umay 12, a small Cray 6 computer was meticulously tracing a kind of multi-dimensional cartography of the gray matter, each type of molecule presenting reverberations for determined frequencies of electromagnetic radiation that allowed for differentiation between them.

After several other sudden, intermittent changes in length, the orange lines stabilized, and at this precise moment the lights corresponding to dials 1 and 4 lit up orange.

End of the first stage.

The two dogs remained calm. Marc was generous with the sugar. He'd managed to keep them in the necessary immobile position for the N.M.R. analysis. He was delighted that he had avoided the delay and any problems that the use of tranquilizers would have presented.

As soon as the orange lights came on, dials 2 and 5 lit up as well, activating two pale brown luminous lines, a sign of advancement into the second stage, the simplest of them all. Electrodes placed inside the armbands were transmitting electromagnetic stimuli (not only painless, but barely perceptible, the equivalent of a ticklish sensation) that allowed Marc to record the cerebral activity in the two dogs, in order to reconstitute each of their individual neuronal circuits.

Marc continued to pet them, talk to them, and ply them with sugar. Cookie and Mana had gradually realized that if they were good, they would be permitted to eat themselves into oblivion, true to the innate gluttony of their species.

Then, at once there was a simultaneous stabilization of the two brown lines, as the two warning lights above them simultaneously flashed on.

Now it was time to launch the third and shortest phase—the most delicate, the most uncertain, the one that defied pure technique, the one that would validate Marc's creative hypothesis, or reveal its speculative nature, totally theoretical, illusory, mad—the appearance of four blue lines on dials 3 and 6.

The most integral, most extraordinary, most incredible phase had perhaps begun to take place. The second superconductor magnet—was it still a magnet? for the time being, Marc was calling it N.I.B.—guided by the two Cray 6s, all of which were still controlled by the implacable Umay 12, this second electromagnetic apparatus was now activated. It radically modified the metallic cones attached to the dogs' heads and the armbands around their necks: if all went as planned, a little of Cookie would pass into Mana, and a little of Mana into Cookie. They would exchange a bit of their "psychic energy," that which made them irreducibly unique creatures. Marc's original concept in designing the apparatus was to confute this "irreducible factor." If the Umay 12 was the brain of the whole machine, the N.I.B. was its soul.

Empirically, yet without precise scientific control of its functioning, man has long known how to intercept what one might call a person's psychic energy—the nerve impulses, the vital impulses—to capture and redirect it outside of the body, as if it were being extracted from him. A hypnotist is capable of this, up to a point and to a certain degree. What Marc had sought to devise was a machine capable of carrying out, as scientifically as possible, the same type of procedure; receiving and storing the bioelectric consequence of all the forces at work in the neuronal circuits, which are the expression of the most intimate part of our personality—both our innate genetic potential as much as the sum of actual experiences acquired through our central nervous system. Such a machine was theoretically conceivable, and feasible in practice—discounting the formidable complexity in its fabrication and perfection, and most importantly, the need to invent a magnetic alloy whose properties would surpass all other existing alloys. Without this, the machine was doomed to perform with reduced efficiency, and therefore, unusable results.

Marc wasn't discouraged by these complications. He had the time, the competence, and the passion to make it work. The invention of the alloy didn't deter him either. After a month and a half of reflection and four months of trial and error, of quickly aborted endeavors, near-failures and immediate, glaring failures, he had an ingenious idea. An exhaustive computer analysis of the structure of magnets prompted him to perfect an alloy made of neodymium-iron-boron, a substance which heretofore had been intended for more or less covert applications, such as spacecrafts. He obtained a highly efficient magnetic alloy, which produced an energy that was three or four thousand times superior to that of a typical ferrite. Such a great difference in quantity gave rise to a difference in quality, and in the very nature of the object. The term *superconductor magnet* was no longer appropriate, and Marc simply called this essential part of his psycho-computer "N.I.B.," for neodymium-iron-boron. (Almost all the names were temporary; he'd figured he would choose the definitive terms after the success of his experiment.)

Consequently, he'd had to confront two new, major technical problems. The first concerned something that Marc, who was as much philosopher as scientist (and as much artist as philosopher), had come to call "psychic energy." Something that was neither matter, nor soul, but that a pure spirit, some sort of deity, would lack. It was not unlike the positive corporality the German theologian Jakob Bohme had called *Wesen*, a substance that defines the veritable being of man. But even if this energy was retained as a nervous impulse, which would allow Marc to tame a sufficient amount of it, it would lose its specific characteristics once outside of the brain that produced, emitted, and discharged it. At that point it would be nothing more than energy with no content, an empty impulse that was of no use. And therefore the need for a new, original combination, between the N.I.B. and a Cray 6 computer—a combination that would be capable of restoring its structures and initial content (according to the cerebral reading ensured by phases one and two of the experiment), and also capable of sending it back in that reconstituted form via the same electromagnetic circuits in the brain of a second subject. This was Marc's grand scheme. Following these various maneuvers, despite the inevitably considerable loss, that small part of the "being" would be uniquely transmitted, an attenuated cerebral image that would circulate—attenuated but complete, and faithful to the original.

It was at this stage of his research that Marc had named the entire apparatus a psycho-computer.

As for the second problem, Marc conquered it with a clever plan.

Every individual expends his psychic energy just like physical exertion; he consumes or conserves it according to a balance that must be maintained. This balance is indispensable, and is achieved almost automatically. If a machine, outside of the person, were to capture this energy (in this case using the N.I.B.), store it, then utilize it according to its own needs, the cerebral balance would be jeopardized for the "receiving" subject as well as the "donor" subject.

This difficulty was unavoidable. Marc realized he would have to employ some kind of artificial device. Then a logical solution dawned on him, simple in its principle: the two subjects in the experiment had to be both donor and receiver; there would have to be a transfer in each direction, so that at the precise moment that a little of Cookie was on its way toward Mana through the devious channels of the psycho-computer, a little of Mana was simultaneously following the opposite trajectory. That is why Marc had to construct the machine with absolute symmetry, so that the experiment, by means of the most rigorous exchange, would leave each subject with his original quantity of being, in a manner of speaking. There would be no risk of an undesirable loss or accumulation of energy. For several moments, long enough for the experimenter to observe, Cookie would be Cookie, minus a little of Cookie plus a little of Mana, and the bulldog would undergo a mirror alteration.

Would a transfer of this nature present any difficulties once Marc himself and Michel Zyto were the two subjects? No, Marc was certain of it. On the contrary, not for either of them.

Meaning that Marc would have two observation posts, one in his brain and the other in Zyto's. And he would actually surpass the goal that he'd set for himself, that had obsessed him for years: to observe and comprehend his subject—his memory, his present, and his plans; transmitted without mediation, therefore with no need for interpretation, which was always risky. He would know him from one thought to the next, their thoughts would be intermingled yet distinct, he would be someone else but remain himself, without having to modify his behavior during the experiment. He could simply "take a look."

And then he would see. He would know immediately and without question whether or not Michel Zyto was guilty of the murder of Marie Poterjnikoff. And if his patient intended to kill again. He would know how Zyto's oppressive pathological system, his mental prison, functioned from the inside. Perhaps he would even find out how to eventually rescue him from it, rather than merely opening the pitiful air vents that, at best, kept the prisoner from asphyixating himself, a condition that had sometimes pushed him into seemingly liberating acts of violence. For a few minutes, he would be a little of Michel Zyto, just long enough to see everything, understand everything, know everything, and perhaps change everything.

And Michel Zyto would undergo an equal experience, which by its very nature—a merger with memories, reasoning, and desires other than his own—could only be to his benefit.

Yes, Marc couldn't help telling himself again and again, it would be a momentous event in the history of science, one of the most important, perhaps the most important of all time.

13

*T*he *four blue lines* began to quiver—but more than they should have, they weren't extending far enough. It was a bad omen, this vibration, Marc immediately told himself. Like wriggling carp thrown straight into the frying pan. Seething with agony.

What a disaster! The lines crowded together to the left of the dial, then disappeared. Marc anxiously observed the dogs, watching for a change of behavior on their part. The experiment, if successful, was supposed to bring about a change. Barring all constraints and any scientific problems, the two pups were supposed to be struck by a new momentum and inner drive, that they would either yield to or resist, that would stimulate them—in short, an acute, visible behavior modification would have been the sign of success. But Cookie continued to lick his paw like a cat and Mana kept up his little growls with a deceptively vacant look in his eyes. Actually, he was waiting for more sugar.

And the blue light remained dark.

A failure. It was a failure!

The first idea that came into Marc's head was that he would never be able to make love to Marianne again.

He was seized with an overwhelming sense of discouragement, despite the hope deep down that all was not necessarily lost.

He got hold of himself. It had to work, it had to! Maybe he'd forgotten or underestimated some factor, maybe he hadn't sufficiently considered... No. He'd thought of everything. He had taken everything into account. It was supposed to work. (Marc's face had turned a sickly color, his brow furrowed with concentration.) It was supposed to work, but maybe it wouldn't work each and every time. Now, there was an interesting thought. Not every single time, like a hypnosis session or a magic show (no, that has nothing to do with it), or like a memory that sometimes escapes us, a word on the tip of one's tongue, something like that... The challenge faced by the psycho-computer was so unusual, so tenuous, so fragile...

He would have to start over, immediately. If it turned out that Marc had to leave the laboratory without succeeding... He didn't dare think about it. In just a few months, the anguish would do him in. No one would be able to help him. Not even Marianne. Not Marie, not Leonard, not a soul.

He fought back a fierce desire to cry. He stuck two sugar cubes in his mouth and crunched on them. The two dogs craned their necks in envy, as if they hadn't had any sugar in weeks and weeks. Marc made another general distribution (meaning he didn't forget to include himself). If he kept this up, he'd kill off his guinea pigs by the most unique means ever recorded in the annals of scientific research, by sugar indigestion.

The second of the three buttons in "Cookie's booth" could stop the experiment at any given moment. The first one started it and could also, after a pause, trigger it back into operation. The third one was used for going backwards, to restore everything to its original state through pure and simple inversion of all of the electromagnetic circuits, thus cancelling the effects of the experiment—in a split second, Cookie would be Cookie again and Mana, Mana.

My God, it was a failure!

Marc had made up his mind. He pushed the first button.

Nothing, except the same wriggling four blue lines, rapidly breaking off.

The perspiration on his forehead followed the line of his brow and trickled down his face, onto his cheeks.

He pushed it again.

Just then, a massive clap of thunder—the likes of which Marc had only heard in the mountains, leading one to assume that lightning must have struck nearby—a brief, ear-splitting crack resounded. The two dogs stiffened, frozen with terror, and began to tremble, their fur standing on end, but calmed down again after only a moment. Even Marc had jumped.

Quick, some sugar.

His eyes were glued to dial number three. The lines grew longer, then shorter, trying to find their place—and then it happened.

The blue light came on.

Marc thought he was going to faint.

Success.

He had the confirmation almost immediately after he placed the sugar cubes into the dogs' mouths. Why? Because of a phenomenon that was both exhilarating and somewhat frightening—after receiving the sugar, Cookie let out an unfriendly growl, he who had surely never growled during his short lifetime. And he didn't look at Marc with exactly the same kindness, or the same gratitude as before, Marc was sure of it, absolutely sure! As for Mana, the change was even more distinct: for a few seconds, the smooth-haired white and reddish monster lost his contempt for the world around him. He timidly held out a paw to Marc, his eyes brimming with tenderness, surprise, and a look awaiting affection that replaced his usual annoying expression.

These changes subsided, but the two dogs remained undeniably different.

Marc took several deep breaths and hastily mopped the sweat from his brow. It had been a success. A success, but why? Because of some freak electricity in the air, from the storm? Of course not. He immediately rejected this erstwhile notion from another era, even though it did go through his mind. On the other hand, could the fright and shock prompted by this thunderclap have quite simply and efficiently contributed to the refined working of the machines, the Umay 12, the Cray 6, and the superconductor, N.I.B.? Was it perhaps the strong emotion—fear—that had depolarized the neurons (this was Marc's hypothesis) and permeated the membranes, thus permitting better circulation and assimilation of nerve impulses, providing the decisive finishing touch? Though it seemed trivial compared to the complexity of the entire operation, was it possibly necessary for a successful transfer and exchange?

Exhilarated, his heart pounding painfully hard, Marc pushed the third button. The psycho-computer readily retrieved that which it had so excellently intercepted and restructured, as if having tamed it. It now gave back to each his due: an instant later, the blue light went out, and the dogs became "normal" again. It was extraordinary. Marc held back a nervous laugh. Then he pushed the first button to start it up again, to relaunch the last phase.

The same hopeless quivering blue lines. Nothing. Nothing more was happening. And what if he couldn't get it to work again . . . ? No, he was going to do it! He had confidence in his hypothesis.

Something frightening, an intense emotion: would physical pain play the same role? He handed out two sugar cubes each to his accomplices, who had remained docile, and hurried into the machine room.

Because the incredible had just occurred, Marc, for the first time since the beginning of his research, was actually intimidated by his psycho-computer, and by the series of purring, smoking, and glowing machines, suddenly mysterious to his own eyes.

He rummaged through the wires. A simple connection was required, that could be carried out in no time by the local electrician—Marc did what needed to be done and hurried back to Cookie and Mana.

Back into operation. Third phase. But this time the button also triggered an electric shock into the dogs' necks, through the armbands. A painful but bearable shock—Marc and Zyto would have to bear it—a momentary burst of pain, that . . .

It worked! It had the same effect as the thunderclap, just as

Marc had imagined, hoped, and foreseen that it would. A success, which could be made to recur at will. Violent emotion rendered the brains of the two subjects identical, so to speak. For that matter, Marc had once written an article in which he'd contemplated the possibility of such a phenomenon. He'd happened to have seen a broadcast of a live rock concert on TV. He hated this type of music, but he'd been struck by the young people in the first row who were screaming, fascinated, hypnotized, their eyes bulging and glued to their idols. At this precise moment, Marc had written, their brains were theoretically interchangeable. The fans wouldn't have even noticed.

Pain, an emotion, a violent passion. Or laughter. True uncontrollable laughter, the kind that totally invades the field of consciousness and unites two or more people for a certain amount of time. In his enthusiasm, Marc could imagine the scene, Zyto and he watching vaudeville films together, shaking with uncontrollable laughter, the psycho-computer taking advantage of the moment to freely exchange their brains!

He was dying of excitement, of happiness, and of impatience.

He gave the dogs what was left of the sugar at the bottom of his pockets.

Then he was suddenly calm. He pushed the third button one more time. He freed the two animals. He went to the refrigerator and gulped down half a bottle of soda. He was overcome with a kind of serenity.

Something important and essential had changed. For him and for the rest of the world.

He drove to Rue Longue, in Neuilly, and left Mana in a kennel that couldn't have been more luxurious, a four-star kind of place. He asked the manager, a man with asymmetrical, crinkled ears, the ears of a half-wit, to pamper the bulldog. Soon, photographers from the four corners of the world would want to take pictures of Cookie and Mana.

Still in Neuilly, he bought a fish sandwich (filet of lemon sole with homemade mayonnaise) at a fancy delicatessen he knew, and hungrily devoured it.

And some ham for Cookie.

As he petted Cookie, who was pressed against his thigh, and told her a million stories, the perfect regularity of the Terrano motor like music to his ears, Marc headed toward home, Chemin du Maréchal-ferrant, about four miles from downtown Versailles.

Suddenly, he was anxious to get back to his wife and son.

14

"*W*hiskey?" asked Leonard, feigning innocence.
"No, Westie, you little smartypants. Westie. W-e-s-t-i-e."
"How come you brought it back from the laboratory?"
"It's a birthday present for Marie-Thérèse."
Marc hugged his son, stroking his hair. He gave him a little tap on the shoulder, a little spank on the behind, and went back to his hair, this time tousling it. Marc was even more excited than Leonard at his greatest moments of excitement.

Cookie was patiently waiting her turn, and it had finally come. While Marc was hanging up his jacket, Leonard crouched down and gently pet the dog on its back, but that was all. Yet Cookie was the model of kindness. He seemed content, and wagged his tail, turning his snout toward Leonard, who stood up.

"You weren't frightened by the storm?" asked Marc.

"No, not at all, it was great! We almost got caught in it on our way back from Marshall's."

He was about to tell him about the pinball machine when Marie entered the hallway. The dog turned its head toward this new person. What a day, what a day! They were all very nice, but when would they be taking him home to his mistress?

Marie gazed at the dog, at Leonard, then back to Marc.

"His name is Cookie," said Leonard. "He's a whiskey."

"So now the torturer is bringing home his victims?" Marie said, giving Marc a kiss.

Marc felt like shouting, I did it, I did it!, but he preferred waiting for the "real" experiment. He wanted to take it to the limit. It was a decision he'd made from the very beginning.

And actually, he didn't mind keeping his joy and his secret to himself for a few more hours.

"Are you kidding? Cookie had a great time passing through a magnetic field. Teslas have never hurt anyone. This precious pet has become the darling of the lab. Right, Cookie? No need to call the S.P.C.A. for our Cookie."

Marc told them about his visit with Germaine Halbronn, without specifying the date.

"He'd be too miserable in a kennel. I was trying to think of a solution, and I finally came up with one. Can you guess?"

Marie was scratching the dog's neck. Leonard was waiting attentively for his mother's reply: would she guess right?

"You want to give him to Marie-Thérèse," she said without hesitating.

"Bravo. What do you think? A Westie that's barely a year old. It's exactly what she's looking for, isn't it?"

"Why not? Marie said, straightening up. "A hat and a dog—that's a nice birthday present."

"I hope she doesn't mix them up," said Leonard.

"What do you mean?" Marie asked.

"The fuzzy hat and the whiskey dog. I hope she doesn't mix them up, put Cookie on her head and serve the hat dog-tails instead of cocktails."

Marc and Marie smiled. When it came to jokes and puns, Leonard took after his father.

"Don't make fun of Marie-Thérèse," Marie said. "She adores you. She and Marshall both adore you."

"I like them too," said Leonard, gravely. "If you only knew how much I want to see them! Can we have dinner real quick and go back over there?"

Marc shot a questioning glance at his wife.

"Today, he likes them even more than usual," she said. "Believe it or not, Marshall bought an antique pinball machine, one of the first imported to France. Redone to look brand new, and it works. This afternoon, Leonard had a real picnic, as my mother would say. And if I'm not mistaken, I think he's counting on a few more rounds tonight. Right, Leonard?"

"No Mooo-mmy. I'm gonna play a few hundred rounds."

He never shortened "Mommy" to "Mom"; on the contrary, he had the habit of drawing out the first syllable.

Marie kissed him on the forehead, and gave Cookie a pat on her way out to fix dinner.

"Can I give him a sugar cube?"

"No, no sugar," his father said a bit sternly.

Tomorrow, he'd make his pitch to Zyto. And Zyto would say yes. And the next step would be incredible. Marc was almost afraid to picture it; he was superstitious. Afraid he'd be dreaming and wide awake at the same time. And yet, this afternoon, he hadn't been dreaming, that was for damn sure. He stretched out his arm to pet Cookie, who curled up next to him on the couch. Too bad about the dog hair. Baby had never been allowed on the couch, or on their beds, for that matter.

Marc realized that he hadn't even been listening to *La Frescobalda* by Frescobaldi. He reset the compact disc to the beginning with his remote control. The starting notes of the first of five brief parts of *La Frescobalda* came on again. Aside from his old favorites, Marc would frequently fall in love with a piece of music, discovered more or less by accident, and then listen to it every day as soon as he returned home from work. It was a ritual. Marie sometimes made fun of him, she'd refer to his "record of the month." In fact, the average duration of these passing fancies was indeed a month. After that, he played the record less and less, or not at all—still, he might always have a change of heart.

These days, he often listened to the piece called *La Frescobalda* by Girolamo Frescobaldi, with Rafael Puyana on harpsichord. One of Marc's greatest regrets was that he'd never studied music. His parents had not been music lovers. It was rare to find anyone as insensitive to music as his father. And Marc was afraid that Leonard was following in his grandfather's footsteps, at least as far as classical music was concerned.

He took a sip of his mint-flavored lemon soda.

Despite the late hour, the sky, dotted with red, was still quite visible outside the bay window. What a storm! Marc thought about it again. O providential storm and blessed lightning bolt!

He heard Leonard's hurried steps on the wooden stairs.

He had lost track of the music again. He didn't bother switching it back to the beginning.

At certain moments, he had a feeling of such intense elation that it almost frightened him. Tomorrow, tomorrow . . .

The door to the living room opened slowly. Cookie pricked up his ears. Leonard entered. Marc kept his right hand on the dog's neck, scratching it with steady regularity. The dog was ecstatic. And Leonard, a trifle jealous all the same. He sat down and snuggled against his father.

"What are teslas?"

Marc automatically thought of the definition: production of a flux of one weber per square meter by uniform induction.

"A tesla, my little man, a tesla is a unit of measure for magnetic fields. It measures what's happening in a magnetic field, in front of a magnet. A unit of measure. It's like quarts for water. Or pounds for potatoes."

"It's a funny name, tesla."

"It's the name of a physicist. A Croatian scientist, Nicolas Tesla. He invented lots of things. That's why his name was used to designate something important, to honor him."

"OK, I get it. And what about pound, was that also some guy?"

End of *la courante*, final section of the piece.

Marc turned it off, let go of Cookie, and put his arms around his son.

"Will you come down to the basement with me?"

"Yeah, sure. Why?"

"I want to get my leather gloves. You know, the old ones."

"Those worn-out things?"

"Yes. So I can play pinball in them, later on."

"That's a good idea. That'll look cool, with those gloves on. Like a real-l-l tough guy."

The expression was nothing new between them, but it always worked with Leonard, who smiled.

"Do you want me to go down and get them?" asked Marc.

"No, I'll go with you."

The couch hissed as soon as they stood up. They went into the hallway. Marc opened a door that led downstairs. He was watching Leonard out of the corner of his eye. He seemed more anxious than usual.

Once, as a young child, Leonard had managed to lock himself in the basement. It hadn't taken long for his mother to find him, but he'd been panicked with fear, alone in the dark for several minutes, screaming and pounding on the walls, incapable of turning the key in the opposite direction, or finding the light switch.

Those few nightmarish minutes had left their mark.

Ever since then, the basement door had remained permanently open. And, in addition to the key hanging in the hallway beside the others, there was a second key hidden downstairs, in a hiding place that only Leonard and his father knew about: if ever, by chance, the vampires succeeded in locking them in, they'd know how to escape.

Leonard tended to talk about vampires whenever he went downstairs to the basement. He had a whole batch of little stories he would tell them, or tell himself, in which he always ended up vanquishing these supposed vampires. Marc hadn't discouraged him. He expected that this old fear, still engraved in Leonard's mind, might subside with the help of childish stories. He had to respect the natural way Leonard had figured out how to deal with this fear, to get the upper hand, fighting off what was still slightly traumatic.

So Marc played along with him.

The key was hidden in one carton, and some pruning shears in another (to cut through the rope, just in case they were tied up). Most importantly, with Marc's help, Leonard had invented a magic formula that only the two of them knew—*vakoo sipaldess teronock*—especially feared by vampires, that inevitably made them flee.

These little strategems had been fruitful, they reassured Leonard. Until the day he ceased to believe in vampires, Marc told himself.

Marc turned on the light and went down the stairs first, whistling a few bars of *La Frescobalda*. Leonard followed.

"Watch out all you little vampires hiding in the corners, you're gonna get it! Vakoo sipaldess teronock . . ."

Marc stopped whistling. Then, to make it sound even better, he added:

"They're going to be sorry they chose to hold their general assembly in Versailles," he said. "We're going to make them run like mice."

They entered the basement, which was clean, well-lit and practically empty. There were cartons full of toys and books stacked against the right and left walls. Also against the left wall was an old piece of wooden furniture, its varnish cracked in several places, that contained some discarded clothing. That was all. Marc had made the place look as unthreatening as possible.

The key to the basement door was in the first carton near the entrance, underneath some toys. The pruning shears (there were three: a large, a small, and a medium-sized pair that Marc had once bought, thinking at the time he would take up gardening) were also under some toys in the third carton down the row. Two cartons farther down was the chest of drawers from which Marc pulled a pair of worn-out gloves.

He held them out to Leonard.

Leonard did not show the slightest sign of anxiety.

"*What did you say?* Filet of wild boar in a bed of sauerkraut with..."

"Juniper berries, that's right," said Marie. "Thirty-six minutes in the pressure cooker. I went to a lot of trouble." Then, gently chiding him: "Basted with lemon-peppermint soda. It's going to be delicious."

Lemon-flavored soda was Marc's favorite drink. Plain lemon soda, or mixed with a meticulously measured shot of mint syrup.

"You're going to like that, aren't you, Whiskey?" said Leonard, straightening up in his chair to examine what was inside the pot.

Cookie did not take offense at the new name that the boy had given him. He ran to Leonard with eager friendliness.

"Don't call him Whiskey anymore," said Marc rather sharply.

Apparently, Leonard didn't notice, but Marie did.

"He doesn't care," said Leonard.

"Yes, you're right, he doesn't care," Marc said gently, as if he had surprised himself by this little outburst.

Marie put the cover back on the pressure cooker, screwing it on tightly.

"There, now it won't get cold."

They began with a salad.

They dined in the kitchen, large, luminous and white, which they preferred to the dining room when they weren't having company, which was most of the time.

Marie liked to cook. (It was one of the reasons the Lacroixs didn't have a live-in maid.) She hardly ever followed the recipes the way they were written in the various books she owned. She invented, she improvised. Tonight, for instance, the juniper berries and paprika had been her idea.

"Do you like it?" she asked Marc.

Marc, absorbed in his thoughts, didn't answer immediately.

"Hey Dad! Do you like it?" Leonard asked, with his mouth full.

Yes, Marc liked it, he loved it. He gave them an odd smile. Ever since the experiment, he felt like he was in another world. He was probably worried about his X-rays that afternoon, Marie thought. She suddenly felt like putting her arms around him.

Cookie had decided to take a little nap. The whiskey dog was taking a snooze from all that booze, as Leonard had put it during dessert.

Marie's hair kept slipping out of the ribbon she'd tied it back with during her shower, and now it spilled onto her shoulders.

Marc was convinced he'd heard his wife in Leonard's room, helping him get ready for bed. He was surprised to find her in the bathroom, still drying herself, rubbing her beautiful legs with a towel. He nearly apologized.

"I thought you were in Leonard's room," he said.

Marie came toward him and kissed him on the cheek, without saying a word. She smelled good, of plain soap. Before leaving the bathroom, she opened a tiny safe with a combination lock, wedged in the back of the medicine cabinet. She took out a bright red necklace. She had very little jewelry. She simply wasn't that keen about jewelry, any more than she was about eccentric clothing.

Marc gazed at her, reflecting on his experiment, his magnificent experiment. Tomorrow. Afterward, everything would be fine, he told himself. With Marie, with Marianne, with the entire world.

"Are you worried about your X-rays?" Marie asked after a moment.

"No, darling. Not at all. No one can tell how it's going to take its course. And it could take a long, long time. There's a slight risk. I'm susceptible to a slight risk. But then again, aren't we all?"

"All right," Marie said with a smile. "Well said. You're a good con artist."

"Oh yes, I almost forgot—about Cedric. He's having lunch the day after tomorrow with a new E.N.T. surgeon from Lariboisière who lives in Versailles. I invited him to have a drink here first."

"Got it. Cedric for drinks the day after tomorrow."

The day after tomorrow—will I have already communicated the results of my experiment to the world by then? Marc wondered. Perhaps. Definitely. Cedric would go nuts!

Marie pointed to the towel she'd been using.

"I don't like that brown one. The only towels I like are the big blue ones."

"No problem, sweetheart. I'll buy you a dozen large blue towels, and we'll throw all the others away."

"Good idea," she said.

On her way out of the bathroom, she gave him another kiss, a kiss that demanded nothing in return, but simply meant: don't worry, I'm here.

She went downstairs.

Marc shaved—as he always did when they went out at night, since his beard grew back so quickly—took a shower, and changed his underwear and shirt.

Then, from the bedroom, he made a quick call to Marianne.

"I just wanted to tell you that I love you and I think of you all the time."

"Me too," she said.

"I'll call you back soon and we'll get together."

After the experiment, he thought. She'd also go nuts. So would Marie, so would Leonard. Even Germaine Halbronn would go nuts. His mother- and father-in-law, his colleagues, everyone—nuts. The entire world would go completely nuts!

He hesitated, then called Germaine Halbronn. The kind old woman seemed a little down in the dumps, but hadn't fallen apart. He conveyed Cookie's best regards and told her he'd call back soon; it wouldn't be long before they would all see each other again.

Then he went downstairs. Leonard was watching TV. Marie was leafing through a book, a biography of the composer Adrian Leverkühn that she'd started reading the night before. She, too, had her passing fancies. These days, Adrian Leverkühn had the honor.

She was wearing a black dress and a red blazer.

She closed her book and stood up.

"Shall we go?"

Cookie wagged his tail. Leonard turned off the TV—zap!—and said to the dog: "C'mon! We're off to see the pinball!"

15

*W*hen they arrived, Marie-Thérèse was on the telephone. She was chattering away, taking down an appointment with one hand, holding the receiver and a cigarette with the other, managing to write, smoke, talk, and once she'd noticed the Westie, mime a whole series of exclamations—silent but emphatic Ohs and Ahs.

Marie-Thérèse was a tall, thin blond who was almost elegant, almost pretty. She almost could have been a model. In fact, she often claimed that if she had wanted to . . .

She was enchanted with Cookie. Nothing could have made her happier. She never would have gotten a dog for herself, not right now anyway, but since it had come from out of the blue like this . . . he was marvelous. She thanked them, and gave them all kisses. She was truly touched. She'd go see a vet, and find out everything she needed to know about Westies, their diet, their illnesses, and their special traits.

Marc and his wife glanced at each other at the same moment as if to say yes, this gift had been a good idea, and they were both genuinely happy for Marie-Thérèse.

She gathered Cookie in her arms, hugged him to her breast, and did not let go of him for the entire evening.

As for the hat, she tried it almost shyly. It would have looked ridiculous on most women, but not on Marie-Thérèse, just as Marie had expected.

Marc understood completely why a man like Marshall would have been attracted to Marie-Thérèse. But he could also see why this same man was interested in a gem like Marie. Quite a coup for Marshall, to have them both, Marc thought, telling himself he was being ridiculous. There was nothing between Marshall and Marie, and there never would be. No, Marc could ignore their intimacy, he knew for a fact that Marie wouldn't cheat on him.

Seeing Marie again, after all his scheming and his implicit declaration that afternoon, Marshall was, alas, almost convinced of the same thing.

They all went upstairs to admire the pinball machine. Leonard pulled the tattered gloves from his pockets with studied nonchalance, and immediately got down to work.

Marie-Thérèse and Marie were chatting. Marshall and Marc were finishing a game of chess they'd begun three weeks ago. Marshall won. He always won. He spent at least two hours a day practicing his game, figuring out chess moves, studying famous matches.

They drank a bottle of wine between the four of them.

Around eleven o'clock, Cookie suddenly began to whine and cry. This went on for ten minutes. He must have finally realized that he wouldn't be seeing his elderly, adorable mistress. Marc and Marie-Thérèse worked at calming him down, and did a fairly good job of it.

Shortly thereafter, Leonard came down to join them. Exhausted and perspiring, he flopped into a chair and fell asleep.

At midnight, his mother woke him with a kiss on the forehead. They all wished Marie-Thérèse a happy birthday.

Then the Lacroixs went home.

"See you soon, Whiskey," Leonard said before getting into the Nissan Terrano.

Cookie looked a bit sad, but obediently remained in Marie-Thérèse's arms.

Once they'd arrived at their home on Chemin du Maréchal-ferrant, an extremely disturbing incident took place. Leonard did something foolish that surprised both Marie and Marc.

He had gone upstairs to get ready for bed. His parents were downstairs, on the couch, chatting as they listened to Leverkühn's violin concerto, playing softly in the background. They talked about the evening. Marc was exhausted, plus he wasn't terribly fond of Adrian Leverkühn's music. They went upstairs soon after Leonard.

Once on the landing, Marie immediately noticed that their bedroom door was slightly ajar, a crack of light shining through the doorway. She called out her usual "Ready or not!" just in case, certain that Leonard's unfailing "Here I come" would not be echoed back: no doubt, the child was not in his room; he was in theirs, and it wasn't too hard to guess that he was up to something naughty.

And indeed, there was no "Here I come" in reply. Leonard appeared at his parents' bedroom door, however, flushed with emotion.

He was holding a gun.

In his confusion, he didn't even have the presence of mind to put it back where he'd found it, or at least to put it down before he left the room. Instead he stood right in front of his parents, with the incriminating object in his hand. And he looked so ashamed! So incredibly awkward and ingenuous that he was instantly forgiven, even though they did scold him a little, as a matter of form.

Marie had been especially frightened. The weapon was loaded with blanks, and even though the barrel was locked with a fixed cam, an accident was always possible, and although the bullets couldn't kill anyone, they could cause minor injuries, particularly if fired at close range. It was a first-rate starter's pistol, a perfect copy of the Swiss 6 mm SIG P2 10. It could fire eight bullets.

Marshall had given it to Marc as a gift the year before. Leonard had never seen it.

Ordinarily, it was hidden under the handkerchiefs in the drawer inside the huge provincial armoire. The drawer was under lock and key, and the key was kept, along with several other objects, inside the night table on Marc's side of the bed.

Marie had secretly approved when Marc had lied to Leonard, telling him that the gun fired real bullets. Marc decided shortly thereafter to hide the weapon in the safe in the bathroom. It wouldn't be very practical in case of an emergency, but it was in a secure place, as far as Leonard was concerned, extremely secure. Plus, Marc told Marie, to close the incident on a light note, there never would be an emergency: before a burglar could break open the doors of the house and get upstairs, Marc would have ample time to set up a double row of loaded cannons on the spacious landing of the first floor.

A while later, they were both in bed with the lights out.

Marc moved closer to Marie. He brushed his hand affectionately over one hip, then to her soft mound below, her belly, her shoulders and finally, her cheek, where he stopped. He wouldn't ordinarily have gone any further than that. But tonight, he needed to touch her, needed the contact. Marie only vaguely responded, she simply put her arms around her husband and snuggled up against him in a sleeping position.

Marc listened to her breathing. He was also very tired. He'd have no trouble falling asleep, contrary to what he'd feared. He whispered: "What really bothers me isn't the fact that he did something stupid. There's nothing wrong with that, every now and then. No, it's the pursuit of certain ideas he gets in his head. Bad ideas. Do you realize the kind of perseverence required to dig around in the drawer, find the key, fit it into the lock . . . ?"

"It was those hoodlum gloves," Marie breathed.

"Gloves?"

"They gave him the soul of a hoodlum. Never mind, darling. Go to sleep."

Her hand went limp on Marc's back.

Marc smiled to himself in the dark. Marie was wonderful. The whole world was wonderful.

Tomorrow, tomorrow!

He mentally hummed a few bars of *La Frescobalda*.

He'd always wished Leonard would take an interest in music. That he'd become a musician. Oh well. Still, he couldn't help wishing it.

His final, fleeting thought was about Cookie, then he promptly fell asleep.

16

The presto movement of Vivaldi's *Summer* concerto blasted out of the four speakers of the Nissan Terrano. The effect was spectacular but made conversation difficult, so Marc turned down the volume.

Michel Zyto was dressed in a light blue shirt and dark blue pants (just as Leonard was the night before, Marc thought). He was also wearing a thin black jacket that went well with the blue and with his chestnut hair.

He'd had a good night's sleep. Not the slightest pain in his throat, not the slightest discomfort. He was happy about the beautiful weather, the outing, the music in the car, and the company and trust of Dr. Lacroix. Marc. How he would have liked to call him by his first name, and for Marc to call him Michel! Maybe after the experiment. Wouldn't he then become a sort of partner to the doctor? Anyhow, that was pretty much what Marc had told him. Not a guinea pig, an associate.

No reason to refuse. And every reason in the world to say yes.

Marc had taken the scenic route by the quays, just for fun. They sped along the Seine. The bridges flew past. The water level was high because there hadn't been a drought that year. Michel Zyto stared at the Seine, the people, the trees.

The sun was warm on the side of his face. It felt good.

The experiment. Nothing to lose and everything to gain. With Marc's help, he had become involved in an exciting enterprise of mastery. Someday, he would step out of Stéphen-Mornay a free man, truly free. And he would continue treatment with Marc, the doctor had given him his word on that.

He made himself comfortable in the plush seat of the Nissan Terrano and pondered the only question that had him a little worried: "Are you sure there aren't any risks? None? You're positive?"

"Positive," said Marc. "It's less harmful to the system than watching television too close to the screen. There aren't even any drugs. You're still taking your Maktarin, aren't you?"

"Oh, yes."

"The only potential problem would be a power failure. But that's impossible, the generator would take over immediately. Of course, you know that if there were any danger involved..."

He paused. Zyto finished the sentence.

"You wouldn't perform the experiment on yourself?"

Out of the speakers came the *presto*, turned down low. The car seemed to float along with the music.

Marc smiled.

"No, maybe I would. But not on you..."

Zyto smiled back, with that charming smile that lingered on his face just a shade too long. Marc added: "Not only is there no danger involved, but, as I mentioned, I even foresee positive results for you on a psychological level. For a few minutes, you'll feel what it's like to be different than you are now. You won't understand it rationally, which is the most important thing. Neither rationally nor emotionally, like the slight disturbances that our sessions may have sometimes triggered. You'll understand it through true, radical experience, by actually becoming someone else. That is, of course," Marc said jokingly, "if I'm really that different than you. Well, you'll see, you're going to know everything about me."

"Does that bother you?"

It sure doesn't bother me, Zyto thought, pleased and excited to be given the actual chance to identify with the one man in the world whom he most admired and envied, and for whom he cared the most, Doctor Marc Lacroix.

"No," said Marc.

Despite his fatigue (he'd had three hours of deep sleep, then had woken up and couldn't fall asleep again), Marc felt fresh and more relaxed than he had the night before. Because he was certain it would be a success, and thrilled by the idea. And because, strangely enough, Michel Zyto had a calming effect on him.

He thought intensely about Marianne, and when they'd next make love. He'd call her tonight, or tomorrow morning. Evenings were a bit tricky. Then he thought of Hugues d'Oléons. The distinguished doctor would surely be chagrined by Marc's secret research. Not to mention the illegal aspect of the project, which would shock him. But Marc would figure out how to explain it to him. Hugues would understand, he wouldn't hold a grudge. He was a simple and straightforward man with a heart of gold, the likes of whom Marc had rarely encountered.

After following a rather diverting route that took scarcely longer than usual, but permitted them to see the sights of Paris, Marc and Zyto arrived at the edge of the city, Porte Maillot.

The sky was clear.

"No storm today," said Marc. "Mademoiselle André told me so."

"Mademoiselle André?"

"Yes. Whenever she has pains between her shoulder blades, it's the sign that a storm is brewing. I'll have to congratulate her about yesterday, she wasn't wrong."

"I love big thunderstorms," said Zyto. "Would you mind if we put this back on . . . ?"

He gestured toward the tape player.

"Not at all," said Marc. "We could barely hear it before."

He reached out at the same time as Zyto and their hands grazed against each other. He pushed down on the "stop" button of the Kenwood tape player, then pressed "rewind," and turned up the volume. Three seconds later, strains of the *presto* flowed from the four-wheel drive again.

They'd reached the highway, direction: Rouen.

They sped the entire way.

"This is a really nice place," said Michel Zyto, taking a seat in an armchair. "You don't see very much wood these days."

He picked up the glass of lemon soda Marc had just served him.

"It's not against doctor's orders?"

Marc had seldom seen him so relaxed, so good-humored.

"Not at this dosage," he said.

"You're not going to mix it with mint syrup?"

"No. I save the mint-lemon cocktail for the evening. Sixteen milliliters mint, a hundred and eighty of lemon soda."

Michel Zyto laughed noiselessly.

"Cheers," said Marc.

They took a sip and put their glasses down on the coffee table at the same time.

Marc pushed himself up by the armrests of the chair and they both stood.

Now they were impatient to begin.

At the clinic, Marc had described to Michel Zyto precisely what would transpire in their brains and in their consciousnesses during the experiment. And, upon arriving at Louveciennes, he gave him a tour of the property, telling him about his parents, and the house, where he could work in peace, all alone. Marc then gave him every possible explanation that a layman could comprehend about the way the machine worked. He felt these explanations were important, along with the fervor and familiarity with which they were presented to Zyto: the experiment involved two people, it was a partnership, Zyto had to be made to feel Marc's equal as much as possible.

Zyto fully grasped everything Marc told him, as evidenced by his questions. He enthusiastically admired the psycho-computer—and showed equal respect for the self-portrait watercolor, which he examined at great length: he thought Marc looked handsome and that the drawing truly resembled him, despite the bizarre colors. Marc couldn't help being flattered by the various compliments.

Michel Zyto attached the armband to his wrist by himself. Easier to fasten than a watch. He glanced above his head, where the booth became narrower, like the tip of a small rocket that would soon take off, and transport them far away. . . .

"Everything is ready," said Marc. "Shall I go ahead?"

"Yes."

Marc, installed in the booth on the right (that would always be "Cookie's booth" for him), pushed the first button.

The red warning light came on.

They could hear the vague rumbling of machines behind the partition. Dials 1 and 4 lit up, the three orange lines did their little snake dance, then stopped, and the orange warning lights 1 and 4 flashed.

"Perfect," said Marc.

Zyto's eyes were riveted to the dials. Dials 2 and 5 lit up at once.

The two light brown lines briefly flickered across the screen.

"It's almost over," Marc said. "Here comes a little electric shock . . ."

Michel Zyto smiled at him, a relaxed, confident, bright smile, the most beautiful and engaging he had ever given him, thought Marc. And Marc felt a rush of gratitude that he expressed with a return smile—probably the nicest one he had given Zyto, Marc thought, considering he wasn't particularly fond of his own smile.

This moment of total complicity marked the pinnacle of their "friendship," a feeling of profound sympathy, bonding therapist and patient.

The electric jolt, coinciding with the sudden appearance of the blue lines on dials 3 and 6, was fairly powerful, more powerful than Marc had expected. It made them both wince and cry out in pain. They closed their eyes. And during that swift third phase, their minds were emptied, or more precisely, their minds actually shared in the emptiness of that one, sole pain that enabled the psycho-computer to finish the work it had begun.

The pain ceased. Marc opened his eyes again.

It was over.

And it was a failure, for nothing had happened. Nothing whatsoever, he thought, realizing that he had remained entirely himself, Marc Lacroix, in his own mind.

Then things happened very quickly.

Suddenly, the horrible surprise, it hit him right in the gut: the blue warning light was on. And yet this light, which during the experiment had been the closest to him of the three, was now the farthest away. And his right hand, groping for the control buttons, was reaching out into thin air. Plus the wooden partition was now on his left!

Marc still refused to comprehend.

But the certainty of catastrophe was almost simultaneously confirmed when he found himself face to face, not with Michel Zyto, but with his own image, Marc Lacroix, the body of Marc Lacroix, his body, his face, his eyes, staring at him in surprise—then, seconds later, with a gleam of malice—for it was Michel Zyto he was looking at, Michel Zyto in Marc's body, while he, Marc, occupied the body of Michel Zyto; in a fleeting glance, he saw *his* black jacket, a long arm sticking out of the sleeve, and a strong hand, a hand that was not his own, covered with fine red hairs.

A failure? No, it had worked all right, but only too well!

The psycho-computer had functioned, but was unable to control the final phase of the experiment. The N.I.B. had been overzealous, it had done more than had been required: the "void" in the neuronic chains produced by the violent pain had been so complete, and had elicited such a strong response, that the N.I.B. and the piloting computer had worked desperately to fill this void. Thus, all of Marc's psychic energy had gone into Michel Zyto and in return, all of Michel Zyto's being had taken possession of Doctor Lacroix.

Of course, the error could easily be corrected. Theoretically, the reverse procedure would work without any problem. But Marc's immediate reaction that he was confronted with an abominable catastrophe, was due to the fact that he'd instantly divined from the scheming look in Michel Zyto's eyes—*his* eyes—the horror that would follow, that was just beginning. And already, he could do nothing to stop it.

17

Marc tried not to panic long enough to tell Michel Zyto, in a voice that startled him, and sent chills up his spine, for it was Zyto's voice: "Quick, push the third button, push it all the way down. Gently, but all the way. Don't you see what has happened? Push it, now!"

His "partner" was stunned, but not horrified in the least.

Quite the opposite.

The heavens had just granted his dearest wish.

The idea forced itself upon him with the clarity and strength of a vital necessity, an exhilarating twist of fate.

And his decision was immediate.

He would take advantage of the situation to fulfill his wildest dream, as impossible and vague, but just as constant and strong as the wish for immortality, a dream that was miraculously within his reach: to become Doctor Lacroix.

He could now appease those mixed feelings of love and hate that he felt for himself and for Marc, reconcile what was previously irreconcilable: inhabit Marc's body and send his own back to Stéphen-Mornay, to the lunatics!

He did not hesitate nor did he ask any questions. He acted first.

Instead of obeying Marc's order, he calmly removed the armband around his left wrist and stood up, awkwardly straightening out this long, thin body to which he would now have to become accustomed.

Then he started to think.

Marc was gripped with a boundless terror when he saw "Michel Zyto" stand up, gazing at him with a cold, calculating stare, rapidly weighing the consequences and risks of his act.

He forced himself to adopt a stern tone: "Will you please sit down and put that armband back on!"

The other man massaged his left wrist in silence. Then he spoke, surprised and delighted by the new voice coming out of his mouth: "Get up, my dear Michel Zyto. We're going home. I'm taking you back to the clinic. I'll let you drive. That way, you'll be able to tell d'Oléons and the rest of them that, not only did you have a good time on your outing, but Doctor Lacroix let you drive his big, beautiful car. C'mon, let's get going!"

He was waiting for Marc to take off his armband before attacking him. He didn't want any damage inflicted on the machine.

Marc stared at him, incredulous, amazed by the rapidity, the ease, and the malice with which Michel Zyto had stepped into "his" shoes, into his new role. It was no use trying to convince him. Zyto had become someone else, far beyond all his hopes and dreams!

Images flashed through his head. He thought of Marianne, his wife, his son.

What a mess, what a horrible mess! And it was all his fault!

He took off his armband, and stood up slowly, painfully—and suddenly flung himself at Zyto—toward his own body. He rushed at him intending to punch him, knock him out, and tie him up, he still had yards and yards of good, solid electrical wire on the other side of the partition. Then he'd be able to turn things around and terminate the nightmare.

Michel Zyto was lying in wait. Despite his now weaker, more delicate physique, he had remained himself, cunning, accustomed to threats and danger, having been brought up in the streets.

Ducking out of Marc's path, he punched him in the stomach. It was both a repugnant and voluptuous sensation; he was his own flesh, pounding with all his might.

Marc stopped dead, the wind knocked out of him, and held his stomach. Tears of pain ran down his cheeks. A hiccuping sob escaped, he thought he was going to vomit.

Michel Zyto quickly grabbed his wrist and twisted his arm behind his back. Then, with a sweeping gesture, he turned the machines back to zero and switched everything off—it was easy, and Marc had explained it all to him so well . . .

He pushed Marc toward the door.

"Don't get any ideas, now. Let's go, we're leaving. Open it!"

Marc was forced to manipulate the keyboard that controlled the sliding door. Zyto took the large key ring out of his pocket, Marc's suit pocket, and handed it to him. Marc, with his left arm still twisted around his back, locked the wooden door of the basement as well.

Zyto snatched the bunch of keys.

"Please, stop this at once!" said Marc. "What do you think you're doing? It won't get you anywhere, except in trouble!"

Zyto brutally pushed him toward the stairs. He twisted his arm even harder.

"Shut up!" he growled, suddenly rude. "This will get me back to your house, all right, where I'll be taking it nice and easy. As of now, my troubles are over. I'm going to see what it's like to be Doctor Marc Lacroix. I'm sure it's a lot better than Michel Zyto. I'll come visit you at Stéphen-Mornay. As usual."

"Look, you're smart enough to know that isn't going to work, you'll give yourself away, and so will I. . . ."

Zyto halted at the top of the stairway, and in an even voice, more ominous than angry, spoke directly into Marc's ear: "You, you don't even count! If you say anything whatsoever, I'll kill your family, your wife and son, I'll kill them both. I'll never be far away from them. And if I am, you'll never know where they are. And I'll always have something on me in case I decide to kill myself, to kill *you*, you understand? Always remember that, don't ever forget it, not for a minute, when you're in your room in the nuthouse. A very pleasant room, you'll like it there, you'll see. Lots of light, good food, music, and a charming staff. And visits from Doctor Lacroix."

He had raised his voice slightly. He laughed contemptuously. No doubt about it, it was a definite transformation. The psychocomputer had worked miracles.

They were outside. It felt almost like summer, like a real August afternoon. Zyto locked the door to the house, and made Marc climb into the Nissan Terrano on the passenger side, roughly shoving him into the driver's seat, then sitting down beside him and slamming the door.

"Drive," he said. "You know the way. Don't get any ideas, like I told you, or else I'll kill you."

Marc started up the engine. He saw himself in the rearview mirror. It was another shock. That mustache, that pimp haircut, those slightly simian features . . . he nearly screamed, had the urge to vomit again, felt an actual spasm, and put his hand over his mouth.

Then, instantly, he regained a semblance of courage. He would attempt something during the drive, or when they arrived at the Center. There, he'd make a scene, he'd start kicking the door of Hugue's office. That way, the distinguished d'Oléons would be forced to get up out of his chair, and move those two hundred pounds of his! Marc would shout at the impostor, he'd say that the "other" man over there was not Marc Lacroix, he'd talk about his experiment in terms that would shock Hugues, he'd provide him with details, precise data of a scientific nature that Michel Zyto could not possibly know. Yes! That was the answer! Hugues would definitely be upset, if not convinced on the spot. He knew about Marc's mad passion for research, his suspicions would be aroused, and everything would turn out all right!

No. It would be best to do something while they were driving.

Marc tried to keep his thoughts clear, not succomb to the madness created by this absurd situation.

"Stop!" said Zyto.

They had just driven past the gate.

"Why?"

"The gate was closed before, wasn't it? We're going to close it."

All of a sudden, he threw himself at Marc, pushing him, then grabbed his wrist again and twisted his arm. They got out of the car. Marc groaned with pain. Again, that unbearable ache in his shoulder . . .

He was flooded with hatred. It was a feeling he had never known before. It made him tremble, he was trembling with hatred.

Once the gate was closed, they got back into the car, and turned on to Rue du Général-Leclerc. Marc was driving, and Zyto was watching him, ready to attack him, as he'd threatened he would.

Zyto had also considered the problem of their arrival. He had a simple plan: he'd knock Marc out before they arrived inside the Center, then he'd inject him with Demerol intravenously. He'd sleep for at least twelve hours. Zyto should know. He knew all about those treatments.

They drove down the deserted street.

A witness—but there weren't any—might have assumed the doctor was simply letting his friend try out his Japanese four-wheel drive.

This was the situation as Marc Lacroix and Michel Zyto departed Louveciennes.

18

*A*t *the first traffic light* past the edge of town, they were supposed to turn left onto a larger road that would lead them to the highway.

The two men were silent now, each absorbed in his own thoughts, each guardedly watching the other's behavior. Time was running out. Marc decided to act immediately. He spotted a tree on another road, to the left of the intersection: he would make the turn, swing around and slam straight into the tree. He'd have the steering wheel and the pedals to brace himself. Whereas Zyto, on the edge of his seat, would be taken by surprise, thrown off balance, sent flying against the windshield, perhaps even knocked unconscious.

Alas, this is not what occurred. Zyto was expecting some kind of desperate move on Marc's part. He was alert, wily, and coiled like a snake ready to strike. He'd recovered all of his boyhood insolence and resentment, and was now eager to put it to work.

Right away, he'd sensed what Marc was up to. So when Marc turned left with his usual caution, trying to appear as if nothing were wrong, and then suddenly stomped on the accelerator, Michel Zyto instantly pounced on him, grabbing the steering wheel out of his hands. The car, lurching forward like a missile from Marc's powerful acceleration, veered slightly off course. Missing the tree by a few inches, it rolled onto a patch of wild grass, then plunged into the thick undergrowth, which brought the vehicle to an abrupt halt.

Marc told himself that he didn't have a chance. He would put up a fight, but he knew he'd just exhausted his last bit of energy. The two men threw themselves at each other. Zyto had the upper hand without any problem. He ignored Marc's awkward attempts to hit him, he immediately grabbed him by the hair—*his* hair, his magnificent, thick, straight, chestnut locks—and smashed his head, the back of his skull, against the window. Michel Zyto fought desperately with his own body, he banged it twice, three times, drawing Marc's face close to his, then flinging it backward with all his might against the window. He continued banging Marc's head even though he had lost consciousness, delighting in his own brutality. He scrutinized this face, contorted with pain, he revelled in the sound, a dull thud, one after the other . . .

He would show him it didn't pay to fight back, that bastard!

Finally, he let go of him. Marc sank lifelessly into the seat.

The window was splattered with blood.

Zyto—an unrecognizable, transformed Marc Lacroix metamorphosed into a wild beast—Zyto tried to catch his breath, noisily panting through his nose and mouth.

He noticed the blood. He grabbed Marc by the ear and turned his head around. There was a bright red wound several inches down his scalp, oozing and throbbing at the edges. The blood trickled out, forming droplets on the ends of his hair.

And what if he were to kill him, right then and there? Legitimate defense. They'd soon forget about Michel Zyto. He was always trying to kill himself. Here was the perfect opportunity, the ideal moment to "commit suicide."

He toyed with the idea for a second. But he wasn't ready to give up his body. And he needed Marc . . .

He got out, walked around to the other side of the car, opened the door to the back seat, then the passenger side. He leaned over slightly, pulled Marc toward him, and gently lifted him onto his left shoulder.

Then he put him down in the back, carelessly tossing him across the seat. In the process, Marc's head knocked against the metal edge of the roof. Oh well, that'll be one more stitch, Zyto thought maliciously.

He folded Marc's legs at the knees and slammed the door.

Just then, a car stopped on the road and a well-dressed young man with a mustache, short hair, and a plaid shirt got out hastily. Had he seen Michel Zyto putting an unconscious man in the back seat of the Terrano like a bundle of dirty laundry? No, there was nothing about his behavior to indicate that.

Zyto walked toward him.

"You have an accident?" the young man asked.

"A little one. I felt kind of faint, sort of dizzy. It didn't last very long, but I ended up on the grass. Fortunately, I wasn't going very fast."

"Are you all right? You're bleeding a little, right there."

He gestured toward his own forehead. They were now face to face, approximately twelve yards away from the Terrano. Michel Zyto brought his hand to his brow. He had taken that moisture for sweat. It was blood. He had cut his forehead on the rearview mirror when he'd flung himself onto Marc.

"I must have had a close encounter with the rearview mirror."

"Nothing else hurts? No broken bones?"

"No. Besides," Zyto added with a smile, "I'm a doctor."

"Oh. That's good. Straight from the maker to the consumer," the young man said stupidly. "Is there anything I can do for you?"

You can get the hell out of here, real quick, Zyto said to himself.

"No, thank you."

"Will you be able to get your car back on the road?"

"No problem."

"Right, with an engine like that . . . Isn't it Nissan's new four-wheel drive? I read an article about it in *Cars Today*, it's supposed to be incredible."

"Incredible," said Zyto. "With any other car, I would definitely have been on the roof."

"You sure you don't want any help?"

"No, thanks, please don't bother. I'm just going to rest for a few minutes and then I'll be off. I'll stop at a pharmacy on the way."

"OK, whatever you say. Goodbye. Well, hey, have a nice day, anyway."

"Thanks, you too."

From his car, the affable young man gave another little wave to Michel Zyto and started his engine.

Good riddance. Zyto sat down at the wheel of the Terrano. He readjusted the mirror. It was indeed splattered with blood. He found some Kleenex in the glove compartment. He dabbed at the cut under his brow, wiped the blood off the corner of the mirror and the window, and stuck a handful of tissues under Marc's head.

The car would need a good cleaning.

He backed up, pulled onto the road without any problem, and sped off toward Paris.

He checked the time on Marc's handsome nautical watch, the one he'd always admired.

Another adventure was about to begin.

He kept glancing behind him, to keep a close watch on Marc.

At the traffic lights, he went through Marc's wallet. He discovered his exact address on a personal card with his wife's first name printed on it. He already knew Marc's son's name, but not his wife's. *His* wife and *his* son, from now on.

He would call them as soon as he arrived at the Center.

It felt like he had sand in his suit pockets. No, it was sugar. Sugar for the dogs. Marc had told him everything. He shook out the pockets.

He looked at himself in the rearview mirror. Doctor Marc Lacroix. On his way to the psychiatric Center Stéphen-Mornay, bringing back a patient who'd had a fit, and suddenly turned aggressive. Marc had been obliged to defend himself. Not easy, when you're in the car. Luckily, in this case, the vehicle had gone off the road.

There had been an accident, violent impact, Michel Zyto's skull had been thrown against the front windshield, a terrible shock. . . .

Doctor Marc Lacroix. He saw the world in a different way with different eyes. His exultation erased any anxiety.

Marc was still unconscious. Thank goodness for that. Otherwise, he would have had to knock him out again.

He had reached Place d'Italie. Michel Zyto's heart began to pound wildly. But he felt confident. He could now trust himself.

19

*M*ichel *Zyto collapsed* into the Louis XV armchair near the window. What an odd chair, and what a curious man Doctor d'Oléons was to have such an old thing in this ultramodern office.

Above all, he had to act naturally.

"There we are!" said Adeline, the young nurse who had just placed a bandage on his forehead.

She had been quick and precise, she had scarcely hurt him while disinfecting the wound. This Adeline was new to the Center. Top-notch care, only one of the many reasons for the efficient operation of the clinic. Patients were more rapidly cured here than in most similar establishments due to the strict selection of employees, from the three head doctors down to the two cleaning women. Hugues d'Oléons supervised everything with a constant and unwielding diligence. Everyone had to be "first rate," even those who had no direct contact with the patients. For him it was a standard, a theory, almost a religion. The fact that Mademoiselle André was a remarkable administrator had some bearing on the improvement of the state of fifteen patients, though she never laid eyes on them. Right or wrong, this was his belief, and therefore (Marc Lacroix had often thought) it was actually somewhat accurate.

Not only had Hugues gotten up from his pivoting chair, he was pacing up and down, slowly and heavily like a battleship, while Adeline took care of poor Lacroix. Now she was dabbing ointment on the bruises that adorned his face.

Mademoiselle André entered.

"Please, sit down," said Hugues, indicating his rarely empty seat.

"No, that's all right. Thank you, Hugues."

It was the first time she had ever called him by his surname. It must have been all the excitement. She was as pale as a ghost. Her violet hair looked even more violet, and her little pointed nose, more pointed. An hour earlier, she'd been inside the entrance to the Center when Doctor Marc Lacroix had gotten out of his big car, wounded and haggard. She'd been extremely upset. She adored Marc, as did everyone.

After a while, she sat down in her boss's chair.

"Well, that's that. The only thing left now is the suit," she said. "But I can't help you there."

"Thank you," said Michel Zyto. "Thanks a lot."

She gave him a warm smile, and acknowledged Hugues d'Oléons with a nod as she very discreetly left the room.

"She's really terrific, that new girl," Hugues said to himself.

Then he thought about what Doctors Onizian, Verhoeven, and Fabricant would say, something like: this is what happens when you let someone from outside the Center get involved. But they would soon dismiss such foolish thoughts. They knew very well that Marc's methods were consistent with their own, and that unless a patient was tied down to his bed in a prison cell . . . no, there wouldn't be any trouble with the doctors. The real problem was poor Marc, who was wounded, in shock, and disappointed. How would he get over this terrible business? As d'Oléons well knew,

Marc was so fragile deep down, so easily depressed, particularly during these last few months.

Mademoiselle André sensed the two men had things they wanted to discuss. She stood up again.

"Well, I'm going," she said. "Doctor Lacroix, if you only knew how sorry I am to see you in this state!"

Michel Zyto, beneath his "Doctor Lacroix" facade, didn't need to make any effort to appear tense and distraught. This was a formidable test. You had to think of everything. His voice, for instance. He consistently had to imitate Marc's poised manner of speaking, the finesse of his intonations. And watch his vocabulary, make sure he spoke "properly." Plus knowing how to act—how would the real Dr. Lacroix behave? How should he address Mademoiselle André? Should he shake hands with her in parting or kiss her on the cheek, or the forehead? What did he do when he arrived at the clinic, when he departed, what were his routines?

Zyto reassured himself: surely nothing out of the ordinary. And today, certainly no one would reproach him for changing his routine a little. And frankly, he told himself, he could do whatever he wanted, walk on his hands if he felt like it, use filthy language, smack the old lady on the butt, and they'd still never guess the truth! No, ha, ha! Nothing too terrible could possibly happen to him!

He shook the hand that Mademoiselle André held out to him, giving her a feeble smile: "Bravo for yesterday's weather forecast. What a storm! I certainly thought of you."

Mademoiselle André was charmed.

"I could gladly do without those pains, you know. But Doctor d'Oléons insists that it's incurable. So did you, you told me the same thing one time, do you remember? Dorsal neuralgia, that's the only thing I've been able to get out of the medical profession. A name. A label.

"Labels are one of the functions of the medical profession," said Hugues, with a smile playing at the corner of his lips. "You know what Georges Sand said about a head cold? That the only remedy doctors had found was to call it coryza."

After the departure of this kindly little violet mouse, Mademoiselle André, Hugues d'Oléons got back into his chair and confronted Zyto with one of the problems raised by this folly of the "prisoner at will," as Marc sometimes called him: should he be transferred elsewhere? Hugues was not in favor of this, and Zyto, who was bent on having Marc under his control, even less so.

"No," said Zyto to Hugues. "It would be a mistake. It would be making him pay for his little tantrum. In my opinion, he's already going to pay dearly for it. No, in the future, we'll have to take into consideration what happened today, that's all. We can reflect on it. However . . . I'm afraid he's going to try to call me at home, on my private number. I'm sure he's going to try. And I think that for the time being . . ."

"Very well," said Hugues, "we'll take the phone out of his room, for as long as you feel necessary."

"Yes, it's better that way."

No more telephone for Marc Lacroix. It was a wise precaution.

Then Hugues gave Zyto a pompous speech punctuated by his noisy breathing: "My dear Marc . . . the only thing that disturbs me is the scare you've had, and how disappointed you must be. I know how much you take your work to heart. Every time I'm on the phone with a member of your staff at Sainte-Anne, all anyone can do is sing your praises. As for your friends on Avenue de Verdun, they talk about you constantly in their bulletins ever since you began directing the lab." He indicated one of the journals lying on his desk. "And for my part, at Stéphen-Mornay, I can vouch that your work with Michel Zyto has been miraculous, considering the state he was in when he was first brought to us. Need I tell you that you still have my complete admiration and trust? No, that would be insulting, for you and for me both. You did nothing wrong, you know that. But you've got to get over this anxiety as soon as possible, I hate to see you so worried, the way you are today. The way you've been for quite a while, my dear Marc," Hugues d'Oléons added shyly, lowering his voice. "You must have realized that I noticed . . . If I'm taking liberties by mentioning this, it's simply because I don't want today's unfortunate episode to make it worse . . . In any case, you know you can count on my friendship. . . ."

D'Oléons stopped, embarrassed and exhausted by his tirade. If they would only finish taking care of Marc so I could get away from this windbag, Zyto thought.

He listened carefully nonetheless, registering what was useful, perhaps precious information. From now on, it was best to take everything in and memorize it. So, Doctor Lacroix had been in a troubled state for a long time. Was it depression? That's what the head of the Center seemed to be implying. Come to think of it, Zyto was hardly surprised.

"I'm very touched," he said in a hollow voice. "Nevertheless, it was a failure, a total failure."

"So what?" said Hugues. "That's life. That's the way things go. Would we be as passionate about our work if we didn't take risks? On the other hand, you know very well that it wasn't a total failure. It's not as if we have to start from scratch again. The work you've done with Michel Zyto is still valid. You have to consider what happened today as a passing incident".

Zyto gazed intently at the enormous, bald, Dr. d'Oléons, whose belly looked like a cushion that had been placed on the chair, on which he himself might sit. Hormonal problems, everyone at the clinic knew that. As everyone knew he lived alone. Well, he wouldn't make any blunders along those lines, Zyto wasn't about to shout: "Give my best to your family!" when they said goodbye. Ha, ha! Poor guy. He probably didn't get laid very often. About as often as I do, thought Michel Zyto. Meaning never.

Zyto had to admit that Dr. d'Oléons had always been decent to him. Not like Marc, but in a different way, a way that he couldn't have hated him for, the way he was capable of hating Marc. Nor could he have liked him as much.

"You're too good to me, Hugues. And what about pride? Do you hold my pride cheap?"

Had he used the expression, "to hold cheap," correctly? It was something he'd come across in his reading but had never said before. Yes, he was pretty sure he had. As for his declaration of pride . . . a bit risky, perhaps? Would he, proud Dr. Lacroix, have uttered such a thing at that moment?

Yes. Zyto could have jumped for joy when d'Oléons replied:

"We've known each other for a long time and this isn't the first time I've seen you reproach yourself for having pride, as if it were a shameful flaw. I know you have pride! So do I, in my own way. You wouldn't be the doctor and the researcher that you are without that nerve, that ambition."

Zyto took on a pensive look. "I feel guilty," he said. "Toward Zyto, and even a little toward you. I'll be back to see him, very soon. I've got to take care of him, follow up on the treatment, particularly now. I must."

Strange to talk about yourself and to hear yourself being talked about as if it were someone else. Zyto, I have to take care of Zyto; it isn't the first time I've seen you reproach yourself for having pride, my dear Marc. And on the subject of pride, bravo for my little speech; if anybody were to try to tell this tub of lard here that it was really Michel Zyto, not Marc Lacroix, sitting across from him, d'Oléons would send him to shock therapy, ha, ha! Zyto had to suppress the desire to laugh.

Someone was knocking on the door.

It was Dr. Antoine Fabricant, the eldest of the doctors at the Center. As a military doctor at the outset of his career, he'd distinguished himself by his extreme competence in nearly every branch of medicine, including surgery. And he always had a solid diagnostic. One glance, a few questions, a quick exam, and he could already tell a lot about a patient. At the Center, his specific job was to attend to the physical health of the inmates, treating them for anorexia, bulimia, traumas provoked by attempted suicide, digestive problems, or high blood pressure due to antidepressant medication, etc.

He was always in a jovial mood.

"How are you feeling, doctor?"

"A lot better, thanks," said Zyto.

"Good. As for your goddamn crazy, bloodthirsty patient . . . it wasn't easy, shaving his neck with that gushing wound! Had to disinfect it, give it a few stitches, and throw in a tetanus shot with antibiotics, just in case. As for the rest, well, he did have a slight cerebral concussion. Very, very slight," he added, noting d'Oléons' dismay. "I've got him on cortisone and decongestants, he'll be out of it for a few hours. His blood pressure is high, and he's been having muscular spasms in the face and stomach. And in the calves. In my opinion, he's going to be extremely agitated when he wakes up."

"Nothing too serious?" asked Hugues.

"No. When I worked the emergency room at Hôtel-Dieu, the guys who arrived in his condition were sent home with a pat on the back. Or a kick in the ass, depending how busy it was."

Zyto couldn't help laughing. Marc would have probably laughed as well, he had a good sense of humor.

"And what about us, what should we give him?" Hugues asked.

"What do you think? Demerol?"

"Yes. Better he doesn't wake up right after his concussion."

"That's exactly what I think," said Zyto.

"You go on home now, Marc. I'll keep you posted."

"All right," said Zyto, gingerly lifting himself out of his chair as if he hurt all over. "I'll drop by tomorrow morning."

D'Oléons protested as a matter of form, but he knew "Marc."

Dr. Fabricant walked toward the door.

"Antoine, Marc won't be pressing charges," Hugues told him. "We decided to keep this business hush-hush, if possible. We don't want it spread around. It wouldn't serve any purpose, for the time being."

"Of course," said Antoine Fabricant.

He left the room.

"Would you mind if I gave Marie a call?" asked Zyto, who had been repeating the number, "his" number, in his head over and over again.

"Go right ahead."

Hugues pushed the phone toward him.

"Would you like me to step out?"

"Not at all. I'm just going to prepare her a little. If I turn up looking like this . . . Marie? It's me . . ."

Marie didn't answer right away. Zyto added:

"Marc."

20

He turned onto the Chemin du Maréchal-ferrant at full speed.

He had the four by four under control. He had a way with cars. He used to drive a dilapidated old truck, owned by his Uncle Nicholas, who lived in Pantin outside of Paris. On the truck, his uncle had painted in lopsided letters: "Nick's Spic 'n' Span Cleaning Service." They had ridden around the suburbs, and once in a while someone had wanted something cleaned, an attic, an overgrown garden, or a ceiling black with soot. This had guaranteed their livelihood for at least a few days.

The Terrano was a cinch to drive. Zyto had examined the contents of the car. He'd opened and closed the front and back doors, and the hood. And he'd practiced operating the tape deck. Nothing to it. He was clever with his hands and caught on quickly.

He'd had a hard time finding this damn street, despite the two maps he'd found in the glove compartment. One was old and crumpled, and the other, brand new, probably never used, of the Paris suburbs on a scale of one inch to five miles.

Obviously, it was out of the question to ask for directions.

He saw the house. No other neighboring homes in sight. In fact, it didn't have a number, it was the only one on the Chemin du Maréchal-ferrant, which trailed off into a little forest.

Zyto was immediately besieged by the fears he'd somehow kept at bay since he'd left the Center. How would the meeting with Leonard and Marie go? (He repeated "Marie" and "Leonard" to himself to get used to their names.) Granted, he appeared as Marc, but what about the rest—his habits, his behavior, the phone calls that Marc regularly made or received, people who came to visit? Was there perhaps some social event that had already been planned for tonight? Did Marc take showers or baths? When? And what about the way he laughed? Zyto had never heard him laugh outright: what would he sound like if he were to laugh wholeheartedly? (For tonight it wouldn't be a problem, Zyto thought, no one would expect Dr. Lacroix to roar with unrestrained laughter.) How did he talk to his son, and about what, and in what tone? Did they talk a lot or hardly at all?

The most terrifying part, by far, would be the intimacy with Marie, his wife. . . .

And a thousand other things.

And there remained one other thing among the thousand that Zyto couldn't stop thinking about: had Marc kept silent, and resisted the temptation to confide in Hugues? Yes, he was convinced he had, and equally sure that Marc would take his threats seriously. Besides, they were serious. Marc must have sensed that deep down inside. Still, Zyto was obsessed with a distant yet tenacious doubt founded on pure anxiety.

He was coming up on the house. He began to sweat from sheer nervousness. If he let himself get tangled in the web of his own questions and fears, he wouldn't last five minutes.

He concentrated for a moment to try to fight them off.

It worked. He wanted to enjoy being Marc Lacroix, not be tortured by anxiety and tension. He reassured himself. He should see the least number of people possible. Have his wife answer the phone. Play on the fact that he was depressed, therefore a little bizarre and different than usual, especially since the attack.

As for the rest, he'd keep using whatever he could learn from others, first and foremost, his wife, and he'd improvise, make up for mistakes in due time, only when necessary.

So he must not panic yet.

He had to wait, feel certain that nothing irrevocable could occur.

"What, you're brushing your teeth right after dinner?"

"Yes, and again before bed. I've decided to follow the rules of dental hygiene down to the letter. It's important. C'mon everyone, into the bathroom!"

Or: "What are you going to wear tomorrow?"

"I don't know. Some green trousers and a policeman's hat?"

"Very funny. How about your navy suit? It's going to be a very chic crowd tomorrow."

"And what if I didn't go?"

"Not go to Henri's wedding? That might be a little difficult. You should have cancelled much further in advance."

"Oh I know, I know! But what if I tried to get out of it? I'll have to find a good excuse. You could help me, instead of siding with the enemy."

Or something like: "So, how's that new guy at the lab? You haven't mentioned him lately."

"Yes, that's true. I got a little carried away about him. I have nothing in particular to report. . . . He's new, and I wasn't that way when I was new, that's all."

Et cetera. Zyto calmed himself down with these little fantasies. Better still, he was suddenly amused and excited by the idea of improvisation, problems that had to be quickly and efficiently resolved.

He was going to enjoy being Marc Lacroix.

The house, his house, was a rich person's home, large, beautiful, and all white. It was perpendicular to the Chemin du Maréchal-ferrant. One side faced a garden, and the other, the countryside. He drove past the gate, and parked in what resembled a courtyard next to a small red Austin (a second car, did it belong to Marie or to a visitor? Probably to Marie), rather than the garage, although the doors were open. On a day like today, Marc wouldn't have parked in the garage, he would have done the easiest thing possible.

He turned off the engine.

Two questions came to mind, important questions that hadn't as yet occurred to him.

Did Marc Lacroix have another woman in his life? No.

Had Marc Lacroix really kept his research absolutely secret, the way he'd sworn he had? Yes.

No to the first, yes to the second. He hoped he'd guessed right. Yes, he believed he had.

He got out of the car.

He wouldn't even have known which door to enter.

But a woman and a child were already on the doorstep, coming toward him.

21

The woman was a slim brunette, with long hair that floated around her shoulders as she walked. A nice figure, in a long clinging red dress that normal men would probably find sexy. A real woman, the kind Zyto had seen only in magazines or in soap operas on TV. A beautiful face, too, mature and very youthful at the same time. The moment their eyes met, Zyto sensed something about her that was reassuring, something that did not repel him, that didn't really threaten him at all.

"Everything is fine," he said to her with a little smile. "It's over now."

The kid went galloping ahead to get to him first, and leapt into his arms. Embarrassing. Michel Zyto lifted him up, kissed him very gently on the cheek, then blew playfully into his dark bangs. Why not?

"You gotta tell me how it happened, OK?" said Leonard. "How long will you have to wear the bandages?"

He was about ten, Zyto already knew that. Tall for his age, with an intelligent gleam in his eye, and a natural elegance, all decked out in his sports clothes—probably expensive, especially the shirt. He was a good-looking little boy. Marc was handsome as well, with his finely chiseled yet perfectly proportioned features. It was an attractive family.

Of which he was now a part.

He set Leonard back down.

"Ah ha, your mother told you. There isn't much to tell, you know. A little cut, a little bruise. Nothing happened to the car. The bandages will be off in . . . oh, three or four months."

"No way!" said Leonard, laughing.

"OK. Tomorrow or the day after."

It was Marie's turn, she clung to Zyto, circling his waist with her bare arms, pressing her cheek against his. She said in a near whisper: "Did you tell me everything on the phone? Are you all right?"

"Yes, I'm fine, I promise, darling. I'll tell you all about it later, but . . . well, nothing. It's just that it hasn't been a great day."

Leonard was heading toward the car.

Marie stepped back and looked at Michel Zyto with great tenderness. Was he supposed to kiss her? He gave her a quick peck on the lips. He'd also called her "darling." Did Marc call her "darling"? Maybe. So what if he didn't. Well, he would tonight! It was better than "honey" or "sweetheart." Tonight, it was going to be "darling." He didn't have to worry.

He had to act naturally. Nothing should take him by surprise. He stopped himself from wiping his lips after the kiss. Ugh!

"Leonard, come back here!" Marie almost shouted.

The boy was about to climb into the car. Zyto said quietly to Marie:

"It's OK. I cleaned off the blood. It was on my suit, too."

"Why?" Leonard called to his mother.

"All right, never mind, do what you want."

At which point, he came trotting back.

Through one of the windows facing the garden, Michel Zyto could make out the living room. It looked very fancy. He was going to like it here.

Marie hugged him again, tightly, then let go, and held out her hand to Leonard.

Hugs, kisses, endearing words, Michel Zyto was flabbergasted that he'd been able to put up with so much from a woman, a woman who had come near him, touched him. Like his mother. But, like his mother, could she possibly desire anything less than his total destruction? Wouldn't she want to take him inside her, engulf him, swallow him up, reduce him to nothing?

And he couldn't help imagining what it would be like to hit Marie. Stab her with a knife, make her suffer.

He revelled in this image. This desire to inflict violence on a woman had been repressed during his months at Stéphen-Mornay, but had returned with frightening speed. An instantly powerful, undying desire that lay at the core of Michel Zyto's very being, the clay that had molded his character. No one could change that, not all the Dr. Lacroixs in the world. Because no one could change what was, and there was a vital, fundamental pleasure in being oneself!

The novelty, the prodigious novelty, was that he was both himself and someone else. He was completely Michel Zyto again, but in the body of Marc Lacroix. And as a result, all he felt was the sheer joy, the energy, the fulfillment of his most intimate urges: the guilt and the pain, that was all over! And the self-hatred was gone, too, since it could now be directed toward another person over at the Center, dazed from his cerebral concussion, and in due time, from the intravenous dosages of Demerol. If the goal of a psychiatrist was to suppress the mental suffering of his patients and restore a sense of well-being, Marc Lacroix had done a perfect job, he'd performed a miracle, just like that fat fool d'Oléons had said.

And so, despite the return of his violent impulses, Zyto discovered he was capable of accepting Marie's support. Emanating kindness and serenity, Marc's own wife would help him even better play the role of Marc, better conceal the truth. It would frighten her to death if she only knew!

He laughed derisively to himself.

Then he was revolted by the thought that Leonard had come out of the belly of this woman. It came to him the moment Leonard, who was holding Marie's hand, latched onto his hand as well, pretending to drag them toward the house, straining forward as if he were pulling a team of horses.

Zyto wasn't too crazy about this little monkey. He would rather have been alone with Marie.

"Say, look how filthy your shorts are!"

Leonard, accustomed to joking around with his father, was quick to reply. He stepped back from Michel Zyto and pretended to scrutinize him carefully: "Yeah, not like your suit . . ."

Indeed, the wrinkled summer suit, ringed with stains from Zyto's hasty cleaning, hardly gave its owner the right to be too fussy about the appearance of anyone else's clothes.

Funny, very funny. So now what was he supposed to do? Slap the brat across the face? Zyto wondered, knowing very well the answer was no, it definitely wasn't the way things were done in this house. Marie was smiling. He imitated her expression and smiled too.

They entered the hallway. Zyto hung up his jacket.

"It's nice to be home," he said.

"So are you going to tell me?"

"You already know everything there is to know, my little monkey. Mommy told you the whole story."

"Mooo-mmy? She didn't tell me anything. Well, hardly anything. You know what I think? When you go out with the crazy people, you should always carry a gun. You could have put eight bullets in his head, and . . ."

"Leonard!" Marie said. "Your father is supposed to take care of his patients, not murder them! Why would you want him to carry a gun?"

Leonard was smart. He seemed to be fairly good at guessing things.

"I'm sure the other guy tried to hurt him," he said, suddenly serious, taking his father's hand again in a touching way. "I saw the expression on your face when you were on the phone with him."

"Come on now, my little monkey," said Zyto, rubbing his cheek. "I let him drive and we had an accident, that's all."

This was what they'd agreed to tell Leonard. "All right, all right!" Leonard shouted, tearing around from room to room.

"Marshall called right after you did," said Marie. "I told him what happened."

Marshall? Who was Marshall?

Marie noticed "Marc's" annoyed expression.

"It doesn't matter, does it?" she asked.

"No, but Hugues and I decided we didn't want it spread around."

Marie seemed surprised. Uh oh. His first little slip.

"So what?" she said. "Marshall won't tell a soul."

Zyto followed her into the living room.

"You're right. Sorry. I'm just a little edgy."

More like you're a little jealous, Marie thought, with a surge of tenderness.

He sank into the black leather couch. He was exhausted. He glanced around the room. What a television! Enormous, like a movie screen, with speakers on both sides like a stereo. And all those books, hundreds of them, and the stereo equipment, all black and shiny, as beautiful as a work of art! There was a varnished solid wood cabinet crammed with records, tapes, CD's, enough music to last an entire lifetime.

"Sixteen milliliters of mint, one hundred and eighty of lemon soda," Michel Zyto said casually to Marie.

He smiled ironically just in case Marc had never asked anyone to prepare his drink before—but tonight was an exception.

"Coming right up," said Marie without batting an eye.

She went from the living room to the dining room, and heading toward the kitchen, she ran into Leonard, who was just on his way out, walking this time instead of galloping, his mouth still wet from having gulped down fruit juice or some other beverage too quickly.

He wiped his mouth with his bare forearm and went over to snuggle up with his father.

"Were you scared? Really scared?"

"No, my little monkey. Hardly at all."

"Why do you keep calling me 'my little monkey' today?"

"Oh, just for a change."

"Do you want me to put on your record?"

"Yes, that would be nice, go ahead, put it on."

Leonard planted a kiss on his cheek and stood up. He was a whiz at handling the stereo equipment and the remote control. Zyto watched him to memorize how it worked. The black stereo unit lit up blue in various places, dials and lines stretched longer and shorter . . .

He couldn't help being reminded of Marc's psycho-computer. Zyto, previously obsessed by the need to act, was suddenly struck by the reality of what had taken place in the past few hours. It was only now that he felt the shock, an overwhelming astonishment, a fear of the unknown, as if he were in a dream, or a fairy tale.

The opening bars of *La Frescobalda* rang out. Marie brought him the glass of lemon-mint soda. Everything had become real again. In a way, nothing had truly changed. Or rather, the change was immeasurable and nonexistent at the same time.

Zyto was living in another person's body. But more than ever before, he was himself, Michel Zyto.

He took a sip, feigning an enthusiasm he was far from feeling. But, all in all, the price of his happiness had not been that high. He felt comfortable in this big luxurious living room, surrounded by priceless objects and green plants without a single speck of dust on their leaves, sunk into a couch that was incredibly soft underneath him and around his shoulders, that seemed to completely envelope him on all sides. This was nice and safe, like a cocoon, yet he could still stare out the bay window into the distance, at a landscape tinted with the intense hues of nightfall, far richer than the sunlit colors of day. . . .

. . . Enjoying the company of a wife and son who were waiting on him hand and foot, a wife and son whose affection, for the time being, was bearable without provoking too much anxiety or aggression. How long would it last? And what if he decided to kill Marc? And then kill Marie and Leonard when the ideal moment and the ideal conditions presented themselves? He could be all by himself and in perfect shape, instead of returning to his old body.

Later—he'd think about those questions later!

He should take advantage of the present.

The music had stopped. He'd found it boring. Marie and Leonard would have to get used to a change in his taste.

"Can I watch TV for a little while?" the child asked.

Zyto said nothing, letting Marie decide.

"Yes. Tonight, you can, so you can see for yourself how stupid the programs are at this hour."

Stupid or not, Leonard made a mad dash for the remote control and fiddled with the buttons as if he were trying to prevent a bomb from exploding. Then Marie asked Michel Zyto if he wanted to take a shower and change, making it sound more like a statement than an actual question.

"Into the shower I go," said Zyto, resolutely getting to his feet.

"I'll go with you."

He knew that she wanted to talk to him alone.

The couch went back to its original shape where Zyto had been sitting, making a strange hiss, like a wounded animal. He almost commented on it, like he'd almost addressed Marie Lacroix with the formal *vous* a second before.

Upstairs, he had to recount the accident and the attack in full detail: He had let Michel Zyto take the wheel, which was fine at first; they had driven through the countryside, chatting and listening to music, but at one point, Zyto had refused to take the road Marc had indicated. In fact, it had happened not too far from Louveciennes. Eventually they had come to blows, there'd been no other choice, and the car had gone off the road, flipped over on its side, and fallen into a ditch. The impact had been very violent. He admitted having been very frightened, despite what he'd said earlier, because his patient probably would have killed him, had he been able.

Michel Zyto and Marie walked slowly down the long, wide hallway of the second floor. Zyto took the opportunity to notice the layout of the house, Leonard's bedroom, the guest room, and Marc's office.

The master bedroom. The bathroom, the armoire, the closet. The bed.

The sight of the bed sent butterflies through his stomach. What would happen later on? Granted, tonight nothing would be expected of him. But what about tomorrow? And then, too, there was the physical proximity of a woman lying next to him; this beautiful, terrifying woman.

Once again, he was able to calm himself.

He would see when the time came. Everything was fine, it would all work out.

Before he'd said a word, she laid out some clothes on the bed: underwear, socks, and a shirt.

"Is the green shirt OK?" was all she asked.

"Fine."

He paused, entered the bathroom without undressing, hesitated again, then left the door open. Would she follow him, or wait for him in the bedroom? See him naked? What kind of relationship did the Lacroixs have as husband and wife? How did they act in private? What would he do if she came over and kissed him, or possibly touched him?

But nothing happened. He heard Marie walking away, her light footsteps on the parquet floor.

He turned on the water. He nearly began to whistle the *presto* by Vivaldi.

In the shower, he examined his new body. Tall, well proportioned. A bit on the skinny side. Very soft skin, the skin of a woman or a child. A little too soft around the abdomen. As for his penis—the object of a careful examination—he found it more attractive, more refined, and better shaped than his own. Yet his had its own charm as well, it was thicker and stronger, more enigmatic, perhaps more provocative for a woman, nestled in a thicker clump of pubic hair, a mass of chestnut-colored hair.

He lathered his body admiringly.

Before dinner, using the excuse that he had a few things to do around the house—to help him unwind—he was able to better explore all the rooms and the garage, where he noticed some masonry and unused garden tools; the basement, nearly empty, (mostly books, toys and some clothes); the grounds surrounding the house; and a small meadow that was not part of their property.

He liked this place. He liked everything about it.

They had dinner. He hardly asked any questions, but gathered a good deal of information about the Lacroixs, Marie's parents, Leonard's little friends, the Cazanvielhs, and the pinball machine Marshall had acquired. A pinball machine? Did these people own some kind of bar? No, this Marshall fellow was a collector.

Marie did not have a profession, he'd already established that. She had studied French, Latin, and Greek. In addition to the volumes of medical texts upstairs, he'd spotted other books with the name Marie Leleu on the inside first page, some of them written in a childish script, dating back to junior high school.

There were no calls.

After dinner, Michel Zyto was the first to leave the table.

"I have to call Hugues. I'll just be a minute."

He headed toward the living room.

There definitely had to be a gun in this house, he thought. Surely all rich people who lived in isolated neighborhoods owned guns.

Hugues. He'd make certain that everything was going smoothly on that end.

22

They were lowering the awnings. He wasn't totally unconscious, he could hear the sound of the crank handle. He couldn't seem to open his eyes. It was probably Adeline, the new girl, who could do the work of two nurses and did a good job of it too . . .

Adeline. Marianne. Images flashed through his mind. He couldn't really focus, his thoughts were slipping past too quickly, becoming muddled, evading him. He pursued them—nothing—what had he been thinking a moment ago that had seemed so important to him?

In Louveciennes, there had been a bratty kid who used to leave a change purse or some other precious-looking object lying around in the street, like a small, worthless metal car that would glitter in the sun. A stupid, well-known, practical joke: you bent down to pick it up and, oops, he'd pull on an invisible string attached to the object and it would escape your grasp. Marc had fallen for it several times when he was a child.

He stirred slightly, making minuscule movements, flexing his muscles, opening and closing his fist, shifting an arm or a leg a few inches, but to him it felt like a huge undertaking, a marathon, a fist fight, an endless tumbling downward.

His father had died after falling two stories from a ladder, a terrible fall, his skull split open, his leg dislocated.

Your father didn't feel anything. He died while he was on top of the ladder, before he slipped, that's why he fell. Marc had hated when his mother said that. Or anything else. Or didn't say anything. The old woman's face was glued to his, he would have liked to push it away . . . why was he so weak? And why weren't Marie and Leonard there, by his side? He had to get well quickly so he could see them, return home to the comfort, the affection, the daily routine.

Marianne. It was her image that reappeared the most frequently, and even blocked out the others. Marianne, so blond, so desirable; she was smiling at him, like she did when he came out of the bathroom and she was still in bed; he wanted her, he wanted to drive her mad with pleasure so she'd cling to him, squeezing him so tightly it would hurt, murmuring his name, Marc, and other words of love.

The streets of Louveciennes, the faces, the scenes from his youth, everything filed past in his head.

Everything, except for Michel Zyto.

He didn't feel any pain. Hardly any. Fabricant, no doubt. Good old Antoine. You could count on him to fix up the cuts and bruises. That must mean I'll be going home soon.

His memory had shut down, collapsed, it wasn't functioning properly, something was askew! He thought he was Marc Lacroix in Marc Lacroix's body, the body he had always known.

He made a bigger move this time: he wanted to take the mask off his face, he felt as though he were suffocating under a mask. He painfully lifted his right hand, his fingers found some hair, a nose, a mustache. The mustache on Zyto's face. What in the world was going on . . .

And everything came back to him in a flash.

Marc wanted to scream, and thought he had, but he'd only produced a muted groan. Drool fell from his lips. Michel Zyto, the car accident, the fight, his poor skull banging against the heavy window of the Terrano, the face of a psychopath so close to his, suddenly far away, then close, far, close . . . the psychopath was in his home, with his family, capable at any given moment of killing his wife and son!

And that mustache he'd just touched . . . how revolting!

He winced from the shock of unbearable mental anguish. Once again, he tried to scream—then calmed down, as other images invaded his consciousness. The concussion prevented him from doing anything too physically violent; he couldn't cry out, he couldn't get out of bed and start shouting in the corridors, couldn't bang his fists against the wall. Now, other images flooded his mind: Marie, radiant behind the steering wheel of her brand new Austin; those hoodlum gloves of Leonard's; Marie-Thérèse cackling away on the phone; his mother, Gertrude Lacroix, and her twenty different illnesses. He calmed down. Some horrid fluid from deep in his bowels had trickled from his mouth onto his chin and neck. He barely noticed it.

Marianne, Marianne!

He'd simply said he'd get back to her soon, as he often did. Marianne wouldn't start worrying right away. If too much time went by, she'd be a little glum, but she'd tell herself something had come up and he'd be calling her at any moment.

And how right she'd be! He was going to escape from this place. Call her, explain it to her. And make sure Zyto could do no harm. For a brief second, this was what he imagined happening. He would escape, call Marianne, convince her. Naturally, she'd believe him, he'd give her irrefutable proof of the truth . . . and then he'd have to . . . Zyto . . .

Zyto . . . The unbearable agony was on the verge of returning, but everything got confused in his brain, blurry, distant, farther and farther away.

Light.

Someone was sponging his mouth, chin, and neck. It felt fresh, cool.

A shot in the arm.

An IV. Demerol. I'm done for, he thought. Trapped in someone else's body. For how long?

He forced his eyes open. Using every ounce of energy, he was able to keep them open and let out a gurgle of words once he recognized Hugues d'Oléons, seated in a chair near the bed.

He wasn't able to see the nurse who was setting up the IV, he couldn't turn his head around far enough, but he knew she was there, a moving, white blur to his right, a blouse, probably Adeline.

His eyes met Hugues's, who was observing him in his usual kind way, looking sad, very sad.

"Doctor Lacroix . . . Where is Doctor Lacroix . . . ? I want . . . to see him . . ."

Only the vowels were audible, pushing their way through a path of bitter saliva, "do . . . or . . . a . . . oi, roix . . . ere . . . i . . . e . . . ?" but Hugues understood him perfectly.

He leaned his heavy torso over the bed and gently placed his hand on the shoulder of the wounded man.

"Don't worry, everything is fine now. Dr. Lacroix is at home, he just phoned me a second ago to find out how you were doing. You see, he isn't deserting you, he's concerned about you. He's coming to see you tomorrow morning. Now you should get some sleep and rest up, and everything will be fine, I assure you."

Doctor Lacroix! Michel Zyto, in his house, with his wife and son!

A new sensation swept him away, the fluid in the IV tingling through his arm, throughout his entire body.

His strength was gone, no more energy, no more thoughts.

His eyes closed again.

Fat tears rolled down his cheeks, staining the pillow.

The distinguished Hugues d'Oléons found this truly distressing.

23

They went to bed early, at the same time as Leonard. Marie Lacroix liked to turn in early and read in bed, and Michel Zyto went along with her.

What a delicious meal! He hadn't enjoyed himself this much in ages! Marie was a terrific cook. The hot apple pie she served for dessert was great. If it hadn't been for that little pig Leonard, Zyto would have gladly helped himself to another piece. And Marie knew how to make the simplest recipes taste good, like her pasta salad. For the pasta, the competition with Leonard had been less fierce, and Zyto had been able to eat his fill.

The phone call to Hugues had made him more relaxed. He was less apprehensive about spending the night with Marie. And Marie was docile, you could make her do whatever you pleased. And she never argued back. He felt in control of the situation. He would act however he liked.

Leonard gave him a kiss before going to his room, but didn't kiss his mother, he hardly even looked at her. Strange. Was he, Zyto, supposed to do or say anything in particular? The child disappeared, leaving the door partly ajar.

Marie walked on toward the master bedroom. Michel Zyto followed.

"Are you going to take another shower?"

"No, I'm too lazy," he said.

Which meant Marc Lacroix was definitely in the habit of taking a shower right before bed. Marie, too: she immediately went into the bathroom.

"There are clean pajamas. I did the laundry today."

She pushed the door behind her, leaving it half open.

Zyto chose a pair of pajamas from the armoire, red with black trim and a low V-neck, that looked like a sort of judo outfit. He undressed and slipped into it.

Before dinner, in addition to the photograph of a young Marc with a mustache that made him snicker, he'd noticed a book in Greek sitting on Marie's night table to the right of the bed. That was Marie's side. Did Marc also read in bed, despite the absence of a book on his side of the bed, where there was another identical night table? Or did he fall asleep while his wife read?

Did they make love every night?

He grabbed a book off one of the shelves, *The Concept of Biolimits*, and stretched out on "his" side, without getting under the covers.

He pretended to read.

Every so often, he brought his hand up to his face. He missed his mustache. He'd worn one since he was young. He preferred Marc without a mustache, but he missed the way it felt.

The noises in the bathroom had stopped.

"Would you please bring me a towel?" asked Marie.

"I'll be right there!"

He got up, randomly selected a big brown towel and entered the bathroom. Marie was comfortably settled into the bath tub, her hair tied up in a ponytail which made her look even younger, her breasts visible above the water.

"Yours is wet. I forgot to take one out for myself before."

She stopped and looked at Zyto, smiling.

"Is this supposed to be a joke?"

His thoughts raced. A joke, what joke? Maybe it had something to do with the towel he was holding out to her? What else could it be?

"You want another one?"

"No, of course not. You're a little distracted, poor dear. Still, don't forget that you're supposed to buy me a dozen blue ones . . ."

She didn't want the brown towel, at least not anymore. She and Marc must have had a conversation about it very recently. Fine, he would buy some blue towels. She stood up, her arm outstretched, and he passed her the towel. She began to dry herself.

Yes, she definitely looked like the women in the magazines, she was just as slim and as curvaceous, with a shapely bottom. He was struck by how lovely it was.

He looked away and walked out of the bathroom.

He went back to reading in bed, this time under the covers with his *The Concept of Biolimits*. He barely understood what he was reading. Not that he was incapable of understanding it, but he was waiting with renewed and increased apprehension for what would happen.

Marie crossed the room, dressed in a white bathrobe. The burgundy bathrobe must be Marc's. His. She went into the hall and shouted: "Ready or not!" and Zyto heard Leonard, from off in the distance, answer back: "Here I come!" So that was it. Their evening ritual, a stupid routine. All this "ready or not" stuff was supposed to come before the final goodnight kiss. And that was why Leonard hadn't kissed his mother before, Zyto thought, laughing contemptuously to himself, but stopping as he recalled the rituals his own mother had established between them.

He was suddenly flooded with hatred. No, he would have to fight it off. Marc had taught him how. First, he had helped him to express this hatred, then explain it, and then to fight it. It was inside of him, but he could control it.

Up to a certain point. And it was all thanks to Dr. Marc Lacroix—to his obstinance and competence as a psychotherapist, and because he had ever so kindly lent his body to Michel Zyto, ha ha!—that Michel Zyto could now bear, up to a certain point, the intimacy of Marie Lacroix, the doctor's wife.

Leonard was tucked in bed, as cute and adorable as could be. As soon as his mother came in, he opened his mouth to show how well he had brushed his teeth, kissed the air loudly, and closed his eyes, pretending to be asleep—all with exaggerated speed. It was all part of the game. His mother drew near him and kissed him on the forehead. He popped up, startled, as if she had woken him, they both burst out laughing, and started the routine all over again.

Now back at Zyto's side, Marie took off her robe and slipped on a nightgown that would have entirely fit in the palm of one's hand.

"Ah, I see you're reading tonight," she said inquiringly, getting into bed next to him.

"Yes. I'm in the mood tonight."

She kissed him on the cheek and reached for *The Odyssey*.

"Good idea, it'll relax you. You'll see, it will help you get to sleep. How do you feel? Does your forehead hurt?"

"No, I'm OK. A little stiff, but nothing hurts."

They turned out the lights soon afterward, neither of them having read very much.

They remained there, lying on their backs in the dark and silent room.

Zyto had the sudden desire to touch Marie.

But he was afraid she'd take it as an invitation to go further, afraid she might touch him back.

But his desire was stronger. For he knew that tonight, and for a while to come, for as long as he wished, he could act however he pleased and she would understand, and even forgive him beforehand. Because he increasingly sensed how reserved and discreet Marie was, contrary to those three women he'd happened to approach and that he'd . . . and besides, it was fear that had made him imagine the Lacroixs' passionate, active sex life. Maybe it wasn't that way at all.

He turned on his side, and slid his hand toward her. He was

expecting to encounter the fabric of her nightgown, but the delicate material had hiked up to her chest and his hand was partially touching Marie's belly. After a few moments' hesitation, he let his hand glide downward, avoiding her crotch, caressing her hip, then her thigh, then all the way down to her knee, and back up again to her breasts, which he found very much to his liking—they reminded him of her gorgeous ass, which he'd seen a little while ago.

He had never gone this far with a woman. With the three prostitutes, right from the start he'd had the urge to rough them up, hurt them; he'd hidden the knife under the bed while they were getting washed, odiously crouched over a bidet. The knife . . . he was suddenly overwhelmed by the memory, the thrill he'd felt when he'd stabbed them. Then, just as quickly, it vanished.

Everything was fine. He could handle it.

He was drawn to her vagina.

His hand slid back down, gently across her belly. Marie turned her head. She kissed him on the forehead, a quick and affectionate peck, nothing more, and then let him continue.

He reached the pubic hair (it slid between his fingers, tickling the palm of his hand), then lower, where he realized there was a little opening, and if he moved his finger in a certain way—a way he quickly discovered, quite naturally—it was slightly moist inside, just a little, and very soft. He didn't dare go any further, he was afraid, exploring any further than that scared him. He quickly pulled his hand away and put it back on her breasts, so smooth and well-defined; no surprises, even if the nipples tended to get erect and slightly larger when he'd brushed against them, but it wasn't frightening, it was almost funny, it made you want to bring them to your mouth and bite them, feel them stiffen under your tongue.

He stopped there. Then Marie began to stroke his arm and shoulder, through his pajamas, then his back and his buttocks, but so cautiously that he hesitated before trying to slip out of her embrace. But he never had to, even when, in passing, she brushed against his new penis, cowering under the fabric of his pajamas, for she simply stroked his cheek, and that was it, what a relief.

Like the night before, Marie had sensed "Marc's" increasing desire to have some kind of physical contact with her, and she'd also sensed his secret fears, totally adolescent fears, an inner tension that kept him from letting go. But it was better than the night before. A tiny step farther. Maybe soon they would go back to making love. The very idea that he might have a mistress, Marianne Matys or anyone else, seemed even more incongruous to her tonight. He was depressed, preoccupied, he was hanging on to his work, he'd had a terrible disappointment today, but she was certain he was beginning to desire her again.

In a rush of tenderness, she put her arms around him and cuddled up to him. For Zyto, the danger had passed. He realized that Marie's affectionate gesture was not terribly significant, it was more like bringing what little had just occurred to a conclusion. He relaxed, put his arms around her, placed his hand on her firm, rounded butt, and held her close, this half-naked woman who was in bed with him, offering him her warmth without expecting anything in return.

Pressed against her, surprisingly content, his hand following the perfect curve of her buttocks, he felt something rise up from the pit of his stomach—a feeling he knew well, but had never experienced with a woman. This was slightly different, it was more than a purely sexual drive—it was a desire for someone else, and this time he was scared, and the violent thoughts came back, making him . . .

"Goodnight, darling. Don't think about that awful business anymore."

"Goodnight, darling."

She fell asleep right away. But not him, he couldn't, despite the exhausting day he'd had.

He realized his jaws were clenched and tense. He relaxed. Otherwise, he'd have a sore throat and an earache again.

Tomorrow he would remind Hugues that Michel Zyto was supposed to continue his Maktarin pills.

The insomnia persisted, but he didn't mind it. At times, he was still amazed to be Marc Lacroix. It was as unthinkable as the concept of infinity, eternity, of something that had no end, that would last forever and ever. As unthinkable as death. And those kinds of thoughts could not endure. They didn't last long; he was soon distracted by the steady breathing of Marie, asleep beside him, and struck by the profound silence of the countryside. He thought about how he would have to get the car washed in a garage, the undergrowth had scratched it, leaving black and white marks on both sides.

Marie had opened the thick brown curtains of the two bedroom windows. The sun flooded into the room.

Michel Zyto woke up as Marc Lacroix.

"I hear Leonard downstairs. I bet he's making us breakfast. He asked my permission a few days ago, but he hasn't tried it out yet."

They had washed and gotten dressed, and were ready to go downstairs.

"I'm going to need a little money," he said.

Zyto had noticed that Marc's wallet was practically empty. He watched for Marie's reaction, pretending to look through the books, tilting his head to the side as if he were looking for one in particular.

"Will a thousand francs do?" asked Marie.

"Yes. I have to dash to the Center and I'd rather not stop anywhere on the way. Oh, by the way, my PIN number just slipped my mind again. The same thing happened to me yesterday. I'm totally absentminded these days!"

"6473," Marie said, going into the bathroom.

Great. He could use Marc's bank card. Easier than checks. For checks, he'd have to go to the bank first and tell them he was changing his signature.

"You haven't forgotten that Cedric is stopping by for drinks tonight?"

"No. I almost forgot, but not quite."

He got a hold of himself. Cedric. He'd work that problem out with Marc.

He followed after Marie, and gave his hair a quick comb.

"Goddamn receding hair line!"

Funny, he'd said "goddamn." That wasn't like him, Marie thought.

"You really don't have anything to worry about, I promise. It's not noticeable. Besides, your head has a nice shape. Even if you didn't have a hair left . . ."

"God forbid!"

He was watching her. She had opened the medicine cabinet. He saw the safe. A little safe was hidden there. Excellent. He walked over to Marie and kissed her on the head.

"If only I had hair like yours! Listen, I won't be very long at the Center. Would you and Leonard like to come along? You can wait for me in a café."

He could never leave Marie and Leonard alone in the house or any other place Marc knew well. In case Marc ever "confided" in someone.

But Marc would keep quiet. It was too dangerous. Zyto's blackmail was completely secure. Zyto would be vigilant. He would take every precaution necessary.

"Of course we'll come," Marie said, delighted by the invitation.

She opened the safe. A simple combination, easy to remember. He memorized it. It was just a little safe for some valuables.

He spied some bills, a few pieces of jewelry, and the gun.

24

Marc Lacroix felt like he was being buried alive. He would have to raise the lid of the coffin, at any cost, before they nailed it shut. Afterward, it would be too late.

If only he could open his eyes. His eyelids were the lid of the coffin.

The back of his head ached. He ached all over. He felt paralyzed.

But opening his eyes also meant waking up, remembering, being inundated with memories that could still be repressed—if he allowed them to nail it shut.

He opened his eyes.

Technically, he shouldn't have been able to scream. It was almost physiologically impossible, he was too exhausted, there were too many drugs in his system. Nevertheless, what he saw made him let out a scream, a long scream of terror, the scream of a doomed man.

Nearly a foot away from his face, as if suspended in midair, was Marc Lacroix—staring at him, scrutinizing him; *his* own eyes, inhabited by the sick mind of Michel Zyto...

An abominable rebirth—Marc Lacroix had just awoke as Michel Zyto.

For a brief instant, he concentrated very hard on Marianne, as if her face could drive away, block out, that other face that was his own and yet someone else's—that *other* man.

He was no longer on earth, he was in hell.

A nurse came running over, the tall one with the deep voice. She apologized when she saw it was "Dr. Lacroix" in the room.

"That's quite all right, it's nothing," said Zyto.

He pretended to examine the pouch of fluid hanging from the IV.

"We'll start reducing his dosage this evening."

"I know," said Zyto. "I saw Dr. d'Oléons a little while ago. That's good."

Besides, he couldn't have kept Marc unconscious forever. And did he want to? No, Zyto needed to talk to him. And wield his power over him, talk to him as doctor to patient, completely reverse the roles—this time for good.

"When he woke up," Zyto added, "he remembered everything that happened yesterday, all at once. It was a shock, which is why he cried out. I'm sure he'll calm down. You can leave us alone now, thanks."

Not bad, the little speech. The nurse listened attentively and left the room.

The son of a bitch is actually getting away with it, Marc thought. The shock he'd experienced, the nightmarish vision he'd been forced to confront when he'd opened his eyes made his blood boil. This mad rage would fight off the dulling effects of the Demerol for a good fifteen minutes. He had to take advantage of it, find something to make Zyto... but as soon as the nurse had gone, Zyto was the first to speak, in a harsh but soft voice: "Save it for another time and try to get a grip on yourself. No screaming. Otherwise I'll make sure that you get an even stronger medication. I'm warning you once again that I wouldn't hesitate to kill your wife. And your son. And if worse comes to worst, I'll even kill myself. I'm capable of it, you know that. If worse comes to worst. I'm contemplating the idea just so you understand that nothing will stop me, I'm the one in charge, you don't have a chance, not a prayer. You can only do what I decide you can. So no screaming, no scenes. I want to hear d'Oléons tell me on the phone when I call that you're a model patient. Like you were before. By the way, speaking of telephones, I had yours taken out. It's just an unnecessary source of aggravation, given the state you're in."

Again, he brought his face close to Marc's, he was panting, working himself up as he spoke.

Right then, Marc could have killed him without a moment's hesitation. Zyto was appallingly correct: he didn't have a prayer, or it was only a vague, confused hope, based on the theory that a situation like this could not last forever. But it would probably last long enough for Marc to lose his mind, do serious damage to his psyche, turn him into a kind of mental patient.

He would be even more like Michel Zyto.

And his "other" would be able to live by Marie and Leonard's side for a long time. He was sly as a fox. In September, Zyto could always say he was giving up medicine, he could get a divorce (he'd have all the money he needed . . .), he could harm Marie and Leonard, he could do anything at all!

Marc was overwhelmed with despair. He almost wanted to give up then and there, in the dusty rose-colored room, without making another move or uttering another word.

No, he mustn't let that happen! He would have to hold his own. Escape. Call Marianne, explain, convince her that something incredible had occurred, and get some moral support. Beg her not to tell anyone. Marc had decided against speaking to Hugues right away. Hugues wasn't good at keeping a secret. He mustn't do anything that could bring on a catastrophe. Zyto was too cunning, too suspicious—particularly now—he'd be on his guard every second; the lives of Marie and Leonard were in danger, and his own fate as well, he, Marc, who didn't want to spend the rest of his life in this loathsome body. This madman was certainly capable of taking his own life—"if worse came to worst"—if he noticed something unusual going on, and if he could find no other way to exercise his malice.

Later on, perhaps, he'd have a chance to . . . But the very idea of "later on" was so upsetting that it threw Marc back into a state of utter discouragement.

Actually, Michel Zyto had been bluffing this time, when he'd brought up his possible suicide. He felt capable of inflicting violence on the false Zyto lying in bed there at Stéphen-Mornay, moaning, wounded, and terrified. But not on himself, Doctor Marc Lacroix.

"You haven't . . . touched . . . Marie?"

Perhaps it wasn't in his best interest to get Marc overly excited and push him into doing something desperate. It was better to measure out the torture in small doses.

"No. You know very well I haven't. She herself hardly seems inclined to touch her husband. It's very nice that way."

Marc believed him. He knew Marie, her reticence since he'd begun neglecting her. And he knew Zyto.

"Would you . . . open the shutters?"

Zyto went to open the shutters. He recalled the day he'd asked the same thing of Marc. He had just been admitted to the Center. He'd been lying helplessly in the same bed, unable to move.

The roles had been reversed.

How gratifying that was, how exhilarating!

Zyto came back and sat near the bed. Marc really looked terrible. He could barely keep his eyes open. At times, you could only see the whites of his eyes, as with someone who was dying. His mustache was all shaggy. In the future, he would have to brush it regularly, two or three times a day. Make an effort to keep up his appearance. That's what Marc had always told him, and he'd obeyed.

"Are you expecting any phone calls? From Sainte-Anne, your lab? Anywhere else? From whom? Are you supposed to call anyone?"

Marc was piecing together his memory. He didn't answer straight away. He was concentrating on this telephone business.

"You'd better cooperate," Zyto said coldly. "I promise you that it's in your best interest."

"No phone calls. Nothing in particular. Everyone has gone away. Except . . . Leonard has some friends who might . . . their fathers might . . ."

"Eric, Victor, Simon, I know."

"We have some friends, in Versailles, who . . ."

"Marshall and Marie-Thérèse, I know that too. No one else?"

God, the son of a bitch was actually getting away with it! Marc told himself he would, in fact, be better off cooperating, to gain his confidence.

Who might call them? Dozens of people. But anyone specific, instantly awkward for the impostor . . . ?

"No, nothing else," he said in one breath. "I can't think of any. What do you intend to do? What do you hope to accomplish?"

"Take advantage of the situation. You were always telling me about the psychological benefits of change, and you were right, I feel better than ever."

"But later on, what do . . . ?"

"I'll decide that later."

The perfect blackmail. No means of resistance, no way to get back at him.

But wait! There was one thing!

Given Marc's pitiful physical and psychic state, his unreliable memory . . . his obsession with the telephone, which Zyto had planted in his mind . . . and sleep already coming over him . . . it hadn't even occurred to him . . .

So there was a way after all. It was Zyto who had just made him realize it, with his questions.

Michel Zyto leaned over him, menacingly: "And Cedric? What about Cedric's visit tonight? Who is he, this Cedric guy? Are you trying to hide something from me?"

Actually, Zyto didn't believe Marc was manipulating him. It was obvious to him that Marc was trying to sort out his thoughts, his memories, that he was totally confused.

Marc had truly forgotten. And on the contrary, far from wanting to hide his visit with Cedric Houdé from Zyto . . .

The tumor. Zyto's hypochondria. A slim chance to tip the scales in their struggle for power.

"Believe me, I forgot all about it," Marc said. "But it's a good thing you reminded me."

He forced himself to keep his eyes wide open, and slowly turned his head toward his persecutor, in spite of the pain. He even managed to speak to Zyto in a tone that sounded curt: "You feel better than ever? Well, not for long, I can promise you that. Pretty soon, you won't be feeling so great."

Zyto sat up straight in his chair.

"Why?" he asked, suddenly alarmed.

"Because I'm ill. You're ill. I found out about it the night before our experiment, from Dr. Cedric Houdé. He's the chief of staff of the E.N.T. at Lariboisiere. An excellent doctor. I was suffering from dizziness and occasional hearing loss, and . . . but you'll be feeling those symptoms soon." (If you ask me, you probably feel them already, you stinking coward, Marc said to himself with malicious glee, noting the change in Zyto's expression.) "I had a scan. I have a small tumor on my acoustic nerve. It's getting bigger. If they allow it to grow, the consequences will be horrible. If they operate on it, it'll be just as bad. Marie knows about it, but she has no idea how serious it is. Please, don't mention anything to her if she doesn't bring it up first."

He broke off, suddenly exhausted. He wondered if he'd be able to utter another word. The medication was overpowering him again. What more could he say to worry Zyto? Cedric would reassure him anyhow. Still, Marc knew that Zyto wouldn't be able to stop thinking about "his" illness and would undoubtedly work himself into a complete panic at certain moments.

A good way to get back at Zyto.

And panicked he was.

And he no longer had Dr. Marc Lacroix to calm him down.

He jumped to his feet.

"You're lying! You're making it up! You want to . . . to . . . You better watch out! Remember what I told you . . ."

Marc thought Zyto was going to punch him right there in his bed, strangle him, give into some crazy impulse. No, as long as he inhabited this sturdy body that only needed a little Maktarin to be perfectly renewed, Marc was in no danger of being murdered. He wouldn't let himself be intimidated. He stared back into the eyes of the other man, and managed to tell him, with his last ounce of energy: "Tonight around six o'clock, Dr. Cedric Houdé is going to stop by the house. He's only coming for drinks, not to talk about the tumor, we've already thoroughly discussed that subject. So steer the conversation toward it in a subtle way. You're not supposed to be worried. And I repeat, don't talk to him about it in front of Marie. The X-rays are in the desk in my study, the second to the last drawer on the right. And don't ask him too many silly questions."

Michel Zyto sat down again.

"What do you mean?" he asked, his voice quavering. "What do you mean . . . What kind of questions?"

But Dr. Lacroix had fallen into a deep sleep, the lid above him shut once again.

25

"There, the tumor is right there," said Cedric. "Do you see it? There. Just at the entrance to the inner ear. It isn't serious in itself. The problem is, it's in the middle of your skull. You see the nerve there that runs from the cerebral stem to the ear . . . wait . . . uh . . . there it is."

Zyto and Cedric Houdé were sitting side by side in Marc's study, the X-rays spread before them. After the initial fear had subsided, Zyto had been seized by a dangerous sense of calm.

Cerebral stem . . . an acoustic neurinome . . . acoustic vestibular . . . the eighth nerve . . . the facial acoustic bundle . . . the seventh nerve . . . the facial nerve . . . total or partial paralysis of the face . . . the words flew by. Zyto made an effort not to faint, to put up a good front and drink his lemon-mint soda without it dribbling down his chin. He resented this tiresome old doctor, with his robust health, and the dispassionate tone he used to explain these unspeakable horrors. Zyto didn't understand all of it, just enough to know that the little blotch on the X-ray was a tiny piece of death inside him that could spread, become larger, turn into death, his death.

And what if they were to operate? There'd be a few problems, fairly serious ones, deafness, partial paralysis of the face....

Even if the operation went smoothly, the middle cerebral artery next to it could go into spasms. An unpreventable, unpredictable risk.

And that meant death.

Cedric Houdé wondered why Marc was bombarding him with questions, particularly questions to which Marc knew the answers as well as he did. He'd seemed much more unruffled when he'd had the scan. Probably an anxiety attack. Everyone had them. Cedric, as a result, decided to calm him down, and Zyto, now impressed by the authority of this elderly specialist, did, in fact, calm down: given the results of the scan, the pessimistic hypothesis of rapid change preceeding a catastrophic operation was statistically nearly impossible. A little check-up now and then, Cedric repeated, and Marc would live to be a hundred and fifty before his neurinome would ever bother him.

Michel Zyto fondled Marie as he had the previous night. Longer this time, better, to the point of arousing her. Marie's breathing quickened, a slight tremor ran through her body. He continued, he didn't stop, and suddenly Marie opened and closed her legs, pressing Zyto's hand between them. She remained still. That was the extent of it. It wasn't exactly what he'd had in mind. He'd been taken by surprise. He found himself in her arms, he let Marie hold him tightly against her.

He was experiencing fear, disgust, and hatred from what had just occurred. But that wasn't all. He was also aroused. And Marie had not made any embarrassing moves. The danger had passed. She didn't seem to expect what he dreaded most, what he was incapable of doing, going inside her. She didn't seem to expect anything at all.

Perhaps Marc Lacroix no longer made love to his wife.

He snuggled up closer to her.

"I was thinking about what Cedric told me," he murmured after a moment.

In spite of Marc's request, he couldn't help whining to Marie. She held him even tighter.

"Don't worry, darling. It won't grow any larger. And even if it did, it would take a very long time. I'm sure of it. I'm sure you're worrying yourself for nothing. You told me so yourself just a little while ago."

She knew exactly what to say to him. The fear, the disgust, and the hatred were swept aside. And his sexual desire was growing. He adjusted his position so that Marie could move more freely, so she could touch him—this was suddenly what he desired.

Marie understood immediately. She took his penis in her hands but only began stroking the man she believed to be Marc Lacroix once she'd sensed that he really wanted her to, slowly at first, gently, skillfully, tenderly.

She wanted to pull back the sheet. But she didn't, and waited for him to do it himself.

At the same time, Michel Zyto was thinking the sheet was definitely in the way, but he still didn't dare . . . then he did it, he flung it aside, no more of that annoying, constrained feeling, his penis was hard and erect in the darkness of the room. Zyto did not feel threatened, no one wanted anything from him, this was only to make him feel good, no one was asking for anything in return. He abandoned himself to Marie's caresses, faster, as fast he wanted.

He felt a rush of incredible pleasure flood his entire body. Marie paused for a moment, just long enough to intensify his pleasure and then she began again, stroking faster, harder, then slower, more gently, a second before his orgasm, and Zyto shook with what seemed an endless ejaculation.

They locked into an embrace, like two people in love.

This morning, for the second time, Michel Zyto dragged the razor over his upper lip. What a strange sensation. He'd need some time to get used to it. On the other hand, he was growing accustomed to his new face and body. He would have liked them even better if it hadn't been for the bad news about his illness. There was no sense being overly afraid, he was convinced of that; it would unnecessarily spoil the pleasure he was deriving from the situation. But a source of anxiety had arisen inside him, it wouldn't let up, not for an instant, as long as he did not inhabit Michel Zyto's body.

An anxiety that would periodically overwhelm him, stifle him. He could already see it coming.

He had slept very poorly.

Not because of the X-rays, that little blurry spot on the nerve fiber, that "acoustical neurinome," as Cedric Houdé had called it. No, because of what had happened with Marie. He was deeply troubled by this unprecedented event and, at this point, he was incapable of gauging its consequences.

"If you'd like, we could go have lunch somewhere in the country," called Marie from the bedroom. "We could stop at the supermarket at the mall on the way back. What do you think?"

Michel Zyto dabbed his face with a towel. A close shave.

Marc Lacroix was staring back at him in the mirror. Quite a handsome face indeed.

The mall? Did the Lacroixs normally do their shopping in a giant supermarket, like everyone else in the suburbs, or was today just an exception?

Funny.

Lunch in the country. Why not? A little family outing would do him a world of good.

He stepped into the bathtub.

"Fine with me," he said.

Adeline removed the bandage.

"There we are . . . we'll leave it like that."

"It won't get infected, Doctor, without a bandage?"

Zyto pretended he was joking, but he needed to be completely reassured there would be no risk of infection.

"No. The risk of gangrene is minimal," Adeline said, smiling.

"Good, I'll take your word for it. Thanks."

She left the office without another word, a smile still playing at the corner of her lips.

"He's very calm," said Hugues d'Oléons. "He's sorry. He's about to enter a stage of guilt. After that, in my opinion, he'll be just like he was before."

"I should have been more careful. He developed an ambivalent relationship with me. I was aware of it, but who would ever have thought . . . ? As a result, I'm going to have to distance myself from him, slowly. . . ."

An ambivalent relationship. Zyto had prepared a little speech before coming. He even had two or three, just in case. At Marc's house, he had paged through a book on psychoanalysis, and had read the chapter on transference closely.

Hugues nodded in approval: "Yes, so you've said. And I, too, would never have thought . . . should we put him back on the IV tonight or . . . ?"

The fat man was perspiring. The summer had finally arrived, it was much hotter than in the past few days, and humid as well. Beads of sweat broke out on his balding head.

It was revolting.

"Maybe again tonight?" Zyto suggested gently.

Marc Lacroix was asleep.

Michel Zyto entered and silently took a seat.

He gazed at him in disgust, his thick, hairy hands, his mustache—truly hideous when it wasn't properly groomed—and his inelegant, stocky, tortured body. As time went on, he had less and less desire to return to that body. Alas, there was no longer any question in his mind. Sooner or later, he'd be forced to become Michel Zyto again, like it or not, because of that damn neurinome. Because he'd be unable to bear the possible physical decline that could follow, a fate worse than death; because of that middle cerebral artery that could suddenly contract during the operation, cutting off the blood to his brain. That would be death. And he no longer wanted death.

He'd had a mild anxiety attack. He'd expected it, but not this soon.

What should he do? Return to Louveciennes with Marc as soon as possible, sit down in the comfortable chairs of the psycho-computer and reverse the process? Then kill Marc and run away? Or should he keep him alive for a while, out of harm's way, carefully plan his departure, and escape to a foreign country, under a new name?

But there was no big hurry, for God's sake, what was the rush? For the time being, the solution to all his problems was simple: have a leisurely lunch in the country, do some shopping with his wife and child in one of those big familiar supermarkets, and that evening, stuff himself on a terrine of duck, the recipe Marie had so skillfully begun to prepare the evening before. And, that night, discover the pleasures of sex with a woman who frightened him less than any other woman in the world.

Marc Lacroix was dozing, he wasn't really asleep. He knew who was there. He was feigning exhaustion. He'd overheard Hugues' remark: "He's starting to relax, he's not fighting anymore, the critical stage has passed, he's going to sleep a lot now." Fine! He'd act like he was asleep, like someone who had given in, who was no longer fighting.

But he was fighting. With every ounce of his strength. The intravenous medication the evening before hadn't been terribly strong. He hadn't been given anything further that morning. The Demerol was gradually being eliminated from his system.

Zyto shook him by the shoulder. Marc stirred, muttering, but didn't open his eyes.

"Don't you want to know how the wife and kid are getting along?" murmured Zyto. "They're not far from here. Everything's going just fine. As for you, hopefully this radical change will improve your depressive state. I'll check on you this evening, after your medication."

The bastard, the bastard! Once again, Marc wanted to kill him.

"Did you see Dr. Houdé?" he asked in a thick, feeble voice.

"Yes. Nothing urgent, you know that. Nothing has changed. So do as they tell you and behave yourself, Mr. Zyto."

The bastard!

Oh! But something *had* changed. He'd been mulling over a plan. And he was fighting, he was simply waiting for the moment when he'd have enough strength and lucidity to execute it.

26

Later that Thursday, August 3, at noon, Dr. Marc Lacroix, transformed into Michel Zyto as a result of an extraordinary but failed experiment, escaped from the psychiatric Center on Avenue Stéphen-Mornay.

With the exception of one incident, it had been almost as easy as he had hoped.

He'd selected some of Zyto's clothing from the closet that he hadn't noticed before; dark, ill-matched colors, a brown jacket and a pair of flannel trousers that immediately made him perspire. In the same closet, he found fifteen hundred francs in cash, and pocketed it.

Marc slid a bottle of Maktarin into his pocket.

He ran a comb through his hair. But that wasn't sufficient. A head of hair as thick and tangled as his resisted all combs. It took him some time before he got it looking somewhat less unkempt.

He gave his mustache a quick comb as well.

No one was in the corridor.

He descended the stairway.

It was an incident of no great consequence, but upsetting nonetheless. Adeline was on her way out of Hugue's office, right near the foot of the stairway. Marc had no choice: he charged, rushing down the last steps at full speed, fist forward, aimed right at the girl. He couldn't afford to waste any time tussling with her. Before she knew what was happening to her, she received the impact of a hundred and seventy pounds on her jaw and silently collapsed onto the floor.

Without losing any of his momentum, Marc made a mad dash toward the lit exit sign at the end of the corridor. He heard Hugues open his door, stammering in surprise, then heard him shout: "Stop!" and nothing more.

Hugues was hardly likely to come chasing after him.

But the police would be notified immediately.

It didn't matter. That was part of the plan. He wouldn't be that easy to find.

Marianne. For the time being, his refuge would be with Marianne.

He ran up the short street, Avenue Stéphen-Mornay, took the Boulevard Vincent-Auriol, and soon arrived, still running, at the metro on Place d'Italie.

No one paid any attention to him, nor did he notice anyone else.

He raced down the stairs.

Then he passed a woman and they looked at each other for a fraction of a second. She wasn't very tall, and had long, curly, chestnut brown hair; a shaggy mane that set off her extremely pale, delicate face, and fine features; a face right out of a painting.

She was casually dressed in a pair of pants and a lightweight leather jacket.

Naturally, Marc didn't have time to scrutinize her. He simply took a mental photograph in passing, as if someone else inside him had clicked the button. A fleeting moment, instantly forgotten, each preoccupied with their respective anxieties. Neither of them looked back, and continued on their separate ways.

Not many people in the metro. Marc dropped onto a bench.

Yes, something had changed, and Zyto must have realized it. Whatever Marc did, Zyto would think twice before carrying out his threats. Marc now had the power to abandon him forever to "his" ailing body.

The smarter and the tougher of the two would win. Ever since he'd found a way to retaliate, a plan of action, Marc felt a new, still unsteady, energy springing up inside him. That neurinome might very well save his life. He'd made up his mind to fight, to win. In his own way, he was strong and unafraid.

He changed trains at Chausseé-d'Antin. Five minutes later, he was out in the bright sun that was beating down on the whole neighborhood of la Madeleine. He quickened his pace again. In no time, he arrived at the café Maritimos, Rue du Faubourg-Saint-Honoré, right across the street from Marianne's apartment. He had called her from there once before. The telephone was located downstairs, usually no one was around.

He pushed one franc into the slot. He would have gladly dropped to his knees and prayed for her to be home. He dialed the number too quickly, the coin hadn't even triggered the dial tone, he had to dig it out and start all over. His heart was pounding at a frightening speed. Hopefully, she'd be home. She had to be there, she had to!

Of course she'd be there, at this hour, probably even waiting for Marc's phone call, impatient and a bit worried about why she hadn't heard from him.

Busy.

She was home, but how long would she remain on the line?

He tried over and over, twelve times. He was shaking like a leaf.

The twelfth time, the phone rang. She picked it up immediately. He could have wept with relief.

"Marianne... it's Marc. I'm sorry, there was no way I could call you any sooner..."

He was out of breath, he couldn't get out another word.

"Marc, are you all right?" asked Marianne, suddenly alarmed.

"Yes and no. No, I'd better explain it to you."

"Your voice sounds strange. You're scaring me, what's going on?"

She'd lost her usual nonchalance. She realized something serious was happening.

He explained it to her. He told her about the failure of the experiment, the abominable failure, the events that had followed, of his impatience to be by her side, of his terrible fear that she'd be horrified, disgusted, when she saw him.

She believed him right away. No one besides Marc could have spoken to her that way.

"Come upstairs, and hurry!"

But when she saw him, when she saw this man shorter than she was, with that mustache and those thick hands, she instantly recoiled, out of fear and distrust.

"I'm begging you, Marianne, please don't be afraid, I'll explain all the details. Just let me sit down, I'm dead tired. Drained from the medication they've been pumping into me. It's a wonder I managed to get this far."

"Sit down, sit down," she said, ushering him over to the small sofa. "Does the back of your neck hurt a lot?"

"No, I can barely feel it anymore."

Marc dropped onto the couch. The six flights had done him in. He hardly dared look Marianne in the face. Poor Marianne, what a terrible thing for her!

"I know it's incredible, I know what you must be thinking, darling; I understand that the most insane ideas have already crossed your mind; I understand because they're not nearly as insane as what I told you, but I'll prove it to you . . . question me, if you like, ask me to tell you anything about what's happened between us since I met you backstage after *A Midsummer Night's Dream* up until the day before yesterday, just ask me, I'll give you details that no one else in the world could know! For example, about three months ago, I cut off a split end from your hair, and we threw it out the window to see how fast it would fall, do you remember? Question me, ask me anything you want, and then help me, please, do you realize what kind of nightmare I'm living in?"

He was gasping for air, wringing his hands, he was on the verge of tears. He felt ridiculous for having brought up the story about the hair; he felt ugly, repulsive, and only hoped she wasn't disgusted by him! She kept repeating: "I believe you, I believe you, darling!" She had been horrified, then pitied him, moved by this different body in which her lover was imprisoned—yes, it was incredible, insane, but she vowed to herself to help him, she would rise to the occasion!

She sat down next to him and innocently took his hand in hers. "Calm down, calm down! Of course I'm going to help you. No one will ever find you here."

"Thank you, darling. But let me give you some proof, I have to, it'll make me feel better. Even if you believe me, I just have to."

And he gave her some irrefutable proof. He went back to the beginning, his secret research, the experiment with Cookie and Mana; then what followed, the machine that had done its job all too well, the nightmarish hours Marc had endured, Zyto's blackmail, his hypochondria, and Marc's retaliation.

Talking about it, telling her everything comforted him. Marianne listened to him with undivided attention, like an incredulous child who is supposed to believe what she's being told, no matter what. She made an effort to calm herself, to accept as best she could, not only with her reason but with her senses, that this man she'd never seen before was actually Marc. She should help and comfort him with the same enthusiasm and love as if she were sitting at her lover's side.

"You never mentioned anything to me about your illness, did you?"

"No. But it's not serious, I promise."

She ran her fingers through his hair and kissed him on the forehead, forcing herself to make the effort. And because her nature was fundamentally cheerful and fun-loving, she couldn't help telling herself that it must have been worse for Marc; that Zyto, despite his slightly bestial look and that mustache—but a mustache could be shaved off—wasn't all that bad-looking, or frightening or repulsive, he had nice eyes. So she'd stick by him until a solution could be found—but what?

"What are you planning on doing? How are we going to deal with this?"

Marc had noticed the change in Marianne's attitude. He was grateful for it, with all his heart. He kissed her back, restraining himself from kissing her the way he would have liked, on the lips, caressing her and holding her in his arms.

"I don't know. Get him alone, knock him over the head, take him back to Louveciennes. . . . Suddenly I'm tired, Marianne . . . after what he told me, it seems impossible, but . . . talking to you just gave me an idea. But I'll need your help."

"Of course I'll help you. Anything you want."

What joy, what a joy to see her again, and what a disaster to see her while he was trapped in this odious body! How wonderful her beauty, her blondness, and her radiance made him feel, and how nerve-wracking not to be able to show his love more openly.

And how equally nerve-wracking that after being with Marianne, he couldn't go home to Marie and Leonard and their own type of warmth, beneficial to him in another sort of way. Marie and Leonard. Now he finally realized how important they were to him as well.

He had a vague plan. He described it to Marianne. Then he felt an overwhelming drowsiness. The Demerol, the fatigue, the tension. He stood up, and staggering forward he headed toward the small bedroom. Marianne supported him by the arm. He took off his jacket and collapsed onto the bed. A car noisily started up its engine in the courtyard, five flights below. Marianne closed the window. When would he be back behind the wheel of his magnificent four-wheel drive? He glanced at the watch on his wrist, Zyto's big, vulgar watch.

Please wake me in two hours. And if you don't mind, buy me some other clothes. And some sunglasses.

Then he fell asleep.

Two hours later, Marc gulped down two cups of coffee with some bread and butter, shaved off his mustache (as he'd shaved his own mustache many years ago, upon Marie's request), took a shower, changed the bandage on his neck, and put on the clothes that Marianne had bought for him. The gray suit fit him perfectly. The white shirt was a little tight in the shoulders. But it would do.

He slipped on elegant sunglasses with thin metal frames, and he and Marianne left the apartment. Marc brought along Zyto's nauseating brown jacket and flannel trousers, stuffed into a plastic bag. He threw it into the trash bin downstairs.

27

To Marie's surprise and amusement, her friend Dominique Macher was wearing a wig. Marie circled her admiringly, complimenting her as Zyto and Leonard looked on. Zyto was obliged to be ecstatic, but about what? A new color, a new hairstyle, or something else entirely? He hadn't the faintest idea. Just in case, he gave young Leonard, who was clearly indifferent to this whole business, a conspiratorial wink. The child came over and took his hand. His father had never winked at him before. It was kind of nice. Like they were buddies. It made Leonard very proud.

Without thinking, Michel Zyto bent over and kissed him on the head, on his hair. Marie noticed and was touched. Marc had been especially affectionate in the past couple of days.

A wig. That's what it was, a wig.

He was uncomfortable in this narrow office, a hideous green, with furniture that resembled huge insects.

Leonard reached up to Zyto and returned the kiss, with a resounding smack on the cheek.

They walked through the aisles of the food section of the huge market. Zyto was pushing a cart that was filling up rapidly. He felt somewhat ridiculous, the wheels were making a kind of clucking sound, like a hen.

Leonard timidly mumbled something about a Walkman. From Marie's expression, Zyto could tell this wasn't the first time the boy had brought up the subject. What was he supposed to do now?

"Come on! We're going to get you a Walkman!" he said suddenly.

"Wowee!" Leonard squealed under his breath, and dashed over to the audio section.

Marie was taken aback.

"I thought you didn't want your son to have one of those space-age gadgets."

"But he wants one so badly. We'll make sure he listens to classical music. What do you think?"

"It's fine with me. It's just that you were so against the idea . . ."

"Well, everyone changes. I feel like making him happy after the scare I had on Tuesday."

These words made her think back to the night before, and she was moved.

Secretly, this comment almost made Zyto burst with glee. He was pretty sly, all right, he thought: After the scare I had on Tuesday, I've changed, ha, ha!

Leonard got a terrific Walkman out of the deal, with a radio that could tape directly onto a cassette automatically, while it was still playing. Plus, the sophisticated headphones fit right into one's ears without even hurting, and the music was only audible to the person wearing it. Everyone else was left in peace.

First Marshall's pinball machine, and now this, the Walkman Leonard had always dreamed of: his vacation was off to a great start. He was thrilled.

Having finished their shopping, they headed toward the cafeteria—a sort of gigantic mezzanine with a snack bar, inside the store. Zyto concentrated on following the course of events, discovering their routines—a visit to Dominique Macher, grocery shopping, the cafeteria—and registering the information.

Apparently, Marie had an old friend who worked there in the store, and had serious problems with her hair.

The cart was jam-packed with items.

Several yards from the cafeteria, Marie bumped into Marianne.

Marie recognized her immediately from her silhouette. Marianne was reaching for a book. She was leaning on her right leg, which was slightly bent at the knee.

"Marianne!"

She spun around. Her face lit up with surprise and delight. Marianne Matys, so blond, with that pretty upper lip that curled when she smiled, that slightly asymmetrical gaze, that luminosity, the radiance she emanated, her candor, that guileless sensuality. Marianne, the only woman who had made her a bit jealous, although Marc was unaware of it; but Marie had obviously been wrong, she now told herself—with a pang of suspicion that still hurt, all the same.

"Marie! I'm so glad to see you! Hi Leonard!"

"Me too," said Marie.

The two women kissed. Then Marianne kissed Leonard, who vaguely remembered her as someone nice. Now "Marc" . . . she glanced at him twice, briefly, casually. She was frightened. But she'd have to withstand the shock, for Marc's sake.

"Hi, how are you?" she asked, extending her hand.

Who was this Marianne? How was he supposed to behave with her? Obviously, she was one of Marie's acquaintances. He'd make an effort to be cordial, nothing more, nothing less, and listen carefully to what was being said.

As for Marianne, if, for some reason, she'd had any lingering doubts, the look on Michel Zyto's face as he shook her hand was enough to erase them faster than any speeches or any other proof: this man had never laid eyes on her before, this man was not Marc; this man—in spite of his body—was less like Marc than the other one; the thought of having to touch him was so much more repugnant, and he was so much more frightening!

Act naturally, for God's sake, act naturally.

She turned toward Marie.

"I'm really sorry I haven't been in touch. But I just got back to Paris. I was thinking of calling you this weekend."

It seemed perfectly believable. Marie was sure Marianne really would have called that weekend.

"Were you performing?"

"Yes, exactly! I didn't contact you because I was travelling in the provinces and in Switzerland. On tour. I was ask to play the role of Titania again, in the Shakespeare play, do you remember? I had to decide right away. First I said no, in June, but then the actress who took the part got sick. Well, not exactly sick, pregnant, a difficult pregnancy. So I accepted. The director is a friend of mine, and I didn't have any other commitments. Once you're on tour . . . it's another world, another planet. But I thought of you. You forgive me?"

"Of course," said Marie.

If Marianne had been away from Paris, then she and Marc couldn't have been seeing each other . . . but what about before that? Just prior to her tour? No. That was crazy. She couldn't believe it. She was about to ask Marianne to join them over at the cafeteria, when Leonard—who was dying of thirst and really wanted a piece of pie, a soda, and an ice cream, at the very least—made the first move:

"We were on our way to the cafeteria," he said to Marianne, trying to sound funny.

Marianne smiled at him.

"You bought a Walkman. I have one too. They're great, you'll see."

This Marianne was definitely cool, Leonard thought.

And Zyto had the situation more or less figured out: Marianne was a vague friend of Marie's, an actress, Marc barely knew her, she hadn't been in touch for a while, and today they just happened to run into each other. Nothing to worry about.

He thought she was beautiful. Before, he would never have thought that about a woman. But now that he was Marc Lacroix

. . . he thought she was beautiful, but not as beautiful as Marie. In fact, he didn't like her. He could never have done with Marianne what he'd done with Marie. He would have been too afraid. He would have hated her too much. And perhaps he would have been seized with the desire to do what he'd done to the others, the ones before her.

"Will you join us?" asked Marie.

"Why not? You seem to know your way around, don't you?"

She took Leonard by the hand, and he offered no resistance.

"We come here all the time," he said.

"It's kind of far from Versailles, isn't it?"

"Yes, but my Mommy . . ."

He turned toward his mother.

"I have a friend from college who is now the manager here," said Marie. "She was my best friend at the time. She left teaching. Total change of profession. So now I can see her. And what about you, do you always shop at these giant supermarkets?"

"Sometimes, when I get back from a tour and there's nothing in my fridge. I like coming here every now and then. Especially in the suburbs. In Paris, it's different. In the suburbs, I feel totally anonymous, more so than in Paris. I look at the people. It's quite a show. It's the opposite of theater, you know what I mean? That's what I like about this store, out here in Ivry, and we're only a hop, skip, and a jump from Paris."

Zyto was thinking that this girl was no dunce. What she was saying was clever. For an actress, wandering around in a huge supermarket was the opposite of performing on stage: interesting, very interesting.

He felt he should say something. Marc certainly would have.

"Or else you'll become so famous that people will recognize you out here in Ivry. One day, the entire store will begin to applaud . . ."

Not bad either. Marianne was amused by the idea. Zyto was pleased with himself.

"No one will bother me for another few years," she said, smiling at him.

She was having a hard time looking at him as if he were really

Marc. But she managed somehow. It took some good acting. And he, too, had turned out to be a good actor, she thought; a damned good actor who was doing incredibly well, considering the impossible situation.

"And how is your research going?" she asked.

"Fine. And I'm glad not to be doing any for a month. Besides, to be perfectly honest, the more you search, the less you find."

Good answer, Zyto said to himself—and so did Marianne. She smiled at him again, and looked at the overflowing cart.

"You're more practical than I am. I always do the same thing; instead of shopping for useful items, I'll spend an hour browsing through the books, the records, the clothes . . ."

"I look at the clothes too!" said Marie. "They're ugly and cheaply made, but I still stop to look."

Marianne already knew that Marie was an attractive woman, but she found her particularly sexy at that moment. The light blue dress looked fabulous on her, especially because Marie had such a great figure. Nice breasts, nice butt . . . nicer than hers? Probably. And such intelligent-looking eyes, what a lovely face!

Something curious was happening, something Marianne found surprising. Suddenly, she was jealous. It was the first time. And now of all times!

"Every once in a while, you come across something cute. I saw some skirts that weren't too bad before. Everything else was hideous, but those skirts . . . I admit that I almost tried one on. Do you want to go back with me?" she asked Marie, as if the idea had just occurred to her. "Should we let the men order for us and go try one on?"

A great performance. Her invitation sounded absolutely genuine. Leonard, who had been referred to as a man, gazed adoringly at Marianne.

"I already did," Marie said with a big smile. "Believe it or not, I noticed them, too, those skirts. But I actually went and tried one on . . ."

"And?" asked Marianne, feigning enthusiasm.

"Well, they're cute on the hanger, but once you get them on, they're no big deal. Nothing to write home about."

"What a shame," said Marianne. "Or maybe so much the better, it saves me the trouble of trying one on myself. One of these days, if you'd like, we can go shopping for some skirts somewhere a little nicer than here."

"I'd love to," said Marie.

Damn. Of the three schemes Marc and Marianne had thought up, the first and the safest had just failed. Any attempt to persuade her would have sounded suspicious.

Now Marianne wouldn't be able to tell Marie the truth, or decide together what their next move should be.

The second plan was a bit more risky. It meant isolating Leonard rather than Marie, using some infallible pretense. Then the perfect opportunity came along. Leonard surreptitiously began to open the box containing his Walkman.

"You better not do that," Zyto told him. "They're not going to like that at the check-out counter. You're going to get into trouble."

"Trouble? What kind of trouble?"

"Oh! Take your pick! A big fine, two days in jail . . . and of course, they'll take your Walkman away."

As a professional, Marianne could appreciate the astonishing ease with which Michel Zyto had stepped into his role. As for the business with the Walkman, he'd pulled it off perfectly. Marc himself couldn't have been more credible, with that malicious yet affectionate gleam in his eyes. Leonard started to laugh, the way children do when they're told something outrageous they know very well is untrue.

"You're kidding!" he said.

"You're right, I am kidding, my little monkey. But it's not nice to unwrap something before paying for it, I promise you. They don't like it at all."

The boy turned toward Marianne.

"Oh well. You could have shown me how it works. I could have listened to the radio while I was drinking my soda."

Marianne looked at Zyto, then Marie, and again at Leonard, with a heartfelt, sympathetic expression: "Listen, I know what we can do. The two of us can go pay for it, real quick, and then come right back. What do you say?"

"It's OK with me," said Leonard.

Marianne flashed Zyto a slightly conspiratorial smile. She, too, could be perfect in her role.

"That's very kind of you," said Zyto. "But have you seen how long the lines are?"

He pointed to the cashiers. They were inundated with customers.

"Too bad," he said. "We'll try to take off the wrapping more neatly."

"Oh, great!" said Leonard.

Leonard, I'm going to tell you my phone number. You're going to memorize it. You'll tell your Mommy to call me, but only your Mommy, all right? You'll tell her sometime when your father isn't around, when he can't hear you. Your Mommy will explain. But most importantly, your father can't know about it. Your Mommy will explain it to you, it's a game. Do you promise? This is what Marianne would have said to Leonard on the way to the cashier's, and she would have done her best to answer the boy's questions. It might have worked. But it still would have been risky. Marc had told Marianne to judge for herself, depending on the situation.

Damn. Once again, it wouldn't have been wise to insist.

Marianne couldn't help feeling relieved.

Zyto left the cart at the foot of a stairway that led to the cafeteria. They started up the stairs.

Marianne played her last card, the most dangerous one. Neither she nor Marc thought it would work, but she'd have to try it anyway.

As she leisurely climbed the stairs, chatting about this and that—like someone on vacation, with all the time in the world, about to have a nice, cool drink on a hot summer day—Marianne asked Zyto if he had bought that four-wheel drive he'd mentioned a while back.

"You remember that? Bravo," said Marie.

"Yes, we bought one," said Zyto.

"A Nissan Terrano. The latest and fanciest model. Awarded car of the year in America. With lateral triangular windows," said Leonard, who sounded like he was reading an ad, which made everybody laugh, especially Zyto.

A laugh that was slightly forced, thought Marianne. But the impostor still amazed her by his incredible capacity to adapt. And as for the nights in bed with his spouse . . . since he was afraid of women and Marc and Marie hadn't made love in quite some time . . . that maniac had everything in his favor.

She could now casually bring up the subject of her old Peugeot, in a tone that prompted Zyto to ask: "You're not happy with it?"

"Not really. It's always breaking down. Recently, it's been stalling, then it won't start up again and I have to call a mechanic. It happened again just a little while ago; when I was parking in the lot, it stalled."

She paused, deliberately.

There were a few moments of silence. Zyto was thinking.

"I'd gladly offer to take a look at it," he said, "but frankly, I don't know a thing about engines. I'm embarrassed to admit it, but it's the truth. I can check to see if it ran out of gas, but that's about it."

Actually, even if he were a top mechanic, and even though this Marianne was above suspicion, he would have found an excuse not to stray too far from Marie and Leonard. Or they would have all gone to the car together.

Marianne was aware of this. She was certain. *Almost* certain. She'd been forced to exhaust every possibility.

Then it was Marie's turn to be jealous: was Marianne trying to get Marc alone down in the parking lot? Ridiculous, she immediately told herself. How could she even think that?

Besides, Marianne's prepared response to Zyto, just to be consistently careful, also served to erase any suspicion Marie might have had: "Thanks, that's very kind of you, but that's not at all why I mentioned it. I've already left my keys at the gas station near the mall, they'll take care of it. That way, I don't have to worry."

They spotted an empty table and went to sit. Marianne excused herself for a moment to make a phone call—to the gas station, in fact, to find out what was going on with her car.

28

The phone rang in a booth in front of a dingy hotel, on the corner of Rue Robert-Louis and a dead-end street bearing the same name.

Several weeks ago, Marianne had replaced her ancient Peugeot with a small pink Autobianchi, well-tuned and compact. It was in this Autobianchi that Marc was waiting for her, in the driver's seat. He kept the door open because of the heat and so he could dash into the booth more easily when the phone rang.

He picked up the receiver.

Marianne was supposed to call, no matter what. If the plan with the car—as risky as it was—were to succeed, Marc was supposed to go to level three of the underground parking near the exit doors and watch for Marianne and Zyto. Then he would knock Zyto unconscious, stretch him out in the back seat of the car, and

Marianne would drive them to Louveciennes. He felt ready for anything, desperate.

"It didn't work," said Marianne. She sensed Marc's overwhelming disappointment. "But try not to worry too much, hang in there, I'm sure we'll find some other way, soon, another day. I just know it'll be possible. We'll talk about it later."

Her nerves were on edge, after the tension of the last few minutes.

"How are Marie and Leonard doing?"

"Fine. They're doing fine. Say, he's quite a performer, your guinea pig. You'll have to encourage him to go into the theater after all this. . . . We'll get him, you'll see. I know we will!"

He overcame his chagrin. He'd set up ten, twenty plans of action. He was feverish from the continual strain of his agonizing situation, still exhausted, but he did feel better. The effect of the Demerol had worn off, and, despite everything, he'd gotten a lot of sleep at Stéphen-Mornay, a healing kind of sleep. And now he had Marianne by his side, who was courageous and efficient. To a certain extent, he was free to do what he pleased.

He could even, if he wanted to . . .

"What are you going to do about the car? What if they decide to walk you to the parking lot?"

Marianne and Marc had decided to resuscitate the Peugeot under the circumstances, in case Marc were to drive the Autobianchi in the neighborhood of Versailles, for instance . . .

"Don't worry, I'll manage. They won't. I gotta go. We'll be in the cafeteria for a half hour to forty-five minutes. I better run. See you in a little while. Bye now."

"Bye. Can't wait to see you."

Marc went back to the car and sat there for a few moments. Then he stood up again and acted on the reckless but insurmountable desire that had come over him during Marianne's phone call.

He walked, taking long strides.

He was thoroughly familiar with the store and the cafeteria. There was no danger of being spotted as long as he was careful.

He crossed the length of the store, the check-out counters to his left flew by as if he were watching them on a movie screen.

He climbed the stairs that led to the cafeteria.

He found himself in the first area, where the platters were displayed at mealtimes. The restaurant, which was enormous, had been sectioned off by a partition of green plants. He drew nearer, parting the branches of the greenery a little. Behind it was a window.

And behind the window, about fifteen yards away, he immediately spied what he was looking for.

And what he saw was almost as shocking and disturbing as everything he'd been through up to that point. Incredible things could easily happen in his secret laboratory in Louveciennes or in a room of a mental hospital—each place lent itself to those sort of occurrences, making them less extraordinary. But here, now, in this vulgar restaurant, at the mall cafeteria in the suburbs of Ivry . . .

Marie and Michel Zyto were facing him. Marianne and Leonard had their backs to him, sometimes looking at each other. They were sipping their drinks, talking, smiling, engaged in casual conversation.

The horror was invisible.

Only a vision so impossible that it would surely vanish at any moment, fade into unreality. But it didn't vanish. And Marc just stared, wide-eyed, dumbfounded, barely able to stand.

Leonard stuck the headphones of the Walkman into his ears. Marianne fiddled with the buttons.

A Walkman! The bastard had bought Leonard a Walkman!

The boy removed the headphones and made a remark that the others found amusing. Then Marie and Zyto exchanged glances, almost tenderly, it seemed to Marc. Zyto leaned over, kissed Leonard on the forehead, then put his arm around Marie's shoulder.

Marc felt a stab of despair and hatred, which made him even weaker. He would kill Zyto. That's what he'd do, he'd kill him. Soon, he'd have the perfect opportunity, and he'd kill him.

29

The Lacroixs returned to Versailles after an enjoyable day.

The car was sparkling clean. It had been polished by a very young and extremely conscientious employee of the Montcourt gas station, not far from the restaurant where they had lunched. There was no longer any trace of the scuffle or the accident.

The red paint was so shiny, it looked wet.

In one corner of the garage a wheelbarrow, a dolly, a shovel, a hoe, and various other masonry and gardening tools were stored. Apparently, none of them had ever been used. Zyto, already intrigued by this equipment, took another look and decided to find out more about it. He was about to say jokingly, I'd love to know who bought all that and why?, when Leonard spoke up first. He inquired with mock seriousness: "So, are you finally going to build your little wall?"

"Dig up the earth? Plant some fruit trees?" asked Marie in the same tone.

Shortly after they'd moved to Chemin du Maréchal-ferrant, Marc had been seized with a sudden desire for physical labor, getting back to the land. He'd gone out and procured everything Zyto saw in the garage (plus the three pairs of pruning shears, hidden in the basement) and piled it up in the garage. But then Marc had never gone near it again, not even once.

Zyto vaguely understood the situation, enough to guess that by shaking his head "no" and smiling, he wouldn't be compromising himself.

Marie found his smile somehow different. A wider, more direct smile, less fleeting than usual.

They entered the house. The phone rang. Zyto let Marie answer it. She immediately held out the receiver to him: it was Hugues, who wanted to let "Marc" know about Michel Zyto's escape.

Michel Zyto had made his getaway after Marc's visit to the Center. Adeline Ledru had been violently knocked unconscious. Hugues had been calling the Lacroixs every fifteen minutes. And he'd notified the police. This time, there was no other way.

Zyto was stunned by the news, instantly flooded with anxiety. His mind raced in panic. Why escape? If Marc had wanted to reveal the truth to someone, he could have done so at Stéphen-Mornay. But perhaps he had decided to keep quiet and act on his own, just to be on the safe side, out of fear of Zyto's threats. Perhaps this was even what he wanted Zyto to realize—was it some sort of challenge? All right, now you can be sure I haven't said a word to anyone, so don't try anything stupid, and let's straighten out this business between ourselves.

Hugues's voice quavered. Zyto could sense he was terribly upset. They had really and truly committed a grave error in their diagnosis. There was nothing else to do but wait, they both agreed. They would stay in touch, should there be the slightest news; they'd see each other soon.

Zyto hung up. He composed himself before turning around to face Marie and Leonard. Marie had heard and understood what had happened, and so had Leonard, smart little kid that he was.

"He escaped from the clinic," said Zyto in what he hoped sounded like a normal tone of voice. "Another attack. He even knocked out a nurse. It was Adeline, I know her quite well."

"And so?" asked Leonard, moving closer to his mother. "Is he going to come here?"

"Certainly not, my little monkey. On the contrary, he'll try to get as far away from here as possible. They'll find him and then put him away in a place where they'll keep him under close surveillance. I'm beginning to get fed up with this entire business. C'mon, let's take another look at the Walkman. Let's find out how to set the stations. You can program twelve stations, isn't that something?"

Marie shot Zyto a vaguely questioning look: Was there reason to be worried? Zyto responded with a rather dubious expression on his face: No, you never know.... He could have been more reassuring, but he wasn't.

He had an idea.

Marie went into the kitchen. Zyto sat down next to Leonard on the couch.

Marc had escaped! What strength it must have taken, what courage! Zyto admired him. It was what he would have done in the same situation—escape, knocking out everybody in his way.

He had always admired Dr. Lacroix.

But how he loathed him at that moment! Zyto would have to be a thousand times more careful. Yes, if Marc had decided to break out of Stéphen-Mornay, at the risk of falling into the hands of the police and complicating everything, it meant he intended to take some sort of action. In spite of Zyto's blackmail. Why? Because Marc also had a way to blackmail him, a weapon—that neurinome on the acoustic nerve.

His anxiety gave way to anger. Zyto would have liked to dig his hand inside his neck, behind his ear, and take out the small tumor himself; and kill Leonard (the perfect crime: who would suspect the father, Dr. Marc Lacroix?). Marc would read about it in the newspapers, he'd tell himself that Zyto was obviously the smarter one; he'd realize that if he wanted to save Marie, there was only one solution—to go back to the Center, to room number six, and slip right into bed like a good boy!

Zyto was boiling with rage. His edginess had returned. He hardly even noticed Leonard, who was holding the Walkman and a cassette out to him.

"Dad! Hey, Dad! Yoo hoo! Here's a blank tape, I want to try to tape off the radio. She didn't show me how to do it, that lady, when we were at the store, how to tape off the radio."

Zyto did his best to smile.

Take action against him. That lady, when we were at the store . . . was it possible that this Marianne Matys . . . ? No. He reflected for a moment. No, no, of course not. Impossible. He had to be careful, but he couldn't start seeing clues everywhere, acting paranoid, otherwise he'd go mad; he knew himself, he wouldn't be able to go on.

For the time being, the ball was still in his court, and it would stay that way as long as he had Marie and Leonard under his thumb.

He made a couple of attempts to record the radio as Leonard looked on in fascination.

Marie came out of the kitchen with a tall glass of lemon-mint soda. Then the phone rang. She answered.

The Cazanvielhs were inviting them to dinner on the spur of the moment, as they often did.

"I'd love to," she said. "We could use the distraction. We really need it right now, we'll tell you all about it. One minute, I'm just going to check with Marc."

She held her left hand over the receiver.

"Marie-Thérèse invited us over for dinner. She's making gazpacho."

Zyto reflected, asking himself a million different questions in the space of a few seconds, then nodded yes. Might as well go visit these old family friends tonight.

Gazpacho? He'd never heard of it.

"It's fine with him," said Marie. "Yes, see you later."

"There you go!" said Zyto to Leonard. "You can record all the stations you want and run around at the same time."

He showed him how to do it, then erased everything and let him have a try.

Marie went upstairs.

Leonard found a station, programmed it using the "set" button, and began to record as Zyto looked on, pretending to be interested.

What would Marc do now? Prowl around the house, follow the Lacroixs' every move—invisible, yet all too present—waiting for the right moment?

Where would he live, where would he hide? In a hotel? Too risky. And too expensive. Zyto knew exactly how much money Marc had, not enough to be extravagant. Could he be staying with a trustworthy friend, someone whom Zyto had no way of knowing about, and to whom he would confide everything? Someone he knew from work, for instance? Or else, if he'd decided to act alone, in the hideout where Zyto himself had once stayed, that he'd described to Marc in such precise detail, driven by the need to tell him everything, confess everything? Anything was possible.

No, Marc would purposely avoid that hideout. Or maybe he wouldn't avoid it, thinking it was the one place Zyto would never look for him? Or he'd think that Zyto would look for him there, anyway. And in that case, perhaps he'd try to set up some kind of trap.

Zyto ordered himself to stop: enough! Marc had taught him to beware of these endless inner debates that would get him confused, imprisoning him and poisoning his thoughts the longer they continued. A "self-intoxication," as Marc had called it.

One thing at a time. He'd keep playing the role of Marc Lacroix as best he could. And be exceedingly vigilant. Hope the police wouldn't find Marc. Straighten out the business between them, at Louveciennes, in the secrecy of the laboratory. They'd exchange bodies again. Then it would be up to Zyto to lay down the law. Kill Marc and flee, more and more that was what was going through his mind. No one would know, or it would come out later, much later; maybe they'd find Marc's body and the destroyed machines. Mysterious suicide of a scientist in his laboratory. That's it, a suicide!

Or else he'd remain in Marc's body, in spite of the neurinome, hoping that . . . no, he couldn't bear it!

He started to get worked up again, his nerves were on edge.

He'd look for Marc, just as Marc was looking for him. Meaning he'd still be able to get away from Marie and Leonard.

By moving into a hotel with them. It was an idea.

"OK!" Leonard practically shouted. "I'm recording!"

Zyto roused himself from his thoughts. He heard a strange panting, some kind of bizarre music.

"What's that you're listening to?"

"Croc-Rock, the 'ravenous for rock' station," Leonard recited.

"Will you listen to a little Vivaldi every once in a while?" Zyto was playing the tolerant but serious father.

"Sure," Leonard said with sincerity. "Do you want me to put on your record? We won't bother each other. I won't be able to hear yours and you won't hear mine either, you'll see. Gosh, this Walkman's fantastic!"

"OK, my little monkey. My ravenous little monkey."

When Marie came downstairs, she found father and son sitting side by side on the couch, each listening to their own music, holding hands—for Leonard, wild with delight and gratitude, had taken his "father's" hand.

It was a touching sight.

"Leonard, go wash up and change your clothes. Go ahead!"

Leonard, who still had on his headphones, pretended he couldn't hear, or, to be more precise, pretended to pretend he couldn't hear to amuse his parents, something he was always able to do quite well. His sense of humor, at such a young age, was only one of his numerous charms.

"You really can't hear me?" asked Marie.

"Not at all," he said, shaking his head energetically, his thick bangs flipping from side to side.

"And what if I talk louder, like this?"

Leonard's beautiful brown eyes glittered mischievously.

"Even less than before. Now I really can't hear a thing. No, actually, I can read your lips. You told me to stay the way I am, dirty, and not to change my shirt to go to Marshall's, right?"

Then he took off the headphones and burst into laughter, followed by an exchange of kisses. He ran upstairs.

Zyto dug around for the remote control of the CD player that had become wedged between two cushions of the couch. The final notes of *La Frescobalda* rang out. He switched off the record. He liked this music more than he'd thought he would.

He wished he could listen to all of Marc's records.

Listen in peace, gazing out the bay window at the beautiful countryside . . . Alas, it would never be possible. Without that tumor, perhaps he would have decided to remain Marc Lacroix, and eliminate "the other."

Marie sat down beside him. She was wearing blue jeans, a wide, dark red belt and a thin, clingy black sweater, her lovely dark hair spilling down over her shoulders.

Zyto leaned over and kissed her on the forehead. Would something happen again that night, as unexpected and terrifying as the night before—though it had actually been more pleasurable than terrifying?

Deep down, he hoped it would.

"Are you OK?" asked Marie.

"Yeah, I'm fine. But I wonder if we should go away for a little while, just until the police get their hands on him."

"You think so?" Marie asked, suddenly apprehensive.

"No, don't worry. I was just thinking of Leonard. There's absolutely no danger, but after giving it some thought I figure that to be on the careful side, maybe we could go somewhere else for a couple of days, until they arrest him. . . ."

30

Marshall agreed. He invited the Lacroixs to stay at his home, Impasse des Soldats, until the maniac was arrested. They refused the offer. Aside from the imposition, if they were obliged to spend a few days elsewhere, it might be best if it weren't in Versailles. Could they even take advantage of it, go away on a holiday? No, Zyto was bent on not straying too far, he wanted to be present when Zyto was apprehended.

Police protection? No, not in a case like this. And it would inevitably have to be minimal protection, more of a nuisance than anything else. And besides, if one stopped to think of all those heads of state who'd been attacked by madmen, despite an army of body guards . . .

"So why not a hotel?" asked Marie-Thérèse. "A hotel in Paris. It would be fun. Take a little vacation in your own city, in a nice hotel, incognito?"

Zyto pretended to consider this, then gave Marie-Thérèse a look of friendly approval, as though she'd just hit upon the same solution that he'd been contemplating since Hugues's phone call about "his" escape: they could hide in a hotel, he'd leave Marie and Leonard there with nothing to fear, and go out and track him down. An impossible plan if the family did not leave their home. At one point or another, Marc would come back to his house on Chemin Maréchal-ferrant. What if he was already there? Zyto thought, resolving to be extremely careful on his end. Marie would see the point of it, she'd be more convinced than ever that it was preferable for them to leave.

"That's a good idea," he said to Marie-Thérèse, whose eyes shone with pride. "In fact, it's a very good idea."

Marie-Thérèse's eyes shone brighter still when Zyto, deliberately changing the subject to divert everyone's attention from the plan to check into a hotel, gave her the highest compliments on her gazpacho. (A total failure, Marie would later tell Zyto: Marie-Thérèse was a terrible cook.) Marie-Thérèse had always been a bit intimidated by Dr. Lacroix. Zyto had her wrapped around his finger. Yet, God knows, this tall, attractive woman, slightly past her prime (who'd received two phone calls and had made one herself during dinner) was unappealing to him. He'd always remember the moment she'd opened the door with that hat on her head, a little round furry dog in her arms, and that silly smile on her face. He knew about the birthday presents, so he'd been prepared to make some kind of appropriate, stupid remark. So this Cookie was the very same dog Marc had used for his first experiment.

For a few seconds, he told himself, the body of this dog had been "occupied" by the mind of another dog. Marc Lacroix was truly an extraordinary man, a genius!

Zyto pulled off the evening at the Cazanviehls without any difficulty. At least he could be glad of that, without any reservations. He'd never spoken first, he'd tried to look pensive and preoccupied, relying on what he knew and had heard in order to speak with deliberation, and had discovered that he was right on target every time: it was like a stimulating game that he played exceedingly well.

The others did, in fact, notice a few strange but minor details—

"Marc's" awkwardness as he moved around the house, though he knew it like the back of his hand; a moment where he'd hesitated between the familiar *tu* or formal *vous* when addressing them—but from these to ever imagining they were in the presence of a mental patient who'd escaped from the asylum using the body of Marc Lacroix to deceive the world, there was an impassable breach.

Not impassable, however, for the West Highland terrier, who wasn't the sort of dog who could be fooled by appearances: Cookie growled a few times at Zyto, to Marie's great astonishment. Zyto offered her a considerable portion of his meal, called her a number of tender names, but nothing seemed to work. He even renamed her "Cookie pie," as in "come here my little Cookie pie." But the tone was all wrong. The animal, by instinct, did not respond to his advances and ended up taking refuge in Marie-Thérèse's lap, snarling, as if still possessed by Mana's rotten temperament.

"That proves she's really gotten used to us," Marie-Thérèse concluded.

There was an uncomfortable moment when Marshall proposed a game of chess to Zyto, to distract him from his problems.

"All right," said Zyto.

Then he pretended to change his mind, to come up with another idea.

"This may surprise you, but I wonder whether a game of pinball wouldn't be even more relaxing?

As soon as dinner was over, Leonard had slipped on his gloves, mimicking the gestures of a small-time hood. He'd burst out laughing, amused by his own little performance, and had left the table, marking every step with: "Pin-ball-pin-ball-pin-ball!"

Zyto's suggestion appealed to everyone—first and foremost, Marie-Thérèse. But glancing at her watch, she asked whether they could hold off twenty seconds. She had, as she called it, a teeny-tiny call to make.

They waited.

After the teeny-tiny call, they all moved upstairs into the cave of Ali Baba, Marshall's room of treasures. Zyto hid his astonishment, as he had when he'd spied the statues in the garden. He was amazed by the piles of furniture, gold-embroidered antique clothes, chess sets, paintings, mounted animals, carved wooden animals, guns, jewelry, musical instruments, all kinds of things.

And the superb pinball machine, an expensive piece of junk, with the two cowboys drawing their guns ready to shoot.

"Do you know how to play?" asked Marie-Thérèse.

"You'll see, you're going to be impressed!"

Leonard, who was all keyed up, still wearing the headphones, stepped aside.

And impress them he did: he gave them a genuine demonstration of his virtuosity, his hips glued to the machine, a gleam in his eye, using quick, precise, and professional movements, with those typical and slightly obscene little pelvic thrusts, the perfect amount of force to change the course of the metal ball without making the machine "tilt." It was obvious that he could have played for hours, winning free games that were awarded every twenty thousand points, without giving the ball the slightest chance to escape his control.

He stopped, almost disdainfully allowing the ball to slide and disappear into the hole.

Then he looked at the Western scene, the outcome of the shoot-out eternally uncertain.

Marie-Thérèse's exclamations and Leonard's yelping had never ceased the entire time he was playing, but he'd barely heard them. Now it brought him back to reality. He realized he'd done something slightly reckless.

"Why didn't you ever tell me you knew how to play like that?" asked Leonard, dizzy with admiration. "You should be in tournaments!"

Zyto smiled.

"I didn't know about this hidden talent either," said Marie.

"Incredible," said Marie-Thérèse, clapping her hands.

Marie observed that "Marc's" smile continued to be even more attractive than usual, more subtle and prolonged. Definitely. At least to the eyes of his loving wife. Tonight was full of surprises!

"Say, partner, one would think you've been doing that all your life!" said Marshall to Zyto.

Faced with an adversary of that sort, with such diversified talents, he realized he had little chance of winning Marie. But he felt no envy, no bitterness. And he hadn't given up yet. He never gave up. After all, he was a good horseman, a good shot, and a good chess player. A better chess player. His reasoning was childish, he still had hope.

"Believe it or not, I played a lot of pinball when I was a student," said Zyto. "You never forget how to do those kinds of things. It's like swimming or bicycling."

"Bicycling," Leonard echoed joyously.

Marie was pensive. She felt as if "Marc" was avoiding her eyes. How was it possible that he'd never mentioned it, not even once; in a café, for instance: "You know, darling, when I was young, I was really good at that game there. . . ." But he'd never said any such thing. She was sure of it. She would have remembered. It must be part of the little mysteries of life, she thought. Maybe Marc would be surprised to find out certain things about me that I never thought to tell him.

She couldn't really think of any. But perhaps there was something.

All the windows of the Cazanvielhs' splendid villa were open, letting in the night air. A total silence reigned over the Impasse des Soldats and the entire neighborhood.

Suddenly, a telephone rang somewhere in the midst of the jumble of antiques. They started. The house was full of telephones.

"That must be for me," said Marie-Thérèse, rushing to answer it.

"Anything is possible," said Marshall, smiling at Marie.

31

That same night, Michel Zyto made love to a woman for the first time in his life.

At first, things happened the way they had the night before, then Zyto unwittingly found himself lying on top of Marie, though it hadn't been deliberate. She hadn't forced him into doing anything, she simply rubbed his back affectionately, murmuring "darling," and he was suddenly inside her, almost by accident. He didn't realize what was happening. He felt overwhelmed by something entirely different than he'd ever known before, with Marie or by himself when masturbating; it was gentler but more tantalizing, not as rough, yet more complete, more enveloping.

He feverishly thrust himself inside her for a few moments, then experienced a brief, intense orgasm.

Marc's sexual detachment had tormented Marie more than she'd realized, or than she was willing to admit to herself. That night, even if "Marc" had hardly satisfied her physically, she was thrilled to have him back, moved by his awkwardness and timidity. It was as if, after all those months of abstinence, he was rediscovering lovemaking with her.

As for Michel Zyto, he forgot his fears, but it was most definitely because he was in someone else's skin, because he was using Marc Lacroix's body. This deception had given him access to what seemed like normal behavior. However, the sexual act was also, most definitely, the basis of what actually triggered his madness.

At the moment of orgasm, he knew for a fact that he was capable of killing Marie, her and the others. It was then that his fate as a "woman killer" was truly sealed, just as the newspapers had said, though he hadn't even killed anyone. But it was also because he was in Marc's body that he could not give in immediately to his desire to kill. He could keep it at bay, in reserve, and calmly tell himself that making love had been a revelation and that he'd gladly do it again, some other night.

He felt as if he were on a winning streak. Master of his desires, stronger than ever.

What remained was the urgency of straightening out the problem with Marc, as best he could, as quickly as possible. And as a consequence of having made love that night Zyto began to formulate a solution to that problem.

It came up during the conversation following their lovemaking—full of complicity, as tender and intimate as if the real Lacroix husband and wife had truly been reunited.

"I can't stand the way Marie-Thérèse blows out her cigarette smoke," Zyto said out of the blue. "It's that noise she makes, it really bugs me!"

"That's the three-millionth time you've told me that, darling."

"I'm sure I'll say it three million times more . . ."

"Did you notice how Leonard looked at the basement doorway when we got home?"

"No," said Zyto.

He refrained from adding: "How?" He cautiously kept it at no, waiting for what might follow, a declaration, some other piece of information that would enlighten him.

"I can feel it, when he's afraid."

"You think he's afraid?" said Zyto in an almost neutral tone of voice.

"Well, not exactly afraid. But this business is stirring up his anxiety. Your accident, the wound on your forehead, Zyto's escape, having to go live in a hotel, do you realize what that's like for him?"

"Of course I do. But it won't last very long. And anyway, he feels secure when he's with us."

"That's true," said Marie. "I'm not really all that worried."

Leonard, afraid, the basement door stirring up his anxiety... afraid of what, what anxiety? How many explanations could there be? Leonard probably had a big scare one day in the basement. As a matter of fact, the Lacroixs always left the basement door in the hallway open. Surely, there was a link. What kind of scare? It didn't matter. And Marie said no more on the subject.

She was thinking about the pinball game. And the possibility that Marc could keep secrets from her. And about Marianne Matys...

Since the performance of *A Midsummer Night's Dream*, Marie had been fighting off the suspicion. But, out of pride, there was no way she would have communicated these doubts to Marc during the time when he'd turned away from her sexually, and also because she attributed this lack of interest to Marc's worries and his depression. Because she didn't really believe it, deep down. She was certain Marc hadn't noticed anything. She'd been good at hiding her feelings. Now that "Marc" had made love her, ironically enough, she was less capable of thinking clearly, she felt a bona fide jealousy, it was physical, she pictured Marc going through the same motions with someone else, with Marianne, giving and receiving the same affection.

She was jealous, absurdly jealous.

And she felt the need to find out for certain.

She tried to restrain herself, reasoning that she'd forget all about it by tomorrow, yet she couldn't resist. It was like an uncontrollable itch. All she had to do was give in to it, then she'd set her mind at rest. One simple question, to get it off her chest. In a few seconds, if she so desired.

"I'm still surprised you never told me anything about pinball."

Zyto's mind raced. He gave a little laugh, a perfect one, totally natural.

"You know, for years I forgot about it, I never really thought about it. After that, there were a couple of times when it was on the tip of my tongue, I remember very clearly. But you know how it is, all you'd have to do is change the subject and it would completely slip my mind. It isn't that important, is it? Does it bother you?"

He laughed again.

"No, it's dumb," she said. "But . . ."

"But what?"

"Was there ever anything between you and Marianne Matys?"

Whew. It had been difficult. Her voice came out in a whisper and her heart was pounding wildly. Fortunately, they were in the dark.

"Are you crazy? Of course not! How could you ever think that? I hardly know her. I think she's nice, but . . . no, come on, really!"

Zyto was convincing. He was telling the truth. And he'd been fearing a more embarrassing question, so he felt relieved. That was all it was! No, nothing between Zyto and Marianne Matys. Marie snuggled up against him.

"You're not mad at me?"

"Yes, very!"

He took her in his arms and covered her face with kisses. The thoughts of murder engraved on his mind did not stop him from liking her. And tonight, he liked her a lot.

What a relief.

And he was also glad, for he might have just discovered where Marc was hiding out.

He'd been too hasty in deciding Marc didn't have a mistress. He'd dismissed the hypothesis too quickly that afternoon, about this Marianne Matys. Marie's remarks threw everything back into question. Marie was subtle, perceptive. If her suspicions were founded, then Marianne Matys the actress had come to the shopping center in Ivry with precise intentions. Hadn't she tried to get Marie alone, then Leonard, and even Zyto himself? And why, if for no other reason than to attempt to do something against him, according to a plan she'd conceived with her lover, Marc Lacroix?

A while later, he got out of bed: he just couldn't sleep, he said to himself, and felt like a lemon-mint soda. He'd go downstairs for a few minutes.

The phone book. Or, Marie's address book.

But Marianne was listed.

Then he examined Marc's enormous key ring. There were so many that Marianne's could certainly be among them. He, Zyto, would have put it there with the others, along with keys to the house and the various places Marc worked. It was the best hiding place.

But maybe he wouldn't need the key.

He went back upstairs.

If Marie's suspicions were founded, it meant that right then, at that very moment, that night, Marc was with Marianne Matys, at her apartment.

32

Marc—*exhausted,* discouraged, ashamed of his physical appearance, and tortured by Marianne's gaze—felt only disgust for himself. In the dark, he imagined that his detestable body, that pretty boy face now missing a mustache, that ungraceful short stocky build, those feet misshapen from wearing poor quality shoes, those heavy thighs, that thick penis; the excessive body hair, such a different color and texture than his own . . .

And he also pictured Marie and Michel Zyto side by side in the same bed, on Chemin du Maréchal-ferrant. He was fairly certain that nothing would happen, or very little—a kiss goodnight, a tender embrace—but even that little bit was too much; that little bit was excruciating, truly unbearable!

Had Marie noticed anything? Had Zyto made any blunders in his choice of words or his behavior, any huge mistakes that Marie would find incomprehensible? And Leonard—who was so smart, always figuring everything out by himself—had he perceived anything abnormal, was he uncomfortable in the presence of this fake father? Maybe. Or maybe not. Marianne had been struck by the ease with which Zyto played his role as head of the family, his role of Marc Lacroix. The role of his life, Marc said to himself with hatred and bitterness. Mistakes or no mistakes, uncomfortable or not, the bastard always seemed to land on his feet again.

Marc berated himself for having gone through with his experiment. If he hadn't, he would never have been caught in this nightmare. But in his heart of hearts, his ambition and pride still kept him going and helped him remain hopeful. He hadn't given up yet.

They had gone to bed early. Marc had taken some tranquilizers, a strong dose. Marianne had taken a milder dose, but since she rarely used them, she was soon as groggy as Marc. They exchanged a few words, a gradually lagging conversation about possible ways to corner the madman, criminal, impostor. Alas, there weren't too many from which to choose. And a permanent surveillance was hardly practical.

They awoke almost at the same time, at around 1:00 A.M., after an initial, fitful sleep. The tormenting recollection of well-being that Marc had always felt after being with his mistress prompted him to make a few timid advances, to which Marianne vaguely responded, and they found themselves in each other's arms.

The window of the small room had been opened onto the dark blue sky, full of stars. Not a sound in the courtyard. They tossed back the sheet and made love in the silence and profound darkness, much like the atmosphere that hung over Chemin du Maréchal-ferrant.

They moved in a kind of semiconscious state.

Marianne, with her blond hair, long legs that were so attractive (though a bit irregular, even to the touch, when you knew them as Marc did)—Marianne experienced more pleasure than she'd expected. The body she discovered through her caresses was not that of her lover's, but all the rest was so like him—his desire, his gestures, his affectionate habits, his being, his person—and she loved him so much that her initial impression of lying in bed with a stranger had now disappeared. And, at the moment of orgasm, it was truly Marc she was holding in her arms, and who brought tears of happiness to her eyes, just as he always did.

Now overtaken by a heavy drowsiness, a bit stunned by what had just happened between them, they both fell silent.

Marianne's optimistic nature had brought her to the conclusion that everything would work out fine in the end. What would happen next, when Marc became Marc again? Exactly how did he stand regarding Marie? Would he agree to divorce her? Marianne had never asked herself these questions before. Suddenly, she wanted Marc all to herself.

It was the first time they'd ever spent an entire night together.

Marc's mind was also wandering. He'd just made love to Marianne, and was now obsessed by two plans, to bring Zyto to Louveciennes, then to reveal his invention to the astonished world. As radically different as his situation was, the secret was still locked into those same words that only a few days ago . . .

And for an instant, his repulsive body struck him as somewhat less loathsome. It was strong, healthy, and functioned well.

No more tumor on the acoustic nerve.

Before dinner, Marc had swallowed two Maktarin tablets.

He drifted back to sleep.

33

Indeed, Zyto always seemed to land on his feet. He'd become perfectly integrated into the Lacroix family. It was a great art, a combination of natural ease and vigilance, of inspiration and calculated caution.

Marie perceived that he was, in fact, very tense, yet closer to her than ever. As for Leonard, he'd rarely seen his father so attentive, so playful, so "cool." That very morning, Zyto had come into his room and started clowning around in the funniest way. He'd made believe he hadn't realized that Leonard was awake, and had pretended to steal the Walkman, tiptoeing out of the room ignoring the child's shrieks of delight, and the whole episode had ended with hugs and kisses.

Nevertheless, that morning, Zyto had awakened feeling extremely anxious.

And a while later that same morning of August 4, before their departure to the Hôtel Pavillon de la Reine, on the Place des Vosges, he'd had to brave quite an ordeal. He had been alone upstairs. On his way out of the bathroom he had sat down on the bed to put on his socks, when he felt as though his ears were stuffed with cotton. He couldn't hear a thing, only a kind of continual buzzing that came from inside his head. Almost instantaneously, the room had begun to spin around him in every direction, like a merry-go-round at full speed that had been turned upside down. Zyto gripped the bed. Then an overwhelming nausea sent him reeling to the floor. He moaned with nausea and fear.

He crawled all the way to the bathroom, still moaning. He hung onto the toilet bowl and vomited, twice, with revolting profusion and violent spasms.

Then the dizziness abated, the noise in his ears as well. He flushed the toilet several times, wiped his mouth with toilet paper, and remained still, kneeling over the bowl, gasping for air.

The attack was over.

In his panic, certain thoughts came to mind that made him lose his head entirely. While vomiting, he'd felt as though he was rendering his soul, as if Marc's body no longer wanted anything to do with him. He told himself that this malaise was a punishment, the punishment of fornication, and that he'd pay very dearly for the pleasure he'd had with Marie the night before.

And he imagined that Marc's escape might have been faked, a trick being played on him by Hugues d'Oléons, Adeline, the entire clinic, the police . . .

He was scared.

He gingerly got back on his feet. He returned to the bed to sit down, then began to dress. Yes, the attack was over. But had Marc ever experienced such a violent one? If only Zyto could ask him! Maybe the illness was getting worse. Maybe Marc had never undergone anything as painful?

He calmed down. He repeated to himself certain things Cedric Houdé had said that were irrefutable. These spells were totally insignificant right now, in terms of the development of the tumor.

A faked escape? A trap, a plot against him? He could easily get to the bottom of it.

By finding Marc that very day. And by performing the same experiment in reverse, stepping back into his own body.

What a shame. But it was inevitable. And he had become and would now always remain someone different. The mere thought gave him new energy.

They left the Nissan Terrano at the garage of the hotel, on Rue de Béarn, and headed toward the nearby Place des Vosges on foot.

Zyto was extremely pale. Marie had been observing him closely. He really didn't seem to be feeling too well this morning.

He was carrying two suitcases, a large and a small one. Marie had a flight bag, and Leonard, only his Walkman plugged into his ears. The boy hardly touched the radio: the dial was permanently set on Croc-Rock, the station for ravenous rockers.

At ten in the morning, it was already quite warm. Once they'd left the eternally shady Rue de Béarn, it felt like burning-hot clothing had drifted down onto their shoulders as they arrived at the entrance of the sunlit Place des Vosges. Zyto couldn't help thinking of the interior garden of Stéphen-Mornay. The entire square blazed with light. One might very well think that here, too, due to a strange phenomenon of reverberation, the rays of the sun came down from all sides.

Leonard took off his headphones and turned to Michel Zyto. He had an idea, he'd been mulling it over for a while.

"Why don't we use the name Xarcoil?"

"Xarcoil? Why? How do you spell it?"

Leonard was surprised, and so was his mother. She'd figured it out immediately. Why was Marc asking these questions? He and his son often played word games together, and usually understood each other within a half second.

"X-a-r-c-o-i-l. Xarcoil. You get it? It's the same letters as Lacroix, only . . ."

"OK, OK, my silly little monkey. I had my mind on something else. OK, great. We'll use Xarcoil."

It wasn't the first time Leonard had suggested using a false name, he loved the idea of it. Zyto had said yes. It was what he'd intended to do anyhow. Just to be overly cautious, scrupulous about the details: he could hardly imagine Marc phoning every hotel in Paris and the surrounding area.

They turned right, then right again, passing through a sculpted archway. After a few steps, they found themselves in front of the Hôtel Pavillon de la Reine—an extremely luxurious establishment set back from the square, with a pleasant, quiet, and almost cool interior.

The swinging doors were propped open; they marched together three abreast and walked down the hallway, with Leonard in the middle. The receptionist in the lobby, straight down to the left, hung up the phone and peered over at them. They were a nice-looking family, the three of them; they looked good together. Zyto was wearing a beautiful off-white linen suit that wrinkled fairly easily, which was even more chic ("Why don't you wear your linen suit?" Marie had asked. "Yes, good idea."); Leonard was in his favorite denim shorts and an elegant black T-shirt with HELP! across the front in white letters; and Marie was dressed in a long summery red dress that was a bit flashy, not always appropriate. But she wore it well, and she moved along gracefully. Zyto, a little less gracefully, awestruck by the ostentation of the vast hallway—all in wood and leather, illuminated by at least ten lamps, and decorated with antique paintings.

The employee was a young man with impeccable "style." An animated mannequin just out of hotel school, thought Marie. He didn't really inspire anyone's confidence. His features were hard; he had a prying gaze with a touch of slyness and almost arrogance—haughty, subtle, but perceptible to people as sensitive as Marie, or as distrustful as Michel Zyto. Zyto had the impression the man was scrutinizing him, that he could see right through him and had guessed everything. That he could see what was in his jacket pocket right through the fabric, the little Swiss 6mm SIG P2 10 pistol he'd removed from the safe just before leaving, without Marie knowing.

"Madame, Monsieur?"

Zyto averted his gaze and didn't answer, looking at Marie, putting himself in her hands. She understood, she knew "Marc," how ill at ease he was, awkward in social situations that weren't professional, easily unnerved, easily disconcerted by little everyday occurrences.

She smiled at him and calmly turned toward the receptionist.

Zyto parked the four-wheel drive on the sidewalk across from No. 23, Rue des Martyrs, in the ninth arrondissement.

He entered the building and looked for the name on the mailbox: Adeline Ledru, stairway B, second floor, door on the left.

A man answered the doorbell. He was young and fairly handsome, and seemed preoccupied. There was a white streak, extremely white, that stood out in his black, wavy hair. He addressed Zyto in a hurried, brisk tone: "Yes? . . ."

"Hi. I'm sorry to bother you. I'm Dr. Marc Lacroix, I work with Miss Ledru at the Stéphen-Mornay Center."

The young man's expression changed.

"Ah, yes. Jean Citadelle." He almost held out his hand, but decided against it. "Please, come in. I took Adeline to the dentist, we just got home. She was there yesterday as well."

"I'm sorry to drop in like this, I wanted to phone, but . . ."

"That's quite all right. It's very kind of you."

The escape hadn't been faked. Deep down, Zyto had known it all along. But now he could be sure. Jean Citadelle ushered him into the living room, which faced a somewhat gloomy courtyard, and Adeline immediately came out of the bathroom. The bottom half of her face and a portion of her left cheek were purple, almost black in certain places. Terrible bruises. She could barely speak. Good old Dr. Lacroix, he'd really gone for it. . . .

Adeline was very touched, and even shed a tear. Mentally, she was still in shock; she'd been extremely frightened the night before, and was in a lot of pain. And this morning, the dentist had extracted one of her bottom incisors.

Zyto took her head in his hands and gently tilted it back. And did so very professionally, Adeline's friend thought to himself.

"Open your mouth, just a little bit, stop if it hurts . . . there . . ."

The canine tooth could be saved, it was only chipped, Jean Citadelle explained. They'd have to kill the nerve of the healthy incisor to the right, file it down, and insert a bridge.

"That's really the only solution," said Zyto, letting go of the young woman. "Naturally, Dr. d'Oléons told me that the Center will assume all financial responsibility."

"It was so nice of you to stop by."

Her words were barely comprehensible, she had to mumble. Jean Citadelle gazed at her with what appeared to be loving concern.

Well, one thing had been accomplished. He was sure. Now for the next step. Zyto felt a small surge of optimism. His anxiety had suddenly abated. He was accustomed to these mood swings. He turned up the volume on the tape deck; it was Vivaldi, marvelous music, and what a great sound system!

The Nissan Terrano sailed down the Rue de Richelieu, the lights turned green as soon as he approached. Zyto had begun to love this car.

He quickly arrived at Avenue Stéphen-Mornay, the short street—not terribly wide—that had been designated an "avenue," God knows why.

The heat did not agree with the enormous Dr. Hugues d'Oléons. He was short of breath and constantly perspiring. The worst part was the great beads of sweat on his scalp; they looked like blisters, or some kind of skin disease. He was continually mopping his head, but they'd come back seconds later, just as large.

"I called the police station this morning at nine o'clock. They decided to run some photographs on the evening news. Two photos, a frontal view and a profile."

Zyto, comfortably seated in the Louis XV chair, wasn't terribly thrilled to hear this information. Luckily, he had the Marianne Matys lead, which he believed was a solid one. He'd avoid a lot of complications if he got his hands on Marc first.

In a little while.

"He's going to feel cornered," Zyto said.

"Obviously. But we can't do anything about it. To the police, Michel Zyto is dangerous. He might have killed once, therefore, he might kill again. They're doing their job. Besides . . . perhaps he really is dangerous. I confess, I'm a bit mixed up myself."

"Me too. I admit, I feel the same way."

He smiled at him. Hugues d'Oléons, accustomed to Marc's fleeting smiles that would immediately fade as if he were repressing them, was surprised and delighted to see a smile that lasted longer brightening up his friend's face.

"Otherwise, my dear Marc, how are things going?"

"OK."

"You mentioned to me on the phone that you were thinking of checking into a hotel for a few days."

"Yes. Probably today. Poor Adeline," he said, changing the subject.

"Ah! If you only knew how disturbing I find all this!"

"I'm glad I stopped by to see her, she was so happy I came. The dentist is going to put in a bridge."

Hugues remained silent for a moment, lost in thought.

"I should have done the same myself," he finally said.

And it was his turn to smile, exposing all his yellow and gray incisors. Zyto, uninformed about anything in particular concerning d'Oléons teeth, prudently refrained from making any comments and stuck to a knowing, slightly idiotic smile.

"Which hotel?" asked Hugues.

"We haven't decided yet," answered Zyto.

Situated on the second floor, the two large beautiful rooms—decorated predominately in brown—were next door to each other, but not adjoining. They were the only rooms available when Marie had phoned. With the onslaught of tourists, they were lucky to find any vacancies at all.

The advantage, for Leonard, was the TV—a TV all to himself, just like the one in his parents' room, with a remote control. He could watch it in his bed that night (he'd already been granted permission) as long as he liked.

Marie had taken a look around, unpacked the suitcases, and now, sitting on the edge of the king-size bed, she lit up a cigarette. It was something she did only rarely. She'd been a heavy smoker when she'd met Marc. He'd succeeded in getting her to quit in the space of four months. He didn't like seeing her with a cigarette in her hand. He'd say: you're letting yourself fall into a hellish vice. You think it's over, but it's not over for your cells. A cell will still remember what tobacco is. Right now, your cells are pushing you into that vice and you don't even realize it. Although his remarks were always in the form of a joke, Marc still had to say something.

Except for last evening, when Marie had smoked a cigarette late that night and, curiously, he'd hadn't commented.

Leonard glanced out the window. Not much to look at. He turned around.

"I'm hungry."

"Already? It's a quarter after eleven."

"There's no time like the right time," the boy said.

He grinned, then his smile turned into laughter as it often did, and he gave his mother a quick peck on the forehead—he was too adorable. Leonard was taking this hotel business better than she'd expected, he was more relaxed than yesterday. And he was very excited by the whiff of adventure hovering in the air.

"We'll have an early lunch," she said. "There are lots of restaurants surrounding Place des Vosges."

"Can I go there?"

"Where?"

"To the Place des Vosges?"

"In a minute. We'll go together."

"Can I go to my room then?"

"To watch TV, eh?"

He hesitated for a moment.

"Yes," he said, making a funny face.

"Go ahead. You'll see, the programs are incredibly interesting in the morning, you big silly. You'll tell me all about it."

She remained there alone. She stubbed out the cigarette in the ashtray and kept herself from lighting another. Leonard was so sweet and straightforward. How could he have rummaged through their bedroom with such deliberate, cold-blooded, and methodical intention the other night? It wasn't like her Leonard, not at all.

She phoned her parents in La Colle-sur-Loup. She told them that they were making their own little tour of Paris and the surrounding area, just for the heck of it. She'd call them back. They'd see each other soon. For once, she had a pleasant conversation with her father and mother, and with Louis, her younger brother by ten years, who had split up with his girlfriend and was spending a part of his vacation with "the folks," as he called them.

Marie hung up and immediately dialed the Cazanvielhs' number, more or less automatically. At this hour, she was almost sure Marshall would answer. Unless... no, it was Friday. The following day, Saturday, was the day he went out to shoot, hunt, or ride horseback, but today he was sure to be there, busy with his antiques, his garden, while Marie-Thérèse ran around to beauty parlors or to get her legs waxed. Now with Cookie in tow. And introducing him to thousands of idle, overly made-up women from Versailles who would probably kill the poor Westie by petting him too much, plying him with compliments and candy.

She let it ring for a long time. Finally, Marshall picked up, not at all out of breath, although Marie knew he'd had to run to answer it. Physically, he was in great shape. More than ever, she realized how much Marshall's affection meant to her. As strong and courageous as she was, the solid support he gave her was very helpful, and even vital.

"Marshall?"

"Marie! How are you? Still in Versailles?"

"No, we've done it, we're at the hotel."

"Where? Which one? Wait, let me write it down... OK, what is it...?"

Before he'd left, "Marc" had told her not to reveal their hiding place to anyone. He'd emphasized *to anyone*. "Not even to Marshall?" Marie had asked in surprise.

Embarrassed, Zyto had mumbled: "No, not to anyone, there's no point doing things halfway." She'd thought that was a bit much, he was really too jumpy. She hadn't insisted. To avoid making him even more nervous, she'd said, all right, fine, but when Marshall asked her about the hotel, she didn't hesitate for a second. Not to anyone. For her that meant the entire world except for Marshall, her closest friend, whom she trusted completely. Besides, how could that madman ever track them down through Marshall? Such a hypothesis seemed totally absurd. And therefore, it was beyond her control to refuse to answer Marshall.

If Leonard was calmer these days, Marc, on the other hand, was so anxious that it worried her. She'd noticed it while they were driving. It had been obvious, though undoubtedly possible, that no one had been following them—one hundred percent sure—yet Marc hadn't taken his eyes off the rearview mirror the entire time. His attack that morning had made him a little shaky, poor darling. More and more anxious, fragile, and therefore a little more jealous of Marshall than usual . . . she felt a tremendous surge of tenderness for her husband. How they loved each other, and had so much to look forward to!

And she told Marshall about the Hôtel Pavillon de la Reine with not the slightest twinge of guilt.

"We're using the name Xarcoil," she said. "X-a-r-c-o-i-l. It was Leonard's idea, it's an anagram for Lacroix."

"He's a sly one," said Marshall. "You tell him I'm polishing up the pinball machine for your return. Soon, I hope. You'll tell him?"

"Sure, I'll tell him."

She was thinking of asking Marshall not to phone them, that she'd call him, herself. It was a bit delicate. She was too embarrassed. Fortunately, he made the first move.

"There, I wrote it down on the little pad. I won't disturb you, but do keep me posted, if you like. I feel a lot better knowing where you are, that's all. I'll memorize the number and throw it away. If you're hiding out for a few days, there's no reason all of Versailles should know about it. No, I'm being mean. It's just that Marie-Thérèse is a little absent-minded sometimes."

Even if Marie had had an iota of remorse about having told Marshall, it was instantly swept away. Dear, dear Marshall. Another surge of tenderness. Completely chaste, of course. She was trying to be honest with herself.

"My dear Marshall . . . it's so wonderful to have a friend like you. Of course, I'll keep you posted. Big kiss."

Marshall remained near the phone, excited and moved by Marie's final words, his nostrils filled with Opium, Marie-Thérèse's perfume. The fragrance stagnated in this corner of the living room, considering the time she spent there. Even the pen smelled of Opium.

However, it wasn't unpleasant, quite the contrary.

He sighed, tore off the page of the note pad, looked at it for several seconds, ripped it into twelve pieces and tossed them into the wastepaper basket.

Then he returned to his statues in the garden. He cleaned their groins and underarms, where, strangely enough—like humans who don't wash—the dirt tended to accumulate.

Michel Zyto left the four-wheel drive at the end of an alley that intersected with Rue Boissy-d'Anglas. It was practically invisible from Rue Boissy-d'Anglas. Then he turned onto Rue du Faubourg-Saint-Honoré, a few yards away. He immediately spotted the café Martimos, across the street from No. 14; large and anonymous, a good place to make a phone call.

He crossed the street and entered the café. The telephone was downstairs.

With luck Marc would be there! He was going to scare him, make him panic. In two minutes, Marc would be ready to accept all of Zyto's conditions, he'd be on his knees. Zyto would tell him: I've got Marie and Leonard, I've got them right where I want them, don't bother trying to find them, it would be a waste of time. And, as you can see, I also know where you are, and I always will. I'm going to arrange a little rendezvous with you, we have some things to discuss, some things to take care of.

But what if he weren't there? If Zyto got Marianne instead? Or if no one was home?

No one was there. He listened to the fairly long message on Marianne's answering machine.

He went upstairs, perplexed. What should he do? He was about to leave the café when he saw Marianne on the sidewalk across the street, exiting from No. 14. He recognized her immediately. She was carrying the sort of large basket one used for groceries.

As soon as she was at a distance, he crossed the street and entered the courtyard of No. 14. He consulted a list of tenants: Marianne Matys, stairway C, sixth floor.

No elevator. He arrived out of breath. Marc Lacroix's lungs weren't as good as his. He listened, holding his ear to the door. Not the slightest sound. He took the ring of keys out of his pocket and began to try them. Every ten seconds, he listened. No noise at all. Then he found it! A long and complicated key that opened the two locks, and an ordinary one for the middle lock.

Still nothing. Besides, Marianne wouldn't have locked the doors if Marc had been there.

Zyto entered, gun in hand, and made sure the apartment was empty. Then he relocked the door and took a look around the small three rooms. There were two bowls in the kitchen sink. Marc? It had to be. Where was he? In Versailles, looking for Zyto? He'd find out as soon as Marianne came back.

He opened the kitchen drawers where the silverware was kept. He was instantly drawn to a knife with a solid handle of natural, varnished wood and a long narrow blade with a nice curve. He nearly cut himself when he tried out the sharpness of the blade with the tip of his finger, though he'd taken pains to be careful. It was a Finnish knife, used to skin seals. A friend of Marianne's, Gérard Demaland—a film director and an aviation enthusiast—had bought it in London (where he'd learn how to pilot a plane in the fog, for an upcoming flight exam) and he had given it to her as a present. Nothing could beat it to cut up meat, roasts, and fowl, the salesman had claimed.

Zyto examined it admiringly. It felt good in his hand.

He went to sit down on the small sofa in the living room.

And he waited.

34

The morning of August 4, Marc was also feeling ill, a half hour after breakfast. He had a burning sensation in his stomach, cramps, and felt like he'd swallowed a brick that would give him no relief until he'd vomited it. It was his gastric juices coming back up, he thought, due to the horrible stress he'd been under; a drop of acid that surges up in the duodenum and sometimes the esophagus. It only took a drop out of the gallons of acid the stomach contains. That was enough.

He lay down for forty-five minutes, immobilized by the urge to vomit, an uncomfortable weight blocked in his chest, halfway up.

Finally he managed to throw up. Afterward, he felt very weak. He drank some herbal tea, rested a while longer, and left for Versailles much later than he'd planned.

The Autobianchi was finely tuned, fast, and pleasant to drive. But Marc missed the Terrano. He would have felt a little less lost and unhappy behind the wheel of his beloved car, at a time when everything mattered to him.

He took the highway to Versailles just as Zyto, Marie, and Leonard were on their way out. If it hadn't been for the vegetation on the median, in full bloom in early August, Marc might have been able to see them.

He raced full speed ahead.

Marianne had practically no cash at her apartment, so she'd left Marc her bank card, just in case. He'd brought along a sandwich made of chicken liver pâté.

Twenty minutes later, he parked the Autobianchi in what was almost a ditch, a fair distance from the intersection where the Chemin du Maréchal-ferrant meets the interminable Rue Martini. And he kept watch for three hours, hoping that his four-wheel drive would pull up. So he could follow it. And have an opportunity to approach Zyto alone, without Leonard and Marie.

The wait seemed endless. Marianne had a radio in her car, but he wasn't in the mood to listen to music.

His stomach left him in peace and he was able to nibble at the sandwich. He took his time, to avoid provoking any more discomfort, but ate it all, down to the last crumb.

After those three hours, figuring he'd done all he could, and having exhausted the plan as a solution, he started up the engine and drove to a phone booth he remembered in the middle of the countryside, far from Rue Martini.

He phoned his home. Maybe Zyto would answer and Marc would find a way to convince him to get it over with immediately. There was no answer. He hung up. He waited a few seconds, during which time he shifted the glasses on his nose. He wasn't used to wearing them—not even sunglasses during the summer months—and they were pinching the bridge of his nose. He tried again. Still no answer.

So he drove back, near the Chemin du Maréchal-ferrant, got out of his car and approached his house on foot. Hiding behind a hedge, he saw that the bathroom window wasn't even open a crack—it was tightly shut, which threw him into a mad rage.

In the summer, Marie never shut this window completely unless they were leaving for vacation.

The bastard! He'd taken them somewhere else!

He drew nearer, closer and closer. The house was definitely empty. He went so far as to take a look in the garage, through the keyhole. His car wasn't there, only Marie's Austin. Where should he look for them now? He had to do something, anything, take some kind of action. He drove off to the phone booth again intending to call Marshall and tell him everything.

On the way there, he had another idea that seemed even better. He knew the nature of the relationship between Marie and Marshall. And what he didn't know, he could guess. Chances were Marie had confided in Marshall. Marshall knew where they were hiding. Perhaps. Marc could reasonably assume so. Therefore, Marianne would call Marshall. I'm a friend of Marie's and Marc's and I can't seem to get a hold of them. Marie has often spoken of you . . . Marshall wouldn't say anything. He would say he didn't know. All right, then. But Marianne could ask him to give them a message—of course, that was in case they happened to call him, she'd say—it would be really kind of him, it was important: he should tell Marie to call Marianne Matys. Marie would call Marianne and Marc would try to speak to Zyto. The bastard was on the run, but he probably wanted to reach Marc as well, he was probably scared to death whenever he thought about the tumor inside his head, which was probably every second!

In the phone booth, the heat was oppressive, even with the door open. The sunglasses were making him hotter. Marc removed them, took a deep breath and put them away in his jacket pocket.

A branch of a hazelnut tree brushed softly against the glass of the booth, like an animal wanting to be petted. The countryside was in full bloom. Every tree, flower, and blade of grass would soon be at its ripest.

Marc dialed Marianne's number. He was going to say he was on his way back, and tell her of his plan.

And he needed to hear her voice.

35

"*I have a friend* named Marie-Thérèse, you know, the one I've already told you about. Anyway, I think she's the only person I know who outdoes you, as far as the telephone is concerned," Marc had once said to Marianne. Marianne had explained to Marc that for an actor, a ringing phone might mean that the greatest director in the world was offering you the greatest part in the world. And that every actor in the world, without exception, thought the same thing when they heard that ringing phone.

Marianne recalled that little conversation as she hurried to open the door.

She entered. She slammed the door shut with her foot, put her red-and-white checkered grocery basket down on the floor, and went into the living room. The red light of her answering machine was blinking: a message. She listened. Nothing, whoever it was hadn't said anything. She sighed. She didn't like those "hang-up calls," they always made her uncomfortable.

She put away the food. It was mostly frozen food, a wide but disparate assortment of crepes, potatoes, peas, corned beef hash—it was enough to wipe out an army, as Marc would say. She had no talent as a cook. The role of housewife was not one in which she excelled.

Some white bread in a package.

A movie magazine, which she brought into the living room.

She dropped onto the sofa with another sigh. She would have liked to call one of her girlfriends. But she couldn't tie up the line, in case Marc tried to phone.

She remained there for a moment without budging, pensive and a bit anxious. But not all that much. Her cheerful nature allowed her to maintain a certain distance, an almost incredulous attitude that anything too terrible could ever happen to her. This disposition, not completely believing in something bad in order to fight against it, had helped her get through the few difficult moments she'd ever had in her life.

Recently, for instance, when a stranger had appeared at her door who was actually her adored lover . . . and when, in the shopping center at Ivry, she'd seen the body of this same lover inhabited by a foreign, enemy soul.

A transfer of psychic energy, by way of a complicated machine, a psycho-computer built by Marc in the course of several years in the basement of his parents' house. Incredible. Marc was truly a genius. She couldn't get her mind off him. She loved him and, on top of it all, when things went back to normal he'd become the most famous man in the world. And she, if he wanted her by his side, the most sought-after actress in the world. There was no reason why not; she was beautiful, she was talented—beauty plus talent plus a few strings pulled was the surefire recipe for a smashing success.

There was no trace of selfish interest in Marianne's reflections. She was simply telling herself positive, encouraging stories. She needed them right now. What a situation! What a shock, when a stranger had appeared at her door who was actually . . .

She shivered.

The biggest shock of her life. Was it, perhaps, the most amazing spectacle that a human being could ever experience? Perhaps. And she'd been the one who'd had to deal with it.

She shouldn't think about it too much. Nor believe in it too much. She shivered again, despite the heat. If only Marc would get back. In whatever form . . .

She reached out for the movie magazine, picked it up and put it back down. She'd just heard a swishing sound, like the rustling of fabric, out there in her small vestibule, next to the bedroom. She tried to curb her increasing panic.

Yes, she had definitely heard something!

Just as she was about to stand up, Marc's tall silhouette loomed in the doorway of the living room. No, not Marc—his body, and his eyes, gleaming with the other man's evil; the same person she'd seen in the shopping center, diabolically playing the part of model father and perfect husband.

And who, obviously, since he was there, had figured the whole thing out, knew everything. Marc had been too optimistic.

"Whatever you do, don't scream," said Zyto abruptly in a curt voice.

Marianne had already taken a deep breath, her mouth open, ready to scream the moment she saw him. And she saw that he was holding Gérard's knife, the Finnish knife that sank into anything like butter.

Suddenly, she was afraid of dying. What did this monster want from her? He was looking at her with such hostility!

And Michel Zyto was indeed looking at her with hostility. The moment he'd laid eyes on her, he'd felt a surge of hatred and jealousy. It had already started in her bedroom, where he'd hidden as soon as he'd heard Marianne come in. The unmade bed, the sheets thrown aside . . . at least Marie made the bed right away. Zyto's imagination had started to run away with itself. Although, after all, he, too, last night . . . if Marianne and Marc . . . Marc had been inside Marianne, wasn't she his as well? He'd had both women!

"What do you want?" Marianne asked, feeling her strength gradually draining away. Her mouth was dry, and her hands trembled.

Zyto was enjoying her terror. It reassured him.

He advanced one step. Again, Marianne kept herself from screaming. What could she do? Scream? He'd be on top of her in a split second. Impossible to get to the telephone. She reviewed even her impossible choices. Throw herself out the window. Knock him out. But how, with what? With the Walkman lying on the coffee table, next to the telephone and the answering machine. Knock him out, that would be best. Knock him out, then tie him up with anything she could find in the apartment. Bind him like a mummy. Wait for Marc. A perfect plan.

She tried to keep thinking positively, and not fall apart completely.

"So, where is he?"

"I don't know," Marianne said in a low voice. "I promise you."

He brought the knife to her face, pressing the blade against her neck.

"Well, I can only promise you that you'd better tell me."

He noticed she was cross-eyed. A tiny bit, very slightly.

"I don't know. All I know is that he's looking for you."

"So you do know. He went to Versailles. And he's going to call you, right? He's going to say to you: 'It's me, darling, it was a dead end, I'm on my way back, we'll think of something else.'"

"Maybe," said Marianne in a conciliatory tone.

"Speaking of 'finding something else,' I must congratulate you for yesterday. A good performance. Nice act."

"So was yours," said Marianne.

She regained courage. A thimble of courage. She tried to show that she wasn't all that frightened. A pitiful attempt. She was faint with fear, that was obvious. And Zyto revelled in it. Making love with Marie had stimulated him terribly. He was like an adolescent who forgets that his first time having sex didn't go all that well, exalted by the fact that he's done it. Fuck a woman one night and terrorize another only hours later. These were great moments for him. Ever since the experiment at Louveciennes, his life was full of great moments. And he'd continue to have them once he became Michel Zyto again, free of the menacing neurinome.

Twice, Marianne had leaned forward to massage her calves out of nervousness, she was cramped with fear. Zyto had noticed her beautiful breasts under the thin, scoop-necked sweater.

Now she was huddled in the corner of the sofa. He was standing in front of her, a few yards away, with a firm grip on the knife. He wanted to see her breasts again.

And he wanted to kill her.

As for Marie, he thought, she would be next. But he still needed Marie, as long as he remained her "husband." And he still needed her body, to penetrate her, to spill his seed inside her. That way he'd be engendering himself. That was how confused he felt about what had transpired between them.

He too, was a good actor, Marianne had said.

"Not bad, eh? You can be sure that I excel at everything I do. All right, well, we're going to wait together. If he calls, please act as if there's nothing wrong. Anyone can get over stage fright, you know that."

Marianne realized that this maniac wasn't really thinking about what he was saying; his mind was elsewhere, she could see it in his eyes, and her fear was back, as violent and paralyzing as when he'd first walked into the room.

"Please go," she said. "Marc isn't going to call. He's on his way, he'll be here any minute."

"All the better," said Zyto. "It'll make things even simpler."

He advanced toward her, the knife held out in front of him. His movements were slow, as if he were being cautious. With his left hand, he pulled down the neckline of the sweater, so he could get a better look at her breasts.

It wasn't very practical.

"No! Leave me alone," Marianne moaned. "Marc will be here soon. You're not acting in your own interest, what you're doing here. You're acting against yourself. Marc doesn't want to hurt you. He'll accept whatever arrangements you want to make, but don't spoil everything now. Either go, or wait for him quietly, I swear everything's going to be all right, you won't be sorry. You both want the same thing, you and he, and under these circumstances, it's not worth..."

She was panting nervously for breath. She couldn't go on, but Zyto interrupted her anyway. She knew that something had clicked in his mind, something that would be difficult to stop. But what? Did he simply want to scare her, see her naked? Still, he wasn't crazy enough to...

Or maybe he was.

She was fighting, fighting off the panic again.

"Take off your clothes," he ordered, taking a step backward. "Don't keep me waiting."

He didn't even try to reassure her. Because he didn't really mean any harm? Or was it because at this point...

She shook her head. He leaned over, brought the knife to her neck, against her throat. He only meant to apply pressure, but the blade was so sharp it broke through the skin. He withdrew it immediately. A drop of blood appeared. Marianne touched her neck, her eyes wide in horror. What else could she do but obey, hoping that he wouldn't go too far, that Marc would call, that the ordeal would soon be over, otherwise she'd go mad!

"It's either yes, or I cut your throat. What'll it be?"

"Yes," she said, in one breath.

She took off her sweater, revealing her magnificent breasts—perfect and imperfect—and her belly, firm and flat despite her position.

Zyto was mesmerized and uncomfortable, an annoying sense of embarrassment made him even more bad-tempered.

"So what was it like, last night, rubbing up against my body? Against the body of a mental patient?"

"Nothing happened. We didn't do anything last night. It doesn't make any sense, what you're saying. Why don't you go now and leave me alone!"

She recalled what Marc had explained to her the night before, that Michel Zyto was incapable of having sex with a woman, and for that very reason (Marc had elaborated with complicated explanations but she'd been half asleep), Zyto was not a true murderer.

There was no connection to those frequent cases where the murder replaces the sexual act.

"I don't believe you," he said. "Take off your clothes. All of them."

She got undressed. Without standing up, she unbuttoned her jeans, and pulled them down. She had a hard time getting them past the obstacle of her ample bottom. Suddenly the fabric slid down, uncovering her knees. Her jeans were piled around her ankles, where she left them. She was whimpering, tears trickling down her nose.

Zyto was fascinated by her legs, sharply defined and smooth, as if they'd escaped the chaos of the wrinkled jeans. And fascinated by her lower abdomen, it was the first time he'd seen a blond crotch, and with so much hair—a nice, bushy triangle, there was even hair after the fold of her groin and a tiny bit on her thighs. What a difference with Marie! Everything was different, her skin was so fair, so white; her shape, everything.

Marianne had to sniff back her tears to speak.

"Please, leave me alone now, either go or stop scaring me with that knife! This is stupid, you're wrong, I swear to you that you've got it all wrong!"

Wrong? Why wrong? Well, maybe he was, but why, exactly? Now what would happen if . . . he tried to think. But all attempts to reason instantly disintegrated.

He leaned over. With his left hand, he touched her belly. He wanted to do to Marianne what he'd done to Marie, slide his fingers through her pubic hair, move it aside, find the tender folds. But her legs were tightly clamped together. He straightened up again. He was ready to strike her. He held back. He wanted to caress her better. And hate her even more.

And, to hate her even more, he wanted to penetrate her as well. He hadn't yet admitted it to himself, but deep down that's what he desired, penetrate her and then kill her. He repeated, in a sharper tone: "Take off all your clothes."

Marianne got up from the sofa and stood on her feet. She managed to pull her left leg out of her pants. Then the right. She stumbled, and to keep her balance, she put her hand on the coffee table, on the Walkman. Zyto was staring at her breasts. They hardly moved, or only very slightly in spite of Marianne's movements, and were pointed downwards, so that in between the cleavage, in the background, he could see the tuft of hair whose softness he had touched only a moment ago.

"You know, last night Marie and I . . . our friend has a really charming wife, and very beautiful. Don't tell him, but I fucked her. Marc would have a hard time believing it, but it's true."

He spoke without thinking, driven by the need to boast, to valorize himself in Marianne's eyes, and compensate for how much he feared her.

He had spoken the truth however. And Marianne believed him. Still hunched over, she glanced up at him and realized she was doomed. If Marc had been correct in his explanations, then she was surely doomed.

Sharp corners made of plastic could hurt someone a lot. She would hit him in the temple with the corner of the Walkman. She'd take him by surprise. Her instinct for survival helped draw her out of the terror, gave her the courage to act.

Her jeans were now off. Her fingers gripped the Walkman.

Suddenly, as if she'd received an electric shock, her strength renewed and tripled by the realization that her life was at stake, she stood up, her right arm a slight distance from her body, spun around on her left foot and brought the corner of the Walkman down on Michel Zyto's left temple.

Zyto, surprised indeed, initially barely moved his head. But enough so that the Walkman slipped out of her hand. The impact was violent, the cover smashed to pieces, but Zyto wasn't hurt.

And, out of reflex, in a move to counter Marianne's, he stabbed her in the hip, sinking the knife all the way in.

Marianne could feel she'd been wounded. It didn't really hurt. She renounced trying to defend herself. It was hopeless. She'd be risking a more serious injury, she told herself, for she thought her wound was superficial. Something gave way inside her, something abandoned her, perhaps it was partly her power to reason. And she saw that the wound was bleeding, that she was bleeding profusely. She was seized with a violent trembling from head to foot. She looked Zyto straight in the eyes, her arms crossed defensively over her chest, and said in a hoarse voice, broken by terrible sobs: "No, Marc, no . . . you're not going to kill me Marc, not you, I love you too much. . . ."

He did not respond. He stabbed her in the belly, three times. Then, as she was about to scream, he threw his left hand over her mouth, clamping it down over her nose, her upper lip, and a portion of her cheek, and he pulled her toward him, forcing Marianne forward to literally tumble into his arms.

At the same time, he drove the knife into her heart.

The blade plunged all the way into the skin underneath her breast, up to the handle.

He immediately withdrew the knife in a quick, decisive gesture, and pushed Marianne back onto the sofa. She fell backward, her arms crossed, legs spread, in a position of languid repose. But her eyes had rolled upward, and her mouth was contorted in pain.

Zyto was panting. He stared at her. He caught his breath.

Now blood was gushing from the wounds, you could see it, you could hear the sound.

Marianne was dead.

He quickly took another look to make sure, but he knew he'd killed her; he knew she was dead, there was no doubt about it.

He was flooded with joy and exaltation. He had just taken another step in his rebirth.

Outwardly, he appeared very calm. He threw down the knife, next to the body. He inspected himself. Not a drop of blood on him, she hadn't even stained his clothes. Except for his hands, he had a little blood on his hands. He went to wash them in the kitchen and came back. He pulled at his jacket, trying to smooth out the wrinkles, but wrinkles in a linen suit didn't disappear that easily.

It was only then that he noticed he had an almost painful erection. Would he have been capable of penetrating Marianne before killing her? He'd resented her for the aggressive move she'd made with that ridiculous Walkman, which had precipitated the whole thing. He wasn't sure. He thought he probably could have.

He examined the body. The blood was trickling out slower

now. Marianne's belly was bathed in blood, completely red, as if it were painted.

Zyto felt no revulsion whatsoever. He'd done what he'd had to, and its calming effect overpowered all the rest. He knew nothing of disgust or remorse.

He still had a little work to do.

He knew all about fingerprints. Using a damp sponge, he wiped down several objects and surfaces that might have had "Zyto's" fingerprints on them. He worked with the keen, meticulous care he was capable of under certain circumstances.

His erection persisted. He was hungry.

He sat down across from the body and waited for Marc. A phone call, or his arrival. Obviously, a phone call would be preferable. If Marc turned up and saw that Marianne was dead, they'd start fighting like cats and dogs again. He could picture it. Zyto would have the advantage. He'd bring Marc to Louveciennes holding a gun to his ribs. He felt strong—master of the universe—the way things were progressing.

A few minutes passed, and the telephone rang.

After two rings, the answering machine clicked on. There was a silence, the time it took for Marianne's message to play, then a beep, and then Marc's voice came on. Michel Zyto's voice.

"Marianne darling," said Marc, "I'm on my way back, I didn't . . ."

At which point Zyto picked up the receiver and interrupted him:

"Michel, darling, it's not Marianne; it's me, Marc," he said calmly, with only a hint of irony in his voice.

36

The sun beat down on the phone booth on Rue Martini.

Marc, already drenched with sweat, felt his moral strength evaporating when he heard *his* voice on the line.

"Where's Marianne?" he asked, in a voice that was neither his nor Michel Zyto's, a voice that he didn't recognize.

Zyto answered him, calmly as ever: "If you ask me, she's probably out shopping. I saw her leaving just when I arrived, a minute ago. So I took advantage of it, thought it was a good opportunity to come upstairs."

It was possible. Marianne had told Marc she'd buy some groceries and make him a nice lunch.

"Why are you there?"

"I was looking for you. Don't think it was her fault, she was wonderful, yesterday, at the shopping mall. But I'm clever. You've often told me so yourself. Your wife is pretty clever too."

So that was it, Marie had confided her suspicions to him! Marc could hardly believe it, and yet . . . he didn't understand. He was becoming increasingly overwhelmed.

"What did you tell her?"

"I reassured her: 'No, Marianne and I are not having an affair.' "

The bastard!

Marc's thoughts raced. It was urgent to get Zyto away from Marianne's apartment. God knows what would happen if Marianne were to come home right then. The mere shock of opening the door and . . . It was also urgent to keep Zyto from going back to Marie and Leonard. Since he was at Marianne's, he might as well take advantage of the situation. At least Marc could talk to him.

"I've been looking for you, too. Let's see each other right away. We can't go on like this, you realize that. I'll give you all the guarantees you want. I'll help you get away, if that's what you want; I'll help you in any way possible, you have nothing to fear, no punishment, it'll be like it was before, as if nothing had happened. I swear to you. I'll even hide you, if I have to. Please, let's arrange a meeting place, right away!"

"All right," said Zyto.

Get back into his own body. Escape that "acoustical neurinome." It was hard to go on like this, Marc was right. Now was a good time. Before Marc found out that Marianne was dead.

"What about Louveciennes?" asked Marc. "Would you know how to find your way back?"

"No," Zyto said sharply.

"No what? You wouldn't be able to find it?"

"It's not that . . . no, not Louveciennes.

"Why not?"

"I'd prefer Paris. In the heart of the city. We could talk and then go there together. I could make sure that you're not trying to set me up. And I don't have the strength to go to Louveciennes all alone. I want us to go there together, when I'm certain that . . ."

A good actor.

Marc was seething with impatience and suppressed rage.

"You don't trust me?"

"Sure I do, but I'd rather do it this way."

Marc controlled himself. He couldn't afford to spoil this opportunity. Or make the slightest blunder.

And furthermore, he completely understood Zyto's point.

"Whatever you say," he replied. "It's a waste of time. But whatever you say. Where?"

Zyto didn't know what to answer. Paradoxically, he was waiting for Marc to take the situation in hand. Marc immediately perceived this.

"Listen, how about Rue de Médicis, in front of a medical bookstore called Epicure, I think it's number five. It's the street that runs from Rue de Vaugirard to Place Edmond-Rostand, across from the Luxembourg Gardens. You'll find it. Epicure."

"What kind of cure?" Zyto asked somewhat childishly.

"No, Epicure, one word, Epicure, E-p-i-c-u-r-e."

Jean Fine, the bookseller—a former doctor who no longer practiced—was rather droll, and would have been even more amusing if he didn't think himself the funniest man in the world. All his customers were subjected to his puns. Marc didn't much care for him, but his medical bookstore was by far the best in Paris.

Epicure.

"Why there?" Zyto asked, suddenly aggressive. "Are you thinking of turning up with an army of cops and nurses?"

"Don't be ridiculous. The simplest place would be Louveciennes, but you don't agree. So, tell me where. I'm suggesting we meet there just because I know it well, it happened to come to mind, and, also, believe it or not, to reassure you. There's a phone booth about fifteen yards from the bookstore. Thirty yards. I'll park in front of it, in a pink Autobianchi. You'll get there before I will. You can take down the phone number of the booth and call me from the other end of Paris, if you're uneasy about it, but I promise you . . ."

"An Autobianchi?"

"Marianne's car."

Zyto now understood. Marc and Marianne had done a good job trying to fool him the night before.

"Oh! Well done! Bravo!"

Marc didn't catch the irony. He was feverish with impatience.

"I'll wait for you, either you'll show up, or you'll call. If you're the least bit worried, I swear to you that you needn't be—you can change your mind and phone me, fix a meeting place somewhere else, whatever you like. Is that OK with you?"

Zyto was drinking in Marc's words. He had become attentive, docile, childlike again, a mere toy in the skilled and benevolent hands of Dr. Lacroix. It was both pleasant and annoying. And troubling, in the sense that he heard his own voice on the phone, or he was talking to himself. . . .

"All right," he said.

"You won't regret it, I assure you. Leave the apartment right now. I'm going to hurry as well. You won't have to wait for long. See you later?"

"See you later," said Zyto.

They hung up, Marc first.

While he was on the phone, Zyto had nearly forgotten about Marianne's body, still lying next to him.

She was no longer bleeding. Her left arm, which had fallen to the edge of the sofa's armrest during the scuffle, suddenly flopped back next to her thigh. The entire body's equilibrium had changed. Her head leaned more to the left, tugging at her torso, which gradually slid downward. Her body weight continued to pull the inert mass of flesh, and Marianne gently rolled from the narrow sofa onto the floor. Then she was still, lying flat on her stomach, her face against the carpet.

Zyto had observed the macabre fall without being affected by it. He simply told himself, with a sneer, that she wouldn't get any farther than that. He was indifferent to the sight of death and agony. He had been present when his Uncle Nicolas had been in his final struggle against death, gone in the space of a few hours due to an internal hemorrhage resulting from an undetected stomach cancer. Even the young doctor at his bedside had averted his gaze during the final spasm of death. Not Michel Zyto. He had watched the blood violently spurt from his uncle's closed mouth, his eyes fixed in a glassy stare. It hadn't disturbed Zyto a bit.

He had told Marc about this scene many times. And also about a simple dream, obvious in terms of its connection to his fear of women: He'd enter a room in which there was a naked woman, her back to him, tied up and blindfolded, her arms in a V above her head (thus arms that were non-threatening, and wouldn't be able to keep him from doing what he wanted), her legs spread open as widely as possible. Her wrists, ankles, and neck were tied with leather straps to a big board (yes, it was a board), tilted back and mobile if he so desired, through a system of pulleys. He didn't hurt her. She wasn't asleep or drugged; she merely couldn't move, nor could she see. He would touch her, caress her. He wasn't frightened or ashamed. He'd be about to take his clothes off, actually he would only pull down his pants so he could get dressed again quickly in case some threat arose. And he'd imagine what would happen next, how he would lie down on top of her, penetrate her. The dream would end there.

Marc had asked him one day if he ever saw himself, in dreams or daydreams, making love to a dead woman. No. He had answered, no, he never thought about that.

These memories came back to him at the sight of Marianne, stretched out on her stomach, her straggly hair hiding her face.

He telephoned Marie (who had just come back from lunch with Leonard) to explain his absence, longer than planned. He spoke to her in a casual tone. And he left. He had nothing more to do there. Putting his hand on the doorknob, he said to himself that he could leave all the fingerprints he liked. They would be his . . . nothing to fear as far as the law was concerned.

Except if Marc turned him in, he thought, shutting the door.

For after the experiment, Marc would definitely inform the police. As soon as he found out that Marianne was dead, Marc would be bent on destroying him.

Therefore, he would have to kill Marc.

As long as he'd remained inside the apartment, giddy with exhilaration from what he'd done, Zyto had felt as if he were enjoying a kind of impunity, that he was omnipotent in his actions, that nothing mattered. As soon as he'd turned the key twice in the second lock, however, the consequences of his act appeared before him in all clarity.

He'd have to kill Marc.

He no longer had any choice. First, he'd have to go back into that complicated, humming machine at Louveciennes before Marc had the slightest suspicion, and then do away with him. And make the crime look like a suicide. That should be possible. He'd already thought of it. A suicide.

Besides, the gun he was carrying was Marc's.

37

In the Nissan Terrano, he shakily consulted a map of Paris, the old one, the one that was all torn and wrinkled.

He nearly had an accident at Place de la Concorde, at the last light before the bridge; he'd been so lost in thought he hadn't even seen it turn red. A car grazed his fender. The driver honked, and continued his angry honking for a good distance down the road.

Within fifteen minutes, Michel Zyto had gone from total elation to one of the worst states of agitation he'd ever known. Now he felt guilty concerning Marc, terribly guilty. Because of Marianne. And Marie. How could he face Dr. Lacroix now? And the idea of Marc being dead, far from comforting him, gave rise to an unexpected conflict: he had to kill Marc, but without Marc, everything lost its meaning. He had to get rid of him, and yet he needed him to summon up the very strength to get rid of him. This vicious cycle of reasoning was being provoked by his anxiety. Deep down, he wanted to tell Marc that he'd slept with Marie, that he'd killed Marianne, and that he'd kill other women—Marie if possible—but then Marc would go crazy and turn against him. He needed Marc's protection, and needed to protect himself from Marc. That was it, he had to protect himself from the person who protected him; it was insoluable, inextricable, a situation that stopped his breath. There was one solution—to kill Marc—but the other solution was not to kill him!

Driving down Rue de Vaugirard, Zyto also began to dread Marc's cleverness. Wouldn't Dr. Lacroix realize at first glance that something was wrong, seriously wrong?

Zyto tried to think of a means of abusing him, at least to maintain control over the situation if Marc were to become too suspicious and get nervous. He looked at the map again. Instead of taking Rue de Médici, he turned back, drove around the Luxembourg Gardens by way of Rue Guynemer and Rue Auguste-Compte, then parked on Avenue de l'Observatoire.

He had never set foot in the Luxembourg Gardens before.

He entered at Place André-Honnorat. The park was crowded, a lot of elderly people, a lot of children with their mothers or their baby-sitters, people walking dogs, young girls, probably students, who were reading on benches, discretely sunning their legs. A few "skirt chasers"; they were easy to spot.

Zyto was convinced that at least two young women, one quite young, were glancing at him with interest, which reminded him that he had a handsome face and an elegant build and was wearing an expensive suit. He looked at them as well. He could have spoken to them; they certainly wouldn't have rebuffed him, he thought with some satisfaction.

He walked across the length of the garden until he reached the iron gate that ran alongside Rue de Médici. He had no difficulty locating the bookstore, Epicure. And the phone booth.

What kind of cure?! Marc must have been mocking him.

He didn't have to wait very long. Marc was a good driver, as Zyto knew. A pink Autobianchi slowed down and parked next to the sidewalk directly across from the phone booth. He saw Marc inside, he recognized *himself* despite the slight shock—actually not terribly surprising—of new clothes, his hair slicked back, dark glasses, and a shaved mustache. It was what he would have done himself.

Marc got out of the Autobianchi, attentively scanned Rue de Médici, looking in both directions, then sat back down in the car. Zyto should have been there by now. Would he telephone? Not likely. Marc had spoken in all sincerity, and he anticipated, intuitively sensed that Zyto trusted him. As always.

A few seconds later, he heard a whistle, a loud, shrill, high-pitched whistle, the kind made with two fingers stuck in one's mouth. And that you don't often hear on Rue de Médici, but rather in certain neighborhoods when a pretty girl passes in front of a café full of men. Marc didn't pay any particular attention to it, he was too busy watching the sidewalk across the way and the street behind him, using the rearview mirror, constantly shifting his gaze. But when another whistle shrilled, he turned his head in the direction of the Luxembourg Gardens.

The sidewalk was deserted.

No, there was someone behind the iron gate. It was Michel Zyto, his arm upraised, gesturing to him.

Marc Lacroix suffered the shock of seeing himself once again. The gate, that hand-waving of the "other," here, outdoors, in the heart of Paris . . . it made it even spookier, as if he were seeing his ghost beckoning to him, his own death trying to draw him nearer.

He got out of the car and crossed the street, dreading a catastrophe. Why was Zyto standing there? He was about three yards from the gate, frozen in place, his face distorted with grief. Marc fought to stave off the wave of disastrous hypotheses. He approached, took off his sunglasses, and made a vague gesture toward the park.

"What are you doing there?"

Zyto thought Marc was playing his role as "Michel Zyto on the run" quite well, that he was goddamn resourceful. He was secretly annoyed, and even a little unhappy. He would have preferred the meeting of two grumbling derelicts.

"Just taking precautions," he said. "I didn't want to waste time calling you to arrange a meeting somewhere else, but I wanted to be sure . . ."

"Sure of what? That I'd come alone?"

"Yes."

"You knew very well I'd be alone."

"I don't trust you. I'm scared." His voice quavered. "I had an attack this morning, I vomited twice. I was scared it was getting worse, I was really scared. Did that ever happen to you, did you vomit? But really hard? I'm just as much in a rush to get this thing over with as you are!"

This was Michel Zyto's ruse, to shift the blame onto his hypochondria: Marc would see he wasn't in terribly good shape because of that morning, from the vomiting. If Marc bought it, he'd want to take advantage of Zyto's state, his frame of mind. Even if he phoned Marianne, he'd figure she wasn't back yet, that she'd be back any minute, and he'd have only one thing on his mind, to race over to Louveciennes with Zyto, obsessed and excited that the agony was almost at an end.

And if he didn't buy it, well! Zyto could easily get away, thanks to the iron bars between them. He'd return to the hotel and think of something. It wouldn't be so bad. And he could still be Marc Lacroix for a while, a desire he hadn't yet admitted to himself.

The ruse nearly succeeded. That Zyto would be capable, under such extraordinary circumstances, of complaining to Marc and would seek to be reassured was so astounding and yet so typical of him, that Marc was nearly taken in by it and, in fact, he almost felt like reassuring Zyto. But not quite. Marc was wary, he knew Zyto all too well.

Two things alarmed him. First of all, Zyto had remained at a fair distance from the bars to talk to him, on the defensive. If he was scared at this moment, it was Marc he was scared of, Marc in particular. Why, and to what extent? Secondly, Marc knew the different ways Zyto manifested psychological stress, according to whether he was suffering from hypochondria or guilt. In his present state a medical student could readily observe the clinical difference between anxiety and anguish. In the first instance, Zyto was nervous, agitated, his voice more high-pitched than usual, and he did not avoid

Marc's eye; on the contrary, he scrutinized him, as if seeking protection there, or a confirmation of his fears. In the second instance, he was overwhelmed. His voice was muted, he constantly averted his gaze.

And this was now the case. Marc was certain of it, even if he had to determine this by reading *his* face, gauging his own voice. Zyto had done something bad. Something really stupid. And therefore, he was inevitably contemplating similar things. He wasn't about to meekly consent to the plan, allow himself to be shut away in Stéphen-Mornay after stopping off at the house in Louveciennes.

To which the bastard had the keys . . .

This time, the wave of hypotheses came crashing down on Marc. Marianne? Yes, it was probably Marianne. How could he find out?

By holding out a little longer, acting his part. Calmly setting down reasonable terms—the same ones he'd already been using—then observing Zyto's reaction.

"Listen, don't get ridiculous over your little physical problems. Soon you won't have anything to worry about. As for the rest, you know very well you can trust me. Come on, you know it. I don't want to have go over all that again. You're going to tell me where Marie and Leonard are. You're going to call them. I'll listen along with you, so I can hear their voices. That's all I ask of you." Then he came out with what he'd been preparing, as nonchalantly as possible. "First I have to reach Marianne, otherwise she'll be worried and she might notify the police. Then we'll go to Louveciennes, and then, as I promised you, everything will work out fine for you. We'll do it however you like. I promised you, and you can count on it."

At the mention of Marianne, Zyto had paled. He was tense. He remained silent. Marc couldn't catch his eye. It was disconcerting to see *his* body express so much confusion, it was painful to him. And he couldn't bring himself to ask the dreaded question.

Marc made up his mind. He asked it gently—or rather he formulated an affirmative question, to force a confession: "Did you kill Marianne?"

Michel Zyto finally looked at him, with an expression of infinite distress.

Marc felt as if he were going mad.

"I didn't do it on purpose. I took out a knife, but only to scare her, so she'd tell me where you were, but she got scared, she tried to defend herself, she shouldn't have, there was a moment where she thought I was attacking her, but I wasn't, it was only to scare her, she's the one that threw herself onto the knife, it's a dangerous knife, that I found in her kitchen, I'm sure you know which one, she threw herself on it, I swear to you, the blade just . . . it did it all by itself, I swear to you that I didn't mean to kill her!"

Marc listened, the wind knocked out of him. He could no longer control his breathing, he was gasping hoarsely.

"Are you totally positive she's dead?"

Zyto hung his head.

At which point Marc charged against the iron bars, his arm outstretched. He wanted to grab Zyto by the throat and throttle him. At that moment, he could have strangled him.

Zyto was too far away, and he stepped back even further. Marc persisted, he panted and growled like an animal, bruising his face against the bars, as his hand opened and closed in the empty air.

He felt as though he were in front of a mirror, fighting against a disobedient reflection.

Zyto was angry and filled with hatred. Abruptly, he said to Marc, with cruel, brutal, and unexpected sarcasm:

"Calm down, Michel Zyto. You escaped from a mental institution. This morning, you killed my friend, Marianne. And now you're throwing a mad fit right here in public. Please, you must calm down."

Marc let his arm fall to his side. His face still pressed against the bars, he began to cry, a few tearless sobs, his chest painfully heaving.

Then he did, in fact, calm down, as Zyto had asked, or seemed to have calmed down. He straightened up, looked at Zyto for two seconds with total indifference, turned around, and hastily strode away.

Now it was Zyto's turn to throw himself against the bars, his arm outstretched in desperation:

"Wait!" he shouted.

But the real Dr. Lacroix got into the Autobianchi and started up the engine, paying no further attention to him.

There was hardly anyone in the street, and nobody had noticed anything at all.

38

He sped toward Pigalle, driving somewhat recklessly, against his better judgement.

He pulled up in front of the huge Crédit Lyonnais Bank, on Boulevard des Italiens, and withdrew six thousand francs from the automatic teller using Marianne's bank card.

Before setting out again, he removed the bandage from his neck and, leaving the car door slightly ajar, discreetly threw it into the gutter. He wouldn't need it anymore.

On Boulevard de Clichy, he bought a map of Paris and asked the shopkeeper if he'd ever heard of the café Le Terminus: yes, it wasn't far, it was near Place Blanche, if he took Rue Gewels there'd be an alley to the right, a pharmacy on the corner, and the café was at the end of the alley.

Marc parked right in the alley.

The green-walled café was ugly, clean, and narrow—a long corridor with a bar counter at the far end, off in the distance.

Every single seat was taken.

Would "Little Rat," the man Zyto had told him about, be there?

Marc advanced slowly, as the rows of male faces checked him out. Several yards away, a man threw down two ten franc pieces on the table, then stood up. He had a long, straight, scraggly mustache that stuck out on each side, like the whiskers of a cat or a rat. His eyes were so small that they looked abnormal. Was that him?

The man walked up to Marc. They exchanged glances.

"Do you recognize me?" Marc asked in a low voice.

Placing his thumb and index fingers together under his nose, he then spread them apart as he smoothed down his mustache, making it clear that he'd recognized Marc, even without his mustache.

Little Rat had a good eye.

"I'm here for the same thing," Marc said, taking a chance.

"Exactly the same?"

Marc figured he must be referring to the type of gun Zyto had chosen the first time.

"Yes, exactly the same."

"Wait here for me a second."

This so-called Little Rat was skinny, dressed in heavy clothing that made you sweat just from looking at him. He walked off toward the bar. He picked up the phone.

Marc, who had remained standing, suddenly felt sharp pains in his stomach. He raised his hand to his mouth, then mopped his dripping forehead. Fortunately, he didn't have to wait very long; Little Rat was already back and said to him:

"In a half hour. Serge Martic, 31A Rue Véron, fourth floor, door on the right."

"I remember," said Marc, who didn't even know where Rue Véron was.

Little Rat brought his hand to his forehead in a kind of military salute, and left the café without another word, on his way to some unknown destination.

Marc looked at his watch, Zyto's horrible watch. He needed to rest somewhere. He could barely stand on his feet anymore. He headed toward the empty seat Little Rat had just vacated. He was in another world, he was thinking about things—Marianne, all that had happened—as if he were in a fog.

He sat down at the table, across from a woman. He murmured: "May I?," glancing at her. He recognized the young woman from the night before, he'd passed her on the steps of the metro at Place d'Italie, when he was running away. It was her, no doubt about it.

"Go right ahead," she said in a soft, even, pleasant voice.

"Thank you," said Marc, taking the map out of his pocket.

Rue Véron was close by, the third street on the right, off Rue Lépic. Marc sat back in his chair and wiped his forehead again.

There was a lingering scent of cheap soap in the café.

He ordered an herbal tea, verbena-mint.

"Are you all right?" his neighbor asked him in a simple, straightforward tone.

Marc took a better look at her; her lovely almond-shaped dark eyes, and finely sculpted lips and nostrils. Her poignant face was as perfect as a portrait, a painting from one of the old masters, and the disheveled mass of chestnut-colored hair added to her splendid presence.

Like the night before, she was wearing a thin black leather jacket over a white shirt and a pair of pants.

She was drinking tea. Was she, by chance, at Little Rat's table simply because there hadn't been any other empty seats?

Marc was about to reply when the waiter brought over his mint tea. Marc waited until he'd gone.

"No. But I do feel better, thanks," he said, surprised to hear his voice sound so natural.

He began by taking little spoonfuls, his back hunched over, frowning slightly from the pain.

"I passed you yesterday in the metro at Place d'Italie, I remember you quite well," she said.

"Yes, you're right," said Marc. "I remember you too."

At first, he felt as if he were being dragged into a conversation that he didn't wanting to be having. But in the end, he allowed himself to relax a bit; this stranger was a distraction from his grotesque problems. He was struck by her hair. It formed a halo around her face, like a dark sun, and it was extremely tangled, impossibly tangled, so it seemed, but the overall effect was somewhat artistic. At certain moments it looked like countless brushstrokes in the same color family, touched up by a meticulous painter.

Marc sipped his tea trying not to make slurping noises, something that had always horrified him when he was a child. He had told Vérapoutsimila about it the first day of his analysis, in that first session, such a long time ago. Twelve years? Fifteen? Breakfast, during the summer, on vacation, the café au lait in which his parents, despite their breeding, had dipped their bread and their noses, creating a racket of sucking and gargling noises. Unbearable. As an adult, Marc had made a serious effort to eat in silence.

"My name is Katarina," said his neighbor, pouring what was left of the tea from her pot, two fingers of reddish liquid.

Why was she telling him her name? Was she a prostitute? He was sure she wasn't.

"Do you know what that means in Greek?" he asked.

" 'The purest', isn't that it?" she said with a bright, fleeting smile. "And you, what's your name?"

Was she trying to pick him up? No, not her, not like that, in this café, and this neighborhood. And not him. Well, not Michel Zyto. She had some free time, she liked talking to people, she was just making conversation, nothing more.

But still, what was a person with such refined looks, manners, and language doing in a place like this?

"My name? I'm not really sure . . ."

"Excuse me for being indiscreet. And naive. In my opinion, a third of the people here have something to hide. A secret. Maybe you're one of them. I know I am."

She smiled again. She inspired trust. Marc would have liked to tell her everything, talk about Marianne, Michel Zyto, Marie, and Leonard. About his moral anguish. She continued: "In a way, I don't know either, I'm not really sure myself. I'll be leaving Paris for three weeks under an assumed name and false papers. That's my secret. I'm leaving tonight. I can tell you, it doesn't really matter. Unless you're a cop."

So she, too, had come to see Little Rat. Without a doubt. Him, or someone else.

"No, it doesn't really matter. And I'm not a cop."

She finished her cup of tea.

"Would you like something else?" he asked.

"No, thank you."

The desire to reveal his own secret, without compromising himself, had become irresistible.

"I'm sort of in the same situation myself, but more complicated. I can't tell you everything. But I can tell you the most important part. You're going to think I'm crazy. Oh well." He lowered his voice and leaned toward her. "I'm not in my body, my real body. I'm in someone else's body. And this someone else is in my body, somewhere else." He sat up straight again. "So there you have it. Do you think I'm crazy?"

It was impossible to tell what Katarina, the purest, actually thought. She looked at him in exactly the same way as before, without surprise or disbelief.

"No," she said.

"Do you believe me?"

"I can't imagine why you'd lie to me."

Marc told himself that she, of course, didn't believe him. Being kind, she wasn't going to antagonize some poor lunatic who happened to cross paths with her.

All of a sudden, he couldn't wait to get out of there. He looked at his watch again, twenty minutes had gone by. He paid for his tea. He offered to pay for Katarina's, but it had already been taken care of. She thanked him.

"I have to go now," he said, getting to his feet. "Thanks for listening to me. I hope everything works out for you."

"And I hope everything works out for you, too."

She said nothing more, asked nothing more. The conversation was over. They nodded to each other, and Marc left the café, a bit embarrassed that she could see the spot on the nape of his neck, shaved by Dr. Antoine Fabricant.

39

On Rue Véron, a calm, deserted little street, he immediately felt far from the commotion of the city, even though Boulevard de Clichy was close by.

Marc rang Serge Martic's doorbell. A half hour, right down to the minute, had elapsed since Little Rat's phone call. Serge Martic opened the door. He looked foreign, Slavic, in his seventies at least. He was short with broad shoulders, a sort of natural honesty and kindness engrained on his face, Marc mused. His imperceptible smile—a slight stretching of the left corner of his mouth—very expressive nonetheless, seemed to indicate that he'd recognized Marc.

"Come in," he said.

He closed the door and led Marc down a hallway entirely covered with thick, burgundy carpeting—the floors, the wall, and the ceiling. At the end of the hallway, he ushered him into a tiny room with barely any furniture, clean and anonymous, like a doctor's waiting room.

He left him there alone.

Marc glanced out the window. He hadn't expected such a beautiful, panoramic view of Paris. He sat down, but stood up again right away: Martic was back with a big plastic bag out of which he withdrew a heavy cardboard box, and from the box, a leather case, and from the case, a small revolver.

"A Colt .38," he said. "A gem. It's practically new. I'm throwing in the case and six extra bullets."

The gun had an unfinished look about it, since it had a very short barrel and a normal-sized handle. Martic put everything back into the bag.

"Perfect," said Marc. "How much do I owe you?"

"A little more. Five thousand francs. It's not the kind of item that loses its value."

He held out the bag and pocketed ten five-hundred franc notes.

"Thanks," he said.

"Thank you," said Marc.

Marc didn't look as if he were preparing to leave.

"Something else?" he asked very gently.

"Yes," said Marc. He managed a wan smile. "Exactly the same thing as last time."

"Wait here a minute," said Serge Martic very matter-of-factly.

He left, then returned almost immediately.

"The room is free, but only until tomorrow, early afternoon."

"That'll be fine," Marc said. "Rue Piat . . ."

"Number 51."

"Right, 51."

It was completely silent as they walked down the hallway. And you couldn't see anything of Martic's apartment. All of the four doors were closed. The front door was rigged with an impressive armor-plated security lock.

* * *

After studying the map, Marc returned to Boulevard de Clichy, taking it all the way to Boulevard de Magenta, where he veered off to the right. He reached Place de la République. On Rue du Faubourg du Temple, he bought two takeout sandwiches in a supermarket, two boxes of fig bars, two cans of beer, some disposable razors, and shaving cream. Then he continued straight ahead on Rue de Belleville.

Rue Piat, the sixth street on the right off Rue de Belleville (Marc had been repeating it to himself every thirty seconds during the drive), sloped uphill for a short distance, then descended. No. 51 was on the right, just after the crest of the hill. It was the perfect location for a "hide-out," since you could see everything without being seen. No buildings around—a depot, a few garages, and several other houses, but they were all a fair distance away.

Marc pushed open the wooden gate to a little garden surrounding a newly renovated small one-story house. It was sort of fancy yet sinister-looking, with a red roof, green shutters, and flowerbeds on each side.

He rang the doorbell. The door flew open immediately, as if the man had been waiting behind it. This so-called Jacquot was one of those bald men who shave their entire head, the temples, and the nape of the neck as well, to triumph over their baldness, to have the last word, suggesting to others that they had, in a certain sense, chosen their own fate. Indeed, this character was not lacking in style, he had a real "mug," a strong, well-defined nose, and big black eyes that apparently never blinked.

He reached out to shake Marc's hand, and said: "Garage?"

"No," said Marc. "No problem."

Once upstairs, Marc offered to pay straight away.

"Eight hundred," said Jacquot.

Marc handed him the eight hundred francs. He still had the thousand five hundred francs he'd taken from Zyto, and in two days he could withdraw six thousand francs from the Crédit Lyonnais again. But he truly hoped that by then it would all be over.

"Newspapers?"

"Yes, thanks," said Marc.

Jacquot went out.

The room was modest in size, but luxurious, to Marc's surprise: a Persian rug on the floor; soft, textured wallpaper—perhaps it was cloth—bordered by moldings of varnished wood; and heavy navy-blue double curtains at the window. A television, a round bistro-style marble table that gleamed from a recent polishing, and a small refrigerator.

Marc set down the plastic bag in which he'd stuffed all of his possessions—the gun, the food, the razors—and went over to the window. Rue Piat was deserted. He realized he had to urinate. The herbal tea. Through the fanlight of the bathroom, you could see the little garden, and all the similar gardens surrounding other small houses.

An almost rural tranquility prevailed.

He examined the instructions for the Colt .38.

Then he stretched out on the bed. He felt crushed by all his woes. His stomach was still bothering him, the cramps and nausea were starting up again. He moaned, writhing in pain, and turned onto his side, curling up into a ball. He closed his eyes. He waited for the hours to pass.

Marianne, dead. And Marie and Leonard, in some unknown place, in that bastard's hands. A dangerous psychopath. But Marc didn't think Zyto would do anything foolish in the immediate future. He, too, was probably squirming with fear and anguish. A meager consolation. Marc congratulated himself for having left Zyto so abruptly, without a word, as if he couldn't have cared less, and more importantly, as if he were abandoning him. Zyto, panic-stricken, would try to find him again. And he'd find him here, at Jacquot's.

Another thought kept Marc going, from deep inside him: he knew he would kill Michel Zyto.

At six thirty, Marc's host brought him two evening papers. Marc glanced through them. He found nothing relevant. He hadn't really expected to, not this soon, but the need to check was irresistible. On the news, perhaps?

At eight o'clock, he swallowed two tablets of Maktarin, nibbled at a sandwich in front of the TV, and drank one of the bottles of beer. Toward the end of the news, he jumped: they were showing two mug shots of Michel Zyto. A psychopath, definitely dangerous, had escaped from an exemplary mental institution, beware, no leads at the present time. The tone of the commentary was slightly derisive. The writer of the newscast had opted for the complacent, demagogic approach. He was telling the audience what they wanted to hear, clearly implying that murderers and lunatics were too kindly treated.

No news about Marianne. When would they find her body?

Marc went to look in the three-way mirror in the bathroom. He put on his elegant sunglasses, took them off, then put them back on, and decided he didn't resemble the photos all that much.

He smiled at himself, for a split second.

Then he returned to the bed and lay down, the Colt .38 within arm's reach.

The sandwich and the beer had gone down without a problem.

He'd wait for Zyto until the next day. Besides, he didn't have the strength to move. He was exhausted.

He couldn't stop thinking about Marianne. He kept picturing abominable scenes. From time to time, he'd get up with some difficulty and look out at Rue Piat. If Zyto didn't show up sometime between now and tomorrow noon, Marc would think of something else. Hugues, Marshall, the police? He devised several plans but none satisfied him. He had to keep Marie and Leonard from the slightest risk. Marianne, dead . . .

But he was sure Zyto would come. He might as well forget about Hugues, Marshall, the police.

He'd kill Zyto.

Little by little, it was getting darker.

40

The Cazanvielhs' blue and gold bedroom, which gave onto the garden, with its trees and statues, was undoubtedly the most beautiful and the strangest room of their strange and beautiful turn-of-the-century house. And the most spectacular curiosity in their room was definitely the canopy bed, which dated back to 1410 and had once belonged to a niece of Henry IV. Marshall had acquired it for a small fortune at an auction in Arles shortly after their marriage, and had had it transported to Versailles for another small fortune. The foot and headboard of the bed supported a pale gray and gold canopy, and were divided into three panels, which were subtly carved with flowers (they looked like tulips), and framed by four imaginatively sculpted bedposts—a genuine work of craftsmanship.

This museum piece stood in the middle of the room, a geometric silhouette of cloth, the fabric raised simply at the four corners when the curtains were pulled open. When the curtains were drawn—as was the case tonight—you couldn't see the actual bed, hidden by the frame, nor the columns, hidden by drapes, nor the canopy itself, hidden by the trim around it, above the curtains.

And in this bed—a kind of miniature room within a room—on the night of August 4, at approximately eleven P.M., Marshall was making his wife, Marie-Thérèse, faint with pleasure from his vigorous lovemaking, which had been going on for a good hour. Her continual moaning became significantly louder during each orgasm, then she'd drink some water (she always had a carafe within reach under these circumstances), shower Marshall with tender words, and after a while, they'd start thrashing around and moaning again. She seemed less bony naked than when she was dressed. They had sex infrequently, three or four times a month, but it was prolonged and intense. This had suited both of them for quite some time now.

If anyone had told Marie-Thérèse that Marshall was cheating on her, or simply that he was thinking of cheating on her, she would have laughed. She adored her Marshall and trusted him completely. She knew what transpired between them in the intimacy of their bedroom. A man who behaved that way with a woman, who manifested such physical passion—sometimes to the point of frenzy—that they'd laugh about it, ("They've gone crazy, completely crazy!" Marie-Thérèse would say, referring to their genitals), a man like that, in her opinion, could never betray her; a man like that wasn't likely to "shop around" anywhere else.

Of course, right from the start, she'd detected (with great subtlety) Marshall's adolescent side, which encouraged him to escape through his imagination into fantasizing, dreaming.

Dreaming of Marie Lacroix, for instance.

Marie-Thérèse (with great wisdom) had accepted this personality trait, and had put up with it, never mentioning a word, sure of Marshall's fidelity.

At eleven twenty-five, their senses assuaged for another good week, they went downstairs into the living room. Marie-Thérèse brought in a painted and lacquered wooden tray with salted appetizers and the bottle of champagne they hadn't finished at dinner.

They watched TV, the late news on Channel 3, as they nibbled and drank. They heard the name Michel Zyto being mentioned, and then saw him on the screen.

"Oh, so that's what he looks like?" asked Marie-Thérèse. "He doesn't look all that bad. He doesn't look crazy. Do you think Marie will call back tomorrow?"

It was usually Marie who phoned them. Marc, only on rare occasions.

"I think so," said Marshall.

When Marie-Thérèse had gotten home, around six, she'd wanted to give the Lacroixs a call. Don't bother, Marshall had said, they're probably at the hotel.

"How do you know?"

"Marie phoned this morning."

"Oh! Which hotel?"

"I don't know. They haven't decided yet."

Michel Zyto returned to the Hôtel Pavillon de la Reine in a state of panic, solitude, and painful abandonment—longing to see Marc again, to have it out with him, to defend himself, to make peace. The ultimate necessity to kill him, to do away with him, did not seem at all contradictory to Zyto. The two desires simply coexisted in his mind.

On the way back, he'd bought a dozen blue terry cloth towels.

How would he find Marc again? By going to Rue Piat, to Jacquot's place? He could start there. Marc would cool off. He, too, was undoubtedly hoping for another meeting. And another journey through the psycho-computer. Therefore, Marc would somehow manage to be "accessible." So why not Rue Piat? Zyto recalled having been precise in his confessions—in the privacy and calm of the pink room at Stéphen-Mornay, at a time when he'd felt so relaxed with Dr. Lacroix, so close to him, so reassured, so cared for by him. . . .

In Belleville, at Jacquot's place. It was a bold assumption, but it wasn't improbable. And besides, Marc himself was bold. He had never ceased to amaze Zyto, ever since his escape.

Despite his confusion, Michel Zyto was able to appraise the

situation with logic and perspicacity. As for Marc, he had not been mistaken in his predictions concerning Zyto. But these predictions were incomplete. He was unaware of the physical relationship that had been established between Zyto and Marie. Little did he know that the usurper was in no particular hurry to track him down, that Zyto would stop and take the time to seek comfort with Marie before acting again.

Zyto himself wasn't conscious of this. But once he saw Marie again, the immediate relief he felt was so strong, it surprised him. And when he gave her the handsome towels, her obvious delight made him happy as well. He told her about his day, what he was able to tell; he embellished, improvised. He improvised well. He artfully stretched out his story.

"You should have seen the poor nurse, with her face completely beaten to a pulp, all bruised! It was terrible. Afterward, I felt like stopping off at Epicure. There's a new neurology manual that just came out, I know the author well. I mean, I used to know him. It's not what I'm interested in right now, but . . . ."

"I understand, darling," said Marie.

"I parked in front of the bookstore. Then I took a little stroll in the Luxembourg Gardens, to unwind. I missed you. I kept saying to myself: if only Marie were here, now, right this second!"

They were sitting on the enormous bed, covered by a dark brown bedspread with thin light brown stripes. Zyto was stroking Marie's cheek every ten words. She was touched. Marc had never been so demonstrative, never had he confided in her so much. And never had he acted so much like a child.

She ran her fingers through his hair and gave him a kiss.

"And your friend," she asked, "is he still making all those fine jokes?"

"What friend?"

"The bookseller."

"The bookseller?"

Zyto was starting to feel anxious.

"Marc! Fine, the Funny Man, the bookseller, Jean Fine!"

Whew. Obviously, Marc knew the bookseller whose name was Fine, Jean Fine, a name that lended itself to silly word associations.

"Oh! Sorry, darling. I don't know if his jokes are all that fine these days. Actually, I never actually went inside the bookstore, after my walk. Just didn't feel like it anymore."

She gazed at him. He looked slightly pathetic. She leaned over and kissed him again, on the tip of his nose. He noticed her breasts under the red dress, cupped in a lacy white bra. He immediately thought of Marianne.

He was getting an erection.

He told himself he was invulnerable in this hotel room. Out of Marc's reach. He was going to spend a few peaceful hours with Marie. Later, he'd see. But later was later.

"You should try to sleep a little," she said to him.

He fell asleep for over two hours, a deep and dreamless sleep.

Then he went to see Leonard in his room. Leonard was overdosing on television. He was watching everything on the air. He knew that once they were home, he'd be back to the same old rules, and that TV would be a rare privilege.

A Walkman and a TV, Croc-Rock and endless programs. He was perfectly content. For the moment, he wasn't bored, not in the slightest.

Zyto chatted with him awhile, amusing him with a detailed description of a dog he'd seen at the Luxembourg Gardens, a tiny, furry thing with a very flat, squashed-in snout, and a scowl, as though he'd bothered some nice horse and had received the just punishment he deserved, a hoof right in the face.

Suddenly nervous, Zyto mimed the alleged scene between the dog and the horse, finally giving himself a slap in the face with his palm, making a horrible grimace that distorted his speech: "Ever seen those kind of dogs?"

Leonard managed to keep a straight face long enough to imitate his father's grimace and, talking through his nose, he answered: "Sure, I've seen 'em!" Then he burst out laughing and they thumped each other on the back like schoolboys.

Then it was time for an American science fiction program that Leonard absolutely did not want to miss. Zyto remained in the room gazing at the lovely brown-haired child; admiring his thick, slightly girlish bangs; his dark shining eyes; his slender, but well-formed arms and legs; and his knees—even browner, for some reason, than the rest of his legs. He was a handsome little creature.

Even more handsome than Marc, Zyto said to himself. Leonard had inherited the best features from each of his parents.

"Why are you looking at me?" asked Leonard.

He gave a delightful peal of laughter, never taking his eyes off—well, perhaps for a fraction of a second—a chase scene between two space vehicles tearing across the screen.

"I don't know," said Michel Zyto.

He felt a curious sense of well-being.

Later, when the sun was setting, Marie suggested they take a stroll on the Place des Vosges. Zyto went down to the lobby a minute beforehand and (avoiding the cold stare of the receptionist) consulted a brochure that listed historical facts concerning the famous Place des Vosges. That way, he'd be able to deal with Leonard, who was certain to bombard him with questions.

They took a fifteen minute walk.

"Who's that, the statue over there, that guy on the horse?"

"Louis XIII," said Zyto.

"And all those pretty houses, when do they date back to?"

"I already told you the last time we were here. Granted, it was a long time ago."

What an exciting game for Michel Zyto! The last time they'd been there!

"No, you never told me."

"Yes I did."

The child was flustered.

"I forgot."

"They were constructed between 1605 and 1612. Now is that all? Would you also like me to tell you the birthdays of every tenant on the second floor of that building?"

He pointed to a building. Leonard started to laugh. Zyto gloated, he was certain that Marc would have made the same joke, word for word. Even Marie was smiling.

As they were on their way back to the hotel, a minibus pulled up in front of them, parking along the sidewalk on the side of the Place des Vosges. About fifteen elderly people got out. A little old woman advanced toward Zyto with a smile that added a thousand wrinkles to her thousand natural wrinkles. She was panting noisily to catch her breath.

It was Germaine Halbronn.

"Doctor! Hello there! How nice to see you again!"

Who the hell was this mummy? As if he didn't have enough problems today? He had no other choice but to say hello, and shake her outstretched hand. She'd said "doctor": one of Marc's patients, or a nut, but a nice one who'd been cured. In any case, Marie didn't know her. Nor did Leonard. Germaine Halbronn looked at them timidly, surprised that Marc hadn't introduced her to them, and even more surprised that he didn't mention Cookie, that he was acting as if Cookie didn't exist. Finally, she introduced herself, with a kind of natural grace despite her age: I'm Germaine Halbronn. Marie shook her hand, smiling pleasantly, and then Leonard. "My wife, my son," Zyto mumbled. He had to add a few words, hopefully avoiding some grossly irrelevant remark that might disconcert the old lady. He kept it simple: "How are you?"

"Fine," she said without conviction. "I keep busy."

She gestured toward the bus somewhat disenchantedly. Marie noticed Zyto's embarrassment. She came to his rescue:

"Are they showing you the sights of Paris?"

"Yes. They take us to nice places. Afterwards, there's a luncheon or a dinner. Tonight, we'll be going to dinner in a big brasserie at the Place République."

She didn't seem terribly thrilled by the idea. She looked to the right and the left, as if Cookie still might appear. Was it conceivable that Dr. Lacroix wasn't going to say anything about him to her? She asked in a soft voice:

"And . . . how's Cookie?"

So that was it! Cookie, the dog Marc had given to the tall Cazanvielh woman, had been bought from this Germaine whatchamacallit, the asthmatic. The dog who'd been used in the first experiment.

"Oh, he's fine, he's doing just fine!" said Zyto.

Then he fell silent, this time irrevocably. Germaine Halbronn couldn't help feeling sad. It was just that the doctor had said, he'd even promised . . . and he'd seemed so sincere, when he'd been at her house! You really couldn't trust anyone.

She sensed she was imposing. She said her goodbyes and, taking small steps because of the poor circulation in her legs, went back to the group of senior citizens who were merrily chewing their gums, and rolling their furtive eyes.

"Who was that?" asked Leonard.

"The woman who sold Cookie to me."

"She's absolutely adorable," said Marie. "Did you see how sad she was, when she asked about the dog?"

"Yes."

"Poor thing! I noticed she had lovely hands for her age."

In the hotel lobby, the unpleasant receptionist gave them a smile as if he were clicking it on by stepping on a pedal underneath the counter, an automatic smile that instantly and completely disappeared from his face four seconds later. Zyto reflected that the room with its twelve oil paintings (he'd counted them) was even more impressive at sunset. It was a question of lighting. He didn't know anything about art. Were the canvases worth a lot? How much could a knowledgeable thief get from selling all twelve?

He didn't feel like having dinner in a restaurant, didn't feel like going out again. Tonight, he preferred holing up in the hotel, limiting his surroundings to the four walls of the room, taking advantage of Marie's company.

Marie phoned the front desk and room service brought them an excellent dinner—*paupiettes de bar*, a sea bass stuffed with shrimp, accompanied by a nicely chilled Puligny-Montrachet. Leonard gulped his food down greedily. He was eager to get back to his room as soon as possible to watch a horror movie on Channel 6. "In the TV guide, they said that it wouldn't even scare a five-year-old," he'd said to win his parents' permission.

At ten, Marie and Michel Zyto also switched on the TV to watch a program on ancient Greece, the first in a twelve-part series. At ten twenty-five, they heard knocking on the dividing wall; a distant knocking, given that the wall was thick.

Marie went to Leonard's room, said, "Ready or not," as she opened the door, and he called out from his bed: "Here I come!"

"No more TV?"

"No, I'm too sleepy."

"Was the movie any good?"

"No. It was dumb. It wouldn't even scare a five-year-old."

She laughed and gave him a kiss. He'd washed up and had brushed his teeth. He smelled good.

Michel Zyto also came in to say good night. Leonard was half asleep. They left the room.

The program on Greece was over. The final edition of the news came on. They hadn't watched the news earlier in the evening to spare Leonard. The less he heard about Michel Zyto, the better. They saw "Marc," the two photos.

"So that's him," said Marie. "It must be strange for you to see him on TV. I hope they arrest him soon."

"I hope so, too," said Zyto.

"You think he shaved off his mustache?"

"Definitely. Plus, he'll be wearing sunglasses. It's not much, but it can really change the way someone looks. But don't worry, darling."

"And don't you worry either."

He wasn't worried. He still felt good, as if something new and important had taken place, though he couldn't say what it was.

They kissed. He stroked Marie's legs, her belly.

Then they made love; almost as if Marc were present, Zyto thought. He told himself that Marc must have been monopolized by his mistress, and had neglected Marie. It was undoubtedly what explained Marie's reserve during their first contact. But tonight she was far less inhibited. And he was far more daring, emboldened by his success on the previous night, and excited by the memory of the erection he had had while standing before Marianne's corpse.

As for Marie, she almost felt as if it were the first time. She had never experienced such intense pleasure with "Marc" before.

After an hour of entwined embraces and two ejaculations that did not drain him—quite the opposite—Zyto finally dared to put Marie in the same position as the women of his dream. It was then that he understood what the expression "mad with desire" actually meant: her gorgeous white curved ass, nice and round, looked as if it were being displayed on the edge of the bed and it made him mad with desire; he did everything he felt like doing, everything he was always about to do in his dream before it would suddenly end.

Neither his desire nor his decision to kill Marie had diminished. On the contrary, both needs had come together and reached their zenith along with the sexual pleasure he'd experienced with her.

But for the moment he loved her.

They tried to be as quiet as possible. Marie didn't want Leonard to hear noises coming from their room. Then again, you couldn't hear anything from one room to the next. And Leonard had surely been asleep for the past two hours.

Leonard was not asleep, however.

He'd promised himself all day that he'd take advantage of the TV at night for as long as he was capable of staying awake. He'd feigned drowsiness and falling asleep quite well, and fifteen minutes after his parents had left, he turned the TV back on, unfortunately with no sound.

At first, he was bored. The programs were deadly dull. The only movie on showed people who wouldn't stop talking. They talked in their apartments, on the way to their cars, they continued to talk in their car, then in an elevator, and in another apartment. Leonard, who couldn't hear what they were saying, felt like he was watching fish. He nearly dozed off. But he fought off his fatigue, switching channels a thousand times, and eventually his perseverance paid off: on Channel 6 they were showing a series of clips of undressed women, and occasionally half-naked men and women simulating copulation. Of course, you couldn't see "everything." But still, it was new and enticing enough for Leonard.

Later on, a cable channel was showing a porn movie. This time, you could see everything, close up, and get a good look. Leonard was now wide awake, as if someone had poured a bucket of ice water over his head, flabbergasted by the unbelievable spectacle.

And it was then, after three quarters of an hour, in this extremely attentive state, that he thought he heard noises coming from the next room, his parents' room. Was it possible? Weren't they asleep at this hour?

He held his ear to the wall. He pressed his head against it as close as possible. He could hear better. There were strange noises. Panting and moaning, gasping and muted little cries.

His eyes were still glued to the set.

He watched and listened, troubled, intrigued, and slightly disgusted. His little penis had gotten all stiff.

All of a sudden, he'd had enough. He turned off the TV, got into bed, and hid under the sheet, as if someone were after him.

Bernard Berchet, the receptionist in the lobby, was staring down, striking a pose of deep meditation. Anyone present might have thought he was contemplating a serious problem. In fact, he was watching a tiny portable TV that he kept hidden under the counter after a certain hour. It helped him pass the time until Antoine Englenden, the night receptionist, came to relieve him. The owner of the hotel, Hervé d'Ollandier-Ferlet, probably wouldn't have refused Bertrand Berchet permission to kill a couple of hours with the help of a little TV set, since the guests who turned up at that hour couldn't see it, or barely even hear it. But Berchet, secretive and cunning by nature, preferred not to say anything; but simply enjoyed the fact that he was fooling everyone.

When he saw the two photographs on the news, he thought he recognized Michel Zyto. He'd seen that man before. He studied the picture. No, he was wrong, he'd never seen him after all.

He switched channels several times. There wasn't anything good on. He settled for the clips on Channel 6. But with the sound turned down so low, despite the naked women, it wasn't very terribly entertaining. On the other hand, he still delighted in the high quality of his little set, an outrageously priced gadget of an obscure Japanese make that his last girlfriend, Estelle Estevan, had given him. She was one he definitely didn't miss. She'd been rich, but definitely too old and tyrannical.

After all, he had his limits. He wasn't that much of a gigolo.

Antoine Englenden arrived, a short fat man of forty with kinky hair and moist protruding eyes. Berchet quickly stuffed his small TV in his Vuitton flight bag (a present from Sophie Sorrente, the second to last girlfriend). He could have left the set, at least once in a while, so that Antoine could watch it. But he didn't believe in lending. And he didn't like Antoine. He didn't like anyone, for that matter.

Zyto, Michel Zyto . . . no, the name meant nothing to him.

To become himself again, Marc was forced to skin himself alive, to strip off the Michel Zyto "layer," square inch by square inch. It was indeed Marc Lacroix who surfaced underneath, but it caused him such pain that he preferred to put a halt to the procedure, and he found himself both Marc Lacroix and Michel Zyto, an odious, confused intermingling between the two bodies.

In a big bed, with Marianne in his arms underneath him, he'd realize he was embracing a liquid mass in the form of Marianne. At that moment, in a kind of silent explosion, the liquid body disintegrated, collapsing under the pressure of his arms, transformed into a mass of blood that flooded the bed and into which he was sinking, despite his efforts to disengage himself.

Or else Marie and Leonard would start screaming when they saw him and take refuge by Michel Zyto's side. They all pointed their fingers at him. Then Marc could barely distinguish between the three people clutching each other; they became increasingly blurred, forming an indistinct magma. A red film had come between him and all things. His vision was clouding over and he was in pain, someone had stabbed him in the back, suddenly he could no longer see, he collapsed.

Or else, he'd be leaving Paris with Katarina; moments later, they were far from the city, driving very fast in a car; the car went off the road and plunged into the vast sea alongside it, a choppy pink and black sea with huge waves that engulfed them.

Marc was tormented by the same nightmares; they'd come

back regularly each time he tossed restlessly in his sleep, for about ten minutes every hour. He would wake up in a pool of sweat, his mouth open, barely able to stifle the cry rising from his chest that had been suffocating him in his dream.

Then he'd get up. He'd look out the window at the dreary streetlights of Rue Piat. He'd drink water; he drank gallons of water that night. Then he'd lie down again and torture himself with the same thoughts, which always brought him to the same point: he couldn't bear it much longer. If Zyto didn't show up, Marc would put an end to this hell sometime during the next day. At any cost. And what would that mean? he then wondered. What price was he willing to pay? Did it mean allowing that madman to inflict bodily harm on Marie and Leonard? Bodily harm, or even worse? And he'd drift back even deeper in his speculations and anxieties. It was intolerable.

But he wouldn't tolerate it any longer. Tomorrow, he would take action.

At six A.M., he heard stirring noises in the apartment below. He was in such deep distress that he felt like going downstairs and talking to Jacquot—tell him everything, and ask him for help.

But it was impossible.

Amédée Hammond, known in the mafia as Jacquot, had gone to bed early, at ten o'clock, and had risen early, as was his custom. He made himself some coffee. He'd slept well. He always slept well. He'd arranged his life with common sense and intelligence. He didn't make a lot of money, but he figured it was enough to be happy. He'd always resisted the offers that were too tempting, therefore dangerous. He only took small risks, like a gambler betting small sums and eventually winning it all back. He'd never said much to anyone, never repeated anything; he was known for his discretion, which had earned him the ironic nickname Jacquot, commonly given to parrots.

He had only a few friends. He got drunk with them once a week. And, also once a week, he'd call on a prostitute in Belleville, a woman who didn't say much, the same one he'd been seeing for over ten years.

He drank his coffee. Delicious. He knew how to make good coffee, he'd tried thousands of brands and thousands of measured doses.

He'd nearly forgotten about his tenant upstairs.

On *Saturday August 5,* at eight A.M., Marshall emerged from the upstairs bathroom—having just shaved, washed, dressed—smelling of Marc Cross aftershave; in good form and excellent spirits.

He was whistling. He kept whistling but noiselessly, under his breath, when he entered the bedroom where Marie-Thérèse was still asleep. He kissed her on the cheek. She moaned, stretched, hugged him, opened one eye, then turned over onto her side. After the kiss, Marshall started up his silent whistling again. Once outside the room, he went back to whistling normally.

He backed his large Volvo out of the garage, onto Impasse des Soldats. Before driving off, he glanced at the front of the house. He saw Marie-Thérèse at the upstairs window, in her bathrobe. She was waving at him. She'd undoubtedly decided that she hadn't said a proper goodbye. Slightly guilty, she'd dragged herself out of bed, and come running to the window.

She may not be the most brilliant woman in the world, thought Marshall, but she was sure one hell of a nice person! He blew her a kiss. At the same time he hoped the Lacroixs wouldn't remain at their hotel for too long.

He missed Marie Lacroix. He was impatient to see her again.

He accelerated, waving to Marie-Thérèse out the window, and watching her in the rearview mirror. Then he turned left onto Avenue de Paris.

Off to Melun! Fresh air, pigeon hunting, horseback riding, jumping over hurdles . . . an excellent day in store. Following an excellent night.

By mid-morning, Marc felt slightly better, physically. He'd had to shave this coarse beard twice in a row, then washed his hair—lingering in the shower for a good fifteen minutes.

His stomach allowed him to partake in the excellent breakfast that his silent host had brought up to him, without it disturbing him.

One by one, he spread every article of clothing he had brought on the marble table to try to get out the wrinkles as best he could.

He was waiting.

Michel Zyto still hadn't shown up.

What was going on? What had he been doing all that time? Still, Marc refused to entertain the possibility of some new misdeed.

At five after one he left his "hide-out."

He drove to Versailles, Avenue de Paris, to the Cazanvielhs'. Time was running out. He would convince them, at all costs. Marshall would have to listen to him, even if it meant threatening him with the Colt .38.

He'd decided against using the holster. He'd slipped the tiny revolver into the inner left pocket of his jacket.

Immediate disappointment: Marshall wasn't home; the garage was open, empty, no cars, not the Volvo or Marie-Thérèse's little Peugeot. He rang the doorbell. Even the maid, Martine, wasn't in. It was her day off. Otherwise, he would have made up some story. Or he would have locked her up somewhere. And he would have waited. He was ready for anything.

Tough break. He knew how to get into the Cazanvielhs' house. Tough break, or all the better: he could wait there by himself. He hoped Marshall would be the first to return! He preferred having to deal with Marshall ten thousand times over. With Marie-Thérèse, it would be a disaster.

He turned toward Avenue de Paris, drove about sixty yards, then took a right onto a kind of path surrounded by two walls; a narrow, abandoned alley. The path curved right, then left. About twenty yards after the bend to the left, he arrived at the garden level of the Cazanvielhs' house. Using the lowest branch of an acacia tree as a stepladder, Marc managed to grab on to the top of the wall with both hands, hoist himself up with some difficulty, then jump down to the other side. In falling, he bumped his chin against his knee quite hard.

No need to break any windows to get into the house; the door to the laundry room was wide open. Some clothes were drying there. Marshall couldn't bear to have laundry hanging outside in the garden.

Zyto's body was definitely a lot more resistant, and more able to heal itself than Marc's; this body obeyed without restraint, despite fatigue, insomnia, and hunger.

Marc's throat tightened once he found himself in the immense magnificent living room where they'd enjoyed so many good times together. The scent of Marie-Thérèse's perfume and her light cigarettes hovered everywhere. He noticed the tall, elegant metal chess pieces had been place in the starting position. He moved a pawn, e2 to e4, his favorite opening move. Generally, Marshall responded with a c7 to c5. Then Marc would throw out a knight, Kg1 to f3; Marshall would respond with e7 to e6, and they'd be caught up in the rigorous labyrinth of the Latokroyzii system, named after the famous Transylvanian.

He hesitated, then left the pawn where it was.

Had Zyto had the audacity to make a visit to the Cazanvielhs' home?

He brushed his finger across the soft, smooth surface of the chess table. The fragments of precious wood—anise, carob, ebony, and myrtle—were inlaid, not simply glued down, forming diverse, beautifully assembled geometric patterns. Marc reflected that he would have liked to have a magnificent table like this of his own. He'd never placed enough importance on his home's interior, in the comfort of his family, having been too obsessed with his machine. And with Marianne.

How could he live without Marianne, even if everything turned out all right? The idea was unbearable; it wouldn't allow him any peace.

The kitchen faced the Impasse des Soldats. He took up his post behind the curtains and waited. Not for long: a few minutes later, Marie-Thérèse arrived in her little car, with Cookie at her side on the passenger's seat, looking very proud. She pulled into the garage.

Marie-Thérèse, what luck! She was probably on her way back from some brunch in one of Versaille's tea rooms. With Marshall it would have been simpler. How should he deal with Marie-Thérèse without wasting time or bringing on a fit of hysteria?

She'd been to the hairdresser's. She'd had her hair cut short.

He heard the front door open and slam shut.

After having lunch with his family—followed by coffee at the restaurant Le Louis XIII on the Place des Vosges, then a second coffee at the hotel—Michel Zyto told Marie he was going to stop by Stéphen-Mornay to confer with Hugues, and pay another visit to poor Adeline—vaguely insinuating that he felt responsible ("Come now, darling, you're not responsible for any of it, not for anything at all!"). And then he'd go to the police to see how their search was proceeding. He'd do one of the three, or two, or perhaps all three; he couldn't sit still, he had to get moving, to feel as if he were taking some action.

"All right, darling," Marie said to him.

She understood, but understood even less without admitting it to herself, why he'd paid so little attention to Leonard this morning, when the child was obviously out of sorts. He had woken up tired, pale, and morose. After lunch, he'd wanted to take a nap; he, who detested napping. Yet, the evening before, he'd been so cheerful, so relaxed.

"I assure you, it's probably just indigestion," said Zyto before he left. "It's not the first time that fish has disagreed with him."

He threw this out at random, liking the sound of it. In any case, Marie didn't seem surprised. He added: "The sleep will do him good."

She held him in her arms, glad that his last words were for Leonard. They kissed goodbye and Zyto headed for Belleville, Rue Piat.

42

M*arc caught a glimpse* of Marie-Thérèse, with her back turned to him, through two half-open doors. She tossed her purse onto a chair and advanced toward the telephone. As for Cookie, he slipped away, yapping all the way to the kitchen. Once in front of Marc, he hesitated—Marc mimed "shhhh!," putting his finger to his lips—and Cookie stopped yapping, wagged his tail, and rubbed up against Marc's leg.

Definitely the cutest and most intelligent dog in the world.

Marc knelt down and patted Cookie's head. Then he resolutely strode out of the kitchen.

Marie-Thérèse—sprawled in a chair in her telephone nook, an unlit cigarette dangling from her lips—was paging through her address book.

She looked up and saw him. He stopped.

"Please, don't be afraid, Marie-Thérèse! Don't be afraid, let me explain, look, I'm not moving any closer, let me explain!"

He had, in fact, stopped moving, and he was holding his arms out, palms upturned, as an appeasing gesture. But it was no use. Marie-Thérèse, terrified, barely heard him. She suspected she was face to face with "Marc's madman," and then instantly recognized him, despite the shaved mustache. Her cigarette and address book dropped to the floor; she stood up and let out a scream that died away abruptly, so she could muster all her energy to flee from this woman slayer.

She stepped back quickly, faster and faster, turning her head to locate the door through which she'd escape—get out of the room, jump out of a window, then make a run for it, she'd figure out where later—but it was already too late: the door was half-open, and Marie-Thérèse dashed forward and banged her forehead on the edge of the swinging door. The impact was violent; she'd knocked herself out. Marc still hadn't budged.

She slid to the floor, unconscious. Marc drew nearer, preceeded by a disconcerted Cookie pie, who gave his mistress little nudges with his snout, whining with everything he had, which was quite considerable.

Knocked out. Her forehead was bleeding. Nothing serious, Marc immediately observed. No, obviously he wasn't getting anywhere with this birdbrain. Time was running out, he kept reminding himself. He decided to take some drastic measures.

He slung Cookie under his arm, locked him in the kitchen, and went back to Marie-Thérèse with a sharp carving knife in his hand.

At least, he thought maliciously, she'd know why she was scared.

He also noted that her short haircut was flattering.

He straddled her. He turned her face from side to side, slapping her cheeks lightly to rouse her. He kept himself from pricking her with the tip of the knife. Inwardly he cursed her. He resented her for panicking. She'd gotten on his nerves, he was angry with her for making him waste time.

He knew he was being unfair and hateful.

Her lids fluttered several times, then finally opened. She could feel her face was wet with blood.

The psychopath was right there, on top of her, crushing her, and he had a knife in his hand!

She was terrified. She didn't move a muscle.

"Where are the Lacroixs?"

"I don't know," said Marie-Thérèse in a little girl's voice.

The cut on her forehead was still bleeding.

"Tell me this instant, or I'll slit your throat!" said Marc, bringing the blade to Marie-Thérèse's face.

"I don't know," she said in one breath.

He believed her.

"And Marshall? Where is Marshall?"

"I don't know."

She knew. It wasn't the same "I don't know" as the two previous ones.

"Yes, you do! He told you. He always tells you. I have no intention of hurting him, I swear. I just want to know where the Lacroixs are."

"I have no idea," she said. "I asked him, he said he had no idea."

"Where is Marshall?" he repeated. "Tell me where he is, goddammit, right now!"

He raised his voice, nearly shouting. He applied a slight pressure to the blade against poor Marie-Thérèse's neck. Again, she said she didn't know, but no sound came out of her mouth, her "I-don't-know" was only mouthed.

She was braver than he'd thought.

Drastic measures. He suddenly raised the knife, as if he were going to stab her. And she did, in fact, think he was about to do so.

"Wait!" she said.

The word gurgled in her throat. Her face was red with blood. Her eyes were popping out of her head. What a mess! Marc thought. He wasn't terribly proud of himself. But he didn't feel any genuine remorse. He realized how the certainty of impunity tempers remorse.

"Are you going to kill me, after?"

"No!" he shouted. "No, and I won't hurt Marshall either. Where is he?"

"In Fontainebleau. Rue des Frères, on a ranch called 'Les Bloudes.' He's horseback riding."

She turned her head to the side. The blood had stained the carpet. She was sobbing. Was she telling the truth? Most probably. Marshall often spoke of his riding sessions in Fontainebleau. And then, she was too afraid to lie, that was obvious. And Marc had no choice. He'd simply have to settle for that information. Anyway, he wasn't about to hack her into pieces to be sure she wasn't lying.

What should he do with her now? She was noiselessly crying. She was pathetic. But he didn't pity her, not yet. Quite the opposite. Something evil incited him to keep up this charade to the bitter end, in case Marie-Thérèse was still hiding something from him; he wouldn't stab her but he'd do everything else, everything except stab: he sat her up, raised the knife, grimacing—exactly as if he were about to kill her, now that he'd managed to get what he wanted; now that she'd talked.

Marie-Thérèse heaved a huge sigh and fainted. This time, she was fainting out of fear. Still straddling her, Marc could feel the air escaping from her, her buttocks deflating like a raft.

Which was just as well, he told himself, he could take care of her and be left in peace. He tore off the cords of three curtains and tied up her ankles and wrists. He found a silk handkerchief in her purse and stuffed it in her mouth. Then he went into the bathroom. The medicine cabinet was well stocked. He brought back some cotton, some alcohol, and some Sterilstrip, a sophisticated type of band-aid that could replace two or three stitches in the case of minor wounds.

First he used the Sterilstrip as a gag. He stuck a long piece over Marie-Thérèse's mouth. No more chattering for the next few hours. It would do her some good.

Then he became a doctor again. He took a pillow from the sofa and placed it under her neck so she wouldn't suffocate. He felt her pulse. A little weak, but it was normal. He dabbed some alcohol on her face.

The sting from the alcohol revived her. She opened her eyes and promptly began to cry. She attempted to speak. Impossible. She let out a few ridiculous moans. This time Marc took pity on her. He joined together the broken skin of her wound, and carefully applying a half inch of Sterilstrip, he said to her gently: "Forgive me, Marie-Thérèse. And don't worry, nothing will happen to Marshall, I promised you that. All I want is to find the Lacroixs. But nothing will happen to anyone, don't worry."

Marie-Thérèse, lost in the depths of her terror, couldn't grasp what he was saying, she wasn't listening, she could barely hear him. At this point, Marc thought, she'd be better off firmly believing she'd been attacked by Michel Zyto—a bizarre, unpredictable madman who certainly could have gleaned some information about her and Marshall during his rather unusual therapy with Dr. Lacroix.

He looked away and stood up.

Les Bloudes, Rue des Frères, Fontainebleau. What effort and time it would take to find Marshall! Marie-Thérèse was rolling her eyes. She was beginning to hope she'd escaped her death. The madman was walking away from her.

Marc crossed the living room, passing near the phone nook. His gaze fell upon the bizarrely shaped green telephone, the three ashtrays—clean except for the middle-sized one—the square notepad. And the wastepaper basket.

He stopped, just in case.

He sat down in the leather chair by the window. Nothing on the pad. The first sheet was blank. And nothing in the wastepaper basket—at least not much, it must have been emptied recently: an empty pack of cigarettes; a cancelled check; a big sheet of wrinkled white paper; a large, red metal paper clip; nothing.

He picked up the pad.

In the adventure novels of his childhood, there were times where the hero had held a blotter in front of a mirror, and in the mirror would appear a message to help him in his search. Or, even more simply . . . Marc examined the first page of the pad. It was blank, but what had been written on the preceding page, now discarded, could be deciphered, through the slight indentations. He tilted the notepad so that the light would hit the grooves and the letters would stand out more clearly. Capital letters. He also saw some numbers. A phone number? It wasn't even hard to read. He picked up a pen and tried to trace the outline of the letters:

XARCOIL

P de la R

42 19 45 26

Incomprehensible.

No, it was totally comprehensible! A trick that little monkey Leonard had come up with. Xarcoil stands for Lacroix. Marie had indeed phoned Marshall, probably without "Marc's" knowledge.

A small twinge of jealousy stirred in Marc. Marshall and Marie had their little secrets. For of course Marshall hadn't said a word to Marie-Thérèse.

P de la R ... He consulted the phone book. Hôtel P de la R ... Pavillon de la Reine. The phone number matched, 42-19-45. Room 26.

Marie-Thérèse couldn't see him. What was he doing? His back was turned to her, hidden behind the potted plants. Why was he staying?

Ah, there, he was leaving ...

Saved!

Marc left the house the same way he'd come.

Xarcoil. He'd just gained hours' worth of risky maneuvers.

Once on the other side of the wall again—taking better precautions to break his fall, to spare his aching chin—he looked at Michel Zyto's watch, which said a quarter after two.

43

*P*lace de la République, Rue du Faubourg-du-Temple, then straight ahead to Rue de Belleville.

Zyto refolded the worn map and started up the engine.

To exit from the garage on Rue de Béarn, you needed a ticket provided by the hotel. He put it in the slot, the gate lifted, and the ticket was immediately returned.

Three minutes later, Zyto was driving down Boulevard Beaumarchais, briskly shifting the gears.

He'd gotten an idea the day before, in the afternoon. A muddled idea at first; one that he found comforting, he could already sense it. As the idea took shape and consistency, it became increasingly necessary. It allowed him to foresee a way out of his unsolvable deliberations; an unprecedented relief, one that would liberate him from a tormenting conflict without much effort by simply casting the whole thing aside, in one fell swoop. The relief of escaping from the prison of "either this, or that," as Dr. Lacroix would say.

He parked on Rue Belleville, a few yards from Rue Piat, in front of a butcher shop. Despite the holiday period and the afternoon heat, there were a lot of people strolling up and down Rue de Belleville. But Rue Piat, a residential street, was deserted.

Zyto didn't see the pink Autobianchi. He'd kind of expected to see it.

He determinedly strode across the little garden of No. 51, not really caring if anyone saw him. He noticed that the blue curtains on the first floor were drawn.

As soon as Amédée Hammond opened the door, Zyto shoved the barrel of a Swiss 6 mm SIG P2 10 pistol into his stomach.

"Greetings, Jacquot. Get inside, quick!"

Jacquot scrutinized him without batting an eye, then obeyed. He was neither surprised nor frightened. He simply reflected that from a physical standpoint, this man here didn't look anything like his usual clients, nor the people with whom he generally associated. They entered the small house. Zyto shut the door. He got right to the point: "Tell me, is your tenant a strong guy about thirty-seven, light brown hair, in a gray suit? Well, he might have changed his suit. His name is Michel Zyto. He's an escaped mental patient. You might have even seen him on TV last night. No? Come on, I'm listening."

Amédée Hammond wasn't put out. He'd been in similar situations and had always gotten out of them without any problem. He figured that he wouldn't be compromising anyone by answering the question. He shook his head no.

"We're going to check," said Zyto.

"It isn't him," Jacquot said, finally speaking up. "There's a guy sleeping upstairs, but it's not him. Please, no altercations; it's not that kind of establishment."

Zyto was in shock. Jacquot didn't seem to be lying.

"We're going to check anyway."

"Don't be obstinate, it's not him."

"Turn around," said Zyto.

He held the barrel of the gun against Jacquot's shaved neck.

"Come on. We're going to walk upstairs slowly. There won't be any altercations. I'd be an ass not to check it out, now that I've made the trip."

Indeed, the tenant was not "Zyto-Marc," it was someone else—a very dark man about thirty, with hair plastered down on his forehead. And he really was asleep, lying on the bed fully dressed. He awoke with a start when Zyto abruptly appeared, shoving Jacquot into the room in front of him.

"Don't be afraid," Zyto said to him. "I'll only be a second. How long have you been here?"

The man, initially dumbfounded, quickly snapped back to his senses. He looked at Jacquot, then at his watch, then at the gun being pointed at him. As Jacquot had a few minutes ago, he considered the question and decided that it wasn't the sort of thing that would trigger a gang war.

"A half hour," he said with a heavy Italian accent.

Then he propped himself up on his elbows and waited for what would come next.

"Fine," said Zyto. "You can go back to sleep and forget I was ever here. And you can still trust Jacquot."

He indicated to the host with the 6 mm barrel that they were leaving.

Back downstairs, with the gun still pointed at him, Zyto looked him straight in the eye, and asked: "This guy I told you about, Michel Zyto, wasn't he staying there before him? He just left, right?"

A more delicate question. Jacquot didn't respond. Was that his way of saying yes? Zyto was almost sure it was. Something in Jacquot's attitude—in his impassive nature and silence—was saying yes rather than no. He couldn't say yes, but the yes was implied. Otherwise, he would have said no. He could have said no if the answer had been no.

Perhaps. It made sense, Zyto thought. Besides, what did it matter? In any case, whether Marc had stayed there or not, he wasn't there any longer.

He kept up the interrogation act for a few more seconds.

"Answer, Jacquot. Your answer might just save your life."

"Up to now," said Jacquot, who had been through this before, "it isn't by answering that kind of question that I've saved my life. And today won't be any different."

Zyto, always ready to admire whatever struck him worthy of admiration, was impressed by Jacquot's calm and self-assurance. He smiled and put down his gun.

"Bravo. You're right. Today isn't any different. I'm leaving now. Oh yes, one thing before I go: Michel Zyto, the lunatic you put up last night, is actually me. I've changed bodies. He's got my body. You get it? Hard to understand, eh? Still, it's the honest truth. You don't believe me? You put me up two years ago. Do you remember?"

Jacquot didn't answer. He remembered Zyto, like all the others; he remembered everything, but he didn't want to remember—he didn't want any part of it. He just wanted this tall, well-dressed guy to leave. He was crazy. Whenever someone accuses another of being crazy, often he's the crazy one, that was Jacquot's experience.

Zyto smiled at him again.

"Bye, nice seeing you again."

He opened the door, walking backwards, not out of caution, but because he still had something to say, something he'd saved for last: "I missed a step going up the stairway. The second to last step. I nearly broke my neck. Think about that, Jacquot."

He slammed the door.

This time, he'd scored. Jacquot remained pensive. How could this man know about such a precise, insignificant detail concerning the other man's first visit, when he wasn't him? Yes, that certainly was strange. But he still didn't give a damn.

Zyto walked across the small garden. He turned around, noting that the Italian had parted the curtains and was watching him. Zyto waved.

He was proud of himself. He'd certainly been the center of attention.

44

Marc had no problem finding the garage on Rue de Béarn. He went inside. No Nissan Terrano. He got back into the Autobianchi and searched the entire neighborhood; no sign of the four-wheel drive. Had they left the hotel? Surely they hadn't. They were probably out. Or else Zyto had gone out alone. Knowing they were safe, he hadn't dragged them along on his little jaunt. On his hunt for Marc.

Zyto had left in the four-wheel drive, Marie and Leonard were at the hotel.

He'd phone Marie, convince her, go up to see her.

He parked on Rue des Minimes, a small street that intersected with Rue de Béarn.

And he made his way to Hôtel Pavillon de la Reine. He'd try a little force.

Two minutes later, he entered the hotel lobby.

The Lacroixs were not wanting for anything . . .

He was watchful. He hoped he wouldn't run into them!

No one was there, aside from the receptionist in the lobby. There wasn't a sound.

"Is Mr. Xarcoil in, please?"

"No, sir," answered Bernard Berchet. "Mr. Xarcoil went out about an hour ago."

"And Mrs. Xarcoil?"

"Yes. Would you like . . .?"

"May I phone her?"

"Of course. The booth on the left. You know the room number?"

"Twenty-six?"

"That's correct. First dial 1, wait for the dial tone, and then 26."

"Thank you."

"You're welcome."

Finally, something was going right. Marc stepped inside the booth on the left.

As soon as he'd closed the door, Berchet—who had immediately recognized him—picked up his own telephone and called the police.

"Police?"

"Yes," someone answered in a deep, brusque voice.

"This is Hôtel Pavillon de la Reine, 12 Place des Vosges. The maniac you're looking for—I think the name was Zyto, he was on the news last night on TV—he's here, in the lobby, on the telephone."

"Who is this?"

"Bernard Berchet, the receptionist."

"Are you sure it's him?"

"Positive."

"Don't move, don't do anything, we'll be there in two to three minutes," the man said.

He hung up.

Berchet was watching Marc from the corner of his eye. He saw him hang up and redial the number. Why? Strange. Yet, the woman and her kid were upstairs in their room.

Leonard slept for an entire hour and woke up in great shape. A good nap had erased the nightmares of the night before, in which his mother—moaning, covered with blood from head to toe—had been giving him distress signals to which he'd been unable to respond; she could neither see nor hear him, though he'd been right next to her.

Marie asked him again about the shrimp they'd had for dinner. Again, he reassured her he'd had no trouble digesting them. He was all flushed. He'd perspired while napping. Marie suggested he take a nice shower. Afterward, they'd go visit Victor Hugo's house, on the other side of Place des Vosges, No. 6.

Leonard took a shower and changed his clothing. He put on a T-shirt that also had HELP! written on it; this one in black letters on a white background, the exact opposite of the other. Marie had purchased the two T-shirts in an American army-navy store on Rue du Faubourg-Saint-Honoré one day last winter, when she was out shopping with Marianne. It already seemed like ages ago. It was like another chapter in her life, she thought a trifle sadly.

They left the room. They were only two flights up, and didn't bother taking the elevator. Leonard walked down the first set of stairs backward; like shrimp walk, he said to his mother. Then he turned around and went down the last flight in a normal fashion.

Still no answer. Could the receptionist have been mistaken? Marc hung up and left the booth, worried.

"Are you absolutely positive that Mrs. Xarcoil and her son aren't out as well? There's no answer."

Bertrand Berchet looked up.

"Absolutely positive, no . . . but I am fairly certain."

It was then that Berchet spotted Marie and Leonard arriving in the lobby. What could this madman want from them, what did he have to do with them? Berchet was extremely agitated.

Marc saw them as well. They'd come downstairs while he'd been phoning.

He was thrown into a state of confusion.

He didn't know what to do first. His luck had taken a turn for the worse. If only he'd been able to reach Marie by phone!

He advanced toward them, his mouth open, ready to say: "Pardon me, madame, I'd like to speak with you for a minute..." but he never got the chance. The employee—what had gotten into him?—shot out from behind the counter, bumping into him, and screamed: "Go back upstairs, madame, quick, run! It's the escaped mental patient! The police are on their way, I called them!"

Marie grabbed Leonard by the arm and disappeared in a twinkling of an eye.

Marc remained there, paralyzed and dazed, for a half second. Quick, he had to do something about that insane employee. He spun around but Bertrand Berchet was already tackling him, or rather, trying to tackle him.

As soon as he'd recognized Zyto, he'd pictured himself handing him over to the police, on the spot. What a coup that would be!

Marc's arms were pinned back, there was no way to reach for his gun. His legs were still fairly mobile, however, despite Berchet's hold. Balancing himself on his left leg and using every bit of strength, Marc managed to thrust his right knee into the man's testicles as though he wanted to send him flying into the air.

The overzealous employee brought his hands to his groin, and let out a brief howl. Marc was enraged. This stupid idiot had messed up everything. Marc pulled the Colt .38 out from his pocket. Berchet became frightened, horribly frightened: the madman was armed, he was going to kill him! He started to scream "Help!" but Marc interrupted by hitting him with the barrel of the gun. It struck Berchet on his lips and upper teeth. He instantly began to bleed. "Waa! Ausk! Mmou!" were the bestial cries he let out every few seconds. Despite the pain, he shuffled behind his counter, where he collapsed onto a chair, his eyes full of tears.

Two cleaning women, followed by a guest, came into the lobby. Marc put away his gun and walked toward the exit without taking any notice of them.

The guest—flabbergasted by the sight of the Colt .38—did an abrupt about-face, already imagining himself behind his door fiercely twisting the key in its lock. More courageous, the two women realized Marc was leaving and remained.

"What's going on?" one of them cried.

"It's Berchet, look, he's hurt!" said the other.

They drew nearer. Berchet's head was drooping toward the floor, almost between his knees. Red, sticky saliva dribbled from his lips.

Marc walked across the courtyard, past the arch, and came out onto the Place des Vosges. Some pedestrians were looking in the direction of Rue des Francs-Bourgeois. The dark, compact police car was moving silently up the street.

Marc turned left, walking at a normal pace all the way to Rue de Béarn. Then, on the deserted Rue de Béarn, he broke into a run.

After his exploits in Belleville, Michael Zyto wondered if he should go see Hugues. He decided against it. Enough for this afternoon. He'd phone him later and say: here's what's been happening, we were in a hotel that didn't suit us, Leonard was sleeping poorly there, we're looking for another one, I'll call you soon. Nothing new? No, me neither, speak to you soon my dear Hugues.

He felt like going back and thinking for a while.

He was perplexed.

But his state of mind remained in the background. Now he knew what he wanted.

Driving along Boulevard Beaumarchais, he turned right onto Rue Saint-Gilles, then left on Rue de Béarn, slowly heading in the direction of the garage.

He saw a man running. Marc Lacroix. Michel Zyto.

He calmly stopped the car, opened the door on the passenger side, and waited.

Marc immediately recognized his Nissan Terrano, and the driver in his handsome off-white linen suit.

The car came to a stop. The door on the passenger's side opened.

Marc didn't hesitate. He kept running, jumped into the four-wheel drive next to Michel Zyto, and slammed the door.

45

"*B*ack up!" said Marc, panting for breath. "The police are at the hotel. Get back onto Rue Saint-Gilles, that street over there!"

Zyto obeyed him. He backed up, with a skillful, rapid swing of the wheel.

If only Marc could have pointed the Colt .38 at his temple at that very moment, what satisfaction he would have felt! Ever since Marianne's death, however, he believed this madman capable of every possible insanity; capable of killing others, killing himself, or allowing himself to get killed.

"We can't go on like this any longer," said Marc. "Can we get it over with now?"

"All right," said Zyto. "I was going to say the same thing to you. I can't take it anymore. But do you promise me . . .?"

"Anything you want," said Marc. "And you know you can trust me."

"In spite of . . ."

They were talking very quickly. Zyto was going to say: In spite of what happened to Marianne. Marc understood.

"Yes. We've got to get this over with now, regardless. I'll still keep my promises. I can't take it anymore either."

Zyto feigned relief.

"How did you find me?" he asked.

"Now turn right, there, on Rue de Turennes. Then you'll be turning left, Rue Vieille-du-Temple."

Zyto forged ahead.

"I'm no dumber than you are," said Marc. "You found me, and I found you."

Zyto turned onto Rue Vieille-du-Temple. He answered for Marc. He'd figured it out.

"Through your friends," he said. "Marshall and Marie-Thérèse. Your wife must have talked to them."

He nearly said "Marie" instead of "your wife." Later. He'd torture him with that later. That, and a whole lot of barbs. For now, he had to be tactful with Marc, gain his trust.

"Yes," said Marc.

He kept turning around. No one was following them. That damn receptionist must be telling the policemen what happened. And dabbing his mouth with a towel every three seconds, so he didn't sound like a gurgling baby.

"We'll be taking a right on Rue de Rivoli," said Marc.

Zyto suddenly had a thought that chilled him to the bone.

"Did you tell them everything? Your friends? Because if you told them everything, then what will happen to me, afterwards? Life imprisonment?"

Now it was Marc's turn to fight off panic. He feared his plans would be thwarted.

He had to reassure Zyto, at any cost, at any cost (no matter what, no matter what)!

"I didn't tell them a thing."

"Do you swear it? So then what did you say?"

"I swear it. I didn't even see Marshall."

And he explained to Zyto, in detail, what had taken place: His unsuccessful interrogation of Marie-Thérèse; the wound on her forehead; how he'd tied and gagged her, then taken care of her; and his idea at the last minute to have a look at the notepad. He didn't need to try to sound truthful: he was telling him the truth. For that very reason, Zyto believed him. For that reason, and because he couldn't imagine that Dr. Lacroix would be capable of lying to him.

They drove down Rue de Rivoli.

After Marc's speech, both men calmed down. They were drenched with sweat.

"Now straight ahead until Porte Maillot," said Marc.

"What happened, at the hotel?"

"I wanted to call you from inside the hotel. To suggest that we do exactly what we're doing now. The receptionist recognized me. They showed mug shots on the news."

"I know," said Zyto.

"He called the police. Marie and Leonard came down from their room precisely at that moment. Marie got scared, the receptionist intervened. There you have it. Did you meet Marshall and Marie-Thérèse?"

"Yes," Zyto answered.

The bastard was truly amazing. He'd succeeded in playing his role with Marie, Leonard, the Cazanvielhs, with everyone!

Marc hated him with all his heart.

There was an awkward moment.

"Not too bad, your disguise," said Michel Zyto. "But I can't wait to have my mustache back."

They looked at each other. Marc forced himself to smile.

The only thing that Marc himself was in no hurry to have back was that acoustic neurinome. He'd thought about that a bit.

"What should I do? Take the Champs-Elysées?"

"Yes," said Marc. "Straight ahead, keep going straight."

Zyto looked at him unhappily.

"When we get there, you can take all the precautions you want.

I'll do what you say. But I swear to you that you have nothing more to worry about as far as I'm concerned. I feel like I'm coming out of a bad dream. I've had that feeling before."

What a superb actor he was. He added: "And I swear to you, I swear, about Marianne, I didn't want to! I didn't do it on purpose, it was an accident, like I told you. Do you believe me?"

"Yes," said Marc with a profound weariness.

He almost believed him. According to his theories about Zyto, and being unaware of his "progress," concerning his relationships with women, Marc was inclined to believe him.

And it was in his best interest to appear as conciliatory as possible with him, since he was going to kill him.

Place de l'Etoile. Avenue de la Grande-Armée.

He detested him for handling "his" car so well.

"I believe you," he repeated. "And again, I also swear that you have nothing to fear from me."

"No one will suspect me?"

"No. Don't worry. If need be, I'll find you an alibi. But it won't be necessary."

"You haven't already turned me in?"

"No."

"Do you swear it, one more time?" asked Zyto, almost imploringly.

"I swear that I haven't said a thing to anyone, not about Marianne, or anything else."

Zyto sensed that Marc was irritated. He pretended to be concentrating on his driving.

"And there? Do I turn right?"

"Yes. In two minutes, you'll be taking the other highway to the right. The highway west. What do you want to do . . . afterwards?"

Zyto gave an immediate answer:

"Return to Stéphen-Mornay. If you can guarantee . . . I must be getting on your nerves, with all these promises I'm asking of you. . . ."

"I can guarantee," said Marc, "that it'll all work out for the best. And I guarantee that I'll publicly choose you as a partner for a new experiment, like I said I would. I don't hold you responsible for what happened. I'll make you completely well. Because I think, despite everything, you've already been partly cured."

Marc also discovered he was a good actor.

They got off the highway at Maupas.

At a traffic light, tailgated by a truck that apparently wanted to flatten them, Zyto missed the curve to the right that Marc had indicated.

"It doesn't matter," said Marc. "You can take the next right."

They drove through the beautiful town of Louveciennes. They passed in front of Château de Voisins, whose neoclassic facade had always impressed Marc.

When they came out onto Rue du Général-Leclerc, Zyto turned left as Marc had directed and they soon arrived in front of No. 101.

"I'll go open the gate."

Marc casually strode toward the gate to open it.

They entered Marc's property by car and parked in front of the stoop.

The view of the pond surrounded by weeping willows, in the middle of the vast park, was refreshing. The gleaming facade of the house sparkled in the rays of the sun. The sculptures on the balconies stood out in almost unreal clarity.

There was total silence.

"You spent the night at Jacquot's place, didn't you?" asked Zyto, as if it had just occurred to him.

"Yes," said Marc. "That was a good tip you gave me."

"I was sure you'd been there. Bravo."

"I was hoping you'd come," said Marc almost jokingly.

Zyto smiled.

"I did come. But you'd just left, from what I could gather."

Did Marc have Martin's gun on him? Probably. A small one (a Colt .38? probably), hidden under his jacket. It didn't matter. Marc wouldn't do anything to hurt him before the experiment.

Zyto handed him the enormous key ring.

They entered the house.

In the hall, Marc flipped a switch. The light in the stairway to the basement came on. Marc determinedly took the first step and went downstairs. He opened the first wooden door, then punched in the code number.

Zyto was watching him: A 2 B 3 4, he remembered that well. He remembered everything, every last detail.

The thick, heavy metal door slid open almost noiselessly.

Marc turned on the lights in the enormous basement.

They advanced forward. Marc shut the door behind them.

They fell silent, both of them somewhat moved to find themselves there—in the midst of that wood decor, both intimate and strange—it even seemed strange to Marc himself.

The two oak booths, each with its curved-legged armchair, seemed to be waiting for them, politely impatient, certain they'd return.

Keyed up, their hearts pounding—each man secretly withdrew into himself, merciless in his own unshakable resolution.

46

Marc's hatred for Zyto was without limits, a hatred that had perhaps even affected his mind. Zyto had taken everything from him, and Marc was going to take it all back. Killing him was a necessity—essential for the restoration of the natural order of things—a desire that he could no longer question; as strong as the desire to invent his machine and to attempt the first experiment.

He wasn't afraid.

He interpreted Zyto's comparative calm and his docile manner as a sure sign that his long crisis had passed, that he'd decided to escape from Marc's diseased body and regain his own.

It was also a sign that he regretted what had happened. As a matter of fact, when Zyto saw the glasses on the round table in the living room—the ones from which they'd drunk just five days ago, he said anxiously: "I don't know what got into me. I wish I could erase the whole thing. I'm ashamed. And I'm scared."

"Scared of what?" Marc asked gently.

Zyto nodded in the direction of the booths.

"You're sure it's going to work properly?"

"Of course."

"Since we were here the other day, it . . . there couldn't be a malfunction somewhere, something that would be dangerous?"

"Impossible. At the slightest malfunction, however insignificant—even one that didn't affect the workings of the machine as a whole—the operational warning light would start blinking."

"And then what?"

"And then, nothing. On the other side of the partition, another light would warn me immediately of whatever the problem was. You have absolutely nothing to worry about."

"OK," said Zyto, relieved. "Would you mind if we had something to drink? I'm dying of thirst."

"I was going to offer you something," said Marc. "I'm thirsty, too. Lemon soda?"

"Lemon soda," said Zyto with a smile.

Marc put the dirty glasses in the sink, took some clean ones out of the cupboard, and a fresh bottle of ice-cold lemon soda from the refrigerator.

They sat down on opposite sides of the round table. The bottle was icy. Marc opened it, and it made a loud "pschchch" that echoed throughout the entire basement.

And they found themselves face to face, each with a drink in his hand. Zyto was contemplating what he was about to say. A simple, direct statement by which he would defeat Marc completely.

Meanwhile, Marc was counting on this interlude to settle the gun problem, however many they had. He was also contemplating a simple, direct statement when Zyto, once again, spoke up first: "I have your gun in my left pocket," he said, opening the jacket of his suit and leaning forward. "Here . . ."

Your gun? Marc concealed his surprise.

"You can take it out yourself," said Marc.

Zyto put the Swiss gun on the table. Marc wasn't surprised that he was carrying a gun. But for it to be the gun that Marshall had given him as a present... ("Since you don't want a real one, my dear Marc... They don't make them any better than this. Even a gunsmith couldn't tell the difference.")

The bastard had gotten into the little safe in the bathroom. And he'd mistaken the starter's pistol for a real gun.

"Bought at Martic's," said Marc, placing his own Colt .38 on the table.

"You can hold on to it," said Zyto. "I'd understand if you wanted to."

"No," said Marc. "If I hold on to it, you'll end up with it after the experiment."

Zyto was sincerely surprised.

"I hadn't thought of that." He reflected for a moment. "So then I should keep a gun on me? That way, you can set your mind at rest. Would you like me to do that?"

"Frankly, yes," said Marc, very firmly. "Don't hold it against me, but I would, in fact, feel more comfortable."

"All right," said Zyto.

And Marc, rising from his seat, stuffed the Colt .38 into Zyto's pocket.

Zyto didn't budge.

"I hope someday you'll be able to trust me again."

"As I said, don't hold it against me," said Marc.

"I won't."

And thus, everything worked out perfectly for both of them. Zyto had won over Marc's confidence, and Marc—sure of Zyto up until the experiment—knew that all he'd have to do next was pull the Colt .38 out of his pocket.

Zyto finished his glass.

"Shall we?" asked Marc.

"Yes," said Zyto.

Zyto abruptly stood up, as if he were forcing himself to assume a firm and courageous pose.

Marc finished his glass as well, placed it on the table, and—

propping himself up on the armrests of the chair—he leaned over and began to rise.

Just then, Zyto grabbed the bottle of soda and smashed it over his head, with a brief, violent blow.

Marc fell back onto his chair, knocked out. Zyto moved the table aside so that he could comfortably stand in front of Marc.

Marc half-opened his eyes. He felt like he weighed a ton, he was incapable of moving. He was barely conscious of what was happening.

"I fucked her!" Zyto screamed. "Not Marianne, Marie. Marie! I fucked her, d'you hear me? Many times!"

Marc perceived the horror of what had occurred.

Zyto observed him, haggard, his mouth open, with a revolting expression on his face. He was still holding the soda bottle, ready to strike.

And he struck again.

Marc tried to rip himself out of his seat. Zyto brandished the bottle, spun it around, and landed a glancing blow on Marc's head as if he wanted to break it all, skull and bottle. He thought he'd heard the sound of splintering bone.

At this point, he was indifferent to inflicting violence on his own body.

He kept himself from striking another blow. He didn't intend to kill Marc. Not yet.

He retrieved the starter's pistol.

Arms dangling, his head hanging to one side, Marc looked like a pile of rags. He was bleeding, only a little. Zyto told himself that "he" had a hard head.

During his detailed explanations, several days ago, Marc had opened the small, handsome cabinet that served as a medicine chest: "Some tranquilizers," he'd said, "but they won't be necessary." Zyto found some Xanax. He knew what it was. He'd taken tons of it. "He" could certainly take a few more.

He took Marc's head by the hair and pulled it back, stuffing a half dozen green-and-white capsules into his mouth and forcing him to swallow them with the lemon soda. The liquid wouldn't go down. He practically shoved the bottle down his throat; there was soda everywhere.

He put the bottle of Xanax in his pocket.

He entered the machine room with some apprehension, and grabbed a roll of electric wire.

Then he slid open the metal door.

It took him over fifteen minutes to drag the dead weight of Marc's lifeless body to the Nissan Terrano. Once inside, he fastened the seat belt around him and placed him in a sleeping position, leaned up against the door so he wouldn't fall over onto Zyto on the way.

He was out of breath. He could hear his heart beating irregularly, at times like bursts of gunfire.

He locked all the doors again.

He found a large rag in the side compartment of the car which he ripped into several pieces. He cleaned Marc's wound, wiped his forehead and the rest of his face—occasionally spitting on the cloth to erase all traces of blood. He clenched a piece of the rag in his hand, in case Marc started to bleed again.

Then he started the engine and left Louveciennes.

47

It was much less difficult to transport the body to the doorway of the basement upon his return to Chemin du Maréchal-ferrant. Zyto didn't have to use the wheelbarrow or the dolly, as he'd first planned: once he'd unfastened the seatbelt that had held up the unconscious Marc, he was able to sling him over his shoulder—legs on one side, torso on the other—and make it across the several yards from the car to the house.

He set Marc down in the hallway and allowed himself a minute to catch his breath. He used the time to search through Marc's pockets. He found Marianne's bank card. In the kitchen, he cut it into six parts with a scissors. He'd scatter the pieces in the woods, later on, before he left.

Then he opened the basement door, turned on the light, went back and grabbed hold of the body under the arms, then pulled it down the staircase walking backward. The brief descent was punctuated by the sound of Marc's heels banging against each stair.

Zyto laid him out in the middle of the basement. The wound was no longer bleeding. There was some dried, dark blood on part of his scalp.

Marc was asleep. He was breathing noisily. Zyto tied his wrists and ankles. The electrical wire was thin, pliable, and strong—just what he needed.

He went upstairs to the second floor and brought back a handkerchief, some adhesive tape, and some gauze, and made a gag (handkerchief stuffed in the mouth, mouth taped shut) similar to the one Marc had concocted to silence Marie-Thérèse.

Then he switched off the light and left the basement, locking the door. He could only hope that Marie wouldn't decide to go down there. Otherwise . . . otherwise, he'd have to modify his plan a bit.

Finally—he was doing everything very quickly: he hid one of Marie's two kitchen knives—the sharpest one—the Swiss pistol, the Colt .38, and the gloves in Leonard's room under a sheet in the bottom drawer of the dresser.

Almost five o'clock. It was urgent that he call Marie. He phoned the hotel and a woman answered, who immediately connected him to Room 26 once he'd given his name, Xarcoil. Marie picked up in the middle of the first ring. She sounded extremely nervous.

"Marc, it's finally you! Where are you?"

"At home, I'll explain it to you later."

"Marc, I'm so relieved to hear your voice! Michel Zyto was here, we were scared—Leonard and I—he injured the receptionist, and before that, he attacked Marie-Thérèse at her home!"

"I know, darling, I know all about it," Zyto said calmly. "I just got through to the police this second, and they told me the whole story. Are you all right? What about Leonard?"

"Yes, I'm all right now."

"We have nothing more to worry about. The latest is that he's been spotted in the train station—la Gare de Lyon. He's going to try and catch a train. This time, they'll arrest him."

"You think so?"

"Yes, definitely."

"But how could he have possibly gone to Marshall's?"

"I must have left one of my address books behind, at one time or another. And perhaps I once mentioned I had friends in Versailles. I don't recall doing so, but it's quite possible. Given how clever he is, and that he remembers everything. . . . What's even more surprising is the hotel. He must have spotted me by a total fluke and followed me. I can't see how else it could have happened. How is Marie-Thérèse?"

"Not too bad. It happened in the early afternoon. Marshall was out horseback riding in Melun. He's been notified, he'll be home any minute now. I called Marie-Thérèse after Zyto had shown up at the hotel. No one answered, but I heard the phone tumble to the floor, and nothing else after that. She was tied up and gagged; she'd managed to move all the way to the phone; when it rang she knocked it off the table. I got scared, I thought she'd fainted. I called the police department in Versailles. Naturally, it didn't even cross my mind that there was a link between . . . I still don't understand."

She'd been talking quickly, feverishly. She stopped, hesitated a second, then said: "Marc, I have to tell you something, right now, this instant . . ."

She was terribly uncomfortable. Zyto rescued her: "I know, darling. I think I can guess. You spoke to Marshall?" He didn't give her time to answer. "Don't blame yourself for any of it, it was only as a precaution that I asked you . . . anyway, it was neither Marshall nor Marie-Thérèse who gave him the address."

"No! Marie-Thérèse didn't know it, and Marshall memorized it. That's why I'm telling you that I don't understand."

"He must have seen me somewhere, near Stéphen-Mornay, and followed me. It doesn't matter, it's over now, darling, you don't have anything to worry about."

"I love you. I can't wait to see you," said Marie softly, suddenly calm. "We'll be waiting for you in the room."

"I love you, too. I'm on my way."

On the way back, he stopped in a pharmacy and bought two sleep masks. He threw away the boxes and put the masks in his pocket.

Marie and Leonard threw themselves into his arms. Leonard repeated at least four times that he hadn't been the slightest bit scared, not at all. Him? Scared? Ha, ha!

I can promise you next time you will be scared, Zyto thought with a silent contemptuous laugh. Which didn't keep him from happily participating in the kisses and consolations. Then he made up a story: "When I left, I nearly had an accident on the Champs-Elysées. Believe it or not, the other driver was a colleague from Saint-Anne. He lost his wife yesterday, poor guy. He wasn't paying any more attention than I was. We talked for a long time. Afterwards, I went to Stéphen-Mornay, but at the last minute I changed my mind, I didn't go inside. I mustn't forget to call Hugues. So I didn't go inside, and . . . I went racing off to the Chemin du Maréchal-ferrant. I figured that Zyto might have gone by there. I absolutely had to have a look."

"That was real smart!" said Marie.

"You see, you should always carry your gun," said Leonard. "That way, if you ran into him . . ."

He was going to say "Bang!" but he restrained himself. Apparently, his parents weren't too pleased by his allusion to the gun, particularly his mother. Perhaps he'd better not remind them of his having been naughty.

And, speaking of being naughty, what he'd seen and heard that night in the hotel came back to him in vivid detail. He tried to imagine his parents behaving like the people in the movie. Impossible.

"What's the matter?" said his mother. "What are you day-dreaming about?"

"Nothing, Mooo-mmy!"

"Don't think about that gun anymore. Besides, your father is going to get rid of it."

Leonard looked at Zyto, who nodded yes in a serious way, then pulled him over and tousled his dark bangs.

"So, what about those fish, did they finally go down?"

"Yeah. They even ran. You know what? The man from the hotel—I heard he's going to have to get a thing put on his teeth, like the nurse."

"A bridge?"

"Yes."

"That damn Zyto!" said Zyto. "If he keeps this up, the dentists in Paris are going to have to pay him a small percentage."

Marie smiled (it was definitely the kind of joke Marc would have made!), then Leonard got it and burst out laughing. Zyto pulled the child's head against his chest, stroking his forehead with his fingertips.

"So, what about Marie-Thérèse?" he asked Marie. "Tell me."

His curiosity sounded completely genuine. Of course he was very curious, but his attitude toward Leonard clearly showed that his paternal affection came first. . . .

"She hit her head against a door, trying to escape. Zyto believed her when she told him she didn't know where we were. He wanted to know where Marshall was. I think she was very brave. He was threatening her with a knife, as if he were going to kill her. She had the presence of mind to give him a fake address. She said he was in Fontainebleau when he was in Melun. He hung around for a while in the room before he finally left."

At that moment, the phone rang. It was Marshall. Zyto told him how sorry he was about Marie-Thérèse. He felt slightly to blame. Marshall (who truly felt he himself was to blame) vehemently protested. Then he went on to enumerate a few bizarre details that greatly troubled him. That troubled all of them, Zyto added, trying to outdo him. The last one, said Marshall, was that Zyto had displaced a pawn from the chess board, from e2 to e4.

"Your usual first move," he concluded.

Zyto addressed the problems Marshall had raised one by one, and tried to solve them: "Zyto is somewhat familiar with the game of chess," he said. "As for your names, he read them one day in my address book. Add to that the fact that he knows how to bluff and perform; he's sly as a fox. And as for his medical expertise—the professional way he applied the adhesive—on the one hand, he himself was just treated for a similar wound, and on the other, he must have found it quite amusing to play doctor. It corresponds perfectly to his pathology."

A praiseworthy little speech. Zyto could still feel proud of himself. But the real question remained, namely the address of the hotel. It wasn't impossible that Zyto had spotted Marc by chance and had followed him, although it was pretty farfetched, "Marc" himself admitted.

"What are you going to do now?" asked Marshall.

"Go home. We might as well consider the whole business over with. It's only a matter of hours."

"Do you want to stop by the house? We'd love to see you."

"Sure," said Zyto. "We'd love to see you, too."

He was all the more delighted, as he'd been on the verge of suggesting it himself to Marshall.

It was necessary for his plan.

Leonard went to collect his things in his room. His mother went with him. He couldn't find the headphones to his Walkman, and he was missing a cassette.

"If you don't find it, I'll come and help you look," she told him.

Then she went into the bathroom to get ready for the evening.

Zyto took advantage of the moment to call Hugues at Stéphen-Mornay.

"Are you at a hotel?" Hugues asked him.

"Yes. Place des Vosges. Not for long. I think we're going to go home. I almost stopped by to see you this afternoon, but our friend was up to his usual tricks."

Zyto filled him in on the events, omitting what had to be omitted, that Zyto would soon be arrested, for example. The distinguished d'Oléons very much wanted to see Dr. Lacroix again. Zyto promised to visit him soon, the day after the next probably.

He picked up the phone again and dialed Marianne's number. As soon as the answering machine came on, he began to speak over Marianne's voice. The message was long enough for him to pull off his little act.

"Hello? Yes, Doctor Marc Lacroix . . . that's right. Is there anything new? . . . Ah! Yes, all right. . . . OK. And I'll give you another phone number if for any reason I'm not at home: 39-69-06-06. . . . All right, thank you."

He hung up the moment the beep sounded, indicating it was his turn to speak.

When Marie came out of the bathroom, carrying a blue-and-white-striped cosmetic bag, he told her about the two calls he'd made.

"They're still watching the train station," he said. "They're searching the compartments. The police have been notified in Lyon and Dijon. They'll call me as soon as they have any news. I gave them Marshall's number."

"If I'd known it was going to come to this, I would have sent Leonard to my parents' house right away. I'm worried about him. This menacing atmosphere . . ."

"It's over," Zyto said. "He wasn't actually scared this afternoon. I mean, he didn't have time to get really scared. Nothing traumatic, I promise you. I'm sure of it."

And he planted a kiss on each eyelid of his lovely wife dressed in her lovely red dress.

The Cazanvielhs and the Lacroixs embraced. Only Cookie displayed a certain reserve. Frozen in place, with his head cocked to one side, he looked at Zyto with big, round eyes. He sneezed twice, then decided to ignore this man who was and who wasn't the man he knew—the same and not the same as the one that afternoon. Quite a puzzle for the dog.

Marie-Thérèse did a good deal of crying. Everyone consoled her. Zyto examined her bandage and admitted that "Zyto" hadn't done a bad job.

Leonard wore a fairly convincing expression appropriate for the circumstances, but all he could think about was pinball. And when Marshall, who had taken him onto his lap like a small child, invited him to go play a few rounds, Leonard said to him: "Is that all right?" before scurrying like a jackrabbit up the stairs.

Then Zyto confirmed what Marie and the Cazanvielhs had known for a long time, that Dr. Marc Lacroix had a superior mind. Shortly after his arrival, he elucidated the one detail that had remained obscure: how the madman, given his sly nature, had figured out at which hotel the Lacroixs had taken refuge. Like Sherlock Holmes, Zyto nosed around the phone nook, examined each object, and lingered over the notepad. He held it up, tilted it at various angles, then brushed his finger over the first page. The others watched.

"Did you write it down on this pad, Marshall?"

"Yes."

"I think I've got it. Look, it's easy to read what was written on the page before it. You must have pressed down pretty hard for your handwriting to have made those indentations. Look."

One by one, they all had a look. They marveled at his cunning. Marie-Thérèse was ecstatic with admiration.

"Bravo!" said Marshall. "In fact, now I remember, I was holding the phone with my left hand and I had to press down very hard so the notepad wouldn't slide. Marc, you're incredible!"

"So is Michel Zyto," said Zyto. "He thought of it first."

He smiled and so did everyone else, now relaxed enough to appreciate that kind of retort. The two couples recounted in detail what they'd been through that memorable afternoon, then Marie-Thérèse invited the Lacroixs to stay with them that evening, and even spend the night.

"We'll have dinner, a quiet evening, you sleep here, tomorrow morning we'll have breakfast together . . . what do you think? Marc? I'd be so glad if you would!"

Zyto thought it over. Why not? Yes, why not . . .

Everyone thought it was a great idea. In no time, everything had been arranged and organized, starting with dinner: Marie and Marie-Thérèse would make a beef bourguignon; Marie-Thérèse had all the ingredients. She declared her friend the head chef and prudently accepted the role of assistant. She even had trouble making hard-boiled eggs, she explained; either they were too soft or else they cracked—thrown against the side of the pot; the boiling water turned too high—or even burned at the bottom of that same pot without a drop of water, so that the pot would have to be thrown away. The number of pots she'd had to throw out since they'd been married . . .

"I'm going to give another call to the police," said Zyto abruptly. "Nothing in particular, I just feel . . ."

He settled into a chair, a few yards from everyone else and launched into the same act as before, at the Hôtel Pavillon de la

Reine. The repetition was effective: he was brief and performed flawlessly during the alleged call, as well as in his account of it afterwards.

He began to speak the moment Marianne's voice came on, and hung up almost as if she'd cut him off and he was still waiting for an explanation.

"According to the police, he took a train, a bullet train. They're sure to arrest him in one of the stations once he arrives. They didn't tell me anything more than that. They're always in a hurry, snowed under with work. You get the feeling you're bothering them. Obviously, for them, it's just another case."

"Not for me," said Marie-Thérèse gravely.

Her remark touched and amused them, prompting another round of affectionate embraces.

"You look great with short hair," Marie told her.

"You think so?"

"Yes, absolutely."

"Well, for that matter Marie, your dress is magnificent. If only I could wear dresses like that!"

The madman, in a train, fleeing Paris. Very smart, that phone call to the police. Now Zyto had nothing to worry about. He took Marie aside and said he felt like going to buy some champagne, to celebrate the outcome of the ordeal.

"Good idea," said Marie. "And pick up a raspberry tart at the Machon pastry shop, a big one."

"I'm going to take Leonard along. He must be tired of being shut inside. Leonard!"

"Marc is going out on an errand," Marie said to the Cazanvielhs.

"Would you like me to stop by the house while I'm out and bring back . . . ?" asked Zyto.

Whether she wanted him to or not, he would stop by Chemin du Maréchal-ferrant. But she did want some things: actually, a fresh change of clothes would be most welcome. And the pills for her circulation, she'd forgotten her bottle at the hotel.

Leonard came running down the stairs, slightly irritated.

"If the stores are still open, I'm going to buy him a little present," said Zyto. "Maybe even a big one. He behaved very well." Then, to Leonard: "Want to come along?"

"Where?"

"You'll see. You won't be sorry. Afterward, you'll be able to play pinball all night: we're sleeping at Marshall's house tonight."

Leonard let out a silent "wowee" under his breath, screwing up his eyes and puckering his lips to show his general approval.

He'd found his headphones, at the hotel, but not the Vivaldi tape.

For a moment, Zyto was afraid Marshall would decide to come along with them; however, it never even occurred to Marshall, since he wanted to stay close to Marie-Thérèse today to be on the safe side, and he also wanted to take a good hot shower after a full day of physical activity.

To have given a phony address while being threatened, when her life was in danger! Marie-Thérèse had amazed him. What an extraordinary woman! In fact, when he'd come home this afternoon, she'd said to him in a choked voice: "Now you know that I'm someone you can trust with a secret."

And she'd burst into tears. He'd never forget that.

Zyto gave Marie a kiss before he left.

This time, he wouldn't see her again. Not in the same way. Never again.

He'd played his part so well at Marshall's, he nearly believed it himself. He would have almost delighted in the idea of an enjoyable evening with good friends, the arrest of the mental patient, then sleeping by Marie's side, and a cheerful breakfast all together the following morning.

And when he kissed Marie, a kind of glimmer of light broke through the darkness of his madness, allowing a glimpse at a tranquil life—a life of pleasure and tenderness with her—and the joy of bringing up Leonard—that other "him" whom he'd love as much as himself, and as much as Marie. And Marie perceived "Marc's" look; a glow, a passion, a fleeting but intense intimacy, in which he seemed to be giving himself to her entirely, and wanting her with all his heart. She kissed him again, murmuring in his ear: "See you later, darling..."

"Come on, lovebirds, you'll see each other later!" said Marie-Thérèse.

Marshall was momentarily vexed, but then fell back into perfect contentment.

Marie-Thérèse dragged Marie toward the kitchen. Cookie accompanied them. Marie-Thérèse bent down and gave him a little pat on the side.

"My poor doggie, locked in the kitchen! You were scared, eh? Well, anyway, now I know you're not a watch dog. Right, my little doggie? It doesn't matter, we still love you."

The dog trotted ahead in front of them.

Marie turned around and flashed Zyto one last smile. He waved, walking off with Leonard.

And he was totally engulfed by the darkness.

48

*S*ix o'clock.

He'd better be quick about it. Speed was a factor in the success of the second phase of his plan.

"Why did you say I wouldn't be sorry, if I came with you?" Leonard asked him in the car.

Zyto casually explained to him that he'd secretly constructed a machine, in Leonard's grandparents' house in Louveciennes.

"A machine?" said Leonard.

"Yes, a fantastic machine, that rejuvenates you."

"Rejuvenates you?" Leonard practically sang, exaggerating his surprise.

"Yup. After a little while, you feel like you're in great shape, you're not sleepy anymore, you feel like running and playing."

They were going to try it out together, right then and there. They'd return to Marshall's like conquering heroes (Zyto became increasingly animated as he spoke), they'd surprise them, Leonard could play pinball all night without feeling the slightest fatigue.

No, not to anyone, he hadn't told anyone about it.

"Not even Mommy?"

"Especially Mommy."

"Why?"

"You know, it's almost always like that with people who invent things. Usually, they don't tell their families anything. They wait until it's finished. Otherwise, everyone would be waiting, and if it didn't work, you'd look silly and everyone would be too disappointed. It's best not to say anything, so afterwards you can say: look, I invented this, I made a machine like this or that, but unfortunately, it doesn't work. Or else: fantastic, it works, come on, you're not going to believe what you see. And that's what's happened, my little monkey, it works! I found out for sure this afternoon!"

"You went to see your machine this afternoon?"

"Yes."

"So, you told Mommy a lie?"

"Only a white lie. And just wait until you see Mommy, later, when we get back! You'll see how we're going to amaze them all! You're the first person I've told. And you're going to be the first to try it, to try out this machine. I mean, both of us will."

"What does it look like?"

Leonard asked questions excitedly during the entire drive. Zyto answered in a way that would make the execution of his plan as easy as possible. The plan had germinated in his mind the night before at the hotel, while he'd been watching Leonard, fascinated by the TV, the flying saucers, and the creatures from Venus on the program.

Or perhaps this plan had begun after his first sexual encounter with Marie...

"Not only will you feel rejuvenated for at least twenty-four hours, but you'll also feel happy; I don't know how to explain it to you, something like the way you felt when we bought you the Walkman, but much stronger and for a much longer time. Soon, there'll be machines like this throughout the entire world. We'll be in the newspapers, on TV; it's going to be great!"

On that early evening of August 5, it took less than eight minutes to get from downtown Versailles to Avenue du Général-Leclerc in Louveciennes to Marc's parents' house, which Leonard hardly knew. Zyto talked almost incessantly, bombarding Leonard with words, working him up into the desired state of excitement and enthusiasm so that he'd be impatient to try the machine, then later return—like a little hero—to his mother, Marshall, and Marie-Thérèse.

Yet the child stiffened slightly in front of the stairs to the basement and cast a fearful glance toward his father. To what extent was Leonard afraid of basements? Zyto cupped his face in his hands, looking him straight in the eyes: "Don't be afraid. You're not afraid with me, are you?"

"No. No," said Leonard. "Vakoo sipaldess teronock."

Zyto, disconcerted, didn't even try to understand. Vakoo . . .? Some improvised fantasy the kid had dreamed up.

"Exactly!" he ventured. "You'll see, this basement doesn't look anything like a basement. First, we'll have ourselves a nice cold lemon soda. One great thing is that after the experiment, you'll feel so strong and happy that you won't be afraid of anything, not even going down in the basement!"

"Are you sure?"

"I promise you."

Leonard, having surmounted his slight apprehension, was enchanted by everything—the silent sliding metal door, the woodwork, the thick light-brown carpeting ("Too bad there isn't a TV!"), the living area, the antique furniture, and the luxurious booths, both strange and reassuring.

While he was examining them, Zyto took a bottle of lemon soda from the refrigerator—the last one—and seized the opportunity to pop two capsules of Xanax into his mouth. Just two, no more.

Leonard came over to join him. They drank. Zyto swallowed the two capsules.

Zyto must have looked at the "start" button at least ten times. It wasn't blinking. Nothing was blinking on that side, and nothing was lit up on the other side, in the machine room, where he explained to Leonard how the energy of their bodies would go through "those superconducting magnets, there, there, and there, measured by these computers, this one here, this one here, and most of all, this one here" (he pointed to the Umay 12), and how this energy would be sent back to them multiplied by sixty. Leonard swallowed Zyto's stories as easily as the lemon soda, but his eyes and mouth were still wide open in astonishment.

"You made all that? All by yourself?"

"You bet I did!"

"It must have taken you a really long time, did it?"

"No, not really."

"Anyhow, you sure are good at keeping secrets!"

"Oh yeah? Come on, kiddo, we've gotta hurry!"

They hurried. Zyto removed his jacket, laid it on one of the armchairs in the living area, and immediately set about installing Leonard in the booth on the left.

He fastened the armband to his left wrist.

"It looks like a rocketship," the child said, looking up.

"Yes, a cannon shell. Actually, a shell is like a little rocketship."

"That's true," said Leonard, impressed by the idea.

Zyto fastened a sleep mask across Leonard's forehead, and put one on himself. The masks had a band of elastic spanning the back of the head, and stayed in place without needing adjustment.

"You'll pull it down over your eyes when I tell you, the same time as me, OK?"

"Okey dokey."

Zyto kissed him on the cheek—a nice big smack—and sat down in the booth on the right.

Leonard looked at him; they were looking at each other, smiling; The child was too trusting and delighted to have the slightest qualm.

An even nicer smile than his father's, thought Zyto. As nice as mine... Marc had once told Zyto that he had a great smile, and that he shouldn't worry about not being attractive.

"In a moment, it's going to hurt just a tiny bit," he said nonchalantly, fastening his armband.

"A lot?"

"No. A little more or a little less depending on the person, but it's bearable, and it only lasts a second. Same for me, it'll hurt me a tiny bit too. We'll say 'Ouch!' at the same time. Okey dokey?"

"Ouch at the same time," Leonard repeated.

The first button: starting it up. The second: the possibility of stopping it at any given moment. The third: back to the beginning. But normally, one maneuver sufficed: setting off the first button.

And Zyto resolutely pushed down on the first of the three tall black buttons, the one closest to him.

"There it goes," he said. "You see, it's not so terrible."

The red light corresponding to button number one lit up, while at the same time they heard a slight purring sound on the other side of the partition.

"Do you hear that?"

"Yes," said Leonard. "It's a rocketship all right. The whole house is taking off."

"You're right," said Zyto. "I didn't dare tell you. Look, look at the dials, and don't move now, stay very still, without moving. You see, they're lighting up, the 1 and the 4, yours and mine, the little orange lines, like I told you . . ."

The analysis of their brains by N.M.R., by multinuclear spectroscopy and nuclear magnetic resonance, had begun. The metal nose cones directed a strong magnetic current to their skulls, and the Cray 6 computer created a three-dimensional graph of their cerebral matter. Zyto remembered this part well.

"There, it's over!" said Zyto.

"Now, the 2 and the 5 in brown, and then in blue," said Leonard, excited and eager to show that he'd remembered everything he'd been told.

The second phase. The orange lights went on, then, the brown dials; the brown lines begin to wriggle . . .

The electrodes inside the armbands carried out the first part of their task, the transmission of imperceptible stimuli. During this stimulation, the cerebral activity was recorded. A banal operation, but essential to the third phase: that's what Marc had told him, and he'd spoken of a ticklish sensation.

"You're right, it's tickling my wrist," said Leonard.

"Yes, it's tickling mine too. So. . . . everything OK? Now, we're going to put the masks over our eyes, come on!"

It wasn't that the rays emitted by the nose cones during the third phase were dangerous, but, on the other hand, they weren't good for your eyes, they made them hypersensitive to light (both artificial and daylight)—especially children's eyes. They would need to protect themselves, a little longer for Leonard, even after they left the basement. Not to mention a couple of secondary, harmless side effects, like their voices, for example; side effects that Zyto had described and that would soon disappear thanks to some medicine he had brought in his pocket.

This was what Zyto had told Leonard.

His goal was to put off as long as possible the moment when the child would start getting anxious. The Xanax would be a big help. Zyto could already feel its calming effect.

They lowered their masks.

"Careful," said Zyto softly, "now it's going to hurt a little. Even if it does hurt you a tiny bit more than expected for a second, remember, don't be afraid, don't worry, I'm here. And right after that, it'll be over."

As soon as he finished talking, as if he'd calculated the length of his speech, the third, brief, and decisive phase of the experiment was triggered.

The brown lines of dials 2 and 5 stabilized, the lights above them came on, and at the moment the blue lines of dials 3 and 6 appeared—when the second superconductor magnet, the N.I.B., piloted by the two Cray 6 computers ingeniously devised by Dr. Marc Lacroix, accomplished its task—at this precise moment a violent electric shock jolted the bodies of Leonard and Michel Zyto.

Leonard cried out in surprise and pain, while Zyto winced.

And once the electric shock ceased to torment them, when all pain had vanished, it was over. The blue lines had stopped quivering, and the blue light went on.

It was over, a success.

The transfer had taken place, the experiment had been carried out to its conclusion.

Zyto knew it even before lowering his mask, when he heard the words: "Daddy! That hurt a lot!" in a voice that wasn't Leonard's, it was Marc Lacroix's.

A voice slightly thickened from the Xanax.

Zyto removed his mask. Marc Lacroix's body sat across from him in the other booth. And Leonard now inhabited this body, his father's body.

No more acoustic neurinome.

"It hurt me a lot too, sweetheart. It's because I put the armband on too tight, to make sure the experiment would be a success. But it's over. Now don't move, and do as I told you."

"But it hurt so much! Do you hear my voice?"

He whined in his adult voice.

Above all, Zyto had heard his *own* voice, Leonard's voice; he was Leonard, a child with a child's voice! He had freed his delicate pretty little wrist from the armband. And he saw his pretty little legs, muscular and tanned, slightly tanner on the kneecaps. He was trembling, his mouth was dry, his heart was pounding out of tension and nervousness but also because he felt happy, supple, healthy, alive, because he was beginning to live life anew!

And he'd begin to live life anew anytime he so desired.

When school started again in September, they'd see that little "Leonard" was taking an interest in science, and later on, he'd major in it. He'd learn to fully understand the machine; its operation, maintenance, and how to repair it in case of a breakdown, if the red warning light ever began to blink.

And one day, the house would be his.

And if something wasn't going right—if he were sick or if death were approaching, or if he simply felt like it—all he'd have to do was bring someone down to this basement, preferably a young child, and take possession of his body.

Zyto was gradually beginning to realize that he was now immortal.

49

He went to unfasten the "child's" armband. The poor boy was whimpering, two fat tears rolled down his cheek from under the mask. Zyto kept talking to him gently, in the deepest voice he could possibly manage. He repeated everything he'd told him: for fifteen minutes after the experiment ("I already explained this to you sweetheart") there would be peculiar, distorted sensations—the impression that his voice had changed; a bulkier body, as if it were swollen; and his eyes, in particular, would remain sensitive. It was time to take the pills to get rid of all these nasty side effects, which lasted fifteen minutes, at the most.

It was no longer a question of relaxing him, he had to knock him out, put him to sleep: Zyto gave him five Xanax tablets with some lemon soda. Leonard drank it down thirstily.

Zyto put his suit jacket, now twice his size, back on. He switched off the machines.

"It's over, we're going back to the car. Come on! You can get up now!"

He took him by the hand. They walked up the stairs, Zyto guiding Leonard as if he were blind.

"Hey, did you take off your mask?" Leonard asked in a pitiful, slightly ridiculous voice. "Do you hear the way I sound? I didn't think the sensations would be this strong. I feel all big and fat."

He said "sensation" like a patient timidly and fearfully repeating a word used by his doctor to describe his condition.

"It'll pass soon. You trust me, don't you? Yes, I took off my mask. My eyes hurt, but not much. In two minutes, you'll be able to take yours off, and in ten minutes it'll all be over and we'll be at Marshall's."

At the top of the stairway, he paused in front of Leonard and, while their heads were the same level, kissed him on the forehead and both cheeks.

"We're going outside. Keep your mask on. I'm locking the doors, there we go . . ."

In the car, Zyto arranged him in the same position Marc had been in several hours before, in the corner with the seatbelt securely fastened.

"Move the seat up a little and make yourself comfortable . . . I'm putting on the seatbelt . . . there we are. Relax, don't move, here we go. Are you starting to feel any better?"

"Yes," said Leonard in a feeble voice. "But I'm sleepy. I feel really big. Like I'm about to doze off. I'm very sleepy."

"Me too. It's the medicine. It puts you in a bit of a daze, but afterward . . . you'll see!"

"Will you tell me when I can take off the mask?"

"Of course. Just a little while longer. Otherwise, your eyes will hurt too much."

Zyto had moved his seat as close to the steering wheel as possible. His head was a bit too low to see through the windshield, but with a pillow he would have had a hard time reaching the pedals. Too bad. He'd have to sit in an awkward position, half-standing, half-sitting, his buttocks against the edge of the seat.

He took the sunglasses out of his jacket, bent the sides to make them fit his new face as best he could, and put them on. With the jacket and the glasses, he looked somewhat less like a ten-year-old child.

He started up the engine.

It was twenty minutes to seven.

He tirelessly murmured the same words to Leonard: it's over, it's normal to feel that, I feel the same way, only two tiny minutes more . . .

The boy was starting to grate on Zyto's nerves.

Watchful, clutching the steering wheel, he shifted into second gear, third—taking care not to drive any faster than thirty to forty miles per hour.

The seven Xanax pills were taking effect on Leonard, who was becoming increasingly limp in his corner. He slurred his syllables when he spoke, and occasionally stopped in the middle of a word. After a few hundred yards, he drowsily reached for his mask to take it off.

Zyto saw him. He hit Leonard's hand with a clenched fist, screaming: "Not yet! Not now! When I tell you!"

The child, completely stupefied, huddled into a ball like a wounded animal. Somehow, he realized that something bad was happening to him. He began to cry, mumbled a few incomprehensible words, tried unsuccessfully to reach for his mask again—then promptly fell asleep.

Zyto ripped off the mask and put it in his pocket.

Leonard was sleeping.

The back streets were deserted, and on the far lane of the highway no one paid any attention to this strange-looking character in oversized clothes who was glued to his wheel.

The four-wheel drive had power steering, the gear shift was easy to handle, but the pedal activity—releasing the clutch, braking, and accelerating—was exhausting. Zyto was perspiring, gritting his teeth. It was a constant ordeal. Plus, he had to make sure to drive slowly to avoid tossing his sleeping prisoner from side to side. He watched him from out of the corner of his eye.

At eight minutes to seven, he entered the Chemin du Maréchal-ferrant.

He pulled into the driveway, stopped two yards from the garage, and turned off the motor. His buttocks ached terribly, right where he'd been supporting his entire body weight.

He got out of the car. He opened the garage. He felt lightheaded. In great form, just like he'd promised Leonard.

He wheeled the dolly over so it faced the passenger's seat. Then he put the wheelbarrow behind it and tipped the dolly over so its handles rested on the legs of the wheelbarrow. This created a ramp, perpendicular to the car, at the same level as Marc's body.

He went back to get the brand-new shovel.

Then he climbed into the car again. He lifted Leonard's legs—Marc's long legs—by the calves and began to pivot the body slowly and steadily, then abruptly yanked it around. Once Zyto had gotten Leonard's back to the door, he braced himself with his back against his own door; he placed his feet on Leonard's haunches—on the hipbones—and pushed with all of his childish might, but with all of his adult rage as well, all of Zyto's rage. Desperate to succeed in this undertaking, he leaned, he pushed and pushed, and thereby managed to move him an inch, and press Leonard's back flat against the door.

When Leonard's torso nearly fell forward, he held it up—positioning himself to the left of the body, half-standing—and unfastened the seatbelt.

Then he opened the door a crack, slipped out, and stepped down, avoiding Leonard, but holding him securely by his shirt collar. His feet touched the ground, to the left of the dolly. He let the torso move toward him, inch by inch, put both arms around Leonard's neck and pulled, until the body weight worked to his advantage: Leonard's buttocks started to slide off the seat. Zyto moved aside slightly, holding Leonard by the hair and left shoulder, so that he could guide his fall with precision. And suddenly, he did, Leonard's body slid and fell flat on its back from the height of about two feet, onto the dolly.

He'd done it.

Leonard's head bounced and fell back onto a metal cross bar on the dolly, so that at the very moment he might have woken up, he was knocked unconscious, which spared Zyto the task of hitting him with the shovel handle, as planned, in case of an inopportune awakening.

He tied him to the dolly with a thick rope that had been in the trunk of the car.

Then he went up to the house and opened the front door. He switched on the lights in the basement and the stairway, barely glancing at Marc, still asleep.

He went back upstairs.

In spite of Leonard's long legs dragging on the floor, Zyto had no difficulty moving the body across the smooth, flat surfaces of the driveway and hall. The descent into the basement was just as easy: Zyto, walking backward, simply guided the wheels of the dolly; holding back slightly at every step, then pulling them gently onto the next step.

Once downstairs, he untied the rope and unloaded the body like a sack of potatoes next to the other body.

He was too warm in his jacket. Aggravated, he removed it, retrieving the sleep masks and the huge key ring from his pocket, and flung it onto the floor.

He realized that Leonard had lost one of his loafers.

He found it on the stairs and put it back on.

Then he tied and gagged him, in exactly the same way as before, and left them—father and son, Marc and Leonard—lying side by side, dazed from the blows and the tranquilizers. Marc, prisoner of Michel Zyto's body, and Leonard, of his father's.

He went into the living room and sat down near the telephone. He opened the phone book and chose a woman's name at random: Marthe Lenoir.

He took out a piece of paper and hastily scribbled down some notes.

He looked at Leonard's small, flat quartz watch: seven o'clock, twelve minutes, twenty-four seconds. Twenty-five seconds, twenty-six, twenty-seven, twenty-eight, twenty-nine: just for the hell of it, he waited until the watch read thirty seconds—seven o'clock, twelve minutes and thirty seconds—before picking up the phone.

He dialed the Cazanvielhs' number.

Marie-Thérèse answered.

He spoke to her in a high-pitched, affected voice. He launched right into his act. It was the only thing to do: play the role to the hilt, forget he was Michel Zyto, forget he was Leonard Lacroix, and for a few minutes become Miss Marthe Lenoir, who worked for the census bureau, and was interviewing approximately one hundred upper-middle-class retired persons living in the suburbs of Paris.

"I have a few questions to ask you, if you don't mind," "Miss Lenoir" literally screamed into the phone. "Your cooperation would be most helpful to us, I won't keep you very long . . ."

Zyto's eyes were riveted to the sheet of paper he held in his left hand.

Of course, Marie-Thérèse Cazanvielh wasn't in the best of shape, and therefore, not in her usual top form for phone conversation. She wished it had been another day—the next afternoon around two o'clock, for instance, after a cup of coffee—but ultimately the pleasure of being interviewed for a poll overrode any other consideration. She put her hand over the receiver and said to the others, with unfeigned excitement: "It's the census bureau. For a poll. Do you mind?" No one minded. She removed her hand. "All right, go ahead."

"Thank you. How long have you been living in Versailles?"

"Fifteen years. Ever since my husband retired. He was in the military. A colonel."

"Ah! That's nice!" Zyto exclaimed shrilly. "And why did you choose Versailles? Because . . ."

She interrupted him, impatient to give an answer: "Because . . ."

Then Zyto interrupted her, so that he could finish his question: "Because you were set on Versailles, or was it by accident?"

"Both. We chose Versailles, but if we'd found something nice somewhere else, we would have taken it. But since we found something in Versailles . . ."

"Thank you . . . on Impasse des Soldats . . ."

"Yes. It's a funny coincidence, isn't it?"

"Yes!" A barking laugh. "Do you have any intention of moving someday—"

"Nn..."

"—or do you consider your present residence permanent?"

"Permanent." Miss Lenoir had stumbled slightly over this question. "She" continued bravely: "Where did you live before? Are you employed? Were you employed? Any children? Who will inherit the house? Do you come to Paris? How many times a month? For what reason (shopping, entertainment, to visit relatives)? Do your closest friends live in Versailles or..."

Marie-Thérèse moved the receiver away from her ear. This Miss Lenoir certainly had an ear-piercing voice.

"Yes, in Versailles. Just outside of the center of town, but it's still Versailles."

"Do they have children?" (Yes. Leonard, the person you're talking to you, ha ha!)

"Yes, one child."

"Do you see them at their home or at yours?"

"Both places, actually."

Four more questions.

And thus, drawing inspiration from his vague questionnaire and improvising according to Marie-Thérèse's responses, Zyto was able to carry on for almost nine minutes playing the role of Miss Marthe Lenoir, census bureau employee, whose strange voice kept fluctuating in delivery, tone, and pitch—a voice that sometimes became a whisper in the high register, a voice that was truly unpleasant to the ears of the person on the other line.

Zyto warmly thanked her and hung up.

He waited thirty seconds, forty, fifty.

Sixty. A minute.

He picked up the phone, redialed Marshall's number and Marie-Thérèse answered again.

"Marie-Thérèse, it's me, Leonard; the line was busy, can I talk to my Mooo-mmy?"

This was spoken in Leonard's normal speaking voice with his distinctive way of pronouncing Mommy, lingering slightly on the first syllable. Marie-Thérèse did not make any connection between these two phone calls; she never for a moment suspected it was a joke, and even if she had, she would have been convinced soon enough that, alas, this was not a joking matter.

She held out the phone to Marie.

"Hello, Mommy? Umm, I'm at home, all alone. When we got here a little while ago, Daddy called the police, and he said: 'There's probably nothing new but I just want to give them a call anyway.' He called, and after that he had to leave; he tried to call you but Marshall's line was busy."

"Leave? Where did he go? Why did he have to leave?"

"Well, they said they were just about to phone him when he called because the crazy man took the train like they thought and when he arrived, he realized that they were going to catch him, so he went into the waiting room at the station and he took someone hostage—a woman who worked at the station."

Zyto was talking very fast.

"When he arrived, where?" asked Marie.

"In Lyon."

"And so? Tell me, sweetheart, don't get flustered, take your time."

She sort of guessed what would follow; she expected something similar to what Leonard then recited:

"So they told Daddy that it would be good if he could take the train at eight o'clock at the Gare de Lyon, actually they even asked him to because the crazy man said he'd give himself up if Daddy came to get him, otherwise, he wouldn't. They told Daddy it wasn't dangerous for him and that it would be best if he went to Lyon, otherwise the crazy man might kill someone. Daddy said he would. He tried to call you. He tried at least twenty times, without stopping, and then he said, oh well, this is what you're to tell Mommy, and he left with the car. After that, I tried to call you again, until it wasn't busy anymore."

"Calm down, darling, it's OK. So he'll be in Lyon by ten o'clock ... did he tell you when he'd be back?"

"Yes! He said to tell you that he'd come back home tonight, even if it's very late; he'd manage it. He also said you should come home, too. He's going to call as soon as they arrest the crazy man. He said the party at Marshall's will have to wait until tomorrow. He said: 'You tell Mommy that beef bourguignon is even better when it's reheated.'"

Marie couldn't help smiling in spite of her distress.

"He's right, darling. It's true that beef bourguignon tastes better when it's warmed up the next day. And what about you, are you all right?"

Zyto murmured unconvincingly.

"No, you're not all right?"

"Yes I am. I'm tired."

"I'm going to ask Marshall to take me home. I'll explain what happened."

"Do you think they're going to stay at our house?"

"No, why?"

"Because . . . I'd rather just the two of us waited for Daddy to call."

"You don't feel well?"

Zyto let her stew uncomfortably for about three seconds, then let out a feeble no.

It worked. Marie's free-floating anxiety suddenly took hold. Was Leonard starting to crack up after all this turmoil?

"I'm on my way," she said. "You're right; we'll wait together, just the two of us. I'll be right there."

"Right away? Really fast?"

"By the time you hang up, I'll be at the door, sweetheart."

"I sure hope not," said Zyto aloud, after he'd hung up.

Once again, he'd have to be quick about it.

He slid behind the wheel of the Nissan Terrano. His buttocks instantly began to ache again. They must be black and blue, he thought. But this time it was a short ride. He drove to the end of Chemin du Maréchal-ferrant, and continued driving on the dirt road that followed. He crossed the little forest, and stopped after the first bend in the road. The car would be hidden by the trees.

He returned on foot, alternately trotting along and walking slowly, bent over, panting very hard.

He put the wheelbarrow, dolly, and shovel back in the garage. He had a harder time pulling the empty dolly back upstairs than bringing it down loaded with the body.

Upstairs, in Leonard's bathroom, he burned the sleep masks, the rags that had been used to wipe up Marc's blood, and Miss Lenoir's questionnaire.

He looked at himself in the mirror. He looked tired and tense, the perfect touch. Strands of his hair were plastered on his forehead from perspiration.

Then he settled onto the couch in the living room to wait. He had just carried out the second part of his plan without a hitch.

His mother would be there soon.

He calmed himself, started to relax. He savored the profound and total happiness he felt inside. He feared nothing. He was guided, drawn, pushed toward one single goal. It was easy, under these circumstances, to relax. He'd never succeeded until now.

When everything was over, later that evening, he'd call Marshall and Marie-Thérèse and recount, sobbing into the phone, the horrible events that had occurred. Marshall and Marie-Thérèse would come immediately. As for Marc's supposed trip to Lyon, Zyto had a story all prepared: at the train station they had told his father that it was a mistake, that it hadn't been Zyto after all, but some madman who resembled him. Yes, another madman who knew Marc, who had been treated by him at the hospital. This other madman had seen Zyto on TV. He was supposed to go to Lyon, and when he noticed he was being followed by the police he got the idea of passing himself off as Zyto, he took a hostage . . .

An unbelievable coincidence.

That, he'd tell them, was what Marc had said to his mother and him, when he got home from the Gare de Lyon. Marc had been about to call Marshall to fill him in, when Zyto had slipped into the house, and then . . .

Only Leonard had been spared in the massacre.

Immobile, staring into space, Zyto waited for Marie. Leonard was waiting for his mother.

50

Marshall pulled up in front of the house in his big Volvo. He realized how nervous Marie was; she was in a hurry to get home to Leonard.

"You go ahead inside. You'll call us, OK? No matter what time it is?"

Marie looked at him gratefully.

"Of course, Marshall. Thanks for everything. We're so lucky to have you!"

She leaned over, held him by the neck and kissed him on both cheeks. He'd never seen her so affectionate before, yet so distant, alas, in terms of any amorous sentiments.

She got out of the car. He turned around and drove off, waving out the window. Marie's hand remained up in the air.

She heard thousands of sounds from the surrounding countryside. The temperature was very mild. There was a slight breeze; it wasn't stifling hot like in Paris.

The taillights of the Volvo disappeared into the night. Marie strode quickly toward the front door of the house.

Leonard ran to meet her. Poor kid! At first glance she could see he'd suffered severely, both physically and emotionally. He had held up well these last few days, but now everything had come crashing down on him.

She covered him with kisses, rocked him with soothing words. She inhaled his childish odor of sweat. She felt emotional. Zyto fought back an intense desire to push her away. Yet, he didn't find it unpleasant to be cuddled like this by Marie, this very same woman with whom, recently, in bed . . .

They sat side by side on the couch. Marie didn't let go of Leonard's hands, she stroked them incessantly while he told her once again what had happened, minute by minute, since they had parted.

"I wonder if I should call the police," she said afterward.

"No, I wouldn't bother," said Zyto. "I told you everything, just like Daddy said I should. He's going to call any time now, as soon as it's over, and then he'll come home."

"You're right," said Marie.

She'd better not call the police, Zyto thought. Just like she'd better not suddenly declare: I'm going down to the basement!

Otherwise, he'd be obliged to precipitate his course of action.

Marie was glad to be back in her home. She put some frozen food into the oven and stuffed the washing machine with dirty laundry—mostly underwear and shirts, and her white robe.

Then, while the machine ran, she prepared one of Leonard's favorite desserts—blueberries with whipped cream, it had been a long time since she'd made it—and did a little vacuuming.

Zyto turned on the TV. Marie did not object. On the contrary, let him be distracted as much as possible, whatever it took! From time to time, on her way through the vast living room, she stopped to kiss and hug him. She sensed that he was tense now, almost rigid. Perhaps during the past few days Marc had been giving him a minute amount of tranquilizers, an infant dosage.

And they'd go away on a holiday. At this point it was no longer up for discussion. It was essential for all of them.

For once, they dined in front of the TV. The television kept them from talking to one another. Zyto preferred not to have to speak to Marie too much.

"Do you think we'll see Daddy?" he asked.

"No."

"They'll talk about him, then?"

Or Marianne? he wondered.

"Maybe. I don't think so. It depends."

"What does it depend on?"

"The other news. When they don't have much to say, they fall back on human interest stories, otherwise . . . anyway, they'll talk about it tomorrow."

That's for sure, thought Zyto.

He ate well, with a hearty appetite. The dessert in particular was a big hit, but didn't prompt the usual comments, from the simple and famous "Woweee!" to the more elaborate "Those blueberries taste berry good!"

If Marc wanted some dinner when he got home, he'd have to settle for another dessert, Marie told herself, her heart softening at the thought of Marc and Leonard at the same time. Maybe Leonard was fighting his anxiety with a kind of gluttony. But she found him so distant at times, so absent and serious, withdrawn, so different!

After dinner, she hurriedly cleared the table to watch *Zorro* with him.

Zyto had a hard time pretending he was paying attention to the program. As for Marie, she stared absently at the screen. Mostly she watched the digital clock on the TV set. Time was passing slowly.

Zyto was also watching the time. He was impatient to act. And Marie exasperated him. Ever since he'd become Leonard, the more time passed, the more she grated on his nerves.

"After *Zorro*, I'm going beddy-bye," he said.

"You're very sleepy, eh?"

"Yes. And what about you, are you going to go to bed?"

"Yes. I'm a bit tired myself, my little lamb. I'll read in bed while I wait for Daddy's phone call."

Perfect, thought Zyto.

"Will you wake me up?" he asked.

"Yes."

"Even if it's very late?"

"Yes. Don't worry. You go get some sleep."

He retrieved the remote control that was stuck between two cushions of the couch, and nervously changed the channels several times.

He'd wait until Marie went to bed to kill her.

He would kill her in bed.

Soon . . .

51

Marc slept for more than five hours. During the last hour and a half he tried in his sleep to rouse himself from his somnambulant state, but his attempts—thwarted by the Xanax, the cords, and the gag—only brought on terrible nightmares.

He regained consciousness around ten o'clock that night, choking and sweaty, his body aching and his thoughts confused.

He opened his eyes. Total darkness.

He'd been gagged, his ankles and wrists bound. Gagged the way he'd done it to Marie-Thérèse. Bound and gagged by Zyto.

"I fucked her, d'you hear me? Many times!"

He remembered the horrible blows, the bottle striking his head.

He hurt everywhere.

He heard someone breathing steadily next to him.

It was perhaps at that moment that he guessed what had happened, when he heard the breathing.

He was lying on his back. He painfully rolled onto his left side, toward where the other body rested. He advanced his feet, then his arms, then his head. His feet touched some other feet; his forehead, a shoulder; and his hands, the belt of some trousers. A man's body.

He'd shown Zyto how the psycho-computer worked all too well!

What other explanation was there, except something even worse than that? And what other insane plans were still in the making?

Where was he? At Louveciennes? No. He wasn't lying on a carpet, it was a rough cement floor.

In the basement, on Chemin du Maréchal-ferrant?

He wanted to speak, to whisper: "Leonard!" He'd forgotten about the gag, the tape, the handkerchief that was choking him. And that must be choking Leonard . . .

In the basement of his house. He'd find out in a minute. He had to act, fight for his life, for several lives, put an end to this evil. Save those who could be saved. Save Marie, who was in danger of sharing Marianne's fate. . . .

Marianne!

He got up on his knees and elbows and moved forward in an animal-like posture and progression, inching along. He reached a wall, followed it to the left, and came upon some cartons.

In his basement, in his own home. Why did that monster drag them down there? What had he told Marie, what sort of elaborate lies? And how had he managed to transport the other body?

Eventually, he bumped against the antique chest full of clothes.

The second carton after the chest. He opened it, turned it over, and rummaged through its contents in the dark.

His fingers closed over some pruning shears, not the large ones, but the middle-sized pair.

He began to cut the cord around his ankles. Electrical wire. From the laboratory, unusually strong. With his wrists tightly bound, his hands awkward, he had a hard time fumbling with the pruning shears to free his feet. He was getting irritated.

It was just as hard to disengage his mouth, to peel off the bandage without tearing off his skin.

He got to his feet, groaning, aching from head to toe, taking small steps toward the door. Groping, he found the light switch.

He turned on the lights.

The other body was indeed Marc's. "His" body.

He drew nearer.

But now he was certain he'd guessed right; the face seemed marked with the expression of a sleeping child. Such an atrocity was inconceivable, Zyto's spitefulness was inconceivable; his ease, his perseverance in carrying out a scheme that the devil himself must have engraved in the most inaccessible, the most secret part of his brain!

What plan, what scheme? Marc fought off the incoherent nightmarish images assailing him, paralyzing him.

Act, he had to act!

He needed Leonard to undo the cord around his wrists. It would take him too long by himself, he'd never manage it.

First, he freed him—his ankles, wrists, and the tape over his mouth—waiting for him to awaken.

But Leonard remained asleep.

He simply moaned in pain when the tape was torn off. Marc gently removed the handkerchief stuffed in his mouth, at which point Leonard mumbled plaintively, then distinctly uttered the word "Mooo-mmy."

Yes, his guess had been correct.

"Leonard! It's me, it's your father . . . Marc."

Leonard heard him in his sleep. He murmured: "Daddy!," then, once again "Mooo-mmy," then "Baby . . .," the name of his dead German shepherd.

Marc felt confused, shattered, seized with an overwhelming pity for his son, stricken by his moaning and call for help, and the very thought of the pain and fear to which he must have been subjected that afternoon. He expressed that pity with a gesture toward his own body, his own face; and anyone witnessing the scene would have seen Michel Zyto cheek to cheek with Dr. Marc Lacroix, murmuring to him tenderly, kissing him on the forehead.

And Leonard woke up. His eyes suddenly opened after the kiss. Marc quickly withdrew. Leonard saw that he was in the basement, that his body was now that of an adult, dressed in his father's clothes—and he saw Zyto's face. But he didn't scream. He merely manifested extreme surprise and extreme distress, then hope, for the first words he heard, which Marc steadily repeated, were "Vakoo sipaldess teronock, we're going to win, Leonard, my boy, we're going to make them run like mice!"

Only two people in the world knew those magic words—not three, but two—his father and him. Kneeling beside him, Marc said: "I'm your father, my darling, don't be afraid, I'm your father. Don't believe what you see, it's as if we were in a dream, and do you know why? It's because of the machine, the machine at Louveciennes, remember? That's what did all these bad things; well, no, actually, it was the vampires; they stole it away from me and they used it all wrong, just to cause trouble. Afterwards, they locked us in the basement. But we're going to escape, right now. They don't know that we have the magic words, vakoo sipaldess teronock; they don't know that we have the key hidden in the carton, there, under the toys; and they don't know that we have the pruning shears either. You see, I already untied you. We're going to escape, make them run like mice, return to the machine and make everything go back to what it was before, we're going to get out of this dream! We're going to win, Leonard, my boy, that's for sure! Here, cut these wires!"

A bizarre sight. Leonard, with what was indeed a childish expression spread over his adult face, drinking in this "other man's" words for, in spite of their changed bodies, Leonard had no doubt that this was definitely his father.

He sat down.

He picked up the pruning shears and cut the bonds.

Then they stared at each other. At the risk of frightening him, Marc gave him a hug.

But it didn't frighten him.

Had "the child" lost his mind? What was going on in his head? What indelible marks, irreversible or perhaps fatal, would be left on him by these terrible moments?

Marc took him by the shoulders.

"I'm going to take care of the vampires and I'll be right back.

I'm going to settle things with them. You know, they're the ones who are scared of us. That's why they locked us in. Don't worry, your Daddy is going to take care of everything. Close your eyes, get a little more sleep, and when you get up, it'll all be over."

He laid him down on the floor. Leonard offered no resistance. But he had absolutely no intention of going to sleep. He never took his eyes off Marc.

Marc stood up, took the basement key out of the carton, and showed it to Leonard as he moved toward the door: "I'll be right back, darling."

He turned his back to him and gently inserted the key in the hole.

The scream he heard just then was so powerful, so piercing, so harrowing that he thought he was dying—that his heart had stopped beating.

Leonard could withstand almost anything, except for his father leaving him alone in that basement. In his disoriented mind, incapable of reasoning—where basic and contradictory instincts stirred, swarming, fighting against each other deep inside him—an old fear was aroused, as old as he was—even older—and he sat up and started to scream, leaning on his hands, his face tilted toward the ceiling, howling like an animal.

Marc rushed over and took him in his arms again. Leonard instantly calmed down.

Was there someone in the house? Had they heard Leonard? If so, what would happen?

"Come, darling, quick, quick! Come with me, stand up. Lean on me, there, that's it. Now, you're going to follow me, OK? Hold on to my hand nice and tight."

Leonard didn't reply, there was no trace of consent or refusal on his face, but he obeyed. He stood up and followed Marc.

Marc turned the key in the lock.

"We're going to keep quiet now, darling, OK? We're stronger than they are. We're going to take back the machine and we'll put an end to this bad dream, and everything will be fine. Let's go!"

He opened the door wide and began walking up the stairs. They climbed a few steps. Marc was in front of Leonard and he gave him his hand. Leonard made an effort to be quiet, like Marc; he seemed to be imitating him.

At the top of the stairs, Marc saw that the lights were on.

52

"Yes," Leonard replied, pushing the door so that it swung open by itself.

Marie barely had to time to wrap the burgundy bathrobe around her naked body. She saw Leonard step into the room, his hands behind his back, hunched forward slightly as if he were clowning around.

She observed his stare, the somewhat forced smile—almost a grimace.

She wasn't alarmed, however. She was only worried that perhaps her son wasn't feeling well. And a bit angry that he'd entered as he'd knocked, without waiting for her to answer; but tonight, a scolding was out of the question.

"Say, you could have waited a moment! What's the matter, you can't get to sleep?"

Just wait, I'll knock you for a loop, Zyto thought, by now used to the family's constant punning.

"No. Can I sit down for a minute, next to you?"

"Of course, darling."

He stopped at the edge of the bed. He felt as if he were returning to his origins. He told himself: "It's her or me." Nothing more; it was all he could think about.

He still had his hands behind his back.

Marie was clutching the bathrobe over her breasts with her left hand. She held out her right hand toward Leonard's head to draw him closer. All the better. He wanted her at her most loving, her most maternal.

The bathrobe slid open about two inches near her navel.

It was there, right in the navel, that he struck first with the knife.

He put his left knee on the bed, turned his entire body—spinning the knife around in an arc—and he thrust it, all the way down to the handle, into his mother's belly.

He quickly withdrew the knife.

Before any realization of pain, Marie perceived the red blade, the gloves; she recognized the gloves that Leonard had used to play pinball at Marshall's house.

She was incredulous for a fraction of a second. Then she took a deep breath and opened her mouth to scream her son's name, but "Leonard" didn't give her the chance: despite the thrashing of her arms and torso, he plunged the knife into her mouth at the moment she was about to cry out, horribly wounding her tongue and palate.

He sunk the blade to the bottom of her throat.

Marie was barely moving, animated only by a spasmodic twitching.

Zyto leapt agilely onto the bed and knelt down. Still advancing the blade, he opened her bathrobe and ripped away the flimsy blue-and-white-striped panties that were hanging by a thread on her hips. Marie, her eyes about to pop out of her head, managed to close her hand over the child's and tried to push away the knife.

But Zyto resisted. He wouldn't give an inch. He was panting. He looked at Marie's hideously deformed face, then at her belly, her long legs, the triangle of black pubic hair around the tightly closed pink lips of her vagina.

He was kneeling between her thighs.

His child's penis was erect and hard. He wanted to do to Marie what he hadn't been able to do to Marianne; at this moment, while she was dying.

He unbuttoned his pajamas.

Marie understood what was happening. Blood gushed from her mouth. Her horror knew no bounds. She let go of "Leonard's" hand and collapsed, unconscious.

Zyto withdrew the knife.

He spread Marie's legs, first the right, then the left, as wide as possible. He would have liked to have gotten rid of her robe completely, but it would have been too complicated. He undressed, took off his pajama top and bottom.

He lay down on top of her, still clutching the knife handle.

He penetrated her easily; he drove his iron-hard little penis into the bushy hair and soft folds.

He thrust himself inside her frenetically.

And then, so great was his excitement, so strong his intense, exalted desire to carry out his task, so imperative were the orders transmitted by his brain to his puerile genitals—barely able to execute what was being demanded—that a drop of sperm, the first ever produced in this child's body, burned in his groin. It was moving, pushing ahead, rushing through him faster and faster, provoking an increasingly thrilling sensation, then a fleeting but clearly perceptible orgasm spilling onto Marie's belly.

He nearly sobbed with joy.

He had reversed some sort of timeless, awesome mechanism.

He'd just engendered himself; he'd actually reenacted his own birth, thought Zyto; he'd engendered himself, and he'd finally been born!

Marie weakly regained consciousness. She was in pain—her throat most of all—an unbearable torture; a fire that devoured her all the way into her belly, even her legs felt as if they were on fire.

She felt the weight of the body on top of her, hair tickling her chest, her left breast.

Leonard on top of her, inside her, Leonard had killed her, stabbed her, raped her!

She gasped for air. She opened her mutilated mouth wide. And she let out a scream that she been unable to express up to that point—a scream of death and terror to drive away death, terror, madness, despair; a hoarse, high-pitched, horrible scream, lifting her out of an unfathomable physical and mental anguish.

Zyto was startled, deafened, paralyzed with surprise and fright. Then abruptly he began to twitch like an insect that hasn't stirred in months and whose stone has suddenly been lifted.

He waved the knife menacingly and plunged it into her left breast.

Marc had just set his foot on the sixth step of the stairway when he heard the scream. He stopped, frozen. What abominable disaster . . . ?

Marie.

Leonard recognized his mother's voice; he knew it was his mother, he knew it instinctively and instinctively, throwing his head back as he had in the basement, he also let out a howl, a kind of response through which he wanted to indicate his own misfortune and his desire to be by her side.

Marc, panic-stricken, turned around and put his hand over Leonard's mouth.

"No, Leonard! You mustn't do that! Let go of my hand, darling, you're squeezing me too hard."

As he spoke, he tried to disengage his right hand.

"Let go of me, Leonard," he said more firmly.

Leonard wouldn't let go, his hand was welded to his father's.

Violently wrenching his entire arm, Marc escaped from Leonard's grip and rushed upstairs.

Without a moment's hesitation, and with surprising speed, Leonard shot up the stairs after him.

* * *

The scream was much closer and more distinct than the one Zyto had heard before entering the bedroom. This time, he understood. They'd managed to escape from the basement. But how? It didn't matter. On the contrary, they would simplify his scenario, make it more believable. Let them come!

He withdrew the knife and blindly stabbed in a rage one last time, between Marie's legs, between the lips of her vagina—barely grazed during his feeble coitus with her; he planted the knife deep inside her.

Marie gave a slight start, turned her head to the side, and began to let out a series of short and rapid little moans.

Zyto ignored her. He bolted out of the room.

In three bounds, he was in Leonard's bedroom. He seized the guns, one in each hand—the Swiss 6 mm pistol in his right, the Colt .38 in his left—and positioned himself near the half-open bedroom door.

An instant later, he heard them come running upstairs.

He felt strong, invulnerable. He was about to carry out the third part of his plan. An admirable plan in its own way, as admirable as Marc's psycho-computer!

He went into the hall, pointing the two guns at them, and shouted: "Stop!"

Marc grabbed Leonard's arm and stopped short, thunderstruck by this diabolical sight; by this child who was blocking their path, naked, wearing only gloves, his torso and face smeared with blood. *His* child, his son, the body of his son, naked, bloody, his thin penis still semi-erect . . .

The door to the master bedroom was open.

Was Marie dead, or only wounded?

He could guess what was supposed to happen next.

Zyto, the escaped mental patient, had broken into the Lacroixs' house; he'd knocked them out, he'd raped and killed the wife. Then he and Dr. Lacroix had killed each other. The child, miraculously, was the only one to survive the massacre.

The child. Alone and free, with all of eternity before him. . . .

Marc immediately recognized the two guns. The Colt .38—

"his" Colt .38, the revolver he'd procured for himself on Rue Véron. And the Swiss pistol. Marc Lacroix and Michel Zyto would kill each other: the monster would shoot Marc, in the body of Zyto, with the pistol. With Dr. Lacroix's weapon. That was why he was brandishing both guns.

Which meant the bastard still didn't know that the pistol shot only blanks.

A slim hope for Marc, his last.

Zyto—vigilant, his arms outstretched—was aiming at both of them, Marc on his right, Leonard on his left.

Leonard, hypnotized by the monstrous little replica in front of him, had turned to stone. Yes, his father was right; they were living in a dream, a dream like the ones he'd had at the hotel the night before, after he'd watched those people on the TV screen, and put his ear against the dividing wall. And, like at the hotel, he was going to wake up—perhaps at the hotel?—then he'd take a stroll around the pretty square with his mother.

Not more than four or five seconds had elapsed since the apparition of the monster metamorphosized into Leonard. Marc was prepared to throw himself at him, Zyto would shoot with the gun loaded with blanks, and . . .

They were two yards apart.

Zyto reacted first. During those four or five seconds, he'd taken perfect aim, pointing at Marc's heart. Immobile and expressionless, with no indication of his intention, he pulled the trigger of the pistol.

He felt no regret. He fired at his own body, conscious of only this after the shot: "Zyto" would no longer exist.

The gun, made during the war, obviously had not been designed to be silent. The explosion in the isolated first floor of the secluded house was shattering. Marc—taken by surprise, his nerves raw, stunned from the deafening noise—closed his eyes in spite of himself, yet instinctively brought his hands to his chest as if he'd been hit. Zyto continued to behave with the cold robot-like efficiency he'd manifested ever since leaving the basement of Louveciennes for the second time. Without reacting to the noise, he let the pistol fall to the carpet and transferred the Colt .38 into his right hand. It was with this gun that he'd shoot the other one, Leonard in the body of Marc Lacroix.

And from then on, he would be Leonard!

Marc opened his eyes. He saw that Zyto's finger was about to squeeze the trigger of the Colt. He pretended to collapse onto the floor but he kept his weight on his right foot for leverage, ready to throw himself onto Zyto before he killed Leonard, before he destroyed his son, his own body, Marc . . .

But something happened.

After the gunshot, at the moment Marc simulated his death, Leonard began to scream.

It wasn't because of the explosion.

Lifting his arm, he pointed to something further down the hall, behind Zyto.

Zyto turned his head, as did Marc.

Then Marc experienced the worst of all possible fates.

The blade hadn't penetrated her heart.

Marie, whose life was hanging by a thread, driven by a superhuman determination to understand what was happening, to put an end to the nightmare, to be helped, saved, Marie Lacroix had managed to drag herself all the way to the bedroom door.

She remained there a split second, standing perfectly straight. The burgundy bathrobe resembled the dark red skin of a metamorphosis, like a skin she was shedding. And the blood continued to stream in complex rivulets down her face, her chest, her legs, like an army of gruesome, liquid vermin.

The knife had remained between her legs. The handle was sticking out of her vagina, its tip dripping with red blood.

It seemed as though time had been suspended.

Then her fear, her desire to know, and her hope were swept away by death, and she suddenly collapsed on the floor face down.

The spell was broken, and time started up again.

Marc threw himself onto Zyto, screaming.

Zyto turned around at the same instant. Stunned, he fired the Colt .38.

Marc knew he'd been hit. He grabbed Zyto's wrist and shook him as if he were trying to strangle a snake. The gun went flying into the air and landed next to Marie's body. Zyto struggled and kicked, his face contorted with rage. Marc resisted him with every ounce of strength. The child fell backward, so violently that the floor shook. But relentlessly Zyto flipped onto his stomach and started to crawl, dragging himself forward, reaching toward the revolver.

Groaning, Marc advanced one step, gathered momentum, and kicked Zyto twice with a brutality beyond his control. The first blow struck the child right in the forehead, between his eyes, and the second, in his abdomen, on his genitals, now shriveled and limp. Zyto let out a yelp, curled up in a ball, then passed out.

Marc fought off the madness that flooded through him. This body he was abusing was his son's. He looked up. Leonard was still in the same position, staring vacantly into space. After his cry, he remained as impassive as a statue.

Then Marc realized he was in pain, that he was bleeding. His thighs were soaked with blood. He looked down. He'd been shot in the lower abdomen. How long could he hold out?

He examined Marie quickly—dead, irreparably dead—then the child's body. The places where Marc had kicked him—badly bruising him—had already taken on a darker hue; the bridge of his nose, the eyes, his groin. But the medical attention could wait. There was no other way.

He said to Leonard, in a hoarse voice: "Come with me, sweetheart, I'm going into the bathroom to wash my hands."

He didn't really intend to wash his hands. He'd said whatever came to mind, the simplest thing, without thinking, just to say something to Leonard.

Leonard followed him like a sleepwalker.

Marc did not wash his hands in front of Leonard, who was absently watching; however, he shoved an entire roll of cotton between his pants and the wound and gave himself an injection of Demerol to kill the pain. It was better than nothing.

He could probably hold out two or three hours. He'd hold out as long as necessary to do what he had to do. There was no choice. There was simply no choice.

Back in the hallway, with Leonard behind him, he lifted Zyto, still unconscious. He wouldn't be able to carry him for very long. He was in too much pain. It would be risky.

He got an idea: he held out the little body to Leonard who took it in his arms and held it close, with no hesitation, no fear, or disgust.

"Come, follow me!" Marc said to him.

And Leonard followed him. He obeyed his father.

They descended the staircase.

They went into the garage. The Nissan Terrano wasn't there. Zyto must have hidden it somewhere, as part of his strategy. Where? Surely not far from the house. Marie's Austin would do. Marc put Leonard in the passenger seat. He helped him prop the child's body in front of him, against him, on the edge of the seat, sitting between his legs.

Then he got behind the wheel and started up the car.

He pulled onto Chemin du Maréchal-ferrant.

The pain was unbearable. He was going to make it. He swore to it. He was going to make it!

He'd go to Louveciennes and then he'd return home.

53

And Marc kept his promise to himself. He proceeded according to plan, at the cost of extreme physical exhaustion and inhuman mental strain, an unknowable agony.

For no one would ever find out about his machine. Marc had come to that decision when he'd realized Marie was dead.

He'd destroy his machine. He loathed the unlimited glory and wealth it could bring him. He loathed the machine for having been the source of a disaster.

And he loathed himself for having made it. It would remain his secret; a secret that would rot inside him, even if it gnawed at him forever!

Michel Zyto, one of Dr. Lacroix's patients—a mental patient whose dementia had been insufficiently gauged—had broken into Dr. Lacroix's home on the night of August 6, a Saturday. Holding them at gunpoint, he'd savagely beaten and knocked unconscious the members of the Lacroix family. He'd tied up the doctor and his son. Then he'd killed the wife, Marie Lacroix, in the most abominable manner. Marc Lacroix had managed to free himself. He only possessed a starter's pistol loaded with blanks, but he'd taken the madman by surprise, and in the ensuing struggle, had been able to grab Zyto's revolver and wound him. Immediately afterward, under the great physical and emotional shock, he'd passed out again, he couldn't say for how long. When he came to, he'd called the police.

As for the tangible evidence, Marc had arranged it to coincide with his version of the story. And he'd already anticipated any questions they might ask him, as well as the answers. His fierce desire never to speak of the machine kept him going. He acted and thought with flawless speed, efficacy, and lucidity.

He'd had little problem finding the Nissan Terrano in the woods, and he now parked it in the driveway.

One last detail before he called the Versailles police station, in the room he hadn't yet dared to enter—the master bedroom.

He saw the unmade bed, the sheets soaked with blood.

He saw the leather bookmark placed on the cover of *The Odyssey*.

And to the left of the bed, he found Leonard's pajamas. He picked them up. "I undressed my son, I examined him while I was waiting for you, I gave him some preliminary first aid."

He walked out of the room. He had to step over his wife's body. An enormous pool of blood formed a halo around her head.

Further down the hall was Michel Zyto, lying on his side, unconscious. He looked as if he were sleeping. Soon, he would die. Marc didn't even look at him as he entered Leonard's room.

The child was resting on his bed, stretched out on his back. Only his hands, free of the gloves, had remained untouched by blood. A huge compress had been placed on his forehead, covering his eyes, and another on his genitals. When he'd come to during the return home, the fact that he was back in his real body, that his father—the man he'd known all his life—was beside him, murmuring comforting words, did nothing to alter his state. He hadn't uttered a word. He hadn't responded to the questions. He hadn't even complained that he was in pain, although he must have been in a great deal of pain. He'd remained shut off behind a wall of passivity.

Marc still felt repulsed by him. He still saw Leonard as the evil little creature who had appeared before him two hours earlier in the hallway of the first floor of his home; bloody, lustful, and ready to kill.

It would pass. It would take some time. Or it wouldn't pass. All of eternity wouldn't be time enough.

He threw the pajamas on the floor and walked toward the bed. Fate had dealt him one final blow.

Leonard had stopped breathing. He was no longer alive. It wasn't his wounds; his wounds weren't fatal. He'd died from the horror. Perhaps he'd waited until he was back in his own body to die.

Too much horror and madness; Leonard had chosen to die.

Marc left the room. He took the Colt .38 out of his pocket. He advanced toward Zyto. He gave him a few little jabs with the tip of his shoe. Zyto came to. With difficulty, he opened his eyes. His gaze fell upon Marc. Marc was standing next to him. His arms were outstretched and he was aiming right at Zyto's head.

The two men stared into each other's eyes for a few seconds. Zyto was incapable of defending himself. Surmounting his pain, he smiled vaguely at Marc without a trace of irony, only the shadow of the handsome smile that once softened his features.

Marc closed his eyes and pulled the trigger twice. The first bullet embedded itself in Zyto's right eye, the second, in the middle of his forehead.

"We were both unconscious. He woke up a little before I did. I could see he was getting closer, that he was going to kill me. I grabbed hold of the gun and fired. I was panicked. I had no choice."

Mechanically descending the stairs, Marc remembered that

when his mother was extremely tired, she'd always said: "My poor Marc, I'm walking because it's the only thing to do!"

He collapsed on the couch. He looked at his watch, his father's watch: 1 A.M. It was now Sunday. Two and a half hours had elapsed since his escape from the basement.

He dialed the number of the police station.

As soon as he hung up, the telephone rang.

It was Marshall, surprised and slightly anxious.

"Marc? So? You're already back from Lyon?"

Marc didn't answer right away. He'd have to impose on Marshall's patience, summon up the strength to concentrate.

"What is it, Marc? Why aren't you saying anything? Did something go wrong with the hostage?"

Marc understood. In a flash, he understood Zyto's ruse; he'd figured out the general outline of the story that Zyto must have told to justify Marc's disappearance for several hours.

His thoughts raced. He had to invent another story, to counter Zyto's fabrications.

"I never went to Lyon. At the train station, I was told it wasn't Zyto after all, just someone who resembled him. A madman. Another madman who knew me, someone I'd treated at Sainte-Anne. And who'd seen Zyto on TV. When he noticed he was being followed by the police, he decided to pass himself off as Zyto. A madman. A coincidence. Incredible, but that's what happened. It worked briefly. He even took a hostage. Don't mention this business to the police or to anyone, Marshall. They told me at the station that they were going to try to keep it quiet, if possible, if I agreed. The police are making too many mistakes these days.

Marshall believed the lie without giving it another moment's thought. His thoughts were definitely elsewhere. He was frightened by Marc's voice—a dull monotone, a voice from the dead. And Marc seemed overly talkative.

"Marc . . . I get the feeling that you're hiding something from me. What happened? Something serious?"

"Yes," Marc said all in one breath.
And he told him.

A while later, the police arrived, then Marshall and Marie-Thérèse.

54

From the moment the Cazanviehls were at Marc's side, and for the ten days that followed, they looked after him as if he were a child, and Marc let them take complete charge. From that night on, they insisted he stay in their big house on Impasse des Soldats in Versailles. They lavished him with attention, they made all arrangements for him, or at least eased the burden as much as possible concerning the formalities. As for the investigation, the formalities were, in fact, minimal: it was a simple matter, the clues and the evidence were in concordance; they left little room for doubt, and the case was closed.

Marie and Leonard Lacroix's burial—a secular ceremony—took place on August 9 at the Versailles cemetery, and was attended only by the most intimate circle, according to custom. Those present were Gertrude and Marc Leleu, Marie's parents; Louis, their other child; Hugues d'Oléons, his great, kind face ravaged by grief; and of course, Marshall and Marie-Thérèse, who were constantly at Marc's heels.

Marc was holding up well. Marshall and Marie-Thérèse were almost surprised. They talked about it at night in their bed, in the operetta-like decor of their room. They feared a sudden collapse, later on. In that same bed, they sometimes quietly wept over Marie and Leonard's death. Afterward, once the burst of sorrow had passed, they were anxious to make love. They had never made love so often as during Marc's stay with them.

Yet, no sudden collapse occurred. Marc's mind was only concerned with an obsession to destroy his machine. Just two days after the burial, under the pretext that he needed to get out a little, be alone, and that going for a ride would do him good, he drove out to Louveciennes in the Nissan Terrano.

First, by the edge of the pond, he burned the diagrams and notes concerning his psycho-computer; an impressive pile of pages that had been locked in a safe in the second story of the house, in a room that had once been his father's study. Then he started on the machine itself. In less than half an hour, he'd ripped out all the wires, unplugged, disconnected, and separated each machine from the others, as if pulling the plug on its vital functions would bring on a swift death.

He returned to Louveciennes every afternoon from the eleventh to the sixteenth of August. He didn't stay away for very long each time, about an hour and a half, because he was hardly up to it and didn't want to worry Marshall and Marie-Thérèse.

Except for these excursions, he lived shut inside their house, most often sitting, waiting for the hours to pass, lost in his ruminations. Marie-Thérèse often suggested he be examined by a doctor, but Marc refused. He also refused a polite invitation from his in-laws to spend some time at La Colle-sur-Loup. He didn't want to see anyone, not even Hugues d'Oléons, who sometimes phoned, but curiously, didn't express any strong desire for them to meet. He ate normally, not any less than usual, and slept without medication. The Cazanvielhs had given him a lovely room that looked out on the garden and its stone inhabitants.

Every day he examined the wound on Marie-Thérèse's forehead, for which he felt responsible, and was pleased by how well it was healing.

From time to time, Marshall was able to draw him into a brief conversation. He didn't dare suggest a game of chess. He really didn't feel much like it himself.

As of Monday, the seventh, Marc had begun to read the newspaper again. He was watching for anything concerning Marianne.

On the twelfth, a news item caught his eye: he knew the victim "well," it was Jacquot. Amédée Hammond, alias Jacquot, had been clubbed and strangled to death the day before while he was having his breakfast. At the same moment, a second assailant had inflicted the same fate on Jacquot's tenant, a Sicilian named Michelangelo Pininfarina. Jacquot had failed to be as cautious as usual. Or rather, he had unwittingly set foot in a world in which he did not belong: Michelangelo Pininfarina, a small-time mafioso from Catalonia, had been sentenced to death by his bosses. The two killers had been at his heels for nine days. As silent and uncompromising as Jacquot himself, they hadn't asked any questions. They would have slit the throats of an entire children's vacation camp if they had found such a thing crammed into the dreary little house on Rue Piat.

On the fourteenth, the police discovered Marianne Matys's body.

One of her actress friends, who thought (mistakenly) that she had a lunch date with her that day—she tended to be overly dramatic, and in fact Marianne wasn't terribly fond of her—became alarmed when no one answered the doorbell or the telephone. Under the circumstances, she'd been right to anticipate the worst, but the reality of the situation exceeded her fears or her hopes.

The inspector in charge of the first findings of the inquiry immediately made the connection with the Versailles affair. But an examination of the fingerprints revealed nothing, in addition to which Zyto was dead, they could no longer interrogate him, the people who were shown his photo didn't recognize him, or weren't sure, and the connection never went any further, just as Marc had anticipated.

He was informed of the news on the fifteenth. As for the rest of the inquiry, he had nothing to fear. He was above suspicion. His affair with Marianne had been kept a complete secret; he'd never been seen with her and in the courtyard of No. 14 Rue du Faubourg Saint-Honoré, which led to offices and four high-rise buildings: dozens and dozens of tenants, visitors, and employees filed past every day. Trying to establish the slightest link between Marc and Marianne was outside the realm of the possible.

Besides, Marc wasn't worried. He wasn't worried about anything anymore. Now certain that his machine would forever remain his secret, he no longer cared about anything else.

As of the eleventh, no one, in fact, could have guessed what all this electronic, computer, and electro-magnetic material piled up in the basement at Louveciennes was for. The entirety was worth a fortune. It had crossed Marc's mind to donate the computers and superconductor magnets to the research center where he worked. He decided against it, however. He was profoundly set against it; his innermost desire was that everything should disappear, that nothing should be recuperated or ever used again. In order to be liberating, the retribution had to fit the crime brought about by the machine; thus, total destruction.

Therefore, day after day, he continued to take things apart methodically, dissect element by element, reducing it all to the smallest units possible; and then, with dejected obstinancy, he destroyed, broke, burned, and threw it all away in two public garbage dumps, until there was nothing left. He also got rid of the chairs, the round coffee table, the small refrigerator, and his self portrait, everything.

He even broke down the partition that separated the basement into two parts. Removing this partition had suddenly struck him as urgent and as necessary as the rest.

On the sixteenth, by 5 P.M., he'd finished the complete annihilation of his work. He experienced a bitter joy, a sense of freedom, but it left him feeling naked, stripped bare.

55

The morning of the seventeenth, when he was getting out of bed, Marc had a dizzy spell. He fell and remained unconscious for ten minutes. Marshall called a doctor. His pulse was imperceptible, and his blood pressure had dropped precipitously.

At his request, he was transported to Lariboisière Hospital, to the general medical unit headed by Professor Douot, whom he knew through Cedric Houdé, and who had returned to work after the August 15 holiday. For four days, Marc was given an entire series of exams. They didn't reveal anything other than a state of extreme exhaustion that resembled, Eric Douot told him, the condition of a man who had spent between six months to a year in a concentration camp. It meant complete rest in a specialized clinic where he would receive various tonics, vitamins, possibly some antidepressants—there was no alternative. A friend of Eric Douot's, Dr. Catherine Hamer, was the director of exactly that sort of establishment, in

Meudon. She was marvelous, the place was marvelous, if Marc wanted . . .

Marc agreed. On the twenty-first, they took him by ambulance to the Angèle-Leclair Clinic at No. 100 Avenue Angèle-Leclair in Meudon. They put him in a magnificent room that looked out onto a park so vast and dense with tall trees that Marc could not even see where it ended.

Eric Douot had been right: Catherine Hamer, a slightly plump brunette, was a marvelous woman and a first-rate doctor. She'd known of Marc by reputation for a long time. After dinner the evening of his arrival she came to see him in his room and spoke to him for an hour. Together, they decided on the treatment that Marc should follow. Marc refused all psychotropic drugs.

"Not even a little Minotaryl?" asked Catherine Hamer with a smile.

Minotaryl was the antidepressant Marc had perfected several years back that, by inhibiting in a radically new manner (by violent surges) the activity of monoamnine-oxydase, calmed, in certain cases the paralyzing ruminations of neurotic obsessives.

From the day of the funeral to the day of his admission into the clinic, he'd lost fifteen pounds. He lost fifteen more in the days that followed. His naturally gaunt face was scarcely changed by this weight loss. And his sharp, striking profile became even more handsome. His eyes acquired a certain depth and an intensity, a disturbing radiance that made it difficult to tear oneself away from his gaze.

Then this wasting away ceased. Marc gained back some of the weight, little by little.

He spent two months at the clinic. Catherine Hamer took care of him personally, every day. She'd understood something important: Marc knew better than anyone what was best for him. It seemed to her that he stayed in his room too much; that he didn't communicate enough with the other patients, if only to exchange banalities about the weather or the food (both in fact admirable), but she left him in peace about that and other matters.

Marshall and Marie-Thérèse visited him daily and sometimes twice a day. They came out of pure affection, loyal and genuine. But also, having been deeply affected by the loss of Marie and Leonard, they needed to spend time with Marc, to share their grief with him. It was a comfort to them, as well as to Marc. He would never forget how they had adored Leonard.

And he knew how much Marshall had loved Marie.

He sometimes asked about Cookie, but he never wanted to see the Westie again.

At the beginning of each month, Marc remembered to send a check to the dog kennel in Neuilly where he'd left Mana. He'd authorized the owner of the kennel to give away the bulldog free to anyone who might be interested.

He never spoke of what had happened. And he never experienced any painful moments, with the exception of one incident. One evening, the Cazanvielhs had dined in a restaurant in Meudon, then went to visit Marc in his room. They watched an American film on TV directed by William Friedkin, set in Los Angeles, that Marshall really liked. Later, they talked about the movie and drank fruit juice (regularly brought to Marc by Marie-Thérèse from a health food store in Versailles), after which Marshall and Marie-Thérèse prepared to leave. And Marc, who hadn't shed a tear since his family had disappeared, sat down on his bed and suddenly began to cry. Marie-Thérèse went to him, took him in her arms, and gave in to the tears she had always held back in his presence. Marshall walked toward them, his eyes moist. He stroked their hair with both hands, one hand on Marc and the other on Marie-Thérèse, in a soothing gesture that he repeated for a few minutes, until the difficult moment had passed.

That same evening, before leaving, Marshall and Marie-Thérèse proposed that Marc come live with them, if he liked, once he got out of the clinic. Marc declined. He nearly started to cry again. He still hadn't really thought about what he'd do afterward, he told them. In any case, he wouldn't live in Versailles again.

Hugues d'Oléons also paid him several visits. Timid and awkward outside of his office, out of his swiveling chair that was almost a part of him, he was somewhat confused by Marc's misfortune. He wasn't terribly sure what to say to him, to such a degree that a slight malaise sometimes pervaded their encounters. One day Marc realized that something was different about his front teeth, two of them were perfectly white. Hugues, almost embarrassed, explained that he'd gotten caps on his teeth; eight of them, incisors and canines. He'd been impressed by Miss Ledru's new teeth, and had decided, well, why not, after all . . .

He'd gotten into the habit of embracing Marc before leaving, as if, by this fervent display of affection, he wanted to compensate and excuse himself for the emptiness of the preceding conversation.

Marie's parents came to visit twice.

Cedric Houdé, with his kindly gangster face, came four times. On the third visit, he asked Marc: "Any more problems with your ear?"

"No," said Marc. "Not for the time being."

"Fine. Those neurinomes can be very strange. Maybe things will stay that way for good."

"Maybe," said Marc. "In fact, I'm sure of it. I mean, I'm confident they will."

Cedric Houdé had found the clinic of his dreams near Tarascon. He'd be leaving Paris within the next few months.

No other visitors. Marc had put Marshall and Dr. Hamer in charge of protecting him, of not letting anyone else through. He didn't want to see anyone for the moment.

In mid-September, he informed Marshall of two decisions he'd made. The first was to give up his practice and go back to painting once he got out. The second was to sell all his possessions, his home, and his parents' house, including the furniture and his library, and to buy a luxury apartment in Paris.

"In what neighborhood?" asked Marshall.

Marc reflected, then looked up and declared, like some kind of simpleton struck by a crazy idea: "The Champs Elysées. Yes, the Champs Elysées."

"What type of apartment? Have you given it any thought?"

"Yes. Big; a penthouse on the top floor of a building with a huge terrace. On the Champs Elysées, or on a street nearby."

"Would you like me to take care of it?" asked Marshall. "I can take care of everything, the selling and the buying."

Marc did not refuse, nor was he politely reticent: yes, he would like Marshall to take care of the whole thing.

Thanks to the connections he had in real estate—prompted by the desire to do Marc a favor, and a bit of luck—Marshall solved the problem in record time. The two houses were sold at the best price (in other words, a phenomenal sum), and he found (for an equally phenomenal sum), an apartment that matched Marc's description, on Rue de Marignan. One afternoon, he brought Marc over to visit it. Marc was delighted: it was the apartment of his dreams. It was situated on the tenth and top floor of No. 10 Rue de Marignan. The space was approximately three hundred and fifty square feet plus a three-hundred-square-foot terrace—a veritable little garden with grass, trees, and various plants that the former owner had left behind. From every angle was a picture postcard view of Paris.

Then, having closely studied numerous catalogs, Marc ordered the furniture. On delivery days, Marshall waited at the apartment. Marie-Thérèse took care of the rest; curtains, sheets, kitchen utensils, everything, even a carton of household cleaning products.

They wanted it to be a surprise.

Several more days went by. On the nineteenth of October, Marc checked out of the Angèle-Leclair Clinic, feeling in relatively good shape.

As he was leaving, he thanked Dr. Catherine Hamer, hesitated, then kissed her on both cheeks.

56

Marc moved in the same day. Marshall and Marie-Thérèse had done an incredible job, like magic fairies: Marc found the apartment ready to be lived in—clean, welcoming, decked with flowers, his stereo set up, and all his clothes put away in closets. He felt a surge of love for his friends. He vowed he'd soon give them a generous gift, proportionate to their devotion.

The next day, he got rid of the Nissan Terrano and purchased a compact car for city driving. Then he bought himself all the painting supplies he needed.

Driving the car crammed with canvases, easels, paint, and brushes, he suddenly thought about getting back in touch with Martin Vérapoutsimila, the psychoanalyst he'd seen as a young man. But then, just as quickly, he rejected the idea.

And he settled into his new life. In the evenings, he went to bed very late. He watched a lot of television, and listened to music. (*La*

Frescobalda by Girolamo Frescobaldi, played by Rafael Puyana, remained his "record of the month" far beyond a month, and was never replaced by a single other piece. Marc never tired of it.) After a half hour of exercise (concentrating particularly on the abdominal muscles), he'd take a walk through the neighborhood and buy groceries. The rest of the day, he painted.

Two mornings a week the concierge of the building, an elderly but vigorous woman, did the cleaning.

He never returned to Versailles. The Cazanvielhs came by often. As for his relationship with Hugues d'Oléons, it was limited to conversations on the telephone.

One morning, he received a letter from John Joseph, the unpleasant, hypocritical owner of the dog Mana. John Joseph didn't seem to know about what had happened to Marc. He was writing because he feared he had a brain tumor, behind his right eye, he was in a lot of pain. As a result, he was unable to get himself to a hospital, he said; hospitals filled him with anxiety. Having learned shortly after the sale of the dog that Marc was a brain specialist, he was taking the liberty of approaching him, though he admitted it was slightly presumptuous: he wished to see Marc in private, at his home, at least the first time . . .

Marc responded that he was no longer practicing and gave him the address of a colleague who worked in the city. Then, as soon as he'd licked the stamp, he called Germaine Halbronn in Montmontre, at her son the tipster's house. Germaine, on the contrary, apparently knew all about it. She remained silent for a long while. Marc wasn't able to say anything either. At last, she awkwardly extended her condolences.

"I could already tell you were worried when I ran into you on Place des Vosges."

"Place des Vosges?" asked Marc.

"Yes, don't you remember?"

Place des Vosges. Hôtel Pavillon de la Reine. Michel Zyto, the usurper.

"Yes, of course," said Marc. "It's true, I was worried. I must have acted strangely to you, forgive me."

She protested.

She was quite touched that Marc had thought of phoning her. Marc said to her: "I didn't forget my promise about Cookie, but..."
She protested once more.
"Sometime soon," said Marc.
"Yes, sometime soon!"
They said goodbye.
Marc was saddened by this phone call, but quickly forgot about it.

One afternoon while taking a walk with Marshall on the Champs Elysées, near the Rue de Marignan, they passed in front of an exhibition of custom-made Italian cars. They stopped to look.
"I'm getting a little tired of that big Volvo of mine," said Marshall. "I think I'll trade it in one of these days. You've got to admit, compared to that one over there..."
"The red one?" asked Marc.
He pointed to a long, elegant, gleaming Maserati.
"Yes."
Marshall seemed truly taken with it, and Marc had just gotten an idea for a present.

Marc thought of Leonard and Marie and Marianne, he still thought of them, every second. But the pain was subsiding.
He was often at home. He hardly ever used his car, parked in the basement of the building. He preferred walking. The few errands he had, he did on foot. He more or less avoided the lower end of the Champs Elysées, because one day he'd inadvertently found himself in front of the Red Dragon. The memory of lunches there with his wife, the good times they'd had, the steamed dishes on the menu, and the smiling Connie Huong, had made him miserable for hours.
He painted a great deal, more and more, and always the same thing. He painted what he saw from his terrace; in other words, the sky and the rooftops. He wasn't concerned about the resemblance, and even less so about the quality of his work. He painted whatever came to mind. When he sensed the canvas was finished, he'd put it

away in a back room, an enormous space that gave onto the courtyard; then he'd set up another canvas on his easel.

They all looked alike: the top half was covered by a large surface of a plain, even, bluish color, with no sun. The bottom part, by a grayish, busy area of rooftops, balconies, and chimneys but, according to Marie-Thérèse, it was also perhaps the ravaged, deserted soil of another planet, or else—said Marshall referring to the overall effect—a coastline and the sea as seen from an airplane at the onset of winter. (Marc was quite content to show his work to his friends from Versailles.)

It was this lower half of the painting that required the most work for Marc. It was full of chaotic designs that escaped definition just when the viewer began to understand them. It was subtle, too, due to the juxtaposition of a multitude of closely related hues; but you could, in fact, distinguish one color from another if you looked carefully, or if the light hit the canvas at a certain angle.

Never any people, no human figures.

One morning toward the end of December—two months had elapsed since he'd left the clinic—he did, however, add a tiny figure to one of the canvases that he'd just finished, on the right, as though the man were standing on top of a chimney, drawn with no concern for perspective: it was him. Not that anyone could recognize him, of course, but in his mind, it was him. He felt better than he usually did upon completing a work—happier, lighter—as a result of having put himself in the painting.

It was eleven o'clock. He wouldn't work anymore today. He phoned the house on Impasse des Soldats and invited Marshall and Marie-Thérèse to dinner. They'd go to an excellent restaurant on Rue Beaujon, right near Place de l'Etoile. Marc had already been there twice for lunch, and Marshall, given what a gourmet he was, would undoubtedly appreciate the food. He asked them to come over to his apartment around six thirty; he preferred to make it an early evening. Marie-Thérèse was a bit surprised, but would never have dreamt of objecting: fine, they'd be there at six thirty.

That afternoon, Marc bought her a gold ring with a diamond in a diamond setting that cost only slightly less than the Maserati.

And he also bought the Maserati. He left it in the showroom and told the salesman he'd be back by seven, before closing time.

As soon as Marshall and Marie-Thérèse arrived, at six thirty on the dot, he said to them: "Let's go right away, if you don't mind. I need to stretch my legs. It's not too cold out. We can have a drink on the way."

He slipped on the navy blue coat he'd bought for himself and they went out.

They walked up the Champs Elysées. They soon arrived at the level of the exhibition hall. Marc stopped.

"Do you still like it as much?" he asked Marshall, gesturing toward the long red car.

"More than ever," said Marshall.

Marc took the keys out of his pocket and held them out to Marshall:

"Well then, here. You can take it and bring it home."

Without giving Marshall a chance to express anything but a vague mumble of surprise and bewilderment, he turned to Marie-Thérèse:

"These cars are so incredibly chic," he said, "that they throw in a ring in the glove compartment for the wife."

And, taking out a small package from his other pocket, he thrust it into her hand.

"Open it. I hope you like it."

Speechless, Marie-Thérèse unwrapped the gift.

"Marc . . .," said Marshall.

"Don't say a thing," replied Marc. "Not a word. I admit that my scheme was rather childish, but it was so much fun!"

They kissed on the sidewalk with such enthusiasm that Marie-Thérèse nearly lost her balance. The hugging went on for several minutes. They were blocking the passage of the other pedestrians.

Marshall went to claim his new car.

They spent an evening in oblivion and well-being, as if time had stopped.

After dinner, they piled into the Maserati. It was fairly late, the Cazanviehls hadn't planned to go back to Marc's apartment. They circled the Place de l'Etoile and went back down the Champs Elysées. Right after the Rue Galilée, Marc spotted the Volvo.

"You can let me off here," he said, "I'll walk home."

"Are you sure?" asked Marshall.

"It's only three hundred yards," Marc said. "Just what I need after a good meal."

Marshall stopped the car.

"What brakes, look at the way it handles, how smooth, how quiet!" he exclaimed.

Out of sheer kindness, he asked his wife if she wanted to take the wheel of the Maserati, already knowing the answer. She said: "No, I'd be too afraid I'd dent it. I'll drive it in the city after I get used to taking it on side roads."

Marc kissed them both. Before now, Marc and Marshall had never kissed each other. They'd always shook hands in the manly fashion.

The two cars slowly drove off into the distance; the Volvo, clumsier-looking than ever, following behind the sleek Italian car.

They waved to each other. Marie-Thérèse leaned out her window and cried: "See you soon!"

Marc nodded affirmatively. He was smiling, a very subtle, very gentle smile that lingered on his face.

He kept waving until they had disappeared.

Then he was gripped with a peculiar feeling, as if he would never see them again.

57

So he set out on foot. The end of the year was drawing near, there were throngs of people in the streets despite the late hour.

He arrived at the intersection at Avenue George V. The light was red. He crossed the wide avenue. He glanced at a woman in a car, perhaps sensing that she was observing him.

It was Katarina.

She was behind the wheel of a vintage black car that had been beautifully restored, whose make Marc didn't recognize. He stopped. He hesitated, then approached. She'd already rolled down the window. She was sumptuously dressed, as if she'd come into a great fortune since their last meeting. He noticed the baggage in the back seat.

He would have liked to say something to her, but nothing came to him. They continued to gaze into each other's eyes. Just at the moment she was about to speak, the light turned green and the cars began to honk.

She leaned over and opened the door on the passenger side.

Marc stepped around the car. He sat down next to her and slammed the door.

She immediately accelerated.

The car crossed the Champs Elysées, arriving at a narrow street between Rue Washington and Rue Berri.

The honking had stopped.

In contrast, and despite the bustling streets, a hush seemed to have fallen on the neighborhood.

The car sped down the little street and soon disappeared.